UNBROKEN

SAVAGE NORTH CHRONICLES, BOOK FOUR

LINDSEY POGUE

AN ENDING WORLD LOVE STORY

Unbroken

Savage North Chronicles Book Six
By Lindsey Pogue

Editing by Lauren McNerney
Proofreading by Letter-Eye Editing
Cover Design by We Got You Covered Book Design

Written and Published by Lindsey Pogue
101 W. American Canyon Road, Ste. 508-262
American Canyon, CA 94503

Printed in the USA

978-1-63848-880-4

For Katie.
We've weathered some turbulent storms
and ridden a horse or two.
And even though I'm the mean big sister, and our journeys in this
life have been different,
you've always been there for me.
We've traveled and laughed, we've fought and sang and danced.

I can't imagine my life without you.
Thank you for being my shoulder to cry on and my best friend.

I love you.
Sister

ACKNOWLEDGMENTS

For my Patreon peeps.
Thank you for going on this new
and unexpected journey with me.
You warm my heart and make me smile.

Mindi Travis
Julie Traina
Melinda Leininger
Stevie
Sabrina Hatfield
Marjorie Conklin
Nicole Hartney
Katelyn Bobbitt
Laura Price
Stephanie Edwards
Amanda Eide

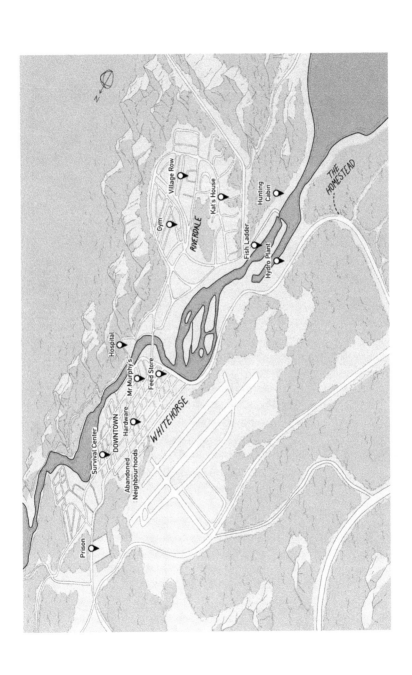

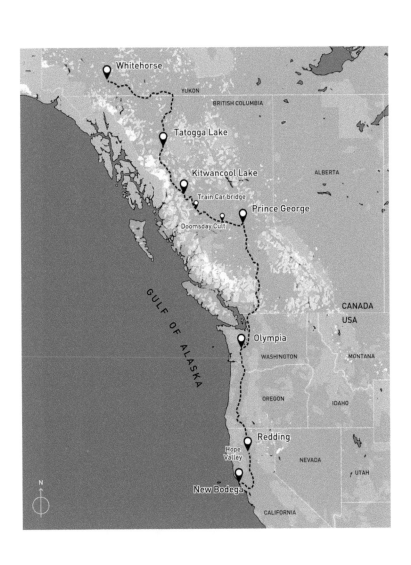

PROLOGUE
THEA

My fingers tapped ceaselessly on the armrest of the F-250 as I sat alone in the truck, peering out the passenger window at Wren's village. All I could think was, *whoa*. Beau was right. Wren's people lived in a time capsule, a leftover place from the world before. I understood more than ever why my brother had wanted Wren, unprotected and so far removed out here, to come back to Whitehorse with him. Their village might've been hidden away, off the beaten path of the main road, but it still wasn't safe.

Our nine-hour drive from home, down the slushy highway, had been a quiet one. Beau and Wren were nervous to return to the village after three months away, especially since my brother had nearly killed Wren and took her away from her family directly after—or so they likely saw it. But a momentary break in the weather made our trip a somewhat urgent one, and with our sudden appearance in the village, I didn't blame Wren and Beau for being anxious. We would be unwanted. We were *Tainteds*.

I imagined meeting the parents was difficult for anyone in a relationship, and under these extreme circumstances, I knew my brother wouldn't be greeted with open arms. It didn't matter if Wren thought Whitehorse was the right call, especially for people like her. They'd never had the Virus, so they had no Abilities, which meant they had no protection against the superpowered crazy people still roaming these lands from time to time.

But I guess Wren wasn't exactly like her people anymore, not since my brother came along. She didn't have an Ability, but she was a Tainted like the rest of us now. Because of him, she was a carrier of the genetically engineered Virus that mutated and changed people—the same one that had changed all of us during the outbreak years ago. But Wren was still alive because of my brother, too. And that made me proud of him.

I watched through the window as the willow boughs trembled in the wind.

Beau was an ass sometimes, for sure, but he wasn't cruel or mean-spirited, and he definitely hadn't known sleeping with Wren could kill her. Knowing how much her family disliked him for what he'd done worried me, but if Hunter was as great as Wren made him sound, I knew her best friend would help her people see that we weren't as bad as some of them seemed to think. In fact, we were normal, all things considered. And if we could relate to anything, it was living in fear, and that was the last thing any of us wanted for Wren and her village.

Heaving the door open, I climbed out of the plow truck, my boots landing on the ground with a soggy crunch. It was still cold as hell, and as a gust of wind blew past, I tugged my purple beanie further down over my ears. Pulling out the small tin of lip balm from my back pocket, I unscrewed the top, dabbed my finger in the raspberry-tinted beeswax, and rubbed it on my lips.

There were two things I would never get used to, living in the North—skin so dry it hurt to move, and lips so chapped they cracked at the slightest twitch. Or maybe it was all just too reminiscent, reminding me of the way the wind whipped around Beau and me in the old forsaken Heston Building the night we thought we might freeze to death in that dank, moldy room. My mother's body, half covered in snow outside the window.

I shoved the lip balm into my back pocket, staring dolefully at the village. It was so . . . sad. I didn't know exactly what had happened here years ago, only that survivors with mind-controlling Abilities manipulated the village to do horrible things, but I knew Wren's mother and brother were dead, and that her family was scarred in ways I could never fully comprehend.

Staring down the muddy road, I eyed the ramshackle homes with frayed tarps on the roofs that flapped in the wind, their eaves dripping with melting snow. I would've assumed the village was abandoned, had I not known any better. There were no cars or people walking about. There were no dogs barking, and what little livestock I could see was in a small stable toward the end of the road, across from Wren's house. She and Beau had been in there for nearly twenty minutes.

A familiar engine rumbled as the old tour bus we used for trips to Prince Rupert came to a stop behind the truck and horse trailer. At least reinforcements had arrived. Aside from the truck that Beau, Wren, and I had driven to plow the snow from the roads, and the trailer we'd pulled to haul the horses home in, the bus could transport the extra eleven bodies back to Whitehorse with us, along with some of their things.

The mechanical doors squeaked open and Jackson stepped out of the bus, the paint-chipped behemoth creaking under his weight. He turned and held out his hand for Jade to step down. The two of them were Beau's buffers, in case things went south and Wren needed people who looked less like us and more like them, with First Nations blood, to help convince her family they were doing the right thing.

Jackson zipped up his jacket and scratched his beard absently as he walked toward me, his hazel gaze set in dark, contemplative features as he assessed the surrounding village. "So," he said. "This is it."

"Yep," I drawled. I imagined Jackson was comparing what would be their new village back home to this one.

At Beau's bidding, we'd worked throughout the winter to ensure Wren's people had a safe, comfortable section of White-horse to move to. Beau had wrangled all of our friends and family together to help and made certain everything was in place —that their new village was stocked with enough food and fire-wood for the remaining weeks of cold, and that his house with Wren was ready so she could be with her family during their transition. It was safe to say that, because of Beau, Wren's people would want for nothing ever again, once they got to Whitehorse.

If what Beau had done for Wren and her family wasn't love, I didn't know what was, and I hoped her people would recognize that. I'd never seen my brother do anything so selfless or persis-tent as what he'd orchestrated for her. He was officially a lovesick sucker now, like the rest of them, and I never thought I'd see the day.

Jade wrapped her arm around my shoulders, and a waft of lavender filled my nose. It was so Jade and reassuring. She had a way of making everyone feel better, which was exactly why she'd been asked to come on the trip. She rubbed my arm and gave me a brief squeeze. "Which one is Wren's?"

Leaning my head against her shoulder, I pointed to the house at the end of the row with brown peeling paint, a crooked awning over the porch, and a glass wind chime hanging from it, clanking in the breeze. Knowing Wren's father was in a wheelchair, I wondered why there was no ramp in and out of the house. *Did he never leave?*

It was no surprise Wren had gotten so depressed living in a place like this. Everything already felt dismal, heavy, and suffo-cating, and I hadn't even met a single person yet.

"Well," Jade said with an exhale. "How do we think it's going in there? Do we think her grandmother and Hunter have been able to get everyone on board?"

I snorted. "They better," I muttered. I liked Wren well enough, I even loved her for making Beau seem more human these past three months, but she'd changed him, or rather, what they'd been through had. He'd be gutted if all their hard work had been for nothing, and Wren ended up staying here with her people. My chest ached for Beau simply considering it. "I don't know if Hunter's even in there. No one's gone in or out—other than Beau and Wren."

"We need to give them time," Jackson said. "They had no warning we were coming. We can't rush them . . . Beau and Wren will shout if they need us." I could tell Jackson wanted to go in and make sure things were all right. Every tendon in his neck and jaw seemed to twitch with tension, but he had promised Beau he wouldn't step in unless he needed to. This was Beau and Wren's fight.

Jackson lowered the tailgate. "Thea," he said as he slid a few empty crates from the back. "Stack these over there, by the shed, would you?" He gestured toward the barn where a gray horse peeked out at me. "Wren wants to use them to pack their things."

I smiled. A visit with the horses seemed the perfect way to keep my restless mind busy. "Gladly."

Taking a stack of plastic crates, I trudged down the road, appraising every house I passed, observing outlines of people on the other side of some of the windows. Mostly adults, from what I could see in the overcast afternoon glare.

Eyeing a small winter garden by the shed, I wondered if Hunter would appreciate the land they would have to sow once the snow melted in the spring. Though I'd never met him, it felt like Hunter was the key to everything that came next. He wasn't only the village leader, but a farmer, one of the only villagers to know a lick about horses, and Wren's best friend and ex-*fiancé*.

As sticky as it all seemed, though, Wren reassured all of us that with Hunter's help, we could convince everyone how important Whitehorse was; they would all understand what needed to come next.

As I continued through the mud, door hinges creaked as villagers poked their heads out. Their skin was tanned, like Wren's, and they had raven black hair. Many of them looked older, with wrinkles around their eyes and mouths, pinched and hardened with fear and uncertainty. It was palpable, and I took a steadying breath, inhaling the scent of melting snow.

Jackson, Beau, and Wren had been preparing for this day, and it was up to us now to make these people feel at ease around us.

I flashed my audience a smile. "Hello," I chirped, only to be met with a mix of furrowed brows and narrowed, distrusting gazes. I understood why Wren's people might distrust us. But more than anything, it was a blaring reminder of how vulnerable they were out here. They were defenseless in a way our community never would be, with our fortified walls, an Ability-wielding police force, the laws we had in place, and a reinforced prison.

As I set the crates down outside the shed, the door to Wren's house opened, and Beau stepped out. His face was shadowed, like he'd aged a decade in mere minutes. He looked down the road to Jackson and Jade by the truck.

"Jade," he said, his voice level, but pleading in a way too. "Jackson." He waved for them to come. He already needed backup, which didn't seem like a good sign.

I swallowed thickly as Beau turned and went directly back into the house, the creak of the porch echoing in the crisp afternoon air. I could hear muffled voices inside, but I couldn't tell if it was as bad—or worse—than they'd assumed it would be.

Jackson helped Jade through the mud and up onto the porch before he slowly opened the door and followed her inside.

With the clearing of horse nostrils behind me and the squish of hooves in the mud, I turned around to find three horses meandering out to greet me. They were shaggy, but stocky and beautiful in a way I'd never seen, almost wild.

A beautiful gray with dappled black spots lifted his nose to the air in curiosity as he stepped closer. "You must be Cricket," I realized, and pulled off my mittens. "I've heard all about you. Your buddy Dancer and I are good friends back home." Hunter's mare had become Cinder's paddock companion over the months.

Slowly, I lifted my hand to Cricket's nose. It was silky soft and prickly with whiskers, and his nostrils flared with unease. "It's okay," I told him. "You can bite me if you want. Or . . . we could be friends too." I didn't have animal-chatting abilities like Beau, but I closed my eyes and left my fate to the broody gray in front of me. "I won't hurt you," I breathed.

He lipped the back of my fingers in answer, but he didn't bite me. Instead, he nudged my hand, and when I opened my eyes, he lowered his furry head, waiting for me to pet him.

I ran my fingers through his dirty forelock happily, and as I glanced at the other two curious horses, my gaze latched onto a man coming out of the woods behind them. There was a tether of dead rabbits in his hands and a rifle strapped across his back. He froze when he saw me.

He was tall with broad shoulders, but it was the longer, ebony hair that hung around his narrowed, distrusting eyes and chiseled features that took my breath away. I'd never seen anyone so severe in all my life, not even my brother.

I straightened, my heart racing as I remembered I was in a foreign place with people who didn't like me. "Hello," I said, as he lifted his chin warily. "I'm Thea."

The man's dark eyes widened slightly, and his jaw clenched. Though he couldn't have been more than twenty, he looked as though the world had hardened him beyond his years.

Without a word, he strode quickly past me.

I bristled as he continued silent and purposeful toward a house, two homes down from Wren's, then he disappeared inside.

"Nice to meet you too," I muttered, and huffing out a breath, I looked at Cricket. "You don't seem to mind my being here, at least," I mused.

I introduced myself to the bay and the chestnut, both excited to have a new visitor as well. But as the minutes ticked on, and the wind blew colder, I debated what I should do. I could continue unloading the crates from the truck and then wait in the cab's warmth for God only knew how long. Or . . . I stared at the front door of Wren's house, cracked slightly open.

My feet began moving before I could tell myself I should leave the others to deal with the convincing and the shouting, but I wanted to know what was going on inside.

I crossed the road and stepped as quietly as I could onto the porch to listen.

"—I won't leave. I don't care what you—"

"Papa, you have to," Wren said, and when I peeked through the crack, she was kneeling at her father's feet. She gripped the handle of his wheelchair as she peered at him, willing him to listen. I knew he'd lost his arm as a result of their unwanted visitors years ago, but I wasn't sure how, exactly. And I hadn't expected the fierceness etched in the lines of his face. "Papa, I promise you—"

"You trust them so easily," he protested, throwing his one arm up, as if trusting us was so hard to do after my brother had saved Wren's life. But as I realized his emotional wounds were probably as scarring as his physical ones, it was hard to fault him.

"*Easily?*" Frustration sharpened Wren's voice as she peered up at Jackson and Jade by the door, then at Beau, sitting on the couch with his hands gripping his hair. "They've taken me in and cared for me the last three months—they've organized all of this for *us*. I was able to come back so soon because of them. Why shouldn't I trust them?"

Her father's eyebrows lifted slightly, like he finally heard and processed her words and felt her frustration.

With a slow exhale, Wren rubbed her brow. "Papa," she said more calmly. "You know me. I would not ask you to do this if it wasn't important—if it wasn't the right thing."

He huffed and shook his head. "Your judgement has been clouded since you met this boy—"

Wren rose to her feet. "Well, think what you want, but I'm going back," she quipped, and her father's eyes widened with a fearful sort of surprise. I wordlessly cheered Wren on. "And I would like you to come back with me too," she added. "To do what's best for everyone. They'll follow our family, and we need to stick together. This village isn't the safest place for us anymore."

An old woman stepped out of the kitchen, wiping her hands on her apron as she scanned the room. Her brow furrowed slightly when she spotted me outside the door, but I didn't move, and she gave nothing away as she glanced back at Wren's father.

"I told her to go back with the boy, Otto," she said as if she were reminding him, and the old woman rested her hand on his shoulder. "The least we can do is listen to what she has to say." It was Henni, I realized. Wren's grandmother's voice was rough, and I got the impression she rarely smiled. She was intriguing, though. I could see where Wren got her gumption.

When Otto finally dragged his stare away from his daughter, and registered everyone's expectant faces, his expression hardened again. "Everyone out," he said. "This is still my house. Out!"

With reluctance, Beau nodded for Jackson and Jade to go, but Beau stayed where he was.

Otto glared at him.

"I'm not leaving Wren, unless she asks me to," my brother told him, obstinate.

Wren flashed Beau a grateful smile, and as Jade and Jackson made their way toward the door, I backed away.

When they stepped outside again, Jackson ran his hand over his closely cropped beard. "Otto will come around," he said, his voice a quiet rumble as he clicked the door shut. But it sounded like Jackson was trying to reassure himself more than us. "He's just afraid."

"Yes," Jade agreed. "It's obvious they've suffered greatly." Her eyes shifted down the road, over the houses and the winter-ravaged trees in the yards.

A reluctant inner voice cut into my thoughts. *Where is the other key player in all of this?* "What about Hunter?" I asked. "He should be in there with them, helping Wren convince her father this is the right thing to do. If Otto sees Wren, her grand-mother, and Hunter standing together in this, he would have to agree, right?"

Jade offered me an uncertain smile and looked to Jackson. "Perhaps we should go to the safe house at Watson Lake for the night and give Wren time with her family. It's a lot for them to have us here, so suddenly. We could come back tomorrow to see if they've gotten everything sorted."

"Maybe," Jackson said, but he seemed reluctant. He stared at the bus and truck. I knew we didn't bring enough biodiesel for numerous trips back and forth, and the safe house was nearly two hours away. "Let's give it more time before we make any deci-sions," he said, thoughtful. I could imagine how helpless Jackson felt because I was beginning to feel that way too. And we were wasting time—and daylight.

"I'm going to wait in the truck," I told them. I was one more new face the villagers didn't want to see at the moment. "Wave if you need me."

Jade's gray eyes crinkled in the corners, and she swept my long brown hair over my shoulder. She leaned in to kiss my forehead. "Take a nap for me while you're in there, would you? That bus is about as comfortable as a bed of rocks."

"Sure," I said with a breathy laugh, but I was too restless to nap.

Jackson winked at me, and I plodded down the steps and up the sludgy road toward the truck.

I still didn't understand why Hunter wasn't inside helping Wren. The way she always talked about him—a man of worth and practicality, who had been groomed to lead this place with her one day—I figured he'd be in there fighting for this. For Wren. For his family and his people's safety. He had to have known we'd arrived, the rest of the village surely did.

A chilling thought filled me. The man with the rabbits was Hunter's age. He hadn't looked happy to see me, but that didn't make sense. Not if he and Henni had been the ones encouraging Wren to go to Whitehorse.

I could feel the attention of onlookers as I continued walking back to the truck, but I didn't look at them this time. Instead, I kept my focus on the slush at my feet, wondering if I shouldn't have come. It wasn't as if they really needed me, even if Wren thought I could help with the horses since she and Hunter would have other things to worry about.

"—don't like it," a woman bit out. I stopped in my tracks and stared at the door to the house where the severe-faced man had disappeared. The window was cracked open, and I strained to listen as the tattered drapes rustled in a gust of wind. "They can't be trusted."

"No, they can't," a man, whom I assumed was Hunter, replied. "But we have no choice."

My eyes rounded and my heart raced with a strange mixture of sadness and indignation. Hunter was supposed to be Wren's ally in this. Even Beau had said they'd parted on semi-civil terms. I knew they didn't like us or trust us, but to hear them say it, and feel the bitterness in their voices like a rake over my skin, was more upsetting than I'd anticipated.

"I still don't like it," the woman said. The grudge she held against us was an anvil weighing each of her words. "We need to think about our family, not Wren's fascination with this man—he nearly *killed* her, Hunter. I can't believe you even let her leave with him."

"I didn't *let* her do anything, Mother. Wren's going to do what she wants. You know that. She was always going to leave with him; it was only a matter of time. I just encouraged her to go before winter set in so she didn't freeze to death." He paused, and my blood began to boil. Hunter wasn't supportive of Wren's decision to go to Whitehorse at all. In fact, he sounded as angry as Otto had looked.

"Bullheaded, foolish girl," his mother bit out. "She's going to get us all killed. You should've killed that Tainted when you had the chance! None of this would be happening right now—"

"That's enough, Mother. You're getting yourself worked up."

My heart thudded harder and faster in my chest. *Should've killed Beau?* Heat flooded through me.

"Of course, I'm getting worked up! This is our lives. You're just blind when it comes to that girl," she snapped.

"I'm not blind," Hunter bit out, and I could hear the anger in his voice. "This is what needs to be done, even if we don't like it. Beau knows where we live—they all do now—regardless of their intentions. We're even more exposed than before. Opposing this will only make things worse."

I glared at both of them through the wall as all hope and intrigue to meet the amazing Hunter withered. He looked as cuddly as a snake, and he sounded like one too. "You're as bad as the rest of them," I muttered.

Clenching my hands into fists, I was about to continue to the truck, to stew someplace where my tongue wouldn't get me into trouble, when his front door opened. The instant Hunter stepped outside, I felt a wash of relief. I wanted him to know I'd heard him, and that I knew what he really thought of us, and Wren.

"Can't be trusted?" I seethed.

Hunter stopped short on the porch, though his severe expression gave nothing away.

"You're an asshole," I blurted, a little shocked when the words left my lips, but it felt good all the same.

His dark eyes narrowed on me. "What did you call me?"

"Did you already forget that my brother was the one who *saved* Wren?" I said, practically foaming at the mouth. "That it was Beau's idea to use the devil's club in the first place? Or did that slip your mind these past few months?"

He took a step closer. "She wouldn't have needed saving if it wasn't for him," Hunter reminded me. His gaze flicked over me, coldly appraising.

"You have no idea what Wren and my brother have been doing all winter—what we've *all* been doing—*for you*," I fumed, my hands fisting at my sides. "She thought you, of all people, would appreciate the lengths we've gone to, to make you all feel welcome in Whitehorse. But you don't even want to go."

"You're making it so appealing," Hunter said sharply.

His mother stepped outside with a stern expression pinching her features, and a younger boy was at her side. "Hunter?" she said with more chill than the north wind as she assessed me. She took the boy's hand in hers protectively.

"Go inside," Hunter told his mother, his glare fixed on me. It was practically a command, and though she scowled in my direction, she did as Hunter said and shut the door behind her.

Hunter stepped to the edge of the porch. "Get out of my way."

It was all I could do not to let my tongue run away from me again, but I knew I had to let this go, before I made things worse. Shaking my head in disbelief, I stepped out of his way. "You're such a disappointment," I muttered, but if Hunter heard me, he had no reply. In two heavy footsteps, he was striding through the mud toward Wren's house.

"Oh," I started, and I spun around, unable to help myself. "And your horse looked half-starved when she got to White-horse, so I fattened her up for you."

Hunter stilled, his back to me.

"You know, in case you want to add that to the list of reasons we're so *untrustworthy*."

Hunter didn't bother looking back as he marched down the road. He stalked past Jackson, who was making his way toward me, without a word, and disappeared inside Wren's house. I noticed Jade wasn't on the porch anymore.

"Making friends already?" Jackson asked wryly, and his furrowed brow raised a little.

I glared at the closed front door, my heart racing with fury. "Something like that," I bit out.

Jackson glanced from me toward the house again. "Are you going to tell me what that was about?"

I met his gaze. What was I supposed to tell him, that all of our hard work was probably for nothing? I'd known none of it was going to be easy, so I wasn't sure why I was letting Hunter's words affect me so much. But I couldn't help but feel unfairly judged and bitter that my expectations had fallen so short.

I cleared my throat. "We just have a difference of opinion," I told him.

Jackson's eyebrows lifted, skeptical, but he didn't press me on it. "Jade's in there now," he explained. "Henni is pulling rank. She and Wren are going to speak with the other villagers. Hope-fully, we'll be home by tomorrow evening."

Hearing the hope in Jackson's voice made me feel like I

should be more excited, and part of me was, for Wren, but I realized this was only the beginning of a messy, complicated situation.

Regardless, I forced a smile. "Good." Because I couldn't get away from this place fast enough.

A YEAR AND A HALF LATER...

1

HUNTER

My father raised me to be a "man of worth". To provide for and defend my family, even if it was my father I had to protect my mother from sometimes. Even if some nights a meal on the table was forgotten when my mother couldn't get out of bed and he'd had too much to drink.

But my father never taught me how to fight against something I couldn't see. He'd never told me how to protect a town from madmen who were hell-bent on terrorizing us. Hurting us. Killing *us*.

A woman's shriek echoed outside the house, her sobbing making my heart thrum like a dribbling basketball inside my chest. It was Nessa, I'd seen the men take her into the house after they bashed Otto's arm to pieces. I'd watched them take her before they'd taken me.

Bile rose in my throat, and tears filled my vision. I could still feel the cool glass against my skin and the tear of my flesh before I'd lost consciousness. Then, I'd woken up in my house, uncertain what happened during the missing moments in between.

Feeling a skin-chilling dread, I squeezed Wren more tightly against me, pain shooting through the raw, raging wounds on my back. I'd been a plaything, and when they finished with Nessa, I knew they would come back. For all of us. Without the mind haze the adults all felt from the madmen's puppet master, everyone could see more clearly; there was no reason for the men to pretend, not anymore.

"Shh . . ." Henni tried to soothe my mother, clinging to little Milo on the couch, completely petrified. My father had been dead for over a year, and still, my mother called his name in fear, as if he could hear her. As if he might come.

I'd been relieved when he'd died. Now though, with strangers in the village, and Wren, my mother, and Milo in danger, I thought I might miss him too. His rage made him as formidable as any of the madmen out there.

"I want my Papa," Wren pleaded as we shuddered against the wall, between the couch and the furnace.

I shook my head and squeezed her tighter. "You can't go out there—"

"What if he's dead! What if they get him like they got Colt?"

Colt's face flashed to mind, fury and fear in his eyes as he aimed the revolver at the man leading Nessa away. I recalled the sudden lurch of his body and the trembling of his arm as he'd fought against the need to turn the gun away from himself. The mind control was stronger, though, and Colt aimed the revolver at his own chest. He pulled the trigger and fell. But even in his last moments, his determination and bravery had won, and with his final breaths, he pulled the trigger again. The moment Colt disabled the mind controller, the veil of oblivion lifted and chaos ensued. Colt was dead, but our community of twenty was no longer under their control, and the screams and torment only worsened.

Wren sobbed.

"Your father's not dead," I promised, though I had no way of knowing. I tried to make my nine-year-old voice sound reassuring, but it was pathetically weak. "I got you—it will be okay."

"—doesn't he shoot them? Why?" my mother shrieked in complete hysterics. I could barely make out her words over my brother's mewling cries. "Why don't they do something!"

Sweat beaded on my skin and fear ripped through me as I thought about Otto's crushed arm and Colt's bloodied body. My vision blurred with tears until I couldn't see Wren anymore. Who was left to save us? Who would stop them from coming back in here? I looked at my mother's swollen face and choked out a sob. I knew the answer was no one. No one was coming. We were going to die. All of us were, it was only a matter of time.

Wren sniveled and jumped as another scream pierced the air outside. My mind told me to get up and do something, but my body wouldn't move. I didn't want to die. I didn't want to watch them hurt my mother or Wren or Henni.

Another scream, guttural and earsplitting.

Still, I couldn't move.

They will come. They won't stop until they've taken everything from all of us.

Another shout and crash outside. Another scream.

When I heard Nessa begging and a cry so despairing it was as if it was ripped from my own throat, I lurched to my feet.

"No!" Wren grabbed hold of my arm. "Hunter!" Her big brown eyes were red-rimmed and pleading.

My chest heaved and a cry ripped from my chest. "I have to do something," I choked out. I was torn, too petrified to leave, but too guilt-ridden not to. There was a way out, an oversized hole behind the washing machine my father had never gotten around to fixing. I'd used it to get out of the house when I needed Otto's help with my father. I tried not to think about the tight squeeze and the feel of jagged wood scraping against the raw flesh on my back.

With another shrill cry outside, my feet were moving. I knew what they were doing to Nessa. The cries were too much like my

21

mother's had been when my father had his way with her. They were too haunting, and I needed them to stop.

"Go to your grandmother," I told Wren, lifting her to her feet. I pushed her into Henni's arms, and heart hammering, I ran for my mother's room, ignoring Wren's pleas. I grabbed the shotgun discarded on the bed.

"What—" Henni rushed into the room. "What are you doing, child?" She tugged at the shotgun, but I gripped it tighter. "Let go," she ordered.

I shook my head and tore the gun from her grasp. "No," I told her. "I have to do something—"

"Hunter," she said more calmly. "Your mother needs you." I'd never seen the staunch woman so scared and sickly looking in all my life. She looked like a shell of the healer I knew. "There are no bullets," she said. "There is nothing you can do. You'll get yourself killed if they see you with that, you foolish boy."

But I knew something Henni didn't. "There are bullets," I breathed.

Her eyes widened.

"And only I know how to get out of here," I told her. I could tell Henni was torn between the two scenarios: all of us staying in the house to be tortured and killed, or a nine-year-old boy risking his life to save everyone.

I lugged the shotgun into my bedroom. It was heavy, but all I needed to do was injure the madmen, for now, to wound them if I couldn't kill them.

Dropping the shotgun on my bed, I crawled under and retrieved the cracker box that hid my most secret possessions: eighteen dollars I'd stolen from my father for emergencies; the stone necklace I'd weaved at Colt's shop for Wren—my future wife—when I was seven; a rap CD I'd gotten from a boy at school, which I was forbidden to listen to; and three shotgun shells I kept for the day I might have to protect my family from my father, or in this case, someone worse.

I couldn't hear Henni's commanding tone over my own whirring blood and rapid heartbeat, and in a blur, the shotgun was loaded, and I was running into the laundry room. I pulled the washing machine away from the wall, feeling the raw flesh on my back burn and stretch.

I'm not sure how much time it took me to get through the hole after I broke a slab of wood to fit, but in what felt like seconds, I was out in the cold.

Another scream. Then a gunshot.

Rocks cut into my bare feet as I ran around the house and out into the open. I ran and ran, past Colt's cold, dead body, gaping mouth, and blood-stained chest, toward his house where they had Nessa, his wife. Only there were no more screams. There was no more shouting.

The screen door of Colt's house opened, and one of the men stepped out, laughing with wild eyes and a bleeding scratch from his temple to his cheek.

The other man came stumbling out behind him, and before they even noticed me, I strained and lifted the shotgun. I had three bullets and I was determined to make them count. Holding my breath, I pulled the trigger.

W hen I opened my eyes, the overwhelmingly vivid memories of twelve years ago dissipated, leaving behind a restlessness I was all too familiar with, and I stared into a dark room filled with moon shadows. A bed. A dresser. A closet. A different room. A different place and time, but the nightmares still made it feel like it was yesterday.

Each time I dreamed of that day, I could hear my mother's sobs and Nessa's screams like they were in the room beside me. I could hear my little brother and Wren's cries commingling in toxic air that filled me with sweat-drenching fear. I could imagine what those men had done to Wren's mother and Nessa

—to the women in the village who were raped, beaten, and killed.

Flinging the blanket off me, the early morning air sent chills trickling over my bare skin. I sat up and ran my hand over my head and down my face with a sigh. No matter the uncertainty I sometimes had living in Whitehorse, I knew my family was safe from madmen, at least. And while that gave me a semblance of comfort, I knew I would always hear the screams. Whether they were my penance or just a haunting reminder of our reality, the deafening sounds would never go away, no matter how far we retreated from that place.

The carpeted floors were warm between my toes as I rose to my feet, and I grabbed the sweatshirt draped over the end of my bed and tugged it on.

It was an unforgettable feeling—terror. It was both numbing and all-consuming. It was a cold sweat and burning fear. It was a haunting memory I could never forget, no matter how much I wished I could.

Walking down the hall, I glanced at my mother's room, glad the door was closed and she was still asleep. I didn't want her asking why I was up so early again.

I stopped outside Milo's bedroom, still shrouded in darkness. I could hear his heavy breaths and see the rise and fall of his back as he slept.

Continuing into the living room, I checked the lock on the front door, the floor creaking under my feet. I walked to the side door that led to the garage next, which we used for canning and food storage, and after I checked the locks on the windows in the kitchen, I made my way to the large dining room, ensuring those windows were secured too.

This house was larger than what I was used to, but size had nothing to do with the uneasiness and doubt I always seemed to have, and as the days and weeks ticked on, I realized it wasn't going away, either.

I stopped at the French doors that faced the fields in the back of the house, stretching an acre deep toward the foothills. The wheat fields were shrouded in mist, and the tunnel-like greenhouse coverings disappeared into the fog. The cobweb on the screen door glistened in the moonlight and everything was calm. Everything was quiet. *Everything is fine.*

Opening the back door, I stepped outside in my pants and sweatshirt. I needed the bite of early morning air to chase away the stalking shadows of my dream. I needed the stillness.

Shoving my hands into my pockets, I peered around at the woods that surrounded the fields. When I was a boy, the old trapper from our village, Sven, taught Wren and me how to listen to the woods, and because of him I'd learned how to hunt; my father was too worthless to know how to do it, let alone teach me. Because of Sven, Wren and I survived and provided for our people, long enough to get here and live a life of unfathomable ease after so much struggle.

Now, Sven was gone, my father was dead, and the old village hidden in the woods was a lifetime behind me. So much was different, and I was grateful for it. More grateful than I knew how to express or could ever repay.

Whitehorse was a place my brother could have an actual childhood and play with kids his age, and one day he'd have a real future. My mother had a chance to start over, too, if she'd let go of the past. So, how was it we had all of this land and our safety, and yet, it didn't feel like home, and it didn't make me happy?

Still, as I peered out at the fields dressed in morning fog, I felt something a little bit like hope.

2

THEA

I stood at the trough, filling it with fresh water for Captain and Benedict, our only remaining horses at the facility. Now that more and more people were riding instead of walking around Whitehorse, we couldn't seem to keep community horses for very long. Those who had space wanted one of their own, and traded goods and services for them in exchange.

Captain, though, was old and gray, and perfect for new riders to practice on. Benedict, on the other hand, was a runner, sorrel and slick as a dart, and I hadn't met someone yet who I thought could handle the young blood. So they were the only two that remained.

Inhaling the comforting scent of hay and horses, I glanced at the paddocks and arena that spread across the west side of the prison. It was still more of a reinforced, just-in-case location that changed based on Whitehorse's needs.

The prison had gone from our fortress against General Herodson, to the Rehabilitation Facility when the rogue gangs were popping up everywhere, and now the property was a catchall—a vehicle parking lot, a storage facility with loading bays, and most importantly, a proper stable area, large enough to accommodate a dozen horses and riders at once.

It had become my second home in many ways. I worked with Kat, the townspeople, and the horses, more than I was at the lodge some weeks, especially between summer storms, when everyone was outside, enjoying what precious time we had without the arctic wind whipping through.

Benedict and Captain clomped up behind me, and Benedict nipped at my shoulder, like a demanding child. "Quit," I told him, nudging his muzzle away with my shoulder. When he nipped at me again, just being ornery, I sprayed him with the hose, laughing as he jolted and trotted off.

"Yeah, that's what I thought," I muttered. Reaching over, I rubbed Captain's withers as he slurped from the trough. "Teach him some manners, would you?" The old boy blinked and slurped again in answer.

When the trough was full, I turned off the hose, grateful as always for the hydro plant that kept this entire town up and running, as if modern civilization hadn't come to a screeching halt twelve years ago.

"I'm getting more next week," Kat said, startling me, and the side door to the old prison shut behind her. She wore riding jeans, like always, a tank top like mine, and her long blonde hair was up in a bun, her sunglasses perched against it.

Kat nodded to Captain. "Horses," she clarified.

"You're getting more horses?" That was surprising. "Where, in Prince Rupert?" Usually, trips were few and far between, and it felt like she and Woody had just returned from their mid-year trip down there to check in with Huck and visit with Phil, who had moved to the trading post a few years ago.

Kat shook her head. "New Bodega. Instead of sending supplies down with the next shipment, we're going to take them ourselves, that way we can pick up some more horses while we're at it."

"That's smart," I said, hosing the dirt and horse hair off my hands. "You take the supplies down in the horse trailer and bring the horses back."

"Two trailers," Kat clarified, and she rested her arms on the fence rail. "And Bert needs to check on one of the radio towers between here and Prince Rupert, since the signal has been spotty the past couple months."

Prince Rupert was the only community we could communicate with because of distance, terrain, and the elements that worked against what few towers we could maintain and keep functioning. They ran off military-grade solar panels and cooling tech to keep things functioning as much as the weather allowed, but routine maintenance wasn't always possible, so it wasn't surprising we'd been having issues.

"So," I said, drying my hands off on my pants, "it will be a multi-purpose trip."

"Yes, which is why it can't wait."

I nodded. "New Bodega this summer and then Prince Rupert in the fall? Ross isn't going to like that," I thought aloud. "And New Bodega is a *way* longer trip."

"Yes, it is. We'll be gone for a few weeks, I think, but it needs to be done sooner rather than later."

I readjusted my sunglasses as Captain meandered closer for more affection.

"We're also taking some of Henni's Seneca snakeroot compound with us, since it's rare down there. And, Alex is going," Kat added, reaching out to give Captain a quick pat. "He wants to see his friend, Zoe, since we're picking up the vaccine they've been working on."

I thought about Wren's fever after she'd slept with my brother for the first time. I couldn't imagine the guilt he would've felt had she died without the devil's club. They'd been the lucky ones; there were other couples like them—Tainted and Untainted couples—who had been intimate but hadn't made it through. At least the vaccine might save people like Wren's family in the future.

I leaned against the rail beside Kat, facing her. "So," I said, realizing it had been over a year and a half since Zoe's letter to Alex had arrived, explaining her scientist and doctor friends were going to work on a vaccine to save what lives they could. "New Bodega figured it out then?"

"I guess," she said, pulling her sunglasses down over her eyes against the blinding afternoon sun. "I'm just the manure shoveler on the trip, maybe a little Ability brawn, if we need it, so I don't know much more than that." Kat sighed as I huffed a laugh, and she shook her head, considering something for a moment. "Sometimes it still hits me that this is our reality. It's like I barely remember things from *before* most of the time, but then there are these moments when . . ." She bit her lip and reached for Captain absently.

"When it all comes rushing back and feels unsettling and unbelievable?"

Kat snorted a laugh. "Yeah, that sounds about right."

Kat could conduct a lightning show with the flick of her hand, and I could move things with my mind in the same way. That was a strange reality sometimes, even now. Especially for me and Kat. She'd struggled with her Ability for years—worried it would hurt someone again, that it was too dangerous and unpredictable after what happened to Ross all those nights ago when he'd tried to save her from Harlon and Cal. And before that, she'd been worried she was broken after she'd zapped Jenny back to life with those same powers, only for Jenny's renewed life to drain away just as quickly when she saved me from Nora.

The same way I felt broken after what I'd done to Luna. There was so much heaviness lingering from the past, and yet so much to focus on for the future. It was a constant push and pull I knew Kat could relate to.

"So . . . I guess I'll be running the center while you're gone," I thought aloud. I felt a mixture of pride to be running things in Kat's absence, and an unexpected longing to see the world south of Whitehorse.

Kat was still and silent for a heartbeat, contemplating. "*Actually*," she started. "I thought Susan could do that."

That . . . wasn't what I'd expected to hear, and I felt a tinge of disappointment. Whatever burst of importance I felt in being in charge while Kat was away smoldered instantly. "Susan?" I repeated, incredulous. Besides Wren, she was the most friendly member of the village, so it wasn't that I didn't like Susan, but in the scheme of things, she was new; she'd only been working with us for a handful of months.

"Yeah," Kat drawled, as if she was waiting for me to catch on, "because you'll be with me this time."

It took me a moment to register Kat's words, and my gaze cut to her.

She grinned.

"Go with you—to New Bodega? Really?" I couldn't suppress my smile. I would finally get to meet the people I'd heard so much about, like mind-meddling Zoe with the hypnotic eyes, and maybe even meet Alex's friend Iris, who made the best lavender honey I'd ever tasted in my life. My mouth watered just thinking about it.

"We obviously have to make sure Susan's up for running this place while we're gone, especially since she has Sutton to worry about. He gets into more trouble than any little boy I've ever met," Kat continued. "But I'm sure Wren won't mind lending a hand."

"I'm so excited!" I chirped. I hurried out of the gate and wrapped my arms around Kat, earning a little gasp and a tight squeeze before she pulled away.

"I figured you could use your own adventure for a change,"

she said with a smirk. "And Lord knows it will be nice to have another female on the trip for once."

I couldn't stop my grin from widening and my thoughts from drifting. Would the accounts I'd heard from Ross and Kat, Beau and Alex—all of them coming back from places I'd never been to over the years—do the landscape and the people justice?

Kat pointed toward our horses in the paddock, ready to saddle for our ride home. "There's something you should know, though," she admitted, chewing the inside of her cheek as we walked over to them.

Lowering my chin, I stared at her over my sunglasses and groaned. I knew that look, half amused and half nervous at the same time. "What is it?"

Her eyebrows rose. "Well, since you asked," she started, and I rolled my eyes. "Hunter is coming."

My excitement drained away a little, but I wouldn't let it vanish completely. "Oh." Hunter and I were not friends, we barely spoke to one another, so I could imagine how awkward a three-week trip together would be.

"Will that be a problem?"

I shook my head. "No," I admitted, and it wasn't, but it did make a road trip with Bert, Kat, and Alex a little less appealing, knowing Hunter's grumpy face would be there at every turn.

We stopped at the covered paddock where Cinder and Puck neighed excitedly, ready to go home. "What's he going for anyway, to trade some of his wheat or corn or something?"

Kat's eyebrows rose. "The vaccine is for his people," she reminded me. "There's a lot to learn about it. Not to mention, he's got specific orders from Henni about the snakeroot."

"Yeah, that makes sense." I forced a bigger smile. "Either way, I'm excited to get away from here for a little while, and see what the rest of the world looks like, you know?"

"Hell yes. This place can get suffocating." Kat nudged me.

"Why do you think I go on these trips? We could all use a little change of scenery once in a while."

We saddled our horses without much more discussion, and as Kat and I climbed into our saddles, she asked, "Are you ever going to tell me why you dislike him so much?"

"Hunter?" I said, glancing over my shoulder at her. I could feel the pink on my shoulders and realized I'd forgotten sun lotion. The weather was so changeable in June, I had a hard time keeping up with it.

"Yes," Kat drawled. "Hunter. What's with you two? You get along with everyone else, so it's weird to see you so icy around him."

"He's . . . aggravating," I admitted with a sigh. It was the only thing I could think of to describe him. "First impressions really do stick, I guess."

"Oh, that's right," Kat said, nudging Puck into a walk beside me and Cinder. Her chestnut gelding was almond-colored beside Cinder's brunette mane and tail. We clomped down the road toward the entrance gate. "You two had words when you first met."

"He just rubs me the wrong way, so severe and cold-shouldered all the time."

Kat reached for the gate latch. "I guess he's standoffish," she said. "But I don't think it's personal. He's like that with everyone." She opened the gate for our horses to walk through.

"Yeah, but you'd think after all we've done for them, he'd drop the judgey, disapproving act, you know?" I turned in my saddle to face her. "I mean, it wouldn't kill him to smile once in a while to make everyone *else* more comfortable."

"Not everyone is as bubbly as you, Thea," Kat chuckled. "Unfortunately," she added.

"And his mother?" I asked. "She's almost worse than him. I'm telling you, they're just . . ." I couldn't think of the word.

"Even Milo?" Kat looked at me over her sunglasses as she and Puck stopped to latch the gate behind us.

I grinned. "No, not Milo. He's adorable, and a happy kid, despite his unpleasant family."

Kat chuckled. "He's definitely a cutie. I always have to stop myself from pinching his cheeks."

Laughing, I shook my head. "And he wants a horse, badly," I told her. He was like me when I was eleven years old. "Every time I see Milo in town, or when I go to see my brother at Village Row, Milo rushes over to say hello and lavishes Cinder with attention."

"That kid could definitely use a little fun in his life." Kat practically snorted again. "It's sad, I feel like most of the village is still living like they're in hiding."

"Yeah, I know," I said quietly. "But Elle and Henni are planning a group dinner," I added. "And Susan and Leo have warmed up to us, which is a start. In fact, I hear Jade and Del have visited with them a couple times in the past few months."

"Wow, tea time with the Ranskins? That is a big step, but not unexpected. They get along with everyone."

"Except for Took," I said with a laugh.

"Yeah, except for him." Old and grouchy as he was, Took mostly kept to himself these days.

I inhaled a deep breath and thought about Hunter's chiseled, narrowed expression. All jokes aside, I did wonder if he ever smiled. "I hope Susan and Leo's gracious spirit catches on," I thought aloud. "Because I'm running out of chipper-Thea juju."

Kat barked a laugh and shook her head, as if I was the incorrigible one.

The clomp of horse hooves on the rutted pavement echoed off the tree line as we continued down the road, using the old abandoned neighborhoods to avoid the people-filled streets in the center of town.

While Whitehorse had been 25,000 people strong before the Virus, there were only a thousand of us now, and we concentrated in the areas of the city we used the most in order to keep us all safe. The unused areas of the city were left to fall to ruin. Without the use of power and heat, and with such extreme weather, the old houses were becoming more decrepit every year they remained empty. The roads were in equal disrepair because of the constant hot and cold. Elle and Bernie's Abilities to melt the snow on the streets during the winter, when the snowfall was too much for the plow trucks to handle, didn't help the pitted streets either. And while Bert and others ran city projects like hole filling, power plant upkeep, and vehicle maintenance, Jackson didn't want to spend the time and resources needed to upkeep the unused areas. So abandoned, leaky, and lonely the outer neighborhoods remained.

When the reinforced walls of Riverdale, the largest concentration of neighborhoods in Whitehorse, came into view, Kat glanced over her shoulder at me, a few paces back. "Want to take the Riverdale way home?" she asked. "I'm going to stop by Village Row and talk to Henni and Wren about New Bodega." She lifted her eyebrow wryly. "I figured you might want to see your brother."

I smiled, squinting in the glinting sunlight off the steel walls that stood a few stories high. "Yeah, sure. I'll go with you," I conceded, realizing it had been nearly two weeks since I'd seen Beau. Between his work at the Survival Center and living full time in Village Row with Wren, I felt like I barely saw him anymore.

When I felt Kat staring at me, I begrudgingly looked at her. "What?"

"Assuming Hunter's there," she started, "try to be nice, would you? Now that we're going to New Bodega together and all."

Heaving out an exaggerated sigh, as if Kat were asking for a miracle, I urged Cinder forward. "I'll do my best."

3

THEA

T he large metal doors of Riverdale were open, allowing us to traipse into the most populated sector of the city without a second thought. But the lack of bars and guards standing sentry at the community entrance was misleading.

A handful of townspeople were always patrolling the perimeter. If not physically, they were doing so with their minds. Guard duty looked a little different when you could feel unnerving Abilities nearby or sense danger. Or, if you were like Woody—the captain of all security teams—who could block people's Abilities with a single thought, just as he'd done during Ross's intervention program some years back. The gangs of renegade youth in the area had been rehabilitated and placed with new families, or they'd moved away from Whitehorse and the surrounding settlements. There was no need for the reform program anymore, and crazy people tended to band together out in the woods, which had given Woody a nice break. Everyone else who'd survived the outbreak had long-settled somewhere else or made a safe haven of their own, so our steel walls and Ross's Ability-strengthened police force sufficed well enough.

Instead of going to the end of the road, where Kat and Ross

lived, the horses plodded down a street that veered toward Gray Mountain. It had been an unused part of Riverdale until Beau and Wren returned from British Columbia looking for a settlement large enough for a dozen people.

The road was pitted like the rest of town, but somehow the area felt like a world of its own—a commune of sorts, where the villagers could remain removed from the rest of us, if they wanted.

We called it Village Row because it felt like a different world than the rest of Riverdale. Glass wind chimes hung from the spruce trees in some yards, a tinkling welcome that met your ears before the houses came into view—or a warning, depending on who you asked. More wind chimes hung from the eaves of the homes, and many of the villagers sat in their yards, tending to their flower and vegetable gardens or weaving willow baskets to trade. It was quiet and peaceful.

Four houses lined each side of the road before butting up to the foothills, though only five of the homes were occupied. With eleven villagers, not counting Beau and Wren, there wasn't a need for all the houses, not yet anyway. The home at the beginning of the row belonged to three older, unmarried women who lived together. Wren joked that they were her crazy aunts, the spinster sisters. They'd helped raise Hunter and Wren and did the same with Milo and Sutton when they were needed, but otherwise, they kept to themselves, speaking in their natural tongue, laughing at inside jokes, and watching the rest of the world with appraising gazes. They seemed happy enough, if a little strange, and liked to weave their baskets on the porch from morning to dusk.

Susan and Leo, a young couple, lived with their seven-year-old son, Sutton, across from the sisters. Otto and Henni lived in the house next to them with a large, glassed-in greenhouse between their lots. And Hunter, Milo, and his mother, Letty, had the largest lot at the end of the street, across from Beau and

Wren. Beau's ranch style house was gray with white trim and rusted gutters, small compared to Hunter's settlement with fields that stretched at least an acre. Over the past year, he and Beau had constructed covered garden tunnels to protect the tomatoes, strawberries, and sunflowers from the summer rains and brisk mornings. Aside from Hunter's expectedly cool demeanor, he was predictable too. He worked the land every day, planting something new, like the sapling apricot and plum trees I'd noticed on my last visit.

Despite him mistrusting us in the beginning, it was because of Hunter's steadiness that everyone seemed to acclimate as well as they had; Wren had been right about that part, at least. The villagers looked to him for guidance, especially in the beginning when so many things were new and uncertain.

When the cornfields came into sight, I noticed Letty first, her tanned skin and her long dark hair braided down her back. She had jeans on and a brimmed hat to shade her shoulders. Her gaze, as always, was unwelcoming.

Milo's head popped out from the towering cornstalks beside her, and the moment he saw me, he gave Kat and me an excited wave. Letty didn't chide him for acknowledging me anymore, she hadn't for a while, so I waved back at him with an irrepressible grin.

"You're right," Kat said. "He's adorable, and going to be trouble one day soon. Mrs. Sour Face over there isn't going to know what to do with him."

I flashed Kat a smile, and we clomped closer to the paddock I'd helped Jackson build behind one of the empty houses. Only Hunter, Wren, Letty, and Susan had a horse. Everyone else walked when they had to leave the comfort of the village, not that they left very often.

When we reached the paddock, Kat climbed out of Puck's saddle and handed me his reins. "I'm going to find Wren and Henni."

"Sounds good," I said with a head bob. "I'll hunt down my brother."

"I'll find you when I'm finished," Kat called over her shoulder, and she disappeared around the side of the house.

As I tied the horses up by the trough, Dancer, my old riding friend, plodded out of her stall to greet me.

She reached her head over the railing. "Well hello, beautiful stranger," I cooed, running my hand over Dancer's white forelock. She and Cinder scented each other in greeting, their nostrils flaring.

Though I saw Dancer sometimes, when I came to visit my brother, it wasn't as often as I liked. I'd grown used to having her around when Wren was staying with us; even Cinder seemed a bit lonely in the paddock back home with only ornery old Big Red to pal around with.

Dancer dipped her head, relishing the attention as I rubbed her velvety, pink nose. Picking a straw of hay from her snowy white mane, I smiled. "You look so elegant when you're not sporting a winter coat."

Her ears shifted back before I heard footsteps behind me, and Hunter came around the side of the paddock, stopping at the fence when he saw me. His expression didn't change much, severe like always, but I'd grown used to it. The way his t-shirt hugged his body, on the other hand, was unexpected. Sweat dappled his light gray shirt, a sight I didn't see in the cooler months. But his chiseled jaw clenched and the hard set of his obsidian-dark eyes quickly squashed such a pleasant surprise. If I hadn't known he was twenty-one, I might've thought him older and much more terrifying.

He rested the shovel in his hand against the side of the barn, and with his bicep, he wiped the sweat from his brow. "Thea," he said flatly in greeting. He'd cut his black hair months ago, no longer hanging in his face, though I wasn't sure if the cropped look made him look a bit more approachable or more . . . something else.

"Hunter," I drawled back.

His gaze shifted from me to his horse.

"Don't mind me," I said before he could voice his displeasure. "I just thought I'd say hello to my old friend real quick." I rubbed Dancer's nose and dropped my hand, motioning toward Otto's house across the street. "Kat needed to talk to Wren and Henni."

"About New Bodega?" The interest in Hunter's voice surprised me.

"Yes, I—"

Without another word, he walked past me and the horses, straight toward Otto's. I tried not to notice Hunter's tanned skin gleaming in the sunlight as he strode across the street, his boots crunching loudly on the gravelly asphalt.

With a huff, I looked at Dancer. "He's always so pleasant," I muttered, and with a purpose of my own, I walked around the paddock to cross the street. When I saw Honey Bear basking in the sunshine outside of Henni's greenhouse, I headed toward the grizzly. If he was out there, it was safe to assume my brother was too.

Honey Bear's head lifted when he sensed me coming, and grinning, I hurried over to him. "Howdy, handsome," I chirped.

He chuffed in hello, and I crouched down to rub his head, loving the way his long fur felt between my fingers. "You don't come home very much anymore, Honey Bear," I told him, realizing how much I missed him. He nuzzled me, knocking me over with playful power, and I giggled as I fell onto my butt on the sidewalk.

"It's *Bear*," my brother corrected from somewhere inside the greenhouse, and I rolled my eyes.

"You should've named him yourself then," I countered. It

wasn't my fault Beau had been so averse to Bear in the beginning. It was laughable, now that they were inseparable.

Henni stepped out of the greenhouse with a basket of bound herbs in her hand. "Thea," she said in greeting. "It's been a while since we've seen you around here."

Although Wren's grandmother was a bit prickly and like Took in many ways, she was more intimidating, and I smiled weakly. "I've been busy with work," I explained and shoved my hands into my back pockets. "Kat's here to talk to you about New Bodega." I nodded toward her house as Beau stepped out of the greenhouse behind her.

"Thank you," Henni said, and she glanced between Beau and me with a dip of her chin and headed across the street.

"Nice to see you!" I called.

"You too," she said quietly. Though Henni wasn't exactly *friendly*, but more reticent and stone-faced like Hunter and the rest of them, I didn't take Henni's reserve personally. Not even when she stared at me for too long like she often did. It didn't seem as offensive as when Hunter or his mother did it, for some reason.

On cue, Hunter stepped out of Otto's house, stopping in the road to say something to Henni before he headed back toward the paddocks. His mother and Milo stood at the barn door, their baskets overflowing with ears of corn.

"He's not that bad, you know."

I looked at Beau. "What?"

"You always scowl when you see Hunter. He's not that bad."

I rolled my eyes. "I don't always scowl—"

"*Yes*," he said with a chuckle, "you do. It isn't like you, which is why it's so damn obvious." Beau eyed me carefully.

Forcing my expression to soften, I waved his concern away, not wanting to dredge up old issues when things were finally starting to smooth out a bit for Wren and her family. "He just rubs me the wrong way, what can I say? I can't like everyone."

Beau left the Hunter topic alone and petted Bear's head absently. The grizzly sniffed my brother's pants like he'd been rolling in food then rubbed his drooly snout against Beau's leg. Beau nudged his face away, as if it were just another day with a grizzly. "Are we doing family dinner tomorrow night?"

"I don't know, I haven't heard anything." I glanced at him. "Cal and I were going to—" As soon as my brother's brow furrowed, I rolled my eyes again. "What?" I said, throwing up my hands. "What is it now?"

"You're still with him?" he asked, skeptical.

"Are you for real, Beau? It's like no one is ever good enough for you—the entire town loves Cal—"

"Yeah, I know, on both accounts. But you guys don't really . . ." He pursed his lips, like he was searching for the right, perhaps least offensive, word.

"What's wrong with him?" I quipped, but no matter what Beau said, it was obvious he'd never fully forgiven Cal for what he and Harlon had done to Kat at her house all those years ago, tying her up and threatening her. It didn't matter that Cal had paid for it, that he still had the fractal scars on his body as a daily reminder of Kat's wrath, or that he was only a kid at the time and his family back then was a gang of miscreants; I knew Beau would *never* forgive him. "Cal has a job with Ross," I said, and began to tick off a list of reasons Cal was wonderful. "He's nice to me, we have fun together, he's well-liked—"

"That's a great resume, Thea, but do you even like him?"

I glared at him. "Of course I do," I deadpanned. "Otherwise, why would I be his girlfriend?"

"No, I mean, do you *really* like him? Because you two have nothing in common."

"How would you know?"

"You're right. How would I? You never bring him around."

I rolled my eyes again. "Why, so you could be an ass to him?"

41

Beau ran his hand over his face and groaned. "Okay, fine. I won't argue with you. Yes, there are worse guys, but I think you can do better."

"Whatever."

"Whatever," he said back, and nudged my shoulder. "Can we please do family dinner tomorrow night? Wren's been helping me and Hunter so much, I think she could use some girl time—and you know she'd never ask for help herself."

That Wren needed me made my heart swell. "Of course we can," I said, never wanting to disappoint either of them. "But *only* if you're nice to Cal the next time you see him."

"First of all, I'm always nice—"

"Ha!"

"What? I am."

I glowered at him. "Fine, then I mean *friendly*."

Beau reached his hand out. "I can do friendly."

I snorted. "Right."

Beau scowled at me and took my hand in his. "It's a deal," he grumbled.

"So, I'm assuming I need to tell Elle we're hosting dinner?"

Beau lifted his shoulder in a half shrug. "I made a comment to Jackson this morning, so I think she might know, but will you make sure? I've been trying to get this final drip system installed so I can be done with the irrigation for good." He sighed, as if he was exhausted, and I didn't blame him. The last year had whizzed by and only half of it had been productive because of all the snowfall. Now that it melted and summer was in full swing, there was a lot to do to get everything ready for the next few months of warm days and sunshine.

"You should be proud of yourself, Beau," I told him, all bantering aside. "Against the odds, you and Wren made this happen." I gestured to the neighborhood surrounding us. "It's exactly like you said it would be, and they all, even Wren, have you to thank for that."

"That might be the nicest thing you've ever said to me, Thea," he joked, and glanced around Village Row like he was taking it all in for the first time.

"I know," I said, smiling ruefully. "Don't get used to it."

"All right, then you better get out of here before my head gets any bigger." He shoved my shoulder playfully.

"Good point. It looks like they're wrapping up inside anyway. Good luck finishing. I'll see you tomorrow."

"See ya." Beau turned and stepped back into the greenhouse.

With a final ear rub, I said goodbye to Bear and started back for the horses. "Hey!" Beau called from the doorway.

I peeked back at him.

"I really do appreciate you staying home for dinner tomorrow," he said.

"I know, I'm the best sister you could ask for and you love me," I called back, shoving my hands into my back pockets.

"Nuh-uh!"

I grinned. "Yeah-huh!"

Beau's chuckle echoed behind me as I headed back down the street to the barn. Bear's grunts and groans followed behind me, and I glanced back to find the grizzly ambling briskly toward the barn too. When Milo came around the side of the building, I realized the cause of the big lug's sudden excitement.

Milo's expression lit up at the sight of Bear lumbering toward him. The old grizzly had finally found a playmate to lavish him with attention, which was heartening.

With a grunt, Bear hurried past me to Milo, nudging him playfully. With a laugh and a hearty pet, the two disappeared into the barn. My guess was to sneak Bear a snack, and I grinned.

I could hear Bear's chuffing inside the barn as I drew closer, but the horses were unfazed by the thousand-pound grizzly's presence. Like all of us, they were used to him by now; he was just another one of us, a misfit member of the family.

"—and things need to change. They can't stay like this,"

Hunter said. I stopped where Cinder was tied to the paddock rail and peered over at him and his mother, standing at the gardening shed a dozen yards away.

Hunter's mother shifted her glare from him to me. Her scowl was unchanged as she registered my presence. So was Hunter's.

I cleared my throat. "Don't mind me," I muttered, and untied Cinder and Puck. I could feel their glares searing a hole in my back. "Like I said, always so pleasant," I uttered under my breath.

I led the horses away as quickly as I could to wait for Kat at Otto's house, only glancing back at the barn as I heard Milo's laughter ring through the afternoon air. I smiled, happy to find him wrestling with Bear in the dirt and hay.

Thank goodness for Milo, who brought a bloom of life to the village. It was like he played and laughed and smiled enough for everyone. Whatever he remembered from his past, it hadn't eternally marked him the way it had the rest, and I was relieved Milo could still act like a kid.

I considered jumping on Cinder and heading home, leaving Kat to deal with her duties alone as Hunter made his way toward the barn. Hurrying my steps, I flashed a final glance in Milo's direction, registering a blur of images that made the hairs on the back of my neck stand on end and gave me pause.

Milo and Bear wrestling in the barn. The horse plow. A rusty plow blade. I saw Milo stumble as he sidestepped Bear's playful swipe, and my adrenaline spiked. "Milo!" I ran toward him, the horses forgotten.

Vaguely, I heard Hunter shout for him too, and as Milo registered what was happening, fear flashed across his face.

I thrust the plow into the far wall with the flick of my wrist, making the barn quake as it crashed. Everything was loud and panicked. The horses spooked in their stalls as Bear skittered out of sight with a yelp, and Milo tumbled to the ground, red-faced and shrieking.

"Are you okay?" I rasped, and fell to my knees beside him. He was unscathed, but the fear in his eyes matched my own as he stared at the bent plow and damaged wall.

My heart hammered in my chest. Restless neighs and whinnies filled the barn, and I tried to catch my breath as I realized my hands were trembling—my entire body shaking in the wave of anxiety that flooded through me.

A cold sweat doused me as I saw Luna flying through the air all over again, and my mother flying out the window with that same haunting look of fear I could never forget. I stared at the damaged barn wall as I tried to catch my breath. "I'm sorry," I breathed as murmurs and rustling surrounded me. "I'm sorry, I didn't mean to scare them—"

"—Hey!"

I stirred. Blinked. Caught my breath and realized Hunter was crouched in front of me.

"Are you okay?" He inspected me up and down, confusion wild in his gaze.

With a brusque nod, I rose to my feet. "Yeah—it's—I'm fine. Sorry. I didn't—" I turned to leave.

"Thea," Hunter bit out.

Pausing for a single moment, I looked back at him, my chest heaving and emotions I didn't want to feel making it hard to breathe.

"Are you sure?" His voice was gentle as he stepped closer. I glanced behind him to see Letty fussing over Milo, and Bear inching his way back into the barn.

But Hunter . . . he was staring at me, his eyes not wide with fear but with concern. "Thea," he prompted again.

"Yes," I rasped, nodding automatically. "I'm fine."

He ran his hand over his short hair and heaved out a heavy exhale. "Thank you," he said, glancing back at his brother.

Dipping my chin, I turned to leave again. This time, Hunter reached for my arm. I froze and stared at his hand, then looked into his umber irises. There was something unexpectedly steady and calming about them and I couldn't look away.

Slowly, he released his grip on me. "Are you sure you're all right?" he asked again, skeptical. "You don't seem like it."

"I—" Of course I was fine. I wasn't the one who had almost impaled myself on the plow. "Yes, sorry about your barn," I said, but it was clear I wasn't fine, every crease in Hunter's brow told me I wasn't. I turned on my heel. "I have to go, but I'll help fix it," I called over my shoulder.

"I don't care about the barn," Hunter called back, but I was jogging toward the horses who'd run down the road before I could hear the rest.

4

THEA

The next day, cross-legged and with piles of pulled weeds beside me, I sat between Luna and Jenny's graves, but it was Rocky's I stared at—the first wolf we'd ever lost, because of Nora and Bear's mother. *My* mother's grave would've been the first in line, if she had been buried there instead of left in the frozen landscape of Whitely after I'd thrown her to her death. All the graves together would've been every bad decision I'd ever made, lined up in front of me as a constant reminder. My mother. Rocky. Jenny. Luna.

When you left remnants of death in your wake, rationality was no longer part of the equation. Regret for certain decisions, yes. Sadness knowing beings I cared about were dead because of them, definitely. It was impossible to forgive myself.

But aside from all the dumb decisions I'd made that led to one horrible outcome or another, my Ability haunted me most.

I told myself that I wasn't the only child who'd survived the fever, then had to use their newfound capabilities to hurt someone they cared about—that my mom wasn't the only one who'd gone crazy from the Virus, even if it felt like it sometimes. It was her face that haunted my thoughts still—that instant her eyes landed on me as an invisible force gripped her, flinging her to her death. The fear and confusion. Telekinesis. Levitation. Mind over matter. Call it what you wanted, but the power in me had been so raw and buzzing, my mind and thoughts swirled and I'd lost control. It was *easy* to lose control. I could still feel it whirling around deep inside me, fed by my fear.

"Hey," Elle chirped as she stepped through the trees.

I smiled weakly. "Hi."

"I thought I saw you come out here." Elle's dark hair was up in a ponytail, away from her neck, and damp soil from working in the greenhouse dirtied her knees and frayed, cutoff shorts.

I smiled as she sat down beside me, indifferent to the wild grasses and weeds I knew tickled her legs.

"So," she said tentatively, "what's up?" It was her concerned mother voice I knew well. She ran her fingers through my hair, long and loose down my back. "Is everything okay?"

My gaze drifted toward the graves again. "Oh, fine, just coming to say hi is all. It's been a while."

"It has, hasn't it," she mused. "I haven't been out here in a while either." There was a hint of sadness in her voice as she stared at her sister's grave, and it needled my heart. "Doesn't mean I don't think about them all the time, though," she said more casually, but the sadness in her eyes gutted me and I had to look away.

"I remember when you used to fall asleep down here," Elle remembered. Her voice was almost whimsical. "I don't know how many times Jackson had to carry you back to the house, your face smooshed and your hair a rat's nest from nestling between Rocky's and Jenny's graves." Wrapping her arm around my shoulders, Elle hugged me against her.

Sometimes I forgot she wasn't my mother. It felt like she was the only mother I'd ever had, and I leaned my head against her.

"You don't have to tell me what's wrong," she said. "But you can talk to me about anything, anytime, you know?"

"I know, but it's not worth talking about." We'd already discussed my guilt ad nauseam, and I wasn't going to put her through that again.

"Well," Elle hedged. "Whatever it is, it's bothering you enough to bring you out here." She was thoughtful for a moment. "You know, Jenny used to tell me it was pointless to be sad or regretful because you can't change the past. You have to think about the future instead."

I stared at Jenny's lichen-covered headstone.

"Of course, she always had a bad attitude when we were growing up, so I thought she was just being a brat, and maybe she was at the time, but there's some truth in it, you know? The past can be a killer if we let it."

I nodded because Elle expected me to, but it was easier for her to move on, especially with the life she had now. She was always busy with a purpose—all of them were. I was just trying to get through each day without dwelling on my every mistake, praying I wouldn't make another one.

Elle tucked a strand of my hair behind my ear, her expression contemplative but certain. "I think this trip with Kat will be good for you."

"You do?"

She nodded against the top of my head, and we sat in comfortable silence for a little while longer. I felt a flare of hope as I realized Elle might be right. And suddenly, venturing to a new place and creating new memories seemed almost too good to be true.

"I'm about to get started on the chili for dinner tonight. You want to help?"

"Oh, do I!" I answered emphatically, sitting up straight.

Elle chuckled. "I'll tell you what, if you take care of the honey cornbread, I'll do everything else. I always burn it. *And* you can have whatever honey is left." She winked at me.

"Bribery is frowned upon," I told her. "Mothers everywhere would be ashamed of you."

Elle groaned as she rose to her feet. "You know me, I'm not above coercion, at least, not when it comes to cooking." She held her hand out to me.

I grunted as she pulled me to my feet. "Clearly."

5

THEA

Lying on my stomach, I stared down at my sketch of Bear. Either he was getting more ragged in his old age, or I was doing a piss-poor job drawing him tonight. Kansas played acoustic guitar in my ears, singing about dreams as they disappear like dust in the wind. As depressing as the song was; the oldies playlist felt apt tonight. Whoever the bulky iPod had belonged to before the world ended had quite a collection of music, and depending on my mood, I could find a little bit of everything.

The last remaining wolf of Beau's pack, Little Foot, was curled on the floor beside my bed, his furry white and gray body rising and falling with slumbering breaths. Smiling, I remembered him as a young wolf, sitting with us around the campfire at the Ranskins all those years ago. Time had gone by so quickly, and yet, it felt like an entire lifetime ago when we'd all first met —Jackson and Elle, Sophie and Alex, the wolves, and the Ranskins. So much had changed since then.

I sketched Bear's muzzle with a pencil, one of the few I had left in my desk drawer. Scavenging trips were few and far between these days since we were self-sustaining, and because so much of the waste left behind was unusable—clothes were moth-eaten, food had spoiled, buildings were weather-beaten and decaying, as were most things inside of them. So unless we needed something substantial, we created it ourselves.

Shading the crease around Bear's eye, I thought of how empty life would be when he was gone, always a bundle of fun and cuddles. What would Beau do then? No more wolves. No more Honey Bear . . . I forced myself not to think about it.

Slowly, my bedroom door opened, and Little Foot and I glanced at Jackson in the doorway. I tugged my earbuds from my ears, and Little Foot's tail thumped against the carpet.

"I knocked, but you didn't answer," he said, his gaze shifting to my sketchbook. "I wasn't sure if you were asleep."

I smiled and shook my head. "Nope. Just drawing."

Jackson opened the door the rest of the way and peered around my bedroom, lit by the overhead lamp and white Christmas lights twinkling across my window. Fleetingly, I wondered if Wren's family had grown used to the electricity, or if they still used fires and candlelight instead.

"I remember when everything you had was pink," Jackson mused. "And bumblebees. You really liked bumblebees."

I sat up, crossing my legs, and pulled my sketch pad into my lap as I glanced around my bedroom. The dream catcher Took had made for me hung at the head of my queen bed, the fringe of feathers fluttering in the evening breeze coming through the window. I studied the slightly sun-bleached movie posters pinned to my walls—depictions of heroes who saved the day, like *Commando* and *Terminator*, whose adventures Jackson told as bedtime stories when I was little. There were the epic love stories, too, which Elle had often requested, like *The Princess Bride* and *Casablanca*. My desk was covered in bits of random-ness, and worn novels filled my bookshelves, framed photos that Elle had taken over the years lining the top of it. It definitely wasn't a little girl's bedroom, not anymore.

"Yeah," I said with a smirk, remembering all the times Jackson had given in and had a tea party with me and Little Foot —the image of my pink plastic cups pinched between his fingers making me laugh. "I did love pink. I bet you're relieved you don't have to tote pink stuffed animals, sticker books, and Disney Princess crap home for me anymore."

He lifted his shoulder. "I don't know, I sort of miss the pink," he admitted, and sat down on the bed beside me. Part of me wanted to ask Jackson if he still thought of his own baby girl and wife who hadn't made it through the outbreak. And another part of me thought to leave well enough alone, hoping that raising Beau and me had given him a little solace, even if I knew it was difficult for him at first.

Jackson leaned his elbows on his knees, his bearded cheeks lifting with a grin as he stared at my iPod. "That thing still works?"

I scoffed. "Barely. I have to keep it plugged in. The battery is shit now." I glanced at him, waiting for Jackson to chastise me for cursing, but he ignored it. Truth be told, I was glad we weren't keeping track of curse words anymore, because I disliked cooking as much as Elle did, and my helping with dinner a few nights a week was plenty for me.

"You didn't mention what happened at the village yesterday," Jackson said, and suddenly, I realized the reason for his visit.

"Oh. Did I forget to mention it?"

"Tell me what's up, squirt." His hazel eyes met mine, concern brimming in them. While Elle was the one who worried the most, Jackson was the protective one. He hated to see me sad, and he was always in my corner, no matter what.

"It was nothing really. I thought Milo was going to hurt himself, so I freaked out."

"I wouldn't call it *freaked out*, Thea. That kid could be seriously hurt if it weren't for you."

I shrugged. "Maybe."

Jackson studied me, and inwardly I squirmed. "What's this really about?" he asked.

"I don't know," I admitted. "I guess I just don't like feeling out of control." It was a shitty feeling to be so powerful and yet feel so powerless at the worst possible times. Acting on raw emotion was terrifying. The incident with Milo could've ended much worse, like it had with Luna.

Jackson wrapped his arm around me, pulling me into his side, and kissed my forehead. "I understand what out of control feels like, in my own way," he said, and his voice deepened. "And I know what it's like to feel blame for something that wounds others."

I peered up at him. "How do you mean?"

Dropping his arm, Jackson turned to me. "When Alex and I left you guys in Slana, and those men came for you, I blamed myself for years for not being there when it happened."

"You did? Why? You didn't know air-sniffing freaks would show up to harass us."

"Regardless, they came, and you kids almost died because I couldn't help Elle protect you. Luckily she's a badass and you didn't need me, but I think about what you all saw and how scared you were—the car accident when you were trying to get away—and I could've helped prevent some of that."

"I think you won all of your points back, though," I said wryly. "With us, this place. We have Whitehorse because of you."

Jackson shrugged, which was uncharacteristic of him. "It doesn't make me feel any better about my failings. Just like nothing I tell you will take your guilt away, or make it fade—not any time soon, anyway."

"Great," I muttered. That Jackson wasn't coddling me made me feel grateful, but that he acknowledged my guilt would linger wasn't very heartening either.

"It's just how we're built, I guess. But the important thing to remember is that you help protect people too. You helped build this town, protected your brother, and now Milo, with that same Ability that scares you so much. And that's not nothing, Thea."

I met Jackson's gaze. His words felt heavy with truth, almost stifling, but I couldn't help but scoff. "I think Hunter would say otherwise. I ruined his wall *and* his plow."

"He's grateful to you, and he was worried about you when I saw him in town today."

"Yeah," I snorted. "Well, it will pass."

Jackson eyed me as I picked at the corner of my sketch paper, and I wanted to ask him what else Hunter had said to him, but I didn't have the guts to.

"You know," Jackson started, "you and Hunter are going on a long trip together. You're going to have to figure out how to tolerate him for more than five minutes at a time."

There was amusement in his voice I didn't appreciate, and my eyes narrowed on him. "In case you haven't noticed, he's not very friendly."

"Well," Jackson said, raking his fingers through his beard. "You haven't put much effort into getting to know each other either." He looked at me from the corner of his eye. "Maybe that will change after this trip."

"Maybe," I echoed, and flashed him a skeptical, sidelong glance in return. "You're okay with me going to New Bodega, right?" I hadn't exactly asked for permission so much as told Jackson and Elle I was going.

"Why? Would you stay behind if I didn't want you to leave?" He lifted his dark eyebrow curiously.

"I don't know," I admitted, though it would definitely give me pause.

"Of course it's fine," he said, patting my leg. "I think it will be good for you. And even if you'll always be chirpy, smiley little Thea to me, you're nineteen now. You don't have to ask for permission to start your own life. You're capable of protecting yourself, and you're smart. Even if I don't care for your taste in boys, I trust you. Elle and I both do."

The thought of Donavan made my stomach churn, and once again, Luna flying through the air flashed in my mind, so did Donavan and Beau standing toe-to-toe because of me. Then I thought of Cal and how he always seemed to make me feel a bit better.

"That doesn't mean we won't worry about you, though," Jackson clarified. "It sort of comes with the territory of being an over-protective parent."

I smiled, but it was weak. This time, my thoughts lingered on Cal. "Why don't you like Cal?" I asked. Unlike my brother, Jackson wasn't one to hold a grudge.

"Are you asking because you know in your gut there's a reason, or because you don't see it?"

I averted my gaze. There were a number of reasons people would question our relationship if they knew all there was to know about us, but none of it made Cal a bad guy. In fact, I think Jackson, and even Beau, might've had a newfound respect for him if they knew the truth. "You just don't know him as well as I do. He's a really good guy."

"Maybe he is, but neither of you have given us a chance to get to know him that well."

"I think you all intimidate him," I admitted. "He still feels horrible about what happened with Kat."

"Well, he shouldn't. Kat and Ross have forgiven him, that's what matters. And I know he's not like that anymore. Meghann's been a good mother for him."

I stared at Jackson, contemplating whether Cal had been keeping his distance or if I'd been the one to keep him separate from my family. I was ashamed and scared they would learn the truth about what happened while Beau was on his adventure with Bear. "We're going to fix that," I said aloud, surprising myself. "You not knowing him the way I do," I amended. A flush of unease burned inside me, and my stomach churned. I stared down at my charcoal-covered fingers.

"Good," Jackson said. "And I never said I didn't like Cal, but I'm not convinced he makes you happy either." His eyes crinkled in the corners, glistening with love and protection.

Why did everyone keep saying that?

Jackson pointed to my iPod. "What are we listening to tonight?"

I grinned, glad to change the subject to something that truly did make me happy and my heart sing. "Your favorite playlist, actually." I handed him an earbud, and the moment he put it to his ear, a smile filled his handsome face.

"It's been a while," Jackson mused with a nostalgic lilt. He sat back against the wall with a contented sigh to listen.

Leaning back beside him, I put the other earbud in. There was something so warm and comforting about Jackson, there always had been. And curled up beside him, like when I was a little girl, was exactly what I needed.

I rested my head on his shoulder, and he wrapped his arm around me as we shut our eyes and listened to a song about country roads, taking us back to where we belonged.

6

HUNTER

My mother and I rode into town, the cart creaking and protesting behind Dancer. I leaned forward, petting her sleek, white neck and peeked over at my mother, silent beside me.

She regarded the town from atop her coffee-colored mare, Juniper, eyeing the people and storefronts, always on alert. Always watching and waiting for something bad to happen, even if she never admitted it. The worry lines on her face gave her away, though. She was still cautious, still distrusting. After more than a year, she still seemed out of place—but then, all of us at the village felt that way sometimes.

Her black hair draped over her shoulders reaching the crook of her elbows; it was grayer now than when we first came to Whitehorse, or maybe I was only just beginning to notice it. But despite how cruel the years had been to her, she was still beautiful—in a stern, grave sort of way.

"Stop staring at me," she said without sparing me a glance.

I watched her a second longer. "I'm getting Milo a horse," I told her, knowing it wasn't something she particularly agreed with.

That got her attention. Her gaze shot to mine. "No," she said. Being in Whitehorse with every necessity we needed at our fingertips, she refused to take more from these people than she'd already had to.

"Yes," I replied. "He's getting a horse."

"Hunter—"

"It's decided, Mother." My gaze hardened. "He deserves something of his own in this place."

"He has everything he could possibly need here, and then some. You act as if he's deprived."

"He *is* deprived—of friends his own age, of schooling with others since you won't let him."

"What's wrong with Jasper?" she said, her brow furrowing.

"Nothing . . . except he's an old, blind man, and Milo should be learning and playing with *kids*. Sophie has offered—"

"He can learn a lot from Jasper."

"That's not the point, Mother. And he will have a horse of his own."

Dancer's hooves clomped on the rutted asphalt, and the jars of dried herbs clanked in the back of the wagon as it lurched over each bump with a thud.

"And it's not charity from anyone or a gift—I'll make sure it's a trade. We won't owe anyone anything." Trade was currency, and between produce, woven baskets and bags, and tinctures, we had plenty in the village to trade with.

I peered up the road at Mr. Murphy's store, nestled between the trading post and the basket shop. I could see our three produce shelves through the large glass window, practically empty and waiting to be filled with our weekly supply of goods for the townspeople. Root vegetables, a few dozen pounds of corn, and jars of sage, lavender blossoms, and wheat was the least we could provide after everything everyone had done for us.

Some people glanced at us as we rode on, but we mostly

went unnoticed now that people were more familiar with us in Whitehorse. It wasn't that we dressed all that different, or even because of our darker skin—there were other Natives and ethnicities in Whitehorse—but it felt different in town because we *were* different. We were the minority because of our blood, something we were reminded of each time we saw people moving objects with their minds or noticed people walking around smiling and laughing at nothing because they were having silent conversations with one another. There were people who could manipulate water and wind, create fire, and bend metal. Here we were outcasts, and it was an indescribable feeling I wasn't sure would ever go away.

"I don't like you going on this trip," my mother said. Her voice was wary but not scolding like it often was. "I don't like you being away from the village and all of us."

"It needs to be done." If I was truthful, part of me was glad to be leaving, if only for more space to think and breathe, away from the watchfulness and expectations of my people.

I didn't mind being their leader on most days, but others felt asphyxiating, when all I wanted to do was go for a ride, or lose myself in the fields without having to worry about setting examples or making decisions . . . or pissing off my mother.

"No, it doesn't *need* to be done, Hunter." My mother's voice was grating. "You're choosing to go. Don't mistake the two."

I had to refrain an eye roll. My mother was a patient woman in so many ways, and yet Whitehorse, Wren, this town, and everything having to do with this new life, kept her on edge unlike I'd ever seen her before.

"What does Wren think about you leaving for this vaccine business?"

"Wren . . . doesn't know yet," I admitted.

My mother looked at me with a disapproving, arched eyebrow. "Afraid to tell her?" she asked with far too much satisfaction.

"Not afraid," I said. "Just postponing an argument."

"Well, you—"

"We're not talking about this again," I told her, and when Mr. Murphy stepped into the window and saw us approaching, a wide grin filled his face. "He never smiles at me like that," I said, glancing at her. "He must be happy to see you."

"Hush," my mother chided as we pulled our horses to a stop at the sidewalk. There were hitching posts lining both sides of the streets, made from old wood beams and metal posts from unused parts of the city.

As my mother dismounted Juniper, it was impossible not to notice the way Mr. Murphy's cheeks reddened, and he seemed to fluster as he fidgeted with his apron.

"Letty, good to see you. You decided to join Hunter today, I see."

"Yes. Hello, Gus," my mother said as she wrapped Juniper's reins around the hitching post. She barely spared him a glance before pointing to the cart. "There is plenty of produce today. And since Hunter is leaving for New Bodega in a couple days, you can come to me if you need more after Tuesday," she offered.

"That's kind of you, Letty. Thank you." His grin widened and he stepped over, hands on his hips as he peered inside. "Strawberries!" he said with excitement. He was a broad-shouldered, talkative man with glasses that rested at the tip of his nose. "It's amazing how much more we can produce with the greenhouses, isn't it?"

My mother's mouth twitched with the barest smile as she began to unload, and I could hardly suppress my amusement. She could fool everyone else, but she couldn't fool me. She was going out of her way not to look at Mr. Murphy, which meant he made her uncomfortable. Which meant she might've liked him, but she would never allow herself to admit it.

I lifted the crate of jars from the back. "The herbs are from

Wren and Henni," I explained as I walked past Mr. Murphy into the shop. "Should I put these by the honey and the jam?" I asked, glancing back at him.

Mr. Murphy heaved out a crate of freshly picked beets. "Yes, but careful you don't break any honey jars. The way Thea goes through them, there's hardly enough for anyone else." As I set the crate down, below the lavender honey shipped up from New Bodega, I thought about Thea's love of the stuff and examined the shop, wondering what else she might enjoy.

The shop was the size of our living room, kitchen, and dining area combined, and despite the ceiling fan and awning, shading the shop from the impending afternoon heat, the faint, earthy-sweet scent of overripe fruit hung in the air. The shelves were lined with goods, everything edible, from teas and jams, to bread and grains and root vegetables. Fruit, vegetables, and dairy were housed in containers and cooling chests lining the walls, and I looked at our nearly empty bins waiting to be filled.

"I didn't bring lemons today, I wasn't sure you needed any, but it looks like you might," I said as I headed back out to the cart.

"Yes, well, I wasn't expecting Meghann to buy everything up for her graduation cakes," he muttered.

"I'll bring you some tomorrow," my mother offered, straining to lift a crate of potatoes.

"I'll get it, Letty—" Mr. Murphy hurried over to take it from her.

Her brow crinkled with indignation. She was about to say something reproving when Mr. Murphy started again. "Now, I hope you'll let me know if you need anything while Hunter's away." Oblivious, he disappeared momentarily into the shop. "Anything at all," he called behind him. "I don't live but two blocks from you." He smiled at her as he returned, but my mother glanced away.

"That's it then?" she said quickly, and looked at me for assurance. There was a quiet plea to leave in her expression.

As Mr. Murphy situated another of the crates farther away from the door, I leaned closer to her and muttered, "Could you at least try to be pleasant?"

"Why," she hissed so only I could hear her. "So he gets the wrong idea?"

"You're right," I breathed, "we wouldn't want anyone to think you have a heart." With a deep breath, I decided my mother's attitude was a problem for another day. "We'll bring you some lemons tomorrow, Mr. Murphy," I said, following him inside with the last of the load. "I don't think we have more than a couple pounds, but you're welcome to them."

"Thanks, Hunter," he said with a nod, and sneaked a glimpse at my mother. She was already climbing back into Juniper's saddle when I stepped back outside.

"I'll get your crates unpacked and have them ready for you to take back when you come tomorrow," he promised.

"All right then," my mother said, and with a final tight-lipped, barely perceptible smile, she turned Juniper in the other direction.

Mr. Murphy turned to go back inside. "I have something I need to do, Mother," I told her, and lifted my chin toward home. "You can head back without me."

She frowned. "What else is there?"

Then her attention drifted past me, and I glanced over my shoulder. Thea and the old man, Bert, rode up the street in an old four-by-four, the truck coming to a stop outside of the feedstore across the street. Thea was in the driver's seat, and two 55-gallon drums of biodiesel were in the truck bed.

Bert climbed out of the passenger side first, waving when he noticed me. He started across the street, toward us, as Thea climbed out of the truck and paused.

Her long hair was up in its usual high ponytail, more of a

tawny-blonde than brown in the sunlight. And if I hadn't seen the fire in her when she was angry, I would've assumed petite, pretty little Thea was all smiles and bubbly laughter.

Our eyes met for a brief moment, and I thought she might walk over and join Bert, before she shoved her hands into the back pockets of her jeans and strode into the feedstore. Even after all this time, she felt like the most distant person of her family, and for some reason, it was starting to bother me.

"Good afternoon, Letty," Bert said in quick greeting. He had a camo bandana tied around his head, his shaggy, gray hair hanging around it. With the dip of his chin, he reached for my hand, giving it a quick shake. "Hunter." Bert, I'd learned, was sarcastic, but the most friendly of the bunch. "Henni's not with you today?" he asked.

I shook my head. "She and Wren are finishing the powders and tinctures for New Bodega."

"Ah. Well, that's too bad," he said with a slightly disappointed smile.

Uncertain what to think of that, I glanced toward the biodiesel in the back of the truck. "For the trip?"

"Yep. We're on our way to the loading bay to drop them off. Thea needed to pick up some provisions for the horses, for while she's gone."

"You only need the two drums?" It didn't seem like enough for two trucks and thousands of miles of road.

Bert chuckled. "Hell no, this is our third trip so far today. Hopefully the last. I figure we'll haul them down in the trailers, and with all the goods we're dropping off, we'll have plenty of room for them in the back of the trucks when we return home." He held up his palm. "Well, that's assuming Kat doesn't load up with a bunch of unplanned goods while we're down there, which she often does on her trips."

I lifted an eyebrow. "She can't if there's not any room. You'll have eight horses coming back this time."

With a chuckle, Bert rested his hands on his hips. "You might be a little rough around the edges, kid, but I like you. You know that?" He glanced back toward the feedstore. "Well, I better get back there and move Thea along." Bert smiled up at my mother. "Ma'am," he said, dipping his chin again. Bert looked at me. "See you Tuesday, kid," he said as he hustled away. "I hope you don't mind long car rides!" he called over his shoulder with another throaty laugh.

I wasn't sure; I'd only ridden in a car a few times. But that wasn't what had been on my mind. When I'd heard Thea was joining us, I considered our constant discomfort around each other, and wondered how, exactly, the next few weeks would unfold.

"Go ahead, Mother," I told her, motioning toward the village. "I'll be home in a minute."

She looked at the feedstore and then at me again, which I thought was strange, then she nudged Juniper into a walk and headed home.

I was about to go back into Mr. Murphy's store when I saw Thea's boyfriend, Cal, walking down the sidewalk, a girl I'd seen with him many times by his side. It was the one Beau worked with at the Survival Center, with blonde hair and bright blue eyes. She fidgeted with her long ponytail, and Cal ambled beside her, his hands shoved in his pockets as they laughed at something. I'd heard about what he'd done to Kat years ago, and I wondered if someone raised the way he had been, unruly with the ability to appear invisible, could really change for the good.

And though I knew I shouldn't care one way or the other if he was seeing Thea, something about the way Cal looked at the girl beside him rubbed me the wrong way. I'd only seen him and Thea together a handful of times, but he was never smiling so much as he always seemed to be with this girl.

Cal placed his hand on her lower back, guiding her as they

disappeared between two buildings, their laughter echoing behind them.

I glanced back at the feedstore. Did Thea know Cal spent so much time with another girl, unable to look away from one another?

I bristled at the thought. Whatever Cal was or was not doing was none of my business, and turning toward the store, I went inside, refusing to think anymore about it.

7

THEA

The sun was setting behind the mountains, and the sky was pale pink as Cal and I walked through the abandoned neighborhoods. It wasn't the most romantic place to go for our last night together, but it was just outside the walls of Riverdale, away from everyone else, so we were undisturbed.

"So," I said, taking Cal's hand in mine. "What are you going to do while I'm gone?"

"Perish, of course," Cal joked, and his blonde hair flopped into his eyes as he turned to look at me. A grin tugged at the corner of his mouth and my heart melted a little. I was going to miss that cocky smile of his.

"Well, that's a given," I said. I shook my head with a grin and peered around at Mother Nature, left to her own devices in this part of our world. Violets grew up through the cracks in the asphalt. Lichen covered rotted roofs. Unchecked garden plants, flourishing in the summer warmth, shaded old steps and porches. There was something hauntingly beautiful about it, when I slowed down long enough to notice it. The old neighborhoods were lush, compared to the steel-lined walls of Riverdale that rose just above the rooftops beyond.

"But really, what will you do?" I asked.

"I'll be on patrol with Ross mostly," Cal said.

With Kat working at the horse facility and going to community meetups, and Jackson helping Beau so much over the past year, Cal had become Ross's newest deputy and righthand man. "And, I told Marica I would help her at the Survival Center since Beau's been busy with the village."

I felt a slight churn in my stomach at the mention of Marica's name, but I said nothing. I'd always felt slightly guilty, knowing they would probably be together if it wasn't for my sudden appearance in Cal's life a year and a half ago when they'd been dating. And while a part of me thought I should worry they were still friends, I also knew the kind of guy Cal was and that he would never hurt me.

"So," he started, scuffing his shoes against the loose gravel in the road, "what time are you leaving tomorrow?"

"Elle and Jackson are taking me to the facility at seven, so we can get things loaded and ready to go," I said with a heavy sigh. "It's going to be an early start to a long day, for sure."

"Meghann said you guys are making a pit stop in Vancouver." Cal's voice held a mix of longing and intrigue, which made sense. Vancouver was where he was originally from before his life with Harlon's gang brought him here.

"Yeah, we have to check on the radio tower," I explained, studying his profile. "You're never going to call her Mom are you," I said. Meghann had been the one to take him in when he first came to Whitehorse, a scared, guilt-ridden boy who had hurt the very people who were trying to give him a second chance.

Cal shook his head. "No. Probably for the same reason you don't call Elle your mom, unless it's for simplicity's sake."

Elle was my mom in every way that mattered, but it always felt strange, ever since I'd been a child, to call her Mom. Probably because she'd never pushed the idea and had always just been Elle to me.

I leaned my head against his shoulder as we cut through some of the overgrown backyards, headed back for Riverdale.

"Are you nervous?" Cal asked in our companionable silence. "About the drive or Hope Valley or anything?"

We weaved around an old metal clothesline, covered in vines.

"I'm not sure if it's nerves I feel, or excitement—if there's even a difference," I said.

We were going to New Bodega, which was Virus ground zero in many ways—where Dr. Wesley had abandoned her family to work with General Herodson and masterminded *the* Virus. In the wake of their devastation, New Bodega had risen up and become the hub of all Virus vaccines, serums, and advancements, and was where the children Dr. Wesley had left behind, Jason and Zoe, had started the only Re-gen safe haven we knew of in their small settlement inland, Hope Valley. It was a community where Zoe and Jason did everything they could to right their mother's wrongs, and I was both intimidated and in awe of them.

We stepped over a fallen fence, into another yard cluttered with evergreens and rusted lawn furniture.

"But I *have* been wanting to see the countryside since we moved here, and now I'm getting that opportunity." California, the coast, rolling hills, and hot summers . . . I'd heard about it all. "Though, meeting a ton of new people and going to the city—which is always unpredictable—that's a little . . . daunting." I nudged him with a grin. "I can't just disappear on a whim, like you can. My Ability is a little more temperamental than that."

Cal's thumb rubbed absently over the back of my hand, and we stopped under an untamed maple tree. "You don't have to worry about anything," he said. His gaze held mine, glistening and blue, like the Yukon fresh with snowmelt. "Alex will be there, and Kat would die before she let anything happen to you. It's not like you need their protection, though."

As he stared into my eyes, I thought I saw something unfamiliar in them. It almost looked like longing, but I wasn't sure why or for what. He studied me a moment longer, then seemed to remember himself and forced a smile. "You can defend yourself in more ways than one."

While that was true, it was no longer the journey that concerned me, but Cal's expression. "Are you okay?" I asked, squeezing his hand.

"Yes." He frowned with confusion. "Why?"

"You just seem . . . a little sad, or something."

Cal rolled his eyes, which was a very un-Cal thing to do. "You're leaving for three weeks, Thea." Maple leaves shivered in the breeze above us, and Cal's smile crept back into place. "It will be weird not having you around." His blue gaze shifted to my lips, as if he was taking the sight of me in, saving it for later. *Or*, a voice told me, *maybe that's apprehension in his eyes, not appreciation.*

Regardless of his smile and reassurances, something about Cal seemed lost and uncertain. "Hey," I whispered, and leaned in to kiss him. The need to feel his lips on mine was more desperate than I expected as I worried a part of him was slipping away, but after his initial surprise, Cal's kiss grew urgent in return.

He was warm and strong, and I didn't feel so alone when I was with him. Even if no one understood it, Cal was the only person who really knew me, and I couldn't imagine my life without him—my best friend, my confidant. My Cal.

His arm snaked around my waist, pulling me closer, and his tongue explored mine more fervently until I gasped and pulled away. "I promised Elle and Jackson I'd be home for dinner since it's my last night home." I grinned sheepishly against his lips. "And I still have to pack."

Cal's head fell back. "Such a tease," he groaned.

"But *one* more kiss won't hurt," I whispered, and pulling his mouth to mine again, I brushed my lips against his, lingering and soft at first, until the rush of heat overcame me. My arms wrapped around him again, and our bodies pressed so close there was no more air between us.

Another groan rumbled in Cal's throat, then a crash behind us startled me. We both spun around to find Hunter standing in the backyard. His expression was a mask of severity, though more scathing than usual.

"What are you doing here?" I bit out, confused and slightly embarrassed, considering I could still taste Cal on my tongue.

"Hiding," he said. "At least, I was." I glanced around, realizing Milo nor his mother were present. I registered what looked like an armful of wood in disarray by a fire pit at his feet. He had a ball cap on, a small ice chest in one hand, and he was wearing a flannel jacket like he was planning on staying a while.

"Then we'll leave you to it," Cal said, taking my hand in his again. If he was embarrassed to be caught kissing in an abandoned neighborhood, it didn't show.

Hunter's gaze was hard on Cal as we walked by, but Cal ignored him and led me out of the yard. "I don't like that guy," Cal said under his breath. Though I didn't look back, I could feel Hunter's eyes spearing us until we were out of view. "And I'm not sure how I feel about you going on the trip with him either."

"Hunter's a grumpy-pants, but he's not dangerous or anything," I told Cal, uncertain how I felt about the sudden bite in his tone. I couldn't tell if Cal was being possessive or if he was actually worried. "Wait a minute," I said with a growing grin. I jerked Cal's hand to force him to look at me. "You're not jealous, are you?" I asked, incredulous.

I giggled as Cal's pinched features relaxed a little, and he glanced away.

"Hey . . ." I wrapped my arms around his neck. "I have to say I'm flattered, but you have *nothing* to be jealous about. Hunter is the last person I'd ever have feelings for."

Cal looked behind me, toward the houses. "Promise?"

I tried to suppress my grin this time, though I found the question absurdly unnecessary. "I promise."

8

THEA

The next morning came quickly. While Jackson and Elle helped load the trucks, Little Foot went exploring the compound, and I made my way over to Captain and Benedict in their paddock to say goodbye.

"You two be good for Susan," I told them, and Captain's gray whiskers tickled my arm as he lipped at it in want of a treat.

Laughing, I pulled a carrot out of my back pocket for each of them. "I stole them from the food bin," I whispered. "Don't tell anyone."

"I won't." Susan's amused voice startled me and I turned around with a smile. "Busted," she said. "And don't worry, you and Kat have trained me well, I can keep these boys out of trouble." Susan's black, bobbed hair was pulled back in a bristly ponytail at the base of her head, and she tucked a few loose strands behind her ears.

"This will be a good test for you," I told her with a wry smile. "Because I think we're bringing eight more horses back with us."

Her eyes widened. "So many?"

"Unless someone's going to start repaving roads, even the

four-by-fours aren't lasting long these days. I have a feeling the riding facility will double in size before much longer."

"Probably true," Susan said with a sigh. She opened the paddock gate and stepped inside to feed the boys their breakfast.

I watched her happily as she whistled, looking like she belonged there, as if she was one of us—a part of Whitehorse. And I was happy for it. But as Hunter and his mother rode their horses through the facility gate, I realized Susan and her family might be the only ones to ever fully acclimate.

Susan moved quickly in the paddock, sifting the grain from the bins under the paddock awning. "Come and get it, boys!" she called.

Susan couldn't have been older than her late twenties, and Sutton was nearly nine years old. It made me wonder what sort of pressure she'd been under to marry Leo, who was much older than her, when they'd wed years ago—the only two people in the village unrelated and old enough to marry. For eleven years, the village strove to preserve their lineage, but now, save for traveling to other untainted communities where they knew no one, they were stuck with Tainteds like us.

The vaccine, I realized, wouldn't just save their lives from cross-contaminated blood but would give them possibilities for their futures. Would Susan regret marrying Leo now that they were living in a new kind of world? I pushed the thought away, knowing she could never regret Sutton and his big, chestnut-colored eyes and freckled face.

She glanced over her shoulder when she realized I was still standing there, watching.

"I promise, I won't kill them while you're gone," Susan jested. "If that's what you're worried about."

I laughed nervously. "Yeah, I know. Sorry. I'm leaving." I pushed off the rail and waved goodbye.

"Don't get into too much trouble while you're gone!" Susan called.

I hurried into the prison and beelined for the cafeteria to grab my things to load. When I saw Wren and Hunter standing in the room, and the horrified look on Wren's face, I froze in the doorway.

"I don't understand why you would throw this at me, right before you leave," she said, wiping the tears from her cheeks. "I hate this."

Hunter stood with his back to me, his broad shoulders straighter than usual. "It's not about you, Wren, it's about us."

I had a gut-churning feeling I wouldn't like whatever Hunter was *throwing* at her, and the tears in Wren's eyes quickly spurred my annoyance. *He's making her cry before we leave?* What kind of friend does that?

"Hunter," Wren started. "No one—"

"I can't argue with you right now," he said, lugging his duffle bag over his shoulder, as if it weighed nothing. "We'll talk more about it when I get back."

Wren shook her head, her sadness hardening into anger. "You did this on purpose, didn't you?" she said, scowling as she shoved his shoulder. I'd never seen Wren look so menacing. "This whole time—"

"Hey," he bit out. Hunter's shoulders squared and he seemed immediately taller and more formidable.

My body stiffened as I felt the sudden need to hold my breath.

"You did what you had to, Wren. Now, I am. I can't keep holding my breath."

My annoyance prickled. Was Hunter talking about her and Beau? I'd always wondered if he harbored some resentment after life had changed for him so abruptly, and Beau had come into the picture.

Despite the sharpness to his tone, though, Hunter leaned in and kissed Wren's forehead. "I gotta go," he grumbled.

"I—" Wren shook her head. "I can't believe you," she growled.

"Yeah, you and my mother both," Hunter muttered as he strode out the door, disappearing down the hallway.

With a deflated sigh, Wren wiped away her tears and ran her fingers through her loose black hair, cursing herself before she noticed me standing there. Her cheeks were stained pink and she offered me a weak smile, like she'd been caught doing something wrong. Or perhaps because Hunter had.

"What was that all about?" I asked, stepping into the room. The protective part of me that had helped Wren feel at home here when she first arrived—that had helped her settle into her new happiness with my brother—didn't like seeing her upset. And I didn't like Hunter talking to her like that, as if she'd done something wrong. "Was that about you and my brother being together?"

Wren shook her head. "No," she said, staring at the doorway Hunter had exited. I waited for her to continue, and when she realized it, she glanced at me. "I'm fine," she offered. "I'm just worried about him." She pulled her bottom lip between her teeth, thinking. "Actually," she started, her gaze hardening. "I'm not letting him leave things like that." She nodded to herself. "I'll meet you out there, Thea—"

"Wren?" Kat called from down the hall. "You get lost in there?"

"Crap, the maps." Wren wiped her eyes a final time and flashed me a quick, watery smile. "Coming!" she called, reaching for the maps discarded on the table as she rushed out the door.

I listened to Wren's receding footsteps as I grabbed my two bags from the corner of the room—my duffle and my backpack. Knowing Kat's was the red one, I hauled it over my other shoulder, the weight nearly knocking me off kilter, and I headed out the door in Wren's direction.

The sour feeling in my stomach stayed with me as I stepped out into the sunshine. And as I drew closer to the trucks parked at the loading bay, I tried to tell myself this was a day to be excited. But I had the sneaking suspicion Wren and Hunter's argument was about something significant, and anger gripped me as I considered how it might relate to my brother.

Even after all this time, Hunter was still making waves. Hadn't he already made things hard enough on Wren? Sure, they'd come to Whitehorse like she'd wanted, but only after Henni stepped in. Hunter had been too busy distrusting us to be in Wren's corner. Now that he was here, he and his mother kept to themselves, scowling all the time. I realized it was possible neither of them would ever be happy because they might not have the capacity for it.

But I instantly forgot all that when I saw Cal wandering closer from the gated entrance, his pack on his back like he'd walked the three miles from Riverdale out here. *To see me.* I couldn't stop grinning.

I dropped my bags and ran toward him. His eyes widening when he saw me. "You came to see me off?" I was elated, even if I knew that was silly. I wrapped my arms around his neck. "How sweet."

"I couldn't let you leave without saying goodbye," he murmured, squeezing me closer.

Whatever insecurities I thought I saw in Cal last night were vanquished, gratitude and a sense of calm filling me instead. "Thank you."

9

HUNTER

Once Cal left and Thea was heading back toward the trucks, I snagged the opportunity to talk to her. I hadn't seen her alone to thank her properly for what she'd done for Milo.

Thea's gaze found mine as I stopped in the middle of the gravel lot. The light, open expression she always had sharpened like it usually did when she saw me.

I clenched my jaw, steadying myself for whatever smart remark she had for me this time.

"Hunter." She grumbled my name in greeting as she walked past me. For being so petite, she exuded ferocity.

"Hello, Thea. It's nice to see you too," I said dryly.

She paused mid-step and turned to me, her ponytail whipping over her shoulder. She was barely as tall as my chin, and her accusatory, honey-brown eyes narrowed on me, more acute than usual. "Did Wren find you?" she asked.

"Yes." I eyed her carefully, surprised by her question. "Why do you ask?"

"Because after the bomb you dropped on her, you just left her

78

standing there, Hunter. She was upset." Thea leaned closer. "Look, I know you're not happy here," she said, her voice low and venomous. "You never wanted to come to begin with—but Wren and my brother have done so much for you and your family, the least you could do is stop throwing their relationship in her face and show some gratitude."

"Excuse me?" A flash of heat whirred through me at the unexpected accusation, and I crossed my arms over my chest, uncertain what, exactly, Thea was talking about. Spoiled, feisty Thea always seemed to be looking for an argument.

"Who pulls that crap and then leaves for three weeks?" she practically hissed.

I tilted my head, unable to keep from glaring at her. "How is it I've thrown their relationship in her face?"

"You said she did what she had to, and now you will."

My muscles tensed and I straightened. "So," I said, holding my hand up. I tried to keep the edge from my voice, but my impatience and disbelief tore at what remained of any gratitude I'd walked over with. "You don't even know what we were talking about?" If I'd had it in me to laugh, I would've, but the fact that Thea was upset with me and had no idea why, was maddening.

"Does it matter?"

I heaved a bored sigh. "No, apparently not."

Thea scratched her brow and took a calming breath, but I could tell she was holding in what she really wanted to say. "You need to get over yourself already," she gritted out. "You've been sulking since you got here. You have everything here, except for Wren, and still, it's not good enough."

My jaw ticked in answer. *This is about Wren?* I was about to tell Thea I'd simply walked over to thank her for what she did the other day, but with her angry words every sleepless night and heavy decision I'd borne since we'd arrived in Whitehorse bubbled up and over, falling at our feet. "You have no idea what you're talking about, Thea," I seethed.

Her eyes widened at the edge in my tone, and I thought she might relent until she shook her head. "So we're *not* untrustworthy, and you're *not* here out of obligation?"

My gaze narrowed on her. "Have I ever said that?"

She leaned closer and I could smell lemongrass and lavender. "You're only here because you were screwed either way, remember?" The first day I met Thea came booming back to life. "Is it really so hard to find some joy in this place?" Her contempt for me was obvious, her eyes burned with it.

That's what Thea thought of me then? That I was a miserable, distrusting asshole who was somehow hurting Wren? I might've respected Thea's loyalty to her family and friends if I wasn't the one she was flinging unfounded accusations at, save for this one. "Of course I didn't trust you when I met you," I admitted. "Your brother nearly killed one of the people I care about most, and then you all showed up expecting us to leave with you? Anyone in their right mind would distrust you. People like you are *dangerous*."

Thea's nostrils flared, and her lips pinched in a thin line. "And how do you feel now?" she said coolly. "Are we still so hard to trust—to *like*?"

"That would depend," I said, feeling the uncontrollable need to sting her back. "Are you lumped in with everyone else?"

More color bloomed in Thea's cheeks, but it wasn't from anger this time. She swallowed. "You're such an ass," she breathed.

"So you've told me," I reminded her, and tilted my head. "Instead of jumping to conclusions and attacking me, why don't you ask Wren what's wrong? Or would that take all the fun out of your tantrum?" Her eyes widened, but I ignored it. If Wren hadn't told Thea why she was upset, then I wasn't about to. Thea could hate me if she was so determined to.

She groaned with frustration and headed toward the trucks without another word.

My mother, Alex, and Elle were watching us from the trucks. Alex and Elle's expressions leaned toward curious shock, while my mother glared at Thea.

Clenching my hands at my sides, I walked toward them, but my mother was in front of me in three furious steps. "How can you let her talk to you like that?" she ground out. I could feel her anger crashing against me in tumultuous waves.

"Leave it alone, Mother," I said with a groan. While I didn't appreciate Thea's attitude, a part of me didn't blame her either.

"I feel like I don't understand you anymore," my mother said, utterly exasperated with me. She shook her head. I hated the discontent in her voice, but that's how she always was— worried, skeptical, rough around the edges. As I stared into her rock-hard gaze—at the lines that crinkled around her eyes in anger—and the scar by her left ear, I thought I saw how Thea might see us. My mother was a harsh woman, she had been for years, and I knew she'd never been overtly warm toward anyone in Whitehorse. It might be easy for someone like Thea, who wore her heart on her sleeve, to assume we were heartless.

My mother wrapped her arm through mine, one of her few motherly signs of affection, and we walked back toward the others. "None of it matters. It's you I'm worried about." Her unspoken sentiment was clear.

"You don't have to worry. I'll be okay." I patted her hand. "And I'll miss you too."

She straightened her shoulders, schooling her emotions as best as she could. "Just come home to me, okay?"

"Of course I will—"

"And . . . be careful, Hunter. If you have second thoughts—"

"I know, Mother. Nothing's set in stone."

With another exhale, I joined the group gathered at the trucks, saying their goodbyes. Alex and Sophie, Beau and Wren,

Jackson and Elle; they were all so close. I noticed it all the time, just like I noticed how Thea's face lit up whenever she was around them. When she was around everyone but me.

10

HUNTER

It rained for the first couple of hours we were on the road, a sudden summer downpour that sent the wipers squeaking over the window incessantly. I wasn't sure how driving with Alex would go after my argument with Thea back at the prison, but Alex hadn't brought it up. In fact, as he drove, he mostly filled me in on his relationship with the folks in New Bodega, explaining how he'd met Zoe, Jake, and Becca, years back at the first Prince Rupert summit.

The rain finally passed, and after another couple of hours, my legs began to cramp. I wasn't used to driving all the time, like Alex was. He was a cool guy, who smiled almost as much as Thea, and he ran the hydro plant with Bert and a small team of others throughout the year. I wasn't sure if it was his dark features, or if it was the quiet thoughtfulness I noticed about him when he was observing others, but something about Alex reminded me of myself.

The wolf exhaled a long, deep sigh behind me. He didn't seem to mind the trip all that much either, sprawled out on the back seat.

"I've been on dozens of trips," Alex started again. "But I've never been to New Bodega. This will be a first for all of us. It's kind of exciting."

Exciting was a word for it. So was overwhelming. Looming. Life-changing.

"What about you?" Alex glanced at me in the passenger seat.

I rolled the window down a little to feel the afternoon air against my skin. "What about me?"

"How are you doing with all of this? I mean, you've always lived in a small village, and coming to Whitehorse was a huge step. Now you're going with us to a different country, to meet a city full of new people, and you—I'm not even sure you like *us*, let alone a bunch of strangers." Alex chuckled, and I looked at him.

"Is that what Thea told you?" I felt my scowl harden in place.

Alex looked from me to the road. "No, man. It's just—I guess I don't know you well enough to tell."

That was an honest enough answer, and I peered out at the rich greens and browns of early summer as they passed by the window. "I like Whitehorse," I admitted. "And I know it's not exactly obvious, but my mother does too."

"Did she tell you that?" he asked skeptically.

"She doesn't have to," I told him, taking in the winding road. "She's just . . . scared."

Alex glanced at me again. "Scared of what? That others will break in and do something to your family, or scared of us?" I knew there was a difference, at least to everyone but my mother.

"Of anyone and everything," I admitted. While I didn't want to overshare with Alex, I also couldn't get Thea's impression of me and my family out of my head. And Alex had said himself he didn't feel like he knew us. "She's built up a hard shell over the years."

Alex was contemplative for a moment. "Yeah, I get it. My situation is different, but it was also the same too, you know? We all—Thea, Beau, Sophie, and the others—we all woke up one day after we thought we were dead and life had completely upended. There were times I wondered if it would've been easier had we died with the others."

I looked at him. Alex's pensive gaze was fixed out the windshield. The diesel engine rumbled. The road bent and turned. The truck shook and shuttered over potholes. Then he started again. "It took us a lot—cost us all *a lot*—to get to this point. We've seen and done things that haunt us. But, it's also like we have this innate need to keep going and make our second chance worthwhile because of all the hard shit."

It was obvious to anyone who saw Alex, Thea, and their family together that what they'd been through had brought them closer together, the same way our village found it difficult to trust or open up to others outside our own people; we'd all been through hell together, which made everyone else an outsider.

"We only left once," I started, watching the faded yellow line in the center of the highway bend with the road. "After the men who came to our village were dead, Henni and I ventured out— we needed medical supplies and food." I exhaled and shook my head. "Everything was a mess. And that's when we put the pieces together from the newspaper clippings, signs on doors and windows, and the bodies in buildings—not to mention the smoke clouding the sky from the fires off in the distance . . . It had been nearly a month since the outbreak, and we realized those men weren't just crazy and could do unnatural things, they were different—everyone who'd gotten sick would be different from us—and nothing would ever be the same again." I felt my palms clam up as I registered what I'd just shared, all of it spoken aloud for the first time.

"That's when you went into hiding?" Alex asked. I appreciated the quiet sincerity in his voice.

"We knew we wouldn't survive something like that again.

The fear and distrust," I continued, "they aren't things some of us can unlearn, I guess. And I don't think Thea understands."

In my periphery, I saw Alex glance at me. "I don't know what's going on between you two," he said, and I looked at him from the corner of my eye. "But whatever your differences are, you should know that she's probably the best of all of us, and she's the one I worry about the most."

"Why?" I asked before I could stop myself. As much as she maddened me sometimes, I couldn't deny that I wanted to understand her better. And it was inconvenient to think about someone who was so frustrating all the time.

"Thea's the most fragile, I think. Or maybe it's just because she's the youngest. She's lived through what we all have, but from such a young age. Sophie and I worry how much of what she's seen and done still affects her—I guess I should say that Sophie *knows* it still affects her."

I didn't have the nerve to ask for details, but I didn't have to. As if Alex could feel my eyes boring into the side of his head, he peeked at me again and continued.

"The day I woke up from the fever, I found her and Beau in an abandoned building. It was the dead of winter, and they were cold and hungry and . . . they were alone and scared. I was a foster kid who could barely take care of myself. I had no clue what to do with two kids, so I took them to Sophie's. And thank God I did."

"You and Sophie were together then?"

Alex chuckled and shook his head. "No, definitely not. We'd known each other a few days, if that. But she was the only one I'd found alive in the entire town besides the kids."

"So their parents died too," I realized. It made sense since Jackson and Elle had assumed that role all these years.

"Not exactly," Alex hedged, more hesitant than before. "Their mother—she tried to kill them, so Thea had to kill her first. She was only six years old."

My heart skipped a beat. I felt my face pale, imagining a tiny Thea frightened and having to kill her own mother. The mere thought of even considering my mother's demise, or Milo's, made bile rise up in my throat.

"Those men that came to your village," Alex continued. "We've seen the likes of them before, too many times. And every single horrible thing I've seen, Thea has seen too, only, she was young and innocent, and confused and helpless in many ways. Just like Beau. It was different for them than it was for us."

Beau was closed off, more reserved than Thea was, and perhaps his past lent to that. But Thea . . .

"She always seems so happy," I thought aloud. "You'd never know any different." Only, that wasn't entirely true. I remembered her expression the day she helped Milo in the barn—the day she'd used her Ability to save him. Beau once mentioned that some survivors had difficulty coming to terms with what they could do, and I realized Thea might be one of them.

"How did Thea kill her?" I asked, unable to help myself. "Her mother," I clarified.

Alex looked at me, as if he could tell I was putting puzzle pieces together. "Her telekinesis," he said. "Threw her right out the window. Sophie's seen the memory. Thea was protecting Beau. She wasn't even fully recovered from the fever, and after that . . . well, they both thought they'd get in trouble for what Thea did, so they didn't tell anyone the truth for months. She lived with that gnawing at her, and the guilt."

They kept it a secret for months? I swallowed the emotions, conjuring the unwanted image of a shivering cold, frightened little Thea. "I guess I know why she was shaken up using her power the other day with Milo."

Alex propped his elbow up on the windowsill and dragged his hand over his buzzed head. "It's more than that too," he admitted. "But yeah, I think it still scares her sometimes. The older she gets, the more I realize Thea's got two sides to her, the tentative, playful Thea I still see from when she was little, and the Thea who's a ball of emotion, which she has a difficult time harnessing."

"I've noticed," I muttered.

Alex smirked and continued. "I think that emotion is what scares her."

Anyone who knew Thea—even me, who seemed to sour her mood with every interaction—could tell she didn't have a mean bone in her body, at least, not really. She practically fumed when she was angry, but the fact that she wore a nearly constant smile and her best friends were animals gave her soft heart away. So having the power to hurt someone . . . I imagined it was something Thea might always struggle to come to terms with.

"Milo seems like a good kid," Alex said. "I was talking to him when I stopped by Jasper's to get some books for Sophie's class. He sure loves animals—he reminds me of Thea at that age, actually."

"Yeah, unlike the rest of us, you don't have to guess how he's acclimating. He's a pretty open book."

Alex chuckled. "Same with Fiona."

We sat in silence for a while, the road stretching out in front of us. I glanced in the side mirror, looking past the trailer we were hauling, to the super duty truck fifty feet behind us. Bert sat in the driver's seat, Kat in the passenger, and I saw Thea's bare feet sticking out the back passenger window.

"What?" Alex asked. "What's so funny?"

I hadn't realized I was smiling. I pointed behind us. "It looks like your sister is enjoying the trip so far," I mused. "She's sunbathing."

Alex grinned. "Sounds about right for Thea."

The truck shuddered again over the road, and as we continued south, further into British Columbia, I thought about my mother and Milo back home, and a strange sense of relief washed over me. It was the first time I was leaving them alone for longer than a handful of hours, but I wasn't worried. No more than the unfamiliar anxiety of being away. They had protective walls and a town of Ability-wielders. They had Beau and Wren and everyone else to look after them if they needed anything.

"I really do like it," I told Alex. "Being in Whitehorse," I said. "I know my mother and brother are safe there, more than they'd be anywhere else."

Satisfaction brightened Alex's features. "Good. That's the point of that place, you know? For everyone to be safe and start over."

No matter what my mother feared, I knew that was true. "Yeah," I said with a sigh. "I guess it is."

11

THEA

All of us waited in the shadows at the side of the road for a sign from Kat that the coast was clear and we could head up to the Tatogga Lake safe house. The sun was finally setting, even though it was well past 9 p.m., and Bert snored in the back, oblivious. Meanwhile, my legs tingled in the driver's seat from sitting too long. I couldn't stop fidgeting. Sure, we'd stopped a couple of times for a break and to switch drivers, but eleven hours in the truck was wearing on my last shred of sanity, and I was ready to let the little Thea inside me out to whine for a bit.

Or maybe I was still restless after my interaction with Hunter. I'd been stewing about it all day. Even if I was convinced he'd handled the situation with Wren poorly, Hunter had been right, I didn't know the whole story or why Wren was crying. Even if my reaction felt justified in the moment, I was beginning to wonder if I might've completely misread the situation. He'd seemed genuinely offended by my accusations, and I couldn't help but regret them.

Regardless of why I was restless, I was. I needed movement. I couldn't wait to stretch my legs. No, bathe. No . . . crawl into a comfy bed—away from wherever Bert was sleeping—to escape his snores ricocheting through the cab of the truck. I glanced into the back seat. His mouth was gaping, and I poked him like a child might poke a sleeping bear—very carefully.

Bert's eyes popped open before his mouth snapped shut, and his gaze shifted over me and the cab interior.

"We're here," I told him, and then I heard the truck in front of me rumble to life. Kat waved us up the road as she shoved her pistol in her belt holster. There was no lightning show or gunshots, so I assumed the coast was clear.

Starting our F-250, I followed Alex's truck up the long, gravel drive to our hidden sanctuary.

"How the hell did Alex deal with your snoring at the hydro plant all winter?" I asked Bert. Alex was patient, but I was starting to think he was more saintly than I realized.

"What do you mean? I don't snore," he rebuked.

"Yeah." I snorted. "Right."

Bert and Alex's first winter at the hydro plant, when the two of them were locked inside together all those months to keep the power running, must have been filled with sleep deprivation and pillow pummeling.

But my annoyance with Bert's deviated septum was forgotten the moment we rounded the curve in the gravel and the property came into view. A farmhouse was washed in orange light from the setting sun and was long and sprawling on a plot of land, hidden within the trees. It wasn't boxy like so many of the houses were back in Whitehorse, with pitched roofs for the snow.

I pulled the truck to a stop behind Alex's and shut off the engine. With twitchy fingers, I opened the driver's door and climbed out of the truck, stretching my legs the instant my boots hit the ground, and I grinned. I didn't have to think about the road or driving for another ten hours.

"Everything's clear," Kat said, pulling her pack of essentials from the passenger floor. "It's musty inside, but empty."

"Thank all that is holy," I muttered, wondering if I'd ever have feeling in my butt again.

Bert began unloading our duffels from under the tarp in the back of the truck, setting them in the gravel drive to lug inside.

"Have you been here before?" Hunter asked Alex as they climbed out of the truck in front of us.

Only then did it dawn on me that Hunter and I would be confined in close quarters for the night, with little room to escape one another. I groaned inwardly. I was too exhausted for awkwardness and arguments tonight.

"No," Alex admitted. He opened the back passenger door for Little Foot to jump out. He instantly began sniffing around, his tail wagging excitedly. If he was beginning to feel his thirteen years, you'd never know it.

"I have," Bert said as he pulled the bandana off his head. "Twice." He ran his fingers through his shaggy gray hair. With his newly cropped beard, he looked even more like Willie Nelson than he did before. *"See," Jackson had said, pointing to a photo of Willie in one of my old People magazines. "Bert and Willie."* It was freakishly uncanny.

Hunter assessed the farmhouse as he pulled his shirt down over the butt of the pistol in his waistband. I wasn't sure why him being armed surprised me; he had no Ability to protect himself if he ever needed it, and nearly everyone I knew carried a weapon, so it wasn't exactly strange. But Hunter was different than everyone else. He and his people were peaceful, and it seemed a stark reality that he would have to bring protection on this trip. It was easy to forget how vulnerable he was, especially out here.

I helped the others unpack what little we needed for the night —our food, bags, and weapons—and secured the bins that might be susceptible to critters. Once everything was latched and locked, we headed inside.

The instant I stepped into the sprawling ranch house, a fusty smell filled my nose—stale air and wood scents. I examined the interior, illuminated by the light that filtered through the draped windows. It was a nice place, a little unkempt with cobwebs in the wooden rafters, but if I had to guess, whoever had lived in the house years before had built it themselves. It felt . . . homey.

The kitchen and living room sprawled out to the right, and I followed Alex to the left, down the creaking tiled hallway, past the bedrooms and additional bathroom. There was an office with a twin bed, a master room with a queen mattress big enough for two, and another room with two bunk beds. Everything was straightened, like someone had been along at some point over the years to clean out what was left behind after the outbreak, so there were no bodies or belongings to worry about.

"Kat and I get the queen bed!" I called out, knowing it was the only thing that made sense.

I dropped my pack, pillow, and sleeping bag inside the door of the master bedroom. The big bed was covered with a white painting tarp to keep the dust off, and the chair in the corner of the room, bedside the sliding glass door, was covered too. That was a relief. I was exhausted and could probably sleep anywhere I laid my head, but I wasn't sure sleeping on months or years' worth of dust mites was very appealing either.

I walked over to the sliding glass door to see what was on the other side of the house. More birch trees. More woods. But they were shimmering in the setting sun, making it look ethereal in a way that reminded me how far away I already was from home. It was a good first day, I realized. No mishaps or lunatics. Just leg cramps and restlessness. It could definitely be worse.

"Let's give the old man the office," Alex said to Hunter in the hallway.

"I resent that comment!" Bert called from the living room. I heard the lid pop off the food container.

Kat's heavy steps echoed through the house next, and I pulled off the bed covering, knowing she'd want to go right to sleep. The bed had pillows and a comforter, but I was still glad I'd brought my own. Kat lumbered into the room with her things.

"Do you think they have running water here?" I asked, hopeful but not overly optimistic. "A shower sounds magical right now."

"Ha! Definitely not." She dropped her bag on the foot of the bed and unzipped it. "But I'm also too exhausted to care too much." She smirked at me. "As long as you don't like to cuddle, I'll be able to handle your stench."

"But," I whined, "cuddling's the best part."

There was a creak in the floor, and I looked across the hall and met Hunter's gaze as he shut his bedroom door. Exhaustion made it impossible to care that he looked as stone-faced as always. Like everyone else, I needed sleep, so I heaved my duffel up onto the bed and unzipped it.

My eyes rounded. "What's this?" I asked, pulling out a jar of my favorite lavender honeycomb.

Kat snorted. "Yeah right, like that's not yours."

I stared at her. "It's not. I mean, I didn't pack it."

"No, I did." Kat looked as confused as I felt. "It was sitting on the dock when I was loading the bags," she said. "I assumed you were bringing it for the trip, so I put it in your pack so you wouldn't forget it."

Suddenly, I realized where it had come from, and a grin engulfed my face. "Cal," I told her. "He came to say goodbye and he brought me this." My heart warmed at the thought. "He must've left it as a surprise."

Kat lifted a brow. "I'm glad I spotted it then."

"Me too—"

"Anyone want a snack?" Bert called from the living room.

My stomach rumbled and Kat paused from pulling her hair out of her signature bun, staring at my gurgling stomach. "You got a live animal in there?" she teased.

94

"Hard to tell," I said, and called down the hall. "I do! I'll be out in a minute—and don't eat all the loganberries."

"I don't think you have to worry about that, Thea," Alex said as he knocked quickly on his bedroom door. As he opened it, I saw Hunter standing beside the bunk beds. His back was to me as he pulled his shirt off, and even in the dying light, I could see it was thatched with scars.

My breath caught in my throat, and unaware, Alex closed the door behind him.

I continued staring at the door, unable to look away. I'd known some of what happened at the village all those years ago. I knew Wren had witnessed very bad things, and that Hunter had helped to save them, but I hadn't quite imagined he had physical scars on top of the emotional ones.

My stomach turned a little with an emotion that felt a lot like guilt. Hunter and I weren't likely to be close friends, but that didn't mean I didn't feel horrible about what had happened to him—to all of them. And seeing Hunter's scars made their past struggles more real than they'd felt before.

"Everything okay?" Kat asked as she went to close the bedroom door.

I blinked at her and focused on the clothes in my hand again. "Um, yeah, I just . . . I was lost in thought, I guess."

"Well, get changed and go get your snack," she said, shrugging out of her clothes. "I'm a light sleeper and I'm trading with Hunter at two for second watch tonight. I can't guarantee what I might do if you wake me from my much needed sleep." She winked at me as she pulled on a pair of sleeping shorts.

"I'll be on watch," I told her. "You drove almost all day."

"Don't worry that pretty little head of yours," Kat said with a smirk. "You'll be doing most of the driving tomorrow, and I can sleep some more."

"Noted." I snorted, and changed into a pair of leggings and a loose t-shirt. When I finished, I grabbed my honey and scampered into the living room on bare feet. Bert studied the family room wall, eating a piece of fruit leather and looking at the photos with a flashlight in the falling darkness.

"Anything interesting?" I asked as I pilfered through the jerky and fruit, deciding on a chunk of bread to eat with my honey instead. I plopped down in the overstuffed chair, ignoring the scent of dust, and opened the jar. Practically salivating, I pulled out a sticky, dripping piece of honeycomb, and bit a small piece off.

"It looks like it was a family house a while back, but the kids were grown. So maybe it was a vacation home after that."

"A vacation," I repeated with a sigh. "I wish we got vacations."

Bert snorted. "What do you call this?"

I bit the inside of my cheek, thoughtful for a moment. "True. Sort of. I guess." And Bert was right, it was better than being stuck at home, adventureless and wondering what lay beyond Whitehorse.

Kat's quick, heel-heavy footsteps echoed down the hall as she came out in her sleep clothes. "Do we have everything we need for the radio tower tomorrow?" she asked, eyeing Bert as she refilled her water bottle from one of the jugs we brought. "If we need to find any supplies, we should do it beforehand. I don't want to linger around Vancouver longer than we have to." Her voice wasn't sarcastic or playful, but serious and marginally concerned. We all knew what awaited us in the cities, especially on the roads that hadn't been used and cleared yet.

"I have my tools and I brought some solar panels, in case they need to be replaced. I'm hoping I won't need anything else."

Kat sighed, but I wasn't sure if it was with exhaustion or relief. "Good." Contented, she turned for the bedroom. "Night," she said with a backhanded wave. "Make sure Jackson tells Ross

I'm alive when you check in tonight." She sidestepped Hunter in the hall.

"Will do," Bert said distractedly.

I eyed Hunter's clean t-shirt, sweats, and unlaced boots as he peered out the window beside the door, surveying the front yard. He checked the window locks first, then he tried to turn the door handle, though the deadbolt was clicked in place.

"Little Foot's out there," I told him, and Hunter looked over his shoulder at me. "He'll keep an eye on things," I explained.

The instant Hunter registered the jar of honey in my lap, his head tilted, his brow creasing slightly. "How did you get that?" he said with an unexpected helping of surprise.

"From Cal," I answered, hesitant, and I stopped chewing my honey-dipped bread. "Wait, is this yours?"

I was going to apologize for not bothering to ask anyone if it was theirs when Hunter shook his head. "No," he said. "It's not mine."

The tension in my shoulders eased and I leaned back in my squeaky chair again. "Oh, good." I smiled and licked the honey dripping down the side of my hand.

"I'm going to check the perimeter," Hunter said, unlocking the deadbolt. He tugged the door open, the hinges protesting.

If I didn't know any better, I would've thought there was a touch of disappointment in Hunter's expression as he pulled the door shut behind him.

12

THEA

After our stop at the solar tower for Bert to check the paneling, and another four hours of Bert and Alex driving, we pulled off at Kitwancool Lake for a break and a dip in the water. The further south we went, the warmer it seemed to get, especially as mid-June inched closer.

"At least the weather's nice," Kat said before cursing a loose rock beneath her feet. Little Foot was already sniffing along the water's edge as we trudged our way down to the shore with our backpacks.

"Well," Bert said, stretching his back as he peered around. "This looks like as good a place as any." While there were trees off in the distance, we set up a blanket and our things in a sandy, open area.

"Pardon me while I *relieve* myself," Bert murmured, and headed toward a small copse of scraggly trees.

"I'm beyond ready to rid myself of the stench under my armpits," Kat said, and untucked her tank top from her cargo pants. "Thea, hold the towel up for me?" She pulled her suit from the bag of clothes and toiletries we'd brought with us. We'd assumed this was going to be our only option to get clean during our trip, at least until we reached New Bodega, so we'd come prepared.

Holding up the towel, I waited for Kat to change into her bathing suit and peered around at the others. While Alex stripped into his boxers without a second thought, Hunter peered around, looking a little anxious. I thought he might be self-conscious about the scars on his back. Before he could catch me watching him, though, I looked away.

Bert cursed as he made his way back, kicking at a rock in his way.

"Let me guess," I said, lowering the towel down as Kat finished. Bert's mischievous, ochre eyes met mine. "You're going to snack, nap, and wait until the last minute to bathe?"

He wagged his finger at me. "Am I that predictable?"

"Yeah," I said with a huff of a laugh. "You are." I grabbed my suit to change into next. Kat held up the towel and I climbed into my one-piece. "Done!" I chirped, and reached for my clothes. My bathing suit and unlaced boots weren't exactly fashionable, but they had to do since I'd forgotten flip-flops and had sensitive feet. "I think I'm going to eat first too," I told her.

"Good, you should," Kat said absently. "Knowing you, you'll get crumbs and honey all over the place and just have to wash again anyway." She winked at me then turned for the water. Kat didn't bother collecting her towel or her things as she pranced down to the lake, as if she couldn't prolong the moment another second.

I spread my blanket out next to the food bin and watched the others. Alex was in the water already, Bert was digging in the food bin beside me, and Hunter . . . When I realized Hunter wasn't at the water's edge anymore, I scanned around for him.

He came out of the same trees Bert had disappeared into earlier, wearing workout shorts and no shirt. The smooth, sculpted planes of his chest and abs were bare and devoid of disfigurements, making it impossible not to notice the single, imperfect scar on his hip.

I tried and failed not to flush as I appreciated the payoff of his hard work in the fields every day.

"Thea," Bert said, nudging my shoulder. He had a smirk as wide as the Yukon River across his face. "Deer jerky?"

"Thanks," I said, and grabbed a sliver from the jar.

"And here are your dried loganberries," he offered.

I grinned, glad he'd saved them for me. Loganberries were the best of the berries, I was certain of it. Supple and sun-kissed, like a ripe raspberry, but with a tinge of the tangy sweetness of a blackberry. "Thank you, Bert," I said, a singsong lilt of appreciation in my voice. I realized, as I plopped a berry into my mouth, that these were loganberries from Hunter's fields.

When I glanced up again, he was standing at the edge of the lake, his clothes and backpack on the ground beside him as he stared out at the mirrored blue of the sky. Kat and Alex were yards away; Kat floating on her back, with her face lifted to the sun, and Alex shaking the water droplets off as he made his way toward shore again. They were content, and Hunter looked, well, a little lonely standing there all by himself.

I couldn't describe the feeling I got when I looked at him after learning about his scars—a tug in my gut, a pity or empathy I hadn't had before that I knew he'd despise me for feeling. And I also knew it must be strange to be here with all of us. Alex, Kat, Bert, and I were family, and Hunter was an outsider.

Even if he annoyed me most of the time, I didn't like how *lonely* looked on him. And another part of me knew that what-ever had transpired between Wren and Hunter yesterday wasn't really my business.

Everyone has good in them. Jade had told me that on more than one occasion. I hadn't been through what Wren and Hunter had, and whatever they were to each other, I knew Wren loved him and that he'd saved her, and I couldn't fault him for that.

Frustrated and disappointed in myself for making such a big deal out of things I didn't understand, I swallowed my pride, rose to my feet, grabbed a few more strips of jerky, and walked over to Hunter.

His arms flexed as he fidgeted with something in his hands, and as always, he looked contemplative and lost in thought.

"Peace offering?" I said quietly as I stepped up beside him. I tried not to stare at his back, and as he turned partially to look at me, I held out a strip of jerky. "I don't think I've seen you eat once yet," I realized. "Which is weird, because you don't get a body like that eating nothing." I practically snorted, then my tongue stilled. My heart raced. My cheeks burned. And I couldn't even blink. "Did I just say that out loud?" Despite my mortification, I couldn't help but look at him.

Hunter's eyebrows were raised and the corner of his mouth twitched.

I cleared my throat again. "Anyway," I said, lifting the jerky in my hand. "You should eat something."

Hunter's fingers brushed mine as he accepted the jerky from me, his gaze searing into me. Or was it just the heat of his proximity? Clearing my throat, I nodded toward the water. "I know we don't necessarily get along, but I figured, for this trip, maybe we should try."

He tore a piece of jerky off between his teeth without saying a word, but his eyes didn't leave me.

"I know you're a deep thinker and a man of few, if angry, words, but . . . could you please say something?" My tone was pitched with impatience, and the longer he remained silent, the more I struggled to hold the acerbic words forming on my tongue.

Hunter's jaw worked slowly as he chewed his jerky. It was like he was testing me, trying to see how easy it was to get me riled up, and I glared at him.

Finally, he swallowed, his Adam's apple bobbing in his

throat. "Yesterday," he started turning what was left of his jerky between his fingers.

I blinked at him. *Yesterday? As in, yesterday when I was having a bit of a meltdown?*

"The reason I'd walked over to you," he continued, "was to thank you."

"What—thank me?" I stuttered. "For what?"

"For what you did for my brother the other day."

All of my bluster deflated. "Oh, well, it's fine. It was nothing," I said, staring out at the water again.

"No," he countered, more softly than I expected, and my gaze gravitated to his again. "You saved my mother and me a lot of heartache, and my brother a lot of pain, doing what you did."

I studied him, noting the shimmering sincerity in the copper flecks of his eyes I'd always thought were cold and black. Blinking, I tore off a piece of jerky and peered out at the water again. "You're welcome," I whispered. "You'd have done the same, if you could."

"But I don't have an Ability," he said. "And I can't do things like you can." I wasn't sure if it was regret that laced his words, or if it was the strangeness of how different we were from his people that still affected him.

"Well, he seemed to be okay yesterday," I said, "which is good."

Hunter plopped the last of his jerky into his mouth. "He's fine—more embarrassed than anything. And my mother hasn't stopped fussing over him."

I smiled, wondering what Milo was doing without his big brother around to wrangle him in. "Is it hard for you to be away from him?" I asked, unable to resist. I found it hard to believe that, as distrusting as Hunter was, he could leave so easily. Picking up the vaccine and meeting the people behind its creation was clearly important for him to leave his family behind.

"Not in the way you might think," he admitted. I must've looked confused because Hunter continued. "I know Wren and your brother will look out for both of them—that all of your family will." When his gaze shifted to mine, and I thought I saw not only truth in his eyes, but relief and maybe a little guilt. "No matter what I've said in the past."

My cheeks burned with shame as I replayed myself throwing his words in his face, especially since he'd only been trying to thank me. Whatever had felt justified then, I couldn't seem to drum up any sort of animosity toward him now.

"I'm more worried about whether my mother would *let* any of them help," he grumbled. "If they needed to."

"Probably not," I blurted.

Hunter looked at me sideways, but before I could regret the words, the corner of his mouth twitched like he might actually smile.

I couldn't suppress a grin. "When was the last time you smile—"

"Hey!" Kat called as she came out of the water. "We're not staying here all day. Are you two bathing or what? I'm not sleeping next to you tonight if you're stinky again, Thea. Fair warning."

"Yeah, yeah," I mumbled, and glanced at Hunter. "Do you have soap and stuff? Or do you want to use mine?"

He nodded at his backpack. "I have what I need, thanks."

His gaze shifted over the lake, and I couldn't help but ask, "You've gone swimming before, right?" He looked so reverent as he peered into the horizon, it was like he was seeing a lake for the first time.

"Yes, but it's been a while since I've been out in nature like this," he said. "Back home, I didn't wander far from the village. None of us really did, other than Wren."

To keep them safe, I realized. Beau and I had the river at the lodge to play in during the summers. We went camping and on hunting trips to the surrounding lakes—we had so much more of a childhood than I'd realized. And Hunter, I was beginning to understand, hadn't had one at all.

Leaving him to his thoughts, I went up to gather my things, flashing a toothy grin at Kat as she snorted at my excessive collection of soaps and scrubs. "What, I like to be clean," I told her. I loved the outdoors and to camp, but I also loved the scent of lavender and honey, of lemongrass and cherry blossom—all the scents that filled my bathroom after a hot shower and a long day of dirt, grime, and horses.

When I reached the shore, I dropped my bag of goodies, and tugging my hair out of my ponytail, I toed off my boots. Hunter was already making his way into the water, slowly and carefully, which made me question its temperature.

Grabbing my rag and soaps, I trudged in, feeling the chills cascade over me, and the slippery stones beneath my feet. While Hunter didn't seem to struggle, my small feet couldn't grip the stones. I screeched as my foot slipped, and Hunter grabbed my arm to steady me.

"Careful," he said, and his firm grip loosened a little. In that fleeting moment, whatever it was I didn't like about him was forgotten as concern and severity warred in his eyes.

Heart hammering, I let out a panicked laugh. "Whoops. That was close."

His gaze shifted to his fingers, wrapped around my upper arm, and he quickly let go.

"Thanks," I said, and with another nervous laugh, I trudged deeper into the lake. "Who would've thought bathing would be such an adventure."

My feet slipped again, and I shrieked before giving in and letting the water consume me. When I came up laughing, I almost missed Hunter's smile before he went under, submerging himself in the lake.

13

HUNTER

I helped Alex and Bert refuel the trucks when we finished at the lake, then we changed into our clothes and gathered our things to load into the trucks.

"I'll drive for a bit," Alex told Bert as we loaded the last of the fuel. "That way you can catch some Zs before first watch tonight."

"I'll take first watch," I offered as I opened the door to reclaim my spot in the back.

"Hey, Hunter!" Kat called, and she gestured to the white truck, the "girls' truck" the guys had been calling it. "You want to ride shotgun?"

I glanced at Thea by the driver's side door as she pulled her damp hair up into a messy clump on top of her head, oblivious to Kat's question. The way her shirt hugged against her chest as she pulled her hair tighter made me think of her generous curves in her bathing suit, and I glanced away.

"What's the holdup?" Thea called. When I looked at her again, she was peering through the rolled down windows. "We're losing daylight, people."

"Since I'm going to nap," Kat said, opening the back door, "Hunter's going to sit up front to keep you company."

Thea's eyes shot to me.

"The guys can take Little Foot," Kat added.

"Wet dog," Alex grumbled. "Fantastic." He shut himself inside the driver's seat.

I blinked at Thea. She'd mentioned wanting a truce, but I wasn't sure close quarters was what she'd had in mind. She forced an awkward smile. "Come on, then," she said, climbing into the truck.

"Go ahead," Alex said. He whistled for Little Foot, who came trotting out of the trees toward the truck. "I'll follow you guys in case Thea gets tired or needs to pull over."

The wolf jumped into the back, his tongue hanging out of his mouth and his fur matted and wet. I guess I didn't envy the guys for having to ride with him.

Body tensing in preparation for whatever was to come, I grabbed my backpack out of the back seat and closed the door.

"I should warn you," Thea said as I approached. She snapped herself into her seatbelt. "I like to listen to music while I drive. It keeps me awake and focused." Thea turned the ignition and the truck rumbled to life.

Kat fluffed her pillow in the back, as if it was just another day on the road.

"Why is that a warning?" I asked. "Do you listen to crap music or something?" I shoved my bag into the corner of the floorboard by my feet and inched the seat back, needing more leg room than Thea seemed to.

"Ha. Of course not," she scoffed. "I listen to the good stuff—well, just about everything, mostly the classics, though." I wasn't sure what that meant, exactly, but then I didn't know much about music. "But," she continued, "I do like to sing—especially while I'm driving, so that I don't get bored, and I've been told I'm horrible at it." She shrugged. "Just ask Kat."

"She's pretty terrible," Kat agreed from the back. She had her eye mask on to keep out the sunlight. While the guys all slept with kinked necks in awkward positions, Kat clearly had a routine down, as if she'd done this same thing a dozen times. "And I'm not exaggerating," she added.

Thea looked at me with doe eyes and shrugged again. "Consider yourself warned."

The image of Thea singing at the top of her lungs made me huff a quick laugh. "I appreciate the warning, but you can't be much worse than Wren."

A genuine grin lifted Thea's cheeks this time, one that showed her dimples. "Ooh, really? Good to know. See, Kat," Thea said, opening the center console. "You don't have it that bad."

"Speak for yourself," she muttered, and shoved her ear plugs in.

Thea giggled and pulled out an old piece of tech I'd seen a long time ago, when I was a kid. "Is that an—"

"iPod, yes. It's ancient, but whoever had this bad boy before had awesome taste. Jackson scavenged it for me years ago— well, I think he got it more for himself but I pretty much stole it from him. There are thousands of songs on here. I've memorized all of them. The day it finally craps out on me"—she shook her head—"I can't even bear to think about it."

Thea attached an adapter to the stereo and adjusted the volume low before she pushed play on the device. In seconds, the cab of the truck vibrated with the rumble of the engine and the plucking sounds of an acoustic guitar.

I stared at the dash as the music played from the speakers. It was one thing to live without power; I'd gotten used to it. Moving to Whitehorse changed all of that, though, and while we still liked to use fire and candlelight, running water and heat during the cold months was a luxury I never thought we'd have again, and I relished it. But of all things, music had never been something I thought about, until now.

"You don't listen to tunes, do you?" Thea asked as she pulled slowly onto the rutted road, the trailer lurching and wobbling behind us. She glanced at me. "Your expression says it all."

"No," I admitted. "I don't listen to music."

"I'm sorry," she said, and when I looked at her, she flashed me a genuinely sorrowful look. "Music is everything, at least to me. I couldn't imagine not having any. When I'm happy or sad—when I'm pissed off—I can always find a song that makes me feel like I'm not alone in the world, like someone else felt that same way once, when they wrote the song."

"You have pissed off songs?" I asked, growing more curious by the second. Reluctantly, I considered she might have one for when she thought about me.

Thea snorted another laugh. "I have tons of them. All of them are by different artists, but the kicker," she said more thoughtfully as she settled back into her seat for the long drive, "is finding that *one* group or musician that gives you all the feels, no matter your mood."

"All the feels?"

She propped her elbow on the windowsill. "Yeah, a voice and sound that resonate and I feel them in my bones. You know?"

No, I didn't know, but I could imagine. "Do you have a favorite band then?" I asked, curious what sort of music made Thea so passionate.

"Linkin Park," she said. "Pissed off, thoughtful, chill, moving—they have it all. Especially if you go back through the years. And Phil Collins," she added. "Don't laugh."

"Why would I laugh?"

She blinked at me. "Right. You have no idea who I'm talking about," she reminded herself.

I listened to the song playing through the speakers. A man

with a bit of a raspy voice singing about a small-town girl and a lonely world. "Who is this? Linkin Park or Phil Collins?"

Thea chuckled. "Neither. It's one of Jackson's favorite bands, Journey. They're pretty rad. This is my favorite song by them."

As we fell into silence, I listened to the lyrics, and wondered if Thea resonated with the words, because they reminded me of her.

"So," Thea said, glancing in the rearview mirror. "I take it you've never needed to drive and that's why you don't know how?"

"No, I've never needed to. When I was a kid my father had a truck, but that was before."

"Before the outbreak?"

I shook my head. "Before he died. He pissed off the wrong people." I felt Thea's attention shift from the road to me. "But yeah, then the outbreak and what happened after changed things. We moved away from the town we'd been a part of, and left what little creature comforts we had behind."

That year had been the longest, most horrifying year of my life, and I hated to remember it. The physical pain as my body healed. Mourning the people we loved and lost in the most brutal ways. Watching helplessly as those I cared about suffered in the wake of everything. The fear that more men would come, and the apprehension that lingered even now. "We went into hiding," I thought aloud. "We had no reason for cars."

The impassioned words of the song filled the cab of the truck, and my skin dampened with sweat at the onslaught of unwanted memories. I rolled my window down a little, needing fresh air.

"I'm sorry about your dad," Thea said, turning the music down a smidgen.

"Don't be," I told her. "He wasn't a good guy. Besides, you've lost more people than I have," I said, remembering what Alex had said about their entire town dying, and about Thea's mother. I couldn't imagine having to kill my mother, whether she was crazy or not.

"Maybe," she said solemnly. "But death is death. It doesn't make losing people easier. At least, not for me."

As we fell back into silence, I hoped Thea wasn't going down a dark road of unwanted memories of her own because of me.

"You drive a lot then?" I asked, noticing how comfortable she seemed behind the steering wheel, and how a big truck suited her, despite her size. "I've mostly seen you on your horse."

"Cinder's great, and I prefer riding her when I can, but Elle and Jackson made sure we all learned to drive, in case we ever have to leave Whitehorse."

The thought sobered me. "You're worried about that?"

Thea's eyes flashed to mine, as if she'd regretted saying it, for my sake. "It's not that we worry about it so much as we know it's a possibility," she explained carefully. "Whitehorse is great, and it's the safest place we can be, but it's not infallible. Bad things can always happen, we've experienced that enough not to settle into a false sense of security."

My curiosity was almost too much to resist. I wanted to know what else Thea had been through in those years between what happened with her mother and now. But I couldn't bring myself to ask.

"What about you?" she said. "Do you want to learn to drive, now that you're here and it's an option?"

I considered it fleetingly as I shook my head. "I probably should, but Dancer's my girl. She's been my horse since she was born, and I'm used to her."

"I'm surprised you let Wren bring her when she and my brother came back with Jasper. You were without Dancer for months." And Thea had taken care of her the entire time; I hadn't forgotten that either. There were certain things she'd said to me that always seemed to resurface. *"Your horse looked half-starved when she got to Whitehorse, so I fattened her up for you. You know, in case you want to add that to the list of the reasons we're so untrustworthy."* Thea had disliked me since the moment we'd met, and even in the heat of our exchange that day, a part of me had still been intrigued.

"I wanted to make sure Wren was safe," I explained. I'd wanted Wren to live, and taking Cricket, exhausted after days of nonstop riding, would have run him into the ground. "And I knew Dancer would take care of her."

I could feel Thea's gaze boring into me again, and could see her chewing on her lip from the corner of my eye.

"Ask it," I said, without looking at her. "Whatever it is." I didn't want her making her own assumptions about me anymore.

"What's the deal with you and Wren?" she said without hesitation, like all she'd needed was a green light. "I know you're best friends, but . . . you're more than that too, right? Or, at least you were."

Surprised, my eyes shot to hers. Thea thought Wren and I had been together? "Is that why you were so mad at me yesterday?" Everything suddenly clicked. I knew she'd been upset on Wren's behalf, but I hadn't realized how deeply skewed her assumptions might actually be, even if the more I considered it, they made sense. "You think I'm trying to weasel my way in with Wren or something?"

Thea glanced at me with red cheeks, then looked back at the road. "I guess," she said, though it was pretty obvious that's exactly what she'd assumed, and if I'd learned anything about Thea in the past year, it was that she was loyal and fiercely protective of the people she cared about. Her brother and Wren's happiness would be no different.

"I've told Beau, and I'll tell you the same thing, Thea," I started. "It's not like that with me and Wren, it never has been."

We sat in silence a few moments, and it was probably for the better. I felt my defenses rising the more I thought about her assuming unpleasant things about me all the time, wondering what else she thought she knew.

After a few miles of staring out the window, watching the woods whip by, and maneuvering around the grooves in the road, Thea cleared her throat.

"Can you, uh, see if there are more honey chews in the side door, please?" she asked quietly.

I looked in the door cubby and saw a flashlight and the maps, but no honey chews. I shook my head.

"Lame," she groused, and I could tell by her furtive glances she was trying to ease the silent tension a bit. "Kat brings them to me from Prince Rupert when she goes. They're really good— some sort of honey and gum tree combination." With an overex-aggerated sigh, she leaned back in her seat again. "Of course I didn't bring enough." Her gaze lingered on me a moment. "Honey's like, my favorite thing, ever."

"I couldn't tell," I huffed, glancing back out the window.

"Yeah, I guess it's no secret." Her index finger tapped the steering wheel. "I still can't believe Cal brought me some," she said almost whimsically; I could hear the smile in her voice. "He even picked my favorite."

I wanted to tell Thea the honey wasn't from Cal, it was from me—a thank you gift for what she'd done for Milo; after our fight at the loading docks, I'd discarded it, and still, it made its way to her somehow.

As she focused on the road with a bright smile, I didn't have the guts to tell her the truth. Once again, I didn't want to be the reason for darkening her mood. And if I was honest, the tension in the cab was thick enough, and I didn't want to admit that I'd been so childish to discard it to begin with.

14

HUNTER

I stared out the window of an old house, just outside of Prince George, at an overgrown backyard shrouded by inky night.

"We continue down Highway 97," Kat said, her voice a rough whisper as she and Alex sat at a three-legged card table propped against the wall, poring over maps and plotting stopping points by lantern light. "Taking Yellowhead is too far out of the way."

Alex scratched his jaw. "Even if we'll be closer to the cities than we'd like?"

Kat sat back in her folding chair "Don't you think the other route will add days, maybe even a week?"

Alex conceded, rubbing his hands over his dark cropped hair. "Let's hope we can drive straight through then."

"If not," Kat said with a tired breath, "we'll figure it out."

We were further south than most of us had been—officially off the beaten path of normal trading routes. Kat and her friend, Jenny, were the only ones to take this course when they'd traveled from Seattle to Whitehorse years ago, but the roads were worse now and we weren't on horseback like they had been. It seemed the further we drove from home, the more Kat and Alex's ease wavered, and my own anxieties loomed.

They continued to mumble and mutter, but my thoughts veered to New Bodega and I leaned against the windowsill. What would my old self have said two years ago, if I'd told him he'd not only leave his home but join a group of tainted, power-wielding survivors, and that I would put my life in their hands as we journeyed to a city packed with even more of them? What would I have said or done if I'd known I would go there to secure a vaccine *created* by them, that could change our genetic makeup for future generations? I was altering everything we'd been trying to preserve so we would survive, and I wasn't sure what cost we might pay because of it.

Somberness settled over me as I remembered Wren, unconscious in Beau's arms the day he showed up at the old village. Risking death, or living and dying alone without families at all was the alternative.

The fact that Wren hadn't been outwardly changed after she'd had the fever was a small comfort, but sleeping with Beau was different than an injected, engineered serum the rest of us would have to take—that my *brother* would have to take if he wanted to have a family in this new world.

I thought about Thea's future with Cal. As much as I didn't like the guy, I envied the two of them. Thea didn't have to think about her future, about a family or surviving her partner in order to have one. Once again, we were the outliers in this and Thea was the normal one.

My mother didn't understand that, even as unnerving as the vaccine was, it was the only option we had. Any hope for a pure bloodline stopped with the children I would've had with Wren. Milo and Sutton had no one their ages. So my mother and Henni—all of them—had been holding their breath for an impossible outcome because they couldn't face the truth. Deep down, I knew the vaccine was my brother's only hope of having a proper life, and I was desperate enough to take the chance.

Bert choked in his sleep, and with a grumble, he turned on his pallet. Little Foot, curled up at his feet, didn't stir in the slightest. Probably exhausted from his playday at the lake.

Alex looked over at Bert as the old man began snoring again, then met my gaze. "You're not tired?" he asked. "I got first watch."

I shook my head. "I can't sleep yet."

Alex perked up, looking around the room. "Is Thea still outside?"

I glanced toward the front door. "I'll check on her." Alex nodded, and I stepped over Bert, then Kat's sleeping bag and pack, and wound my way around a crumbling recliner toward the door.

The house was tiny, only a single room and a nonfunctional bathroom off to the left, but from her travels before, Kat knew it was off the road enough to keep our trucks and trailers out of sight for the night.

"If we stay on the highway, we risk unwanted attention," Alex told Kat behind me. "But if we go off course, there's a whole slew of potential issues."

I tuned them out as I peered through the cobwebbed, single-paned window at the front lawn. It was more like a meadow with a moss-covered patio table and warped chairs that had seen much better days, stacked in the center of it.

Thea sat in one of the plastic chairs, wrapped in a blanket and staring up at the stars. Her hair caught in the breeze and she shivered.

Opening the door, I stepped outside.

"Do you ever stare up at the stars?" she asked, as she lifted her blanket and pulled a small round tin from her pocket.

"All the time," I admitted.

Thea's head snapped to me. "I thought you were Alex." She

rubbed her berry tinted balm over her lips as I walked over to her, careful not to step on anything nestled in the tall grass. "You're not asleep with the others?" she asked.

"The only one sleeping is Bert," I told her, knowing she'd appreciate that.

"Of course he is," she muttered and shoved her lip balm back into her pocket. Leaning her head back, she peered up at the stars again, her features partially hidden in night shadows. "Is it because you miss your family?" she asked, quieter this time.

"My family?" Since my presence didn't seem completely unwelcome, I unstacked one of the old chairs, brushed the dead pine needles off it, and sat down on the other side of the dirt-coated table.

"Is that why you can't sleep?" she clarified.

"No," I said, and crossed my arms over my chest. My family was definitely on my mind for a handful of reasons, but missing them wasn't exactly the reason. "I like my space," I admitted. "Does that make me sound like an asshole?" I knew she would have no problem telling me if it did.

With a smirk, she shook her head. "Trust me, I get it." She nestled deeper into her seat and I watched the way her index fingers tapped on her arms, folded over her knees. Her mind was busy, that much was obvious.

"I've noticed," she started again, "you're very . . . diligent. You check the doors and windows, even when you're not on watch." This time, her eyes met mine, and I couldn't help but wonder what else she noticed about me.

"I like to know my surroundings," I said. "And, I've been thinking a lot about New Bodega, so my mind's too full for sleep." I wasn't sure if I was confiding in her, or answering her question, but either way, conversation seemed to come more easily than usual.

"Me too," she said with a lilt of understanding, though I

knew we were thinking about New Bodega for very different reasons.

We sat in shared silence for a few minutes, and my thoughts began to drift to nothing more than admiring the glinting sky and hoping for a shooting star, when Thea cleared her throat.

"That house you were at," she said, clearing her throat. "The one in the old neighborhood . . . Is that why you were there the other night, to get some space?"

The day I saw her and Cal? I lowered my chin. "I found it a few months after we arrived in Whitehorse."

"Let me guess, you were doing a perimeter check and scoping out your surroundings?" Thea smiled knowingly.

I didn't bother validating her question with an answer. "I remembered the fire pit in the backyard, so it sort of stuck with me."

"And now it's where you go to escape?"

"I guess you could call it that."

Thea's head bobbed slightly, as if she understood, and she gazed up at the stars again. "I have a place like that," she said quietly. "The graveyard at home."

While that seemed morbid in a way, it also sounded peaceful. "The graveyard is special to you—"

Twigs cracked and bushes rustled in the darkness, and Thea and I rose to our feet.

"What was that?" she breathed.

"It's definitely not Little Foot," I said dumbly, knowing he was inside sleeping. I didn't have my gun on me, but I stepped in front of Thea protectively.

The bushes rustled again, another twig snapped, and squinting, I stared into the darkness.

I considered calling the others, but with another rustle and a cooing, skittering noise, a large porcupine tottered out of the foliage, sniffing around the forest floor.

I exhaled the tension in my shoulders as Thea gasped. "I love porcupines," she chirped. Somehow her voice was quiet but still brimmed with excitement.

"Clearly you've never been pricked by one."

She peered up at me, closer to me than I realized, her eyes wide and curious in the moonlight. "You have?"

"No," I said. "But there was a dog in my village once who had."

Thea nearly giggled, and she seemed to realize at the same time how close we were. Her expression sobered.

"I'm not sure why I stepped in front of you," I said, and went back over to my chair. "I should've pulled you in front of me instead. You can protect me a lot better than I can protect either of us."

Thea's eyes rounded again. "Oh my—Hunter, was that a joke?" she asked merrily, and sat back down in her chair.

I allowed myself to smile, and my cheeks warmed. "An attempt at one anyway."

Her brow shot up. "*And* a smile. Wow." With a snigger, she pulled her knees up against her chest again, her gaze on me as she thought of something that made her smile soften. Then, it fell completely, and my ease faded with it.

"Honestly," she said, glancing back at the porcupine as it waddled around the house, undisturbed by us. "I'm not always the best person to have around in tense situations." Her voice was suddenly distant. While I didn't think I was the cause this time, I hated that her smile could falter so easily.

"Your ability—to literally move trouble out of the way—would counter that argument," I told her, attempting another, more lighthearted joke.

"It's not that simple," she said, the lilt gone from her voice.

I knew I needed to find a safer topic. "Maybe—"

"I have a knack for using my Ability at the wrong times," she admitted, and her stare blanked. I assumed what had happened with her mother caused the disquiet in her voice. "Household chores are one thing," she started again, and though she spoke to me, she looked at nothing, as if I wasn't even there. "But the moments when it counts, it's not all that reliable."

"But, you saved your brother when he was little, and mine. That's a good thing."

Thea blinked, and her unfocused gaze sharpened on me. I regretted saying it as she sank deeper into her seat. "Maybe," she hedged, "but that night—what happened with Beau . . . that wasn't exactly what I was thinking about."

My fingers curled into my palm on my lap, and I braced myself. "No?" I whispered, scared that if I said more or asked too much, she'd clam up on me.

"I was thinking about Luna." Thea ran her palms over her knees, as if it calmed her. "Beau's wolf."

I recalled the name, but I'd never been buddy-buddy enough with Beau to ask about it.

"I hurt her with my Ability, and she died because of it."

Knowing Beau had deep connections with animals, I could see how scarring her part in the wolf's death might be, but I found it hard to believe that Thea had done any harm on purpose.

"It's like . . ." Her eyes glazed over again. "I feel something and act instantly—my body takes over and by the time I realize what I'm doing . . . it's too late to stop it. I just—" She peered down at her hands again. "It's not like Kat's or Elle's Ability— it's not elemental. They have to concentrate and conjure, and all I have to do is think about it and look at it. It takes no effort, and in the heat of the moment, when my feelings are amped, there's little I can do to control what happens next." Thea shook her head. "No amount of practicing compares to instinct in a single, heart-pounding moment and . . . I hate it." Like she suddenly remembered she was staring through me, Thea blinked, refocusing as she folded her arms over her knees to rest her head. "It's hard to explain."

"I get it," I said, because I did. I didn't have an Ability to contend with, but I was all too familiar with the aftermath of them. "At least you can protect yourself," I told her. "In this world, you're one of the strong."

Thea exhaled. "An Ability doesn't make you strong. Not always. In fact, I feel sort of broken half the time."

I didn't know what it was like to fear an Ability I'd woken up with one day and couldn't get rid of, but I knew what it felt like to fear the unknown, knowing I wouldn't likely be able to stop it. "Not even Whitehorse makes me feel safe, even though it's supposed to," I realized aloud.

Thea's brow furrowed slightly, her eyebrows delicate dark lines etched in moonlight. "It's why you check the locks and windows so often," she said, as if it just dawned on her. "Is it the memories of what happened when you were little?"

I felt a rush of anxious need to stand up and walk away, but I forced myself to stay there, with her. To give Thea something, the way she had given me a small glimpse of her. "Not so much the memories, but the feeling of helplessness and the guilt," I admitted.

"But," she lifted her head, "you saved them, didn't you? Wren told me you killed those men—"

I shook my head. "There was more I could've done," I told her, my head still shifting back and forth like she might continue speaking if I stopped. "And it's not just that." I clenched my fists, suddenly clammy, in my lap. I allowed my father to do horrible things to my mother before he died. And I'd heard too many screams before I finally found what little courage I had to go outside to stop those madmen. "Otto, Nessa, Colt—"

"Hunter," Thea said, her voice only a whisper. Pulling myself out of the past, my eyes met hers. "You were only a boy," she insisted, and my chest burned as her gaze drifted down my body. "After what they did to you . . ." Her voice cracked a little and she swallowed.

"You don't—" I forced myself to stop. Thea didn't know

how many screams could fill a single immobilizing moment of numbing fear. Or how many hysterical, desperate pleas for help haunted my dreams. Or what I might've prevented if I'd acted even five minutes sooner. Thea didn't know that every movement was an aching reminder that I would carry for the rest of my life. And that, because of my scars, I would never forget what true weakness felt like either.

"I know you're scared of your Ability," I told her, my voice harder than it should've been as I forced out the words. "But because of it, you will never know weakness like we have. You're not broken, Thea, you're lucky." The words felt uncomfortably true.

Her eyes shimmered with emotions I couldn't stomach, and as Thea's lips parted to say something, I rose to my feet. "I'm going to get some sleep." I knew sleep would evade me as I started for the cabin, but her pitying expression made it impossible to sit still any longer. In three strides, I opened the door. "Night."

"Goodnight," Thea whispered, and I refused to meet her gaze as I closed the door behind me.

15

THEA

"I'm not sure why we're surprised," Bert said, tossing a rock into the void in front of us. "Our luck's been too good for too long."

After getting an early start, knowing we had a lot of ground to cover to get to Washington by the end of our driving day, Hunter, Alex, Bert, and I stood along the Fraser River, staring at the ravine where the bridge should've been, according to Kat and our map.

"How old is that thing?" Bert asked as he stared at the map in Alex's hand, the corner flapping in a gust of afternoon wind.

"Who the hell knows," Alex muttered, and squinted down at the river.

The day was warm, and I could feel my shoulders turning pink the longer we stood there, annoyed and feeling a bit defeated.

"But," Alex continued. "I'm beginning to wonder if it's not that bridge over there that's on the map." He pointed downriver.

I followed Alex's gaze to the rust-colored railway crossing off in the distance.

"Well," Kat called from upriver. She stalked around bottle-brush and bramble bushes, Little Foot lagging behind her. "The good news is, I found our bridge."

I looked at Hunter, neither of us very hopeful as she stomped closer.

"It's around that bend," she said, pointing in the direction she came. "But it's in slabs of broken steel and concrete at the bottom of the ravine—pieces of it are sticking out of the water."

Bert looked at me. "You ever moved a truck and trailer with your mind, kid?"

My eyes widened and I stared down into the ravine, it was as wide as a dozen trucks and twice as deep. "Um—"

"He's joking," Kat grumbled.

Bert looked at her with a huff. "I am?"

Tilting her head as if she was bored, Kat looked at me. "Thea, is that something you'd like to try?" I could tell she wasn't serious, but Bert surely was.

I glanced between them. "Um—not particularly." I didn't want to let them down, but if I dropped one of the trucks or trailers down there, we'd be screwed and probably have to turn back. "We'd still have to figure out a way to get ourselves across, even if I could move them," I added. Moving objects was one thing, but people—that was far too dangerous and nerve-wracking.

Kat rubbed her forehead and peered across the river. "Shit," she spat. We were in the middle of nowhere, past what looked like the remains of a small village that wasn't even on the map. We'd accounted for rough roads and bad weather that would undoubtedly slow us down, even the occasional blocked route that we'd have to maneuver around, but the roads were few and far between in Canada, and not being able to cross the river was a huge setback, one I knew might mean we couldn't continue at all.

I looked at Hunter, who was staring down at the river in silence. More horses for Whitehorse could wait. Trading food could wait. Securing the vaccine, however, that was important enough for Hunter to leave the protection and comfort of home.

"I should've thought of this," Kat muttered as she turned toward the truck. "Of course one of the goddamn bridges would be out. It's only been a decade."

"None of us thought about it, Kat," Alex told her in his calming, fatherly voice. "At least, not seriously enough. This isn't on you."

"Regardless," she said, opening the driver's door and pulling out her water bottle. Hastily, she unscrewed the cap and took a swig, greedily gulping it down like it would make everything better. "We backtrack," she said when she finished. Kat licked her lips and peered down the road. "We figure out another way."

The more minutes we waited would become hours, and by the end of the trip a "simple" backtrack could add days, and we were only halfway to New Bodega. Knowing our next checkpoint to communicate with home was in California, we had to keep going; if we fell too far behind, the others would worry.

"We use the rail bridge," I said, closing my eyes so I wouldn't look at it looming off in the distance and change my mind.

When I finally opened them, Kat's expression was wary. "Thea—"

"Okay," Alex said.

I glanced between them. "It might need a little help, but it's still standing," I explained. I felt compelled to do this, even if I was slightly terrified. I didn't want to attempt moving entire trucks and trailers with my mind over such a wide, deep ravine, but I figured I could hold a bridge that was unsafe but still standing together, long enough for them to drive the trucks through.

Kat frowned, but Alex smiled from ear to ear. "We could use the practice," he said, eager to flex his Ability-infused fingers.

"Thea," Kat started again, and took a step toward me. "Are you sure? It's not that I don't think you can keep it all together if something happened, because I know you can, but—"

"But you know I don't want to," I finished for her. I shrugged, as if I wasn't shaking on the inside. "We all have to do things that make us uncomfortable, right? We have to get across, Kat."

Like me, she knew the consequences of using her Ability, and that it could go a bit off-course in the blink of an eye; Ross had the lightning burn scars on his jaw and neck to prove it. But Hunter had been right last night, I had an Ability that would help us.

"Besides," I told her. "The rail bridge can't be worse than this one." I pointed toward the remains upriver. The entire ravine was eroded by years of Mother Nature's free rein on the world, and I had a feeling this was only the start of what I might have to do the further we drove from home. I needed to do this. For them. For me. For Hunter.

Alex nudged me. "We can do this," he said with so much confidence, I wished it was contagious.

With a nod, I turned back to the truck. "Then let's do it," I told them. "Before I change my mind." I whistled for Little Foot as I opened the door for him to jump into the back seat. I met Hunter's gaze as he walked past. I wasn't sure what weighed more heavily on me, the look of shame and fear on Hunter's face last night when he spoke about the weakness of being human, or what Alex and I were about to attempt.

I hadn't stopped thinking about Hunter's words; I had super-powers and they were useful, even if they scared me. As much as my telekinesis felt like a curse at times, I knew that wasn't the only side to it, and I wouldn't allow myself to be a coward, especially since I knew what Hunter had risked to save his family with only his will and courage to protect him.

Everyone filed into the trucks in silence, and Little Foot's head hung out the window. He sniffed the air with curiosity while unease coiled in my stomach as the trucks protested and shook over a gravel path that cut through the empty village.

The breeze carried a warm metallic scent the closer we drew to the railway bridge. And as I glanced around, I decided the place hadn't been a community so much as a gas stop. There was nothing more than a few squat buildings, rotted to the foundation, and a few old gas pumps. All of it was covered in vines—a lot of them—making it feel even more ancient and forgotten than everywhere else.

As we drove closer to the rounded, corroded trusses of the bridge, I reminded myself how strong my Ability had grown over the years, and if I could focus, there was no reason I wouldn't be able to do this. I forced myself to push my anxiety down somewhere it wouldn't distract me, beneath the apprehension and the intimidating memories, and I appraised the bridge. It was rusted antiquity at its finest, but it was metal and steel and I had moved objects just like it a dozen times before in Whitehorse; if I could reinforce a prison and build walls around a city, I could do this. I swallowed thickly.

As Alex slowed at the tracks, I noticed it was blocked at the other end by train cars. He looked at me with a wry grin.

"Yeah, yeah," I said, waving his excitement away. "I know what you're going to say. It's time to practice. "

Alex chuckled. "We could both use a good warm-up anyway," he said, and climbed out of the truck.

"Maybe *you* could," I smirked, my feet hitting the ground with a thud as I climbed out of the truck too. It was time for Alex and me to flex some Ability muscle, whether I was ready or not.

He climbed onto one of the iron bracings, and fleetingly, I imagined him scaling trees as a little boy, then remembered how troubled he was in his youth. Now, Alex was a man—a father and big brother—and I smiled to myself. He squinted into the distance. "I can see five train cars for sure," he said.

"Well, I can only move what I can see," I reminded him. "And I can only see part of two of them." I needed to get closer. "Come on." I gestured down the tracks with false bravado.

I'm not sure why I thought the bridge might sway beneath my feet with each step, but it didn't move, save for the occasional creak or moan in the breeze and hot sun. And although I didn't have the warm and fuzzies walking on a bridge covered in vines and bramble, which made it difficult to assess, I wasn't exactly worried about the bridge crumbling with the additional weight of two mere people either.

"Careful of the wood slats," Alex warned. He pointed to a few rotted ones in front of me, the metal meshing present but rusted beneath them; I could see the rushing water below.

"If you're worried about it holding us, Alex, it's definitely not going to hold the trucks."

He took my hand in his. "Just—be careful. Jackson would *kill* me if I let anything happen to you."

I smiled. Whether or not I needed Alex to amplify my telekinesis, I knew we had a better chance of getting this done together; his presence alone was comforting, so I squeezed his hand as we made our way cautiously across.

As unsettling as the bridge was, it was strangely beautiful too. The sun cast a wash of polka-dotted shadows inside the interior, and hints of paint glimmered beneath the thinnest layers of dust. "What's that?" I asked, pointing to a crossbeam with brighter colors peeking through.

Alex squinted. "It was tagged." I looked at him. "Graffiti," he clarified. "Spray paint. People used to do it when they were bored, just to be assholes."

I vaguely remembered something about that, in my little Thea mind from years ago. The walls in the abandoned Heston

Building. The deserted streets in Anchorage after the outbreak. "I think it looks sort of cool," I told him, wishing I could see all the colors when they were new and vibrant.

"You would," he snorted.

I ignored his insinuation as we continued walking. Bird droppings covered the iron beams, and despite how rusted the bridge was, it was covered in green. Like everything else in the world, the bridge looked forgotten in time, and yet life seemed to have sprung up around it too.

"Look," Alex whispered.

I followed his index finger to the crossbeams above and noticed a large nest. A hawk stood inside, staring down at us with a tilted head.

"It probably doesn't know what to make of us," I realized. "I wonder if it's ever seen a human before."

Alex looked at me, staring for a moment, then shook his head. "That's such a weird thought," he mused.

Finally, four of the five train cars came into view, and I stopped in the center of the bridge. "I'm going to move the one closest out and over to the left," I told him, verbalizing my game plan in case it was idiotic.

"You're assuming they aren't all attached to one another." He looked at me with a challenging smile.

I grinned back. "And you're assuming it matters."

With a laugh, Alex held up his free hand. "Pardon me, Miss *Thang.* I'll just watch from the sidelines until you need me then."

Winking at him, I squared my shoulders, squeezed his hand playfully, and willed myself to focus. I had no idea how difficult this would be, but I still had a bridge to keep together and my family to get across.

With a deep breath, I fixated on the simmering, vibrating power within the fibers of my skin; ignoring the constant hum had become second nature, just like the pumping of my heart. That's how it was for all of us, we'd discovered. Our Abilities were like another organ, always present and alive though we forgot it was there—a whirr that was white noise, lying in wait like a sleeping bear in its winter cave.

Staring at the train car closest to us, I lifted my chin. The base of my skull ached for the briefest of moments, then relaxed, and the hum beneath my skin amplified until the hairs along my arms and neck lifted with the vibration. As I willed the train car to roll toward us, it did.

16

HUNTER

Bert, Kat, and I stood back at the trucks, holding our breath and waiting for whatever might come next. I'd seen the fear in Thea's eyes when she'd mentioned crossing the bridge. After what she'd confided in me last night, about dreading her own powers, I could guess where that fear came from and what thoughts ran through her head. Yet, she'd offered anyway.

But all of that was forgotten when I heard the reverberating whine through the eerily still air, the sound of metal scraping against metal.

A flock of birds burst from the woods lining the canyon ahead, and my heart hammered against my diaphragm the instant I saw the train car shift. Slowly. Loudly. Begrudging the interruption after years of sitting. But it *was* moving, and as much as I knew I should, I couldn't believe it. The bramble that had taken over the bridge and river valley stirred with it, tearing and breaking, and wisps of it snapped and flung into the air as Thea broke its hold.

A sudden surge of awe filled me, and my chest tightened. Even after all I'd observed living in Whitehorse, I'd never encountered anything as jaw-dropping as petite, bubbly Thea, wielding an unfathomable power I couldn't even see, let alone comprehend. She was amazing.

"Don't mess up the bridge," Kat pleaded quietly. "Don't mess up the bridge." Her arms were crossed over her chest and she bit at her thumbnail, her attention fixed ahead. The three of us watched another train car moving along with the first, just as stubborn.

I knew what Thea could do because I'd seen what she did for Milo in the barn, but I had never seen her move something so huge, and she didn't have to lift a single finger.

"Pretty cool, huh?" Bert said, his eyes meeting mine.

"Yeah," I breathed. The first and second train cars shuddered. With his hand in Thea's, Alex stepped closer, like even his proximity might help her. The metal continued to groan and shift off the track toward the cliff, and the third train car skidded as it was pulled off-kilter. As the first one edged over the cliff, I expected it to plunge to the bottom, but it continued to move further over the ledge, floating in the air, its immensity quaking.

"It's going to fall," I said, but Kat shook her head.

"Don't mess up the bridge," she continued to chant, her voice barely a breath.

Only then did I realize what Thea was trying to do; if she let the first train cars fall, she might lose control of the rest. So, she suspended them until each one was clear of the crossing. I had no idea how many thousands of tons she was controlling with her mind, and the sheer awe of it made it impossible to look away.

"How does it work?" I whispered. It was easy to forget what some of them could do. It wasn't like everyone walked around with neon signs and lightning bolts coming out of them as a daily reminder. Mostly, they were just . . . normal.

"Thea's telekinesis?" Kat asked.

I nodded, my eyes fixed on the first train car moving further and further away from the cliff, making room for the others trailing behind it.

"I don't know, exactly. Focus, I guess." Kat tilted her head. "With her—it's changed over time. If she's concentrating, I think she can do it without moving or blinking if she wanted to. But when she was little, she used to point, and she'd have to strain to make things move. Obviously, having Alex makes it easier for her."

"I'd use it a lot more than she does if I could do that," Bert said, and he leaned against the truck like it was just another pit stop and just another day on the road. "I'll tell ya that much."

"Yeah, well you've never hurt someone with it, so you don't know that for sure," Kat reminded him.

Bert conceded with a sigh and we stood there for what felt like a fleeting moment, and yet the sun was lowering in the sky by the time Thea was finished, and the last train car neared the cliff.

Suddenly, the screeching metal became a clanging, clanking cacophony of ear-splitting noise as the train slid the rest of the way off the cliff and into the river. The ground shook, a hawk sprung from its perch on top of the bridge, and Little Foot ran for cover under the truck as the metal frame moaned.

As suddenly as the disruption started, it was over. Everything became still and quiet, save for my heart pounding in my chest. "Holy shit."

Bert whooped, and Kat clapped her hands, rejoicing in Thea and Alex's success.

I watched the water rushing around the newest obstacles in its path, and a stupid thought came to mind: the next people to come this way wouldn't know what happened here today, that a young woman who liked to eat honey and play with animals, whose build was no bigger and whose body was no stronger than the average person, moved an entire train off the tracks and into the river with her mind.

As Alex and Thea made their way back with grins on their faces, all I could think about was the raw power Thea could wield with a single thought, and for the first time, I thought I might've truly understood the burden she carried.

17

THEA

Our camp, settled somewhere along the Fraser River, wasn't up until nearly ten, and by then the sun was only a glow behind the silhouette of the surrounding mountains. But after one of the longest days of my life, it felt more like midnight.

The bridge had been sketchy in some areas, but hauling the trailers over it one at a time and as slowly as we could had been uneventful. Thankfully.

I'd been napping off and on in the truck, but I was still exhausted. It was like the adrenaline and the fear combined had sucked every ounce of energy I'd rallied. It was a feeling I hadn't felt in a long time, if ever. The effects of exuding my telekinesis felt different this time—I felt stronger, even a bit more excited. And somehow, every muscle ached from doing absolutely nothing.

As I wandered through the woods, collecting firewood, I told myself sleep was imperative tonight because, unless a caravan of sorts had passed through Vancouver and Seattle at some point before us and cleared a path, tomorrow I would have leftover road congestion from the outbreak to deal with. Even if Alex was going to be there to supercharge me, I would need all the energy I could muster.

When I had an armful of birch sticks and branches, I headed through the woods back to camp. Our overnight spot was nothing more than a widened shoulder off the road, but we were too tired after an unexpectedly long day to continue driving.

I stepped into the clearing where Bert and Kat were finishing up with the tents, and Hunter and Alex worked on dinner and the fire.

"You look like you're barely standing upright," Alex said, glancing up at me from beside the unlit campfire. He poured a can of beans into a pot.

"I'm fine," I told him. "But I'm sure I'll sleep good tonight." I walked over to Hunter to hand him the firewood cradled in my arms. When his eyes met mine, dark and assessing in the lantern light, they lingered momentarily.

I wasn't sure how it differed from usual, but Hunter had been looking at me strangely ever since the bridge. I felt his attention on me frequently, and he seemed even more contemplative, if that were possible. But was it because he saw me differently after what I'd done today, or because he was seeing me—not the Thea from nearly two years ago—for the first time? Or was it something else entirely?

Either way, I couldn't tell if it was a good thing, or if it was bad. And I didn't want Hunter to look at me like I was a freak, even when I told myself it didn't matter what Hunter thought at all.

I opened one of the camping chairs discarded in the dirt, appreciating the thought of a warm fire tonight. It had been days since I'd gotten to sit beside one, and the night was chilly, which made it the perfect way to wind down after such an exhausting day.

"What's on the menu tonight?" Bert asked as he brushed his hands off on his Dickies.

I opened another chair and began placing them around the fire for our dinner feast.

"Beans and caribou," Alex said as he laid the grate across the stone pit.

Bert strode over to the girls' truck and opened the back door. He pulled out some pillows, stacking them under his arms.

"Bert!" Kat barked as she struggled to finish the final tent. "If my pillow touches your nasty pits, I'm going to strike you down with lightning."

Bert looked at me, and I had to bite back a laugh. "I would never," he called back, and winked at me. He heaved Kat's red duffel out of the truck bed and headed back to the tent with her things. "How could you ever think such a thing?" Though he sounded innocent enough, his eyes were full of mischief.

Kat grumbled something, but I headed for the truck to get my hoodie and scarf. The wind was cool, though not frigid like it often was at home, and I thought that was one more thing I might like about being further south.

"Where's Little Foot?" I asked no one in particular, my back to the group as I tugged my sweatshirt over my head.

"Probably hunting."

I spun around. Hunter stood behind me, the burgeoning fire crackling behind him, casting his profile in shadow. How was it he could seem so ominous and intriguing as he stood there?

"Makes sense," I said. The others moved around camp, finally winding down for food before we hunkered in to sleep. But I stared back at Hunter, waiting for him to say something as he stood there, staring.

I worried that, after today, whatever progress we'd made since our truce by the lake had been for nothing because I was feeling uncomfortable around him again, like he was judging me, and I bristled. "What, Hunter?" I asked, impatiently resting my hands on my hips.

After a few seconds, he lifted the flashlight in his hand. "I was waiting for you to move so I could put this back in the truck," he said flatly. "But if you want to do it for me . . ."

I swallowed. "Oh." I was thankful he couldn't see the embarrassment on my face in the darkness. "Sure." I took the solar flashlight and tucked it into the pocket behind the front seat. "Sorry, I—" When I turned around again, Hunter was no longer standing there. He pulled the plastic bowls and the silverware out of the camping box and headed over to Alex, stirring the meat and beans by the fire.

"Shit," I muttered. My stomach growled, reminding me I was starved, and with an exhausted sigh, I threw my hair up in a messy bun and grabbed my water bottle from the front seat.

"Come and get it, Thea," Alex said. "And grab my beanie from my truck, would you?"

"Sure thing." Closing the truck door, I headed to the other F-250 to grab Alex's beanie and his jacket, just in case, then I headed to the fire.

Alex ladled me a bowlful of beans and caribou meat. "It's nothing gourmet, but . . ." I exchanged the bowl for his beanie and jacket.

"This is great, thank you."

He nodded and draped his jacket over the seat next to him, which left only one chair empty beside Hunter.

Just grateful to relax and eat, I walked over and sat down beside him, telling myself I was going to eat then go straight to sleep . . . I wouldn't be able to make things more awkward between us if I was asleep.

Hunter didn't seem to care I was so close, which made it easy to forget my discomfort, and I dug into my dinner. The beans were tender and warm on my tongue, and I could taste Alex's signature surplus of brown sugar he always added.

"This is perfect, Alex. Thank you," Kat said.

Our heads bobbed and we mumbled in agreement as we shoveled food into our bellies; I could feel it coating my insides, sating the gnawing parts of me that needed comfort and sustenance.

I was scraping the last of the beans from my bowl by the time everyone had finished, too relaxed for much conversation. The fire crackled and popped, and the crickets chirped. The breeze kissed my nose and cheeks, making me appreciate the warmth of the fire all the more.

"Assuming we can make up for lost time tomorrow," Bert said. "We'll be in Olympia for the night. Do we have any idea where we're going to stay?" The low gruffness of his voice was a sure sign he was ready for sleep, and I didn't envy Alex for having to sleep beside him in the tent again. I made a mental note to give Alex a pair of my rubber earplugs, which I'd specifically brought *because* of Bert.

Kat walked around the circle and collected our bowls for the wash bin. "I've only been to a couple places in Olympia," Kat said. "At least that I can remember. I think somewhere near the Puget Sound is the best option, if we can manage it. The cities are too unpredictable, and we've been making a lot of noise in our wake so far. Tomorrow won't be any different."

"I say we get past the cities," Alex said with a curt nod, "and we try to find a place somewhere off the road. The ocean would be nice, but we're going to have to figure it out as we go along, at this point."

"I've never been to the ocean," Hunter said. We all looked at him as he stared into the fire.

"Really?" I asked, though I wasn't that surprised. He'd lived inland all his life, without a reason to go so far west.

His eyes met mine. "Really."

Pulling my lip balm from my back pocket, I leaned back in my chair. "You're going to like it," I told him. He held my gaze, the air between us humming with something I couldn't name until I forced myself to look away. Focusing on the fire, I smoothed the raspberry salve over my lips before sliding it back into my pocket. Then, closing my eyes, I tried to lose myself to the feel of the breeze and the sound of Alex and Bert chattering about who was driving tomorrow. Kat griped at Bert for picking at a scab on his arm, and there were moans and sighs as everyone began to unwind.

The flames warmed my cheeks, nose, and hands, and as I soaked it in, I felt the heavy blanket of sleep settle over me more quickly than I could stop it.

———

The hoot of an owl made my eyelids flutter open. The flames of the fire were low, the wind a bit chilly, and I nestled closer to the warmth of my headrest. There was no one left across the fire, and I thought I was alone for the briefest moment before I registered the scent of someone familiar and that I was resting against something that felt a lot like a shoulder.

Bleary eyed, I lifted my head and looked at Hunter. His gaze flicked from the fire to me.

I blinked as my sleepy haze faded. "Oh—sorry." I jerked away from him. "I didn't mean to—" I wiped any remnants of drool that might linger from my mouth as my mind raced. "You should've shaken me or something."

"You're exhausted," he said, like that was more important than however long he'd had to sit there, probably losing the feeling in his legs from sitting too long, or worse.

I felt my cheeks flush, and not because of the fire. "Still." I swallowed thickly and peered around at the tents, realizing Bert was snoring in the outermost one. "How long was I asleep?" I whispered.

Hunter leaned forward and prodded at the embers in the firepit. "Almost an hour."

I rounded on him. "Hunter—"

"The wolf and I are on first watch anyway," he said quietly. "Don't worry about it."

I peered around for Little Foot, noticing he wasn't asleep by the fire, one of his favorite places. "He's probably out catching his breakfast at this point," I grumbled, and combed my wayward hair back with my fingers. "I hope I didn't drool or something." Leaning forward, I put my palms to the fire, dreading leaving its warmth for the cold tent.

"No drooling," Hunter said. "You only snored."

"What?" I gaped at him. "Are you serious?"

"Just a little."

My apparent horror made his cheek twitch a little as he sat back in his chair, his gaze still fixed on the flames as they grew again.

I shoved him playfully. "You think that's funny?" I couldn't help but laugh. "That's horrifying."

Finally, he smiled and looked at me. "It happens," he said with amusement.

I rolled my eyes as I rose to my feet. "Well then, maybe next time I'll drool on you too," I warned him.

Hunter arched his eyebrow. "Next time?"

I flashed him a grin as I walked past. "Night, brat." I barely heard him chuckle over the crunch of debris beneath my shoes.

18

HUNTER

S leepless nights were nothing new to me, so I welcomed being on watch. I appreciated the evening air, cool against my skin as I walked around the perimeter of the campsite. I weaved my way along the line of brush and gangly trees at the edge of the woods, cast in the pale blue glow of deepening night.

I wasn't looking for anything in particular, but every shadow was a potential hiding place. No amount of reassurance from Thea or Kat or Alex could change the clawing need I had to double-check each of those shadows, even if I wished it would.

I inhaled deeply, the scent of moist earth filling my nose. I'd thought this journey would be long, looming, and uncomfortable —and it was to some extent—but it had been surprising too. I almost smiled, remembering Thea moaning in her sleep against my shoulder by the fire two hours ago.

A rustle in the trees startled me, and Little Foot scampered out of the brush, his nose to the ground as he sniffed around. Just another day in the life of a wolf. His head lifted and his ears perked up when he realized I was standing amidst the trees. He trotted over, as if saying hello was the proper thing to do.

"You know," I murmured as his eyes met mine. They glistened in the full moonlight. "I've never been much of a dog person." Little Foot licked my hand undeterred, then nuzzled me to pet him. "But you're not so bad," I admitted. "You stink, but . . . you're all right." I couldn't help a small smile as he leaned against my leg, basking in the attention.

Having Bear around the village, popping up in the most unexpected places, had become part of our daily lives. The wolf, on the other hand, not so much. He was always with Thea or patrolling the land around the lodge. But just like with the grizzly, it was easy to forget that Little Foot wasn't a pet, but a wild animal, though I wasn't sure there was much of a difference when you grew up alongside humans.

Fleetingly, I felt envious of Beau and Thea. I hadn't had a pet until Dancer was born, when I was fifteen. Meanwhile, Beau and Thea had a zoo most of their lives. It was why I wanted Milo to have a horse so badly—to give him a purpose and sense of independence, like Dancer had done for me. She was a creature I felt a mutual respect for, that got me out of the house and out of my head; I didn't have to be strong for her, or try to be someone else to make her happy or feel safe; I could just be me.

Little Foot's hind leg tapped against the ground in euphoria as I scratched his back harder, and I chuckled. "That's the spot, huh?" He looked longingly back at me when I finally stopped.

Allowing myself a minute of stillness, I leaned back against the trunk of a pine tree and peered deeper into the woods, toward the river that ran somewhere down the hill. I was considering a midnight dip to wash off the burden of the day when I noticed a divide in the tall grass.

A chill trickled down my spine, though I tried not to let my mind wander too far too fast, and I straightened. Little Foot seemed oblivious to it, which meant it wasn't likely problematic and that put my mind slightly at ease. Still, I couldn't help my legs from moving, and I walked over to inspect the path.

An intermittent, wide gait disturbed the grass, and I crouched down, scanning the surrounding woods—the branches and shadows, instinctively looking for movement.

When I saw nothing but leaves and moon shadows, I reached down and fingered the damp earth illuminated by the bright night, scouring it with fresh eyes this time. Shoe prints, heavy and large, matted the path. They weren't exactly fresh, but they couldn't have been more than a day or two old either—old enough that the ground was drying them into place.

I looked furtively toward camp where the others nestled inside their tents, then back into the woods. I could ignore the unsettled feeling needling me, especially since I tended to be paranoid and Little Foot didn't seem worried about them, or I could wake the others, potentially worrying them for what might be nothing—a print much older than it looked; an innocent traveler who'd been in search of water. Maybe I was wrong and it wasn't old at all, but Bert's, from one of his many bathroom trips.

Either way, Little Foot and I could check it out for ourselves and come back for the others, if something wasn't right. If there was one thing I was good at, it was tracking, hunting, and sneaking around. And feeling for the gun in my waistband, ensuring it was there, I scanned the woods again.

With my mind open to the noises surrounding me, I followed the trail, quiet and slow, my steps as light as a fox as I slipped inside the forest.

19

THEA

Shivering, I reluctantly stumbled out of my tent, having to pee despite my desire to stay in the protective warmth of my sleeping bag. I peered around, startled when I saw movement in my periphery. Squinting, I watched as Hunter and Little Foot disappeared into the trees.

"What the hell are they doing?" I muttered.

Kat groaned and turned in her sleep, and I zipped her back inside the tent before wrapping my arms around myself and following after them. Briefly, I considered grabbing a solar powered flashlight, but the moon was high and bright in the sky and I was too groggy and impatient to spare it another thought.

I hurried into the trees, hoping I didn't stumble upon Hunter doing exactly what I was waking up to do. I paused momentarily at a perfectly covered peeing tree. Squatting down, I listened for Hunter as I took care of business, and tried not to groan with ecstasy as my bladder thanked me for finally crawling out of my sleeping bag.

When I finished, I peered around the grassy forest and down the hillside toward the river. My curiosity got the better of me as usual, and I decided to follow Hunter and Little Foot instead of returning to the warmth of the tent. Twigs and pine needles crunched beneath my footsteps as I tried to focus on both the uneven earth and the patch of woods Hunter disappeared into. The spruce were tall and the low hanging branches brushed the top of my head, forcing me to duck between and around the trees.

"Hunter," I whisper-shouted as the shadows of the forest seemed to swallow me. I quickened my pace along the moonlit path in search of them. "Little Foot."

I must've walked for a few minutes before I paused mid-step, hearing what sounded like a crack echo faintly in the air. I held my breath, listening for another sound. When I heard nothing but the crickets, starting up again in my stillness, I continued deeper into the woods, clenching my hands at my side. *I'm not defenseless.* I needed the reminder.

It was strange that Hunter would leave like that, but then, I knew he liked to be alone and never slept, and when the river caught my attention through the trees, glistening as if it was glowing from the night sky, I thought maybe he'd wanted to take a midnight dip, even if the setting was beyond eerie.

I didn't worry about invading his privacy as I weaved my way through the giant spruce, squinting to see in the shadows. I was near the river's edge when I heard a voice.

"—so where'd he go?" The voice ricocheted from beyond a thicket of trees, and I froze where I stood. A cold sweat broke out instantly across my forehead, and I strained to listen. It was *not* a familiar voice.

"You know him, he heard somethin' and took off," a different, more high-pitched male voice replied. "He's always hearing something."

"Yeah, well, we can't all be mind-melders like you," the other quipped.

"Hey—I caught us a sacrifice didn't I? So don't start with that shit."

My spine clicked ramrod straight and I could feel the blood leeching from my face. An image of Hunter flashed to mind, and my breath caught in my throat. *A sacrifice?*

"Well—go get Ricky." The man's voice echoed over the water. "Mother wants him by her side tonight."

"*You* go get him, Fred. I gotta wrangle a hundred-plus pounds —" The man cursed and there was a crash. "Geez! This one's a brute . . . I like the females a lot better."

My stomach soured at his words, and I held my breath as I stepped into the brush against my better judgement, to peek across the river. Despite my instinct to run, I couldn't go back to camp before I knew if it was Hunter they were talking about—I couldn't leave him out here.

I blinked, trying to focus and calm myself enough to take in the scene two hundred yards away. The land surrounding a farmhouse, a barn, and a two-story garage was cleared, and dancing shadows from the fires that flickered on torch spikes scattered throughout illuminated the property.

"The fire's not gonna stop burning to wait for your sorry ass, Denton," Fred bit out, walking to the barn. He wore a white robe that reminded me too much of a ghost. "I would've wrangled him myself, if I knew it was gonna take you this damn long to prep him."

There was another crash inside the barn. "By all means, you're welcome to him!" Denton shouted. "The bastard bit me twice already." More thrashing emanated from inside.

"Hell no, you've already pissed him off." Fred threw up his hands as if he couldn't be bothered, then grabbed a bucket from the side of the barn and headed to a cross that rose in the center of the lot. Torches burned in a square pattern surrounding it, illuminating what looked like a scarecrow sagging from the beams.

I clamped my hand over my mouth to suppress a shriek as I realized it wasn't a scarecrow, but a withered body. Human, and a woman by the looks of the dark bedraggled hair hanging from the head. The remnants of a white dress, tattered and weather-beaten, dangled from her. I nearly fell backward. She was dead, too shrunken and emaciated not to be, but what had they done to her, and why was there a dead body up there in the first place?

The door to the house opened. "Are we ready?" a woman asked as she stepped into the doorway. The torch blaze danced off her, illuminating her in a glowing halo, and it took a moment for my eyes to focus. She wore a white strappy gown that showed her supple body, and a cherub-cheeked face.

"No, Mother," Fred said as he straightened from sprinkling what looked like feathers or petals that floated down around the base of the cross. He pointed to the barn. "I told Denton to hurry," he said defensively. "And Ricky went to investigate a noise."

The woman peered around the property and out toward the reflective water. "The moon is high. It is time. We cannot make the virgin wait."

"Yes, Mother," Fred said, but the woman looked anything but motherly.

I stared at the dead body hanging on the cross again. *The virgin?*

"I'll ready the others and find Ricky," the woman told him, her gaze locked on the moon above. She sounded awed and urgent at the same time. "We must not be late, not on the night of the full moon."

She disappeared into the house again, and I peered up at the sky. We were no longer in the land of the midnight sun; the moon was definitely full, and it was bright.

I wasn't sure if they were crazy people or if they were a doomsday cult reveling the end of the world, but as another crash echoed from inside the barn, Denton, tall and dressed in the same white robe as Fred, wrangled a giant creature from the shadows. The beast was thrashing against him, then charged, making Denton shriek. *A boar.*

I squeezed my eyes shut, barely able to feel relief that it wasn't a human sacrifice, when a quiet owl sound met my ears and my head shot up. Hunter stepped out of the shadows, his eyes wide and his forefinger pressed to his lips to silence me.

"I heard you a mile away," a man's voice cooed quietly in the woods behind us.

Hunter reached for me with rough hands, grabbing my forearm and pulling me into the shadows of the low branches between the trees.

I pointed to Hunter's gun, gripped in his other hand, concerned that it wasn't aimed in the man's direction already. Hunter shook his head and pointed to his ear. *The sound.* I glanced toward the homestead. Everyone would know we were here if he used the gun, and hell would break loose.

I scanned the river, hearing the squealing boar and the sound of the woman's voice. My insides were screaming at me to get the hell out of there. I had no idea how many cult people there were, or what Abilities they could use against us if we were discovered.

Hunter glanced down at my hands, nodded, then his gaze shifted back to me as if he was trying to tell me something. I flexed my fingers as my head shook of its own accord.

Hunter nodded, adamant. *"In this world, you're one of the strong."* His words from the other night had been at the forefront of my mind since the moment he'd uttered them. Once again, I realized how right Hunter was. Train cars and inanimate objects were fun and games, but this, this was our safety, and if ever there was a time to use my Ability, this was it—here with who knew how many possible dangers, whether they were crazy people or not.

Then I remembered Hunter hadn't come down here alone. "Little Foot?" I mouthed to him, but Hunter only stared at me, pensive and listening to the footsteps drawing closer through the trees behind us, a few dozen yards away.

"Where'd you get off to . . ." the man, who I assumed was Ricky, drawled. I wasn't sure if he knew we were human or if he thought we were dinner—or if they were the same thing—but I held my breath, praying Little Foot didn't do something stupid as I heard a wolf's growl, low and menacing.

"Oh, shit—" Ricky spat, and everything after that was a blur.

Determination flared to life. I stepped out from behind the tree cluster, my body already humming with adrenaline. Ricky's rifle glinted in the moonlight, and it all seemed to happen at once —I tore a branch from the tree behind him, bashing the back of his head with it just as he pulled the trigger, skewing his aim. The gunshot missed Little Foot and cracked through the air. Confusion registered in the man's expression, then he fell to the ground with a lifeless thud. I wasn't sure if the blow to the head killed him or rendered him temporarily unconscious, but either worked for me. Little Foot scrambled out of the shadows and inched closer to Ricky's body, sniffing as I forced myself to breathe.

"Ricky!" An eruption of voices rang out across the river and my gaze snapped to Hunter's.

He grabbed onto my hand. "Move light and fast—no noise," he commanded.

I nodded frantically as he pulled me behind him. Hunter's footsteps were silent and quick as we hurried up the hill toward camp, though I wasn't sure I could say the same for each of my steps. I was a trembling mess of nerves and dread at what might come next.

Fred and Denton continued to call for Ricky behind us, their shouts drawing closer. They might have no clue what happened when they found him, or they might find and follow our trail. There was no risking the latter.

When we finally reached camp, Hunter pointed to my tent to wake Kat as Alex climbed out of the one he and Bert were sleeping in, half dazed and crazed at the same time. "What was that—a gunshot?" He glanced furtively toward the woods.

"People by the river—we need to go," Hunter told him, and Alex jostled Bert awake.

Little Foot growled in the same direction, and I shook Kat. "Come on," I rasped, pulling her sleeping bag off.

Her eyes flashed open as her hand went instinctively to her gun. "What is it?" she said, climbing out of the tent, as if she was ready for a fight.

Above my thudding heart, I could hear indistinct shouting from the woods. "There are people. I don't know how many—"

"We don't have time to pack," Hunter told them, grabbing food bins. "Leave the tents—we need to go, *now*."

No one asked questions or argued as we gathered our weapons and necessities, and climbed into the trucks. I didn't hear anymore yelling as the trucks rumbled to life, or as we pulled off the dirt and back onto the road.

20

HUNTER

I *heard Nessa's screams. Otto crying out in pain.*

"The weak smell weak." The madman's voice was right beside my ear.

Wren trembled in my arms, crying against my chest as she prayed the bad men would go away.

"It's okay," I promised, and clung to her tighter. She needed me. "I won't let anything happen to you." And when I peered down, wide, tear-filled eyes met mine.

It wasn't Wren in my arms, but Thea. "Please, Hunter—"

"T hea—" I breathed, and shot up. The truck brakes squeaked, we lurched to a stop, and a discord of cawing crows echoed in my ears. I blinked as the sky darkened. Black-winged ravens blotted out the sun as they launched into the sky.

"Well, shit . . . That's not ominous or anything," Bert muttered, peering out the windshield at the cloud of black disappearing into the distance.

I watched as the birds fluttered toward their new perch on the horizon. I'd been dozing on and off all morning, but my thundering heartbeat ensured I wasn't drifting off again anytime soon. Wiping my sweaty palms on my pants, I inhaled a deep breath. *What dream was that?*

The sleepless nights were catching up to me, and after what happened last night at the river, it felt like my body was finally too exhausted to function anymore. The dreams were reemerging, but Thea was a new addition, which made them more unsettling than before.

With a sigh, I leaned back in the seat. We'd been on the road for hours, not wanting to risk stopping in case the cult decided to look for us, but instead of hours or minutes, it felt like only seconds had passed.

"Where are we?" Alex yawned in the passenger seat.

"Seattle," Bert said, distracted.

"Seattle?" I sounded like a parrot, but the last thing I remembered was driving through the greater Vancouver area surrounded by trees on a long, abandoned stretch of road. But as I registered the jagged cityscape outside my window, I knew we were far from no-man's-land now.

The buildings were strange—tall and boxy, while some were pointed and looked made of glass that glinted in the sunlight. All I could do was stare at their dark facades and at the gaping windows, more ominous than I'd expected them to be. Every crevasse between the looming buildings was dense with greenery, and it was too easy to imagine what sort of survivors might dwell in the cities with so many places to hide and supplies to scavenge.

There was a reason I'd lived with my people in the middle of nowhere, hidden from the world. Now, we were driving right through the heart of old civilization, a place I never thought I'd ever have to go.

I realized Kat and Thea were stopped ahead of us. I tried to see around the truck and trailer, about to ask why we weren't moving, when I noticed the cluttered vehicles abandoned on the road ahead. This was the part they were talking about, the streets so congested we'd have to inch our way through with Thea's help.

"Is something wrong?" I asked, uncertain why nothing was happening.

"I don't know," Alex admitted. "Maybe Thea needs my help." He was about to pick up the radio receiver when screeching metal met my ears and movement to our right caught my attention.

"There she goes," Alex murmured, sounding a bit relieved. Beyond the truck, a red, rusted-out van with a hanging bumper shifted closer to the railing. The frame shook as it settled back into place out of the way.

There was more movement to the left as a small silver car crunched against the median, and the girls' truck began to roll forward again. Slowly, they weaved around the parked cars, the trailer tapping the back taillight of the van that was still slightly blocking the way.

"I guess that's our cue," Bert said, and he shifted the truck into drive and followed carefully behind them.

A rusted, aqua car was next, bumping into a black truck that faced us as Thea shifted it farther to the left.

All too late, I realized I should look away as we passed the first car just outside my window. A skull with a gaping mouth peered back at me. I straightened in my seat, horrified but unable to peel my gaze away. After last night, everything felt too close to the surface—every uncertainty and fear. Every dread. I blinked at the image in the car, taking it in.

Tattered clothes hung from the skeleton's shoulders, and more faded fabrics clung to the other bodies decaying in the vehicle. Smaller skeletons.

Children.

A terrified numbness washed over me.

"I always hate this part," Bert muttered. He kept his eyes in front of the vehicle.

"Sometimes I forget," Alex whispered in front of me. His head bowed forward like he was looking down at his hands or feet—anywhere that wasn't out the window.

Although I didn't want to look either, my gaze shot to the next vehicle we passed and bile churned in my stomach. Inside were the skeletal remains of someone draped over their steering wheel and a four-legged animal in the back seat. I didn't know if the discoloration on the bodies was grime, leathered flesh, or a mixture of both, but I finally forced myself to look away.

This is what the end looks like. A sea of bodies—people whose last breaths were spent in fear and chaos. It was one thing to assume, but to see the remains of humanity's final moments was the most sobering thing I'd seen in so long. It made me realize, with a different sort of gratitude, how lucky I was to be alive. I stared at the butt of the gun I rubbed incessantly, discarded on the seat beside me. *Not even a weapon would've saved them.*

Haunting reminders of the past were somber and thick in the cab of the truck, making it difficult to swallow as we drove in slow silence.

I'm not sure how many colors and cars passed my window before Alex cleared his throat. "I hadn't known Elle, Beau, and Thea more than twelve hours when we left Whitely," he said. His voice was low and lost, like he didn't want to remember, yet he didn't want to forget either. "I'd only known Sophie a matter of days at that point—we were all strangers, and when Thea asked us who was going to give the people in the cars a proper funeral . . ." He cleared his throat again.

I glanced at him in the side mirror.

Alex shook his head, his eyes unfocused as he licked his lips. "I didn't know how to answer her, but I didn't have to. I still remember her expression when she realized the answer for herself."

No one. No one was coming to help them. It was easy to picture a little Thea laughing and playing, but imagining her living through this, scared and sad, and registering all these dead bodies made my chest ache for her.

"That was right after Elle and I had to find Sophie's mom and—all we could do was cover her up. We didn't get to bury her. That was all the closure Sophie got." He blinked a few times and licked his lips again. "I didn't have anyone to mourn, but witnessing Sophie's sadness made me glad for it."

Bert grabbed hold of Alex's shoulder and squeezed. "It's a complicated feeling," he said, the voice of reason and wisdom when it mattered.

Alex looked at him.

"Survival." Bert glanced from the road to Alex. "The guilt. The gratitude. The fear. It's confusing as hell. It makes you question everything that made you who you are, and regret the things you're grateful for, wondering if you deserve them." With a final squeeze, he let go of Alex's shoulder. "Surviving while everyone else is gone seems like it's pretty straightforward, but we know life is never straight, or easy."

I stared at Bert's profile as he watched the road ahead. He was a colorful guy, which made it easy to forget that he'd also lost people he cared about, that all of them had. And while seeing the aftermath firsthand was a shocking revelation for me, it was only dredging up the past for them—a past they'd worked twelve years to overcome.

"Don't forget to feel pride too," I told them.

Both Alex and Bert peered back at me.

"Look what you've all achieved in the wake of it."

They blinked at me, and Alex dipped his chin almost gratefully, and he faced forward again.

Whether it was out of respect for the dead, or an ode to the past, the three of us drove through the rest of the city in silence.

21

THEA

We didn't get to stay on the beach in Olympia. Instead, after raiding a partially collapsed camping store for more supplies, and triple checking what sort of neighbors we might have, we'd found another place to camp off the side of the road. We had ourselves a rabbit stew, since Bert had found and shot one while he was peeing behind a tree, but the vibe in camp was stilted and heavy.

Maybe it was seeing that woman strung up on the cross by the river, or fearing Hunter had been captured, but upon seeing the sea of cars in Seattle, I'd had a small breakdown. The night we'd left Whitely suddenly seemed like it was yesterday, and all the cars on the road filled with the dead and dying bombarded my memories all over again.

I remembered the smell of the cannibals, a sickly-sweet scent that made me cringe the moment we'd walked into the bus depot, even if I didn't understand why at the time. I thought of my mom, not about what I'd done, but about what had happened to her, how she'd changed into something unrecognizable and frightening, and I thought about my dad, who we never found at all. But it wasn't fear and confusion I felt this time, but an indescribable sadness.

Once the emotions were out, and Kat and I had a quick cry, I forced it all back down again, determined to keep us moving forward. None of us talked about the two hours it took us to get through Seattle. We seemed to wordlessly agree that we'd been through enough and mingled in companionable silence for most of the evening.

I was squatting at the soapy bucket, washing the stew pot, Bert's butchering knife, and our plastic bowls and spoons, when Hunter walked over and sat a steaming mug on the camping bin beside me.

"What's this?" I asked, craning my neck to look up at him from my makeshift kitchen sink.

"Hot cider," he said, standing to full height again. "I know you like sweet things, and I made some for Kat, so—" He shrugged.

Hunter *shrugged.*

"Oh." I couldn't help the surprise in my voice. "Uh, thank you."

Instead of answering me, Hunter lifted the mug again and opened the bin. He pulled out a towel and replaced the lid. "I'll dry," he said, and crouched down beside me, balancing on his knee.

"You don't have to help," I told him. "I'm capable of drying them myself."

He glowered at me, and I paused. I was about to glower back when I realized I was being rude.

"Sorry," I muttered. I glanced back down to my dirty suds. "I appreciate you helping."

Hunter reached into the tub of freshly washed bowls and grabbed one to pat dry.

"I'm not sure why I snap at you so much," I thought aloud.

When he looked at me, his hands moving methodically over the bowl, his expression was stern and unreadable.

"Probably," I said with a sigh, "because you look at me like *that,* and it makes me feel uncomfortable."

Hunter's brow twitched and he averted his gaze. He set the dry bowl on the camping bin and grabbed the next one from the tub. "I don't mean to make you feel uncomfortable," he said, thoughtful.

"I didn't mean it like that," I told him.

"Yes, you did," he said without sparing me a glance.

"No, I didn't. I just—I don't know how to act around you, and . . . It's hard to tell what you're thinking."

He stacked another dry bowl on the bin. "You could ask me," he said. His eyebrows lifted as he grabbed another bowl from the wet tub, and his gaze skirted to me. It was the most sincere expression I'd seen on him, and I felt a prick of heat over my skin.

Hunter's jaw flexed. Had I not noticed the scar on his jawline before? I opened my mouth, uncertain what to say. "Okay," came out first, then I smiled. "But you don't think that's kind of *advanced* for us?"

He smirked, and I felt another furl of heat, this time in my chest. "I'd rather you ask me questions than assume something that's not true." Somehow, Hunter made it sound so easy and matter of fact, like he was an open book. I smirked back, finding that hard to believe.

Mulling his words around in my head, I scrubbed the last of the goop on the bottom of the pot and glanced at him through my lashes again. "I guess that's fair. But be careful what you wish for," I warned. It was meant to be another joke but Hunter said nothing, and he didn't look at me again as he finished drying.

Taking his cue for silence, I put the pot on the bin with the other washed bowls and walked the dirty water a few yards from camp, dumping it at the base of a tree.

When I returned, the dishes were all dried and stacked, and Hunter held out my cider mug. "Can I ask you something?" he said. His voice didn't sound inquisitive as much as it sounded concerned.

"Sure . . ." I drawled, hesitating as I took the mug from him. I suddenly wondered if our open invitation to ask questions was going to bite me in the ass, not him, and yet, that he wanted to ask me something made me inexplicably pleased at the same time. I inhaled the sweet steam from the cup as he lifted the clean dishes to put them away.

"I know what you *don't* like about your Ability, but what's your favorite part about it?"

I eyed him over the brim of my mug. "Interesting question."

Hunter looked at me, waiting for an answer.

"Well, to be honest, I don't use it as much as I did when I was a kid," I admitted. But remembering the scent of winter and the feeling of snow on my skin, I smiled. "But one of my best memories was the day I realized I could use my Ability against Beau. He and I were outside waiting for the wolves one day—this was before Elle and Jackson knew what Beau and I could do. Beau pissed me off—" I shook my head. "I don't even remember what, but I chucked a snowball at his head and he got *so* mad at me." I could still see his eyes narrowing on me and his cheeks reddening with annoyance. "Of course it wasn't as funny then, when I knew he had better aim than me, but I realized I didn't have to have better aim in a snowball battle because I could stop his from hitting me at all."

Hunter's lips parted in a grin and my heart melted a little.

I cleared my throat. "Anyway," I continued, and took a sip of my cider before meeting his gaze again. "It was fun then, and it made me feel powerful. Now, I forget I can do things like that. The power is a bit too real, you know?"

Hunter lifted his chin in understanding. "After what I've seen the past couple days, it makes sense." He folded the towel and dropped it back into the camping bin.

"What's that mean, exactly?" After my hesitation to use my Ability last night, when we needed it most, I wasn't certain.

"It means," Hunter said, straightening his shoulders. "It means that even if what you did with the train cars is one of the most amazing things I've ever witnessed, I understand why it scares you." He was close enough I could smell the campfire smoke on his sweatshirt and see his jaw working beneath his skin.

Hunter thought what I could do was amazing? The same Hunter who distrusted people like us, even if it was for good reason? I frowned, unable to stop my thoughts from tumbling out from between my lips. "Why are you so different?" I whispered.

The austere expression I knew so well slid back into place. "Different?"

I tilted my head, scrutinizing every nuance in his face, realizing how difficult it was to see the same Hunter from days before. "You're not the same out here as you are back home."

Per usual, Hunter's expression gave nothing away. "Am I different, or are you only just getting to know me better?"

"I—don't know," I admitted. I didn't understand why my heart was beating so fast or why I felt the urge to avert my gaze, but I wouldn't allow myself to—I didn't want to miss a single change in his expression.

Hunter's lips pursed. His eyes narrowed slightly. He assessed me as I studied him, and I saw questions in his eyes and wondered if they were teeming like mine. Then, Hunter turned. "Goodnight, Thea," he said quietly, and walked away.

Thoughts suddenly scattered, I lifted my cup. "Um—thanks for the cider," I told him in a rush. "And for helping me with the dishes—and for last night." I bit my lip, uncertain what trouble I would've found myself in if he hadn't pulled me into the shadows to hide me.

Hunter nodded but continued walking.

"Hey, Hunter?" I said, uncertain why the words sounded like a timid plea.

Finally, he stopped and looked back at me.

"I'm sorry we didn't get to go to the coast today. I could tell you really wanted to."

He shoved his hands in his hoodie pockets. "There's always New Bodega, right?"

"Yeah," I said with a tight-lipped smile, "I guess so."

"Night," he said again, and then walked past the others sitting by the fire, oblivious to our conversation. "Goodnight," he told them.

"Goodnight," we all said in unison, and I watched as he climbed into his tent.

It dawned on me that it was the first time I'd seen him attempt to get some sleep the entire trip. And it was the first time I realized that, behind his reserve and quiet demeanor, Hunter didn't look severe or disapproving so much as he looked . . . lonely.

22

THEA

After a six-hour driving stretch, Bert, Kat, and I pulled off the interstate, behind Alex and Hunter, for a bathroom break. At first, there was no real difference between British Columbia and the lower forty-eight, at least not in the northwest. But the further south we drove, the more captivated I became as I noticed the changes. Like the far-reaching, gnarled limbs of the wild oak trees that dotted rolling, golden hillsides, and the blue sky that seemed to stretch forever in both directions with no mountains or jagged tree lines to impede it.

"Where are we?" I asked, in awe at how quickly the landscape could change.

Bert shut the truck off with a grin. "Gold country," he said, a merry sheen in his ochre eyes.

"South of Redding, somewhere in Tehama County," Kat clarified from the passenger seat, studying the map. "But I'm going to call it the armpit of hell. It's hot as shit here."

Bert chuckled. "Just wait until the peak of summer, then you'll wish you were dead."

"Wonderful," Kat grumbled, and she shoved the map into the glove box.

"Have you been here before, Bert?" I asked, and I opened my door to climb out.

"Yep, many times." He unbuckled his seatbelt. "After Vietnam, I hopped on my motorcycle and traveled around. I spent nearly five years in California before I headed up to Alaska, where I met my wife." He smiled fondly at the memories and climbed out of the truck. "And boy, did the law and I have our differences."

Curiosity piqued, I hurried around the front of the truck to hear the rest of his story.

"I was in a motorcycle club, and we'd ride from Redding all the way to Stinson Beach, causing trouble along the way."

"What did you do?" I asked, suddenly in awe of him. I loved Bert like the crazy old guy he was, but I never thought of him as a troublemaker.

"Drugs," he said. "That's all you need to know."

Kat laughed as she readjusted her sunglasses, then brought her pinched index finger and thumb to her lips, like she was smoking a joint. "A lot of drugs, " she mouthed.

I couldn't help my laugh as I knotted my hair on top of my head to get it off my sweaty neck, then glared up at the intense rays of the sun. "I wouldn't say hell's armpit," I told Kat, "but I don't think I've ever been this hot before."

"Ha!" She headed for the other truck as the guys finally climbed out.

"Welcome to Cali," Bert said with a stretch. "The summers are dry and hot here."

"Well, since you're so familiar with the place," I said, reaching through the back window for some sunblock. The sun was intense, suddenly too warm now that we'd stopped driving and the breeze was gone, and I rubbed Henni's famous carrot seed lotion on my nose, cheeks, and forehead. "How close are we to Petaluma?" It felt like we'd been on the road for days, and

I was eager to get to Hope Valley, nestled between there and New Bodega.

"Another four hours or so," Bert said. "Well, maybe five with your brother leading the pack," he grumbled.

Alex flipped him off as he grabbed his duffel out of the back of the truck.

Bert blew him a kiss and did a deep lunge to stretch. "I'm gettin' too old for this shit." He groaned. "The long drives are killing my sciatica."

"One more reason for you to retire from this gig, old man," Alex said. "Thea can take your spot," he offered, winking at me.

"I'm actually surprised Cory didn't come in your spot, Bert," I said. "He's a good mechanic too, and could get us out of a pinch if we needed."

"Cory thinks everything can be fixed with his Ability," Bert muttered. "Kids these days don't realize know-how is also important." He held his hand up and wiggled his fingers. "It's not just about superpowers, but skills and practice. It's about wisdom."

I tried not to smile too obviously with amusement. Bert was one of many in the community who were having a difficult transition with the changing times. Whether it was some sort of kinetic energy or electrical charge he exuded through his touch, Bert could make an engine run or keep the power plant functioning if he had to—with help, of course. But Bert's mind was sharper than his Ability these days, and I thought that might be why he held onto the past the way he did. His years of hard work were engrained in him.

"Well, I'm glad you came, Bert. Even if you're feeling your age," I told him. "You might snore louder than anyone I've ever known—even louder than Bear—but Cory would've talked our ears off until they were bleeding."

Bert grinned. "It's only because he likes you."

I snorted. "No, that's not it."

"Suit yourself," he said. "I'm gonna find me a tree." Bert studied the oak-dotted hillside that butted up to the highway. "If I'm not back in ten minutes, it probably means I got bit by a rattler or I broke a hip."

"I'm *not* sucking the poison out," Alex muttered as he followed, leaving a generous distance between them.

Just happy to move my legs, I peered down the abandoned highway. We'd seen big rigs, cars, and trucks along the way, but there weren't a ton of them, at least not yet, and we'd had no issues getting through the stretch of road since Oregon. I headed in the direction Little Foot wandered, sniffing as he explored.

"Grapes!" I chirped, and hurried closer to the overgrown vines along the side of the road.

"Wine grapes!" Bert called from the trees, and I picked a tiny green grape off the vine. "You're not going to like the way they taste." His voice carried through the afternoon, but I'd already put a grape in my mouth. Instantly, my throat tightened and my lips puckered as the juice squirted on my tongue.

Hunter chuckled behind me and I spun around.

"They're that bad, huh?"

"No, they're great," I lied. "You should definitely try one."

A barely-there smile tugged at his lips. "Well, since you're selling it so well . . ."

I picked another grape and handed it to him, anticipating his expression when the tart grape burst on his tongue.

Hunter's eyes locked on mine, almost as if it was a silent dare, and his expression didn't change in the slightest as he chewed and swallowed. "You're right, they're not so bad."

My shoulders slumped with disappointment. "I should've known you'd be able to keep a straight face. That's your MO." I brushed my fingertips over the smooth, perfectly round grapes, wondering if they'd get sweeter as the summer continued to warm them.

"What's that mean?" Hunter picked another grape off the vine and plopped it into his mouth.

"What, your MO?"

He nodded.

"You're the *king* of serious-face," I explained, running my fingers over the thick grape leaves. I noticed Hunter's head tilt from the corner of my eye. "Oh, don't act so surprised." I pried my attention from the foliage and looked at him. "I can count how many times you've smiled or laughed in the year and a half I've known you on a single hand."

His eyebrows rose at that. "Maybe you don't pay enough attention."

I scoffed. "I pay plenty of attention."

Hunter's cheek twitched, and his eyes held mine, curious.

My heart palpitated suddenly, and averting my gaze, I started walking further down the road toward Little Foot. "What I meant was," I continued as Hunter fell into step beside me, "maybe you're different around your family, but when you're around the rest of us, you're pretty—" I glanced at him, trying to find the least offensive word. "Serious."

Hunter stared at the rutted highway as we walked, running a grape leaf through his fingers.

"It's not a *bad* thing," I amended, and I guess it wasn't, even if I used to take it personally. But in the days I'd spent with him, I realized Hunter was too worried about everyone else to be purposefully hurtful or offensive.

"It's not?" His eyes narrowed, like he was gauging whether I was lying. His irises looked like melted chocolate in the sunlight.

Slowly, I shook my head. "It just makes it harder to get to know you, is all." Inhaling a fortifying breath, I turned my attention to the chirping, rustling world around us. Blackbirds flitted to and from broken power lines, and golden grasses swooshed on the hillside in the breeze. Still, I could feel Hunter watching me. The heat and scenery weren't the only differences I'd noticed this far south; his presence had become as comforting as it was unnerving.

"Oh, those are pretty," I said in need of a distraction. I scuttled over to a giant bush of white funnel-shaped flowers that looked almost tropical. "I saw a bunch of pink ones lining the freeway earlier . . ." As I reached for a blossom, Hunter grabbed my hand.

"Don't," he said, his fingers squeezing around mine. "Oleander's poisonous."

"Oleander?" I tried to recall Sophie's drawings and survival journals I'd pored over as a little girl, and Jade's teachings over the years. "I don't think I've ever heard of oleander before."

"It doesn't grow like this at home."

"Oh." My gaze drifted to his fingers gripping mine. *Three times.* That's how many times he'd saved or protected me in some way. At the lake when I'd slipped, in the dark shadows of the forest, and now.

Hunter let go and dropped his hand by his side, tightening it into a fist.

As another confusing mixture of comfort and uneasiness coursed through my veins, I tried to focus on the flowers again instead. "I thought," I started, realizing I'd spent so much time as a child learning about the land we lived on, I didn't know much about the world around me. "I thought maybe I'd missed one of Jade's lectures about it or something." Noticing how far we'd wandered, Hunter and I turned and meandered back toward the trucks. "It was hard to stay focused when we went on nature walks, especially if the wolves were around." I smiled at the thought. "I can't tell you how many times I got *the stare* when I should've been paying attention."

Hunter's footsteps were slow and heavier beside mine, and he was quiet—too quiet. When I looked at him, he was staring at the horizon, lost in thought.

"What's wrong?" I asked gently. I could only assume his change in mood had to do with something I said.

Hunter shoved his hands into his pockets. "I'm just ready for the day to be over," he said, and his sudden soberness surprised me.

"Guys!" Kat called. "If you're going to pee, do it and let's go! The sun actually sets here, remember? I'd like to get to Petaluma before midnight."

I glanced at Hunter. "I guess we're being herded in," I said wryly, trying to make him smile again.

But Hunter didn't smile as he continued toward the truck, his footsteps quicker than before. Although we could find common ground most of the time, it didn't feel like it was enough.

As Hunter put more distance between us, I questioned whether we'd ever be truly comfortable around each other. And suddenly, I realized how temporary all of it might be anyway. Once we returned home, everything could go back to the way it was, and the reality of it made me sad.

23

THEA

I leaned out the passenger window, feeling the warm breeze against my skin. Purple clouds painted the sky as it began to darken, and the fields that stretched on either side of the road were glowing. A rabbit with tall, pointed ears rose out of the yellow and white blossoms spackling the fields, eyeing us as we passed.

Kat laughed in the driver's seat. "What are you, five? If you fall out, I'm not stopping—I have to pee like a racehorse."

I smiled but said nothing as I took in the country road. Alex honked the horn behind us, and when I looked back, he and Bert were laughing at my giddiness. Ignoring them, I let my hair blow wild and free, and I inhaled the scent of dry earth. I'd never seen so much open land as there was in California, and I yearned to climb onto Cinder's back and see how far we could ride before we reached the ends of the earth.

"Perfect—our turn off," Kat said, and slowing, she veered down an overgrown road. Horse droppings and walking trails lined the path, used little by vehicles, it seemed, and within a few moments, small cottages came into view to the left. The settlement spread out over the rolling hills, interspersed by oak and eucalyptus trees. There were sheep and cows grazing on swells of green and gold, and as we passed an intricately hand painted sign that read Hope Valley, my stomach knotted and an unexpected wave of nerves fluttered through me. We'd arrived.

"Finally," Kat breathed, and she sighed with what sounded like both apprehension and relief. She knew some of these people, but I knew none of them. As excited as I was to meet everyone, I also wasn't sure what to expect. Smiling faces? Unease? Stilted conversation?

Kat continued up a gravel driveway toward a large white farmhouse. We passed a barn and animal pens to the left and pulled around a circular lot. I stared at everything, taking it all in. It was a proper farm. Fruit trees extended behind the house and the cottage that flanked it, and next to the barn was a garden the size of Hunter's fields back home.

A German shepherd, old and gray but wagging his tail excitedly, crawled out from under the farmhouse porch and trotted toward us.

Little Foot jolted to attention, his fluffy white tail thumping against the back seat and his stance posed for playtime.

Kat shut off the truck and a smile stretched her lips. "Well, this place looks fun." Her gaze was assessing before it locked on the horses in the pasture beyond the property. I noticed the settlement I saw from the road butted up to the pastures in the distance.

So much of it was similar to home but so much more sprawling and all in one place.

The German shepherd yipped in greeting and Little Foot leapt out the back window, sniffing his new friend excitedly. Briefly, I wondered if Little Foot was lonely without his pack to pal around with any longer.

The screen door of the house screeched open as I climbed out of the passenger seat.

"What do you know, a wolf to add to the mix." A woman in a

long skirt with a pregnant belly and long raven-black hair stepped out, her eyes a jewellike blue.

One of the truck doors slammed shut behind us. "Hey, Zoe," Alex said with contented laughter as he came up behind me.

"Alex." Zoe smiled and she opened her arms to him. The wrinkles around her eyes were subtle, and I noticed a streak of gray in her hair. She must've been in her late thirties. "It's good to see you, old friend."

Alex leaned down and gave her a hug as Hunter and Bert walked up beside us, scanning the farm. The farmhouse doors opened again and others filed out.

"She was *this* close to worrying," a tall, broad-shouldered man said, striding up behind her.

Alex straightened and reached for his hand. "Jake, good to see you. We ran into a few snafus, but nothing we couldn't handle, thanks to Thea." He winked at me.

Zoe stepped past Alex and gave Kat a quick hug, then Bert. "Hey, old man," she said affectionately. Bert gave her a squeeze, muttered something that made Zoe laugh, though I couldn't hear it, and they all continued to greet one another as they likely did at the summit each year.

Finally, Zoe looked between me and Hunter. "Welcome to Hope Valley," she said. "I'm Zoe." She reached for my hand first.

"Hi. I'm Thea," I said, forcing an awkward smile.

Zoe's eyes were assessing but kind and crinkled in the corners, and a small smile curved her lips. "I feel like I already know you," she mused happily, and I assumed it was from years of gleaning information about me from Alex and the others.

Jake shook my hand next. He was rugged like Jackson, but with cropped sandy-brown hair, rich amber eyes, and a slightly crooked nose. And Jake had a gentleness about him I hadn't expected. When I recalled what Alex had told me about the prophecy, Zoe losing her memory, and their epic love story, I realized any man that romantic would have a kind, gentle soul, and I smiled.

A slender framed woman with wavy, brunette hair hanging past her shoulders stepped out of the farmhouse next. A girl a few years younger than me was at her side and had a falcon perched on her shoulder as they headed our direction.

"And you must be Hunter," Zoe said, her attention fixed on him. As she reached for his hand, a flicker of what looked like regret crossed Zoe's features, then remembering herself, she smiled. "I'm happy to finally meet you."

"Same," Hunter said, and dipped his chin as he let go of her hand. It dawned on me how immense the moment was for both of them. Zoe, shouldering some of her mother's blame for all that had happened in the world, and Hunter who was one of only a few like him left. Now, he was relying on her for help, which he could probably hardly believe himself.

"This is my sister-in-law, Becca," Zoe said, gesturing to the wavy-haired woman as she stepped up beside her. The setting sun illuminated Becca's gray-violet irises. "And my niece, Annie." Zoe motioned to the falcon girl.

Annie waved a bit shyly, her wild blonde curls bouncing around her round face. The falcon fluttered on her shoulder as she knelt down to Little Foot, who was wagging his tail as he peered up at her. "He's beautiful," Annie said, and the falcon eyed the wolf carefully. For a moment, Annie seemed to lose herself in Little Foot's eyes, and I knew immediately what she was doing. Her grin widened and she peered up at me. "I had wolf friends when I was little," she explained. "But it's been a while."

"I couldn't imagine my childhood without them," I realized. The pack had been with us since the beginning.

So, Annie was a telepath. I wasn't sure I knew that, though Alex had told us about the rest—Jake could regenerate, Alex had felt his raw power when they'd had to save the honey-maker's father back in Prince Rupert. Zoe's Ability was like Sophie's, but amplified, and she could read minds and feel emotions. Becca was a Re-gen, like Jenny had been, and she had the gift of prophecy. In an offhanded way, I felt gratitude toward Becca, who'd been the one to warn Alex, Kat, and the others about Nora all those years ago, sending them home in time to say goodbye to Jenny before it was too late.

Annie's falcon peered up at me, and as if the falcon had asked her a question, Annie glanced from it to me. "Sorry. I saw the wolf and got excited." She rose to her feet. "This is Perry— I'm an animal telepath, in case you couldn't tell."

I waved to her falcon, uncertain what else to do. "I'm Thea, and, yeah, I recognize the signs," I said, half-joking. "My brother, Beau, is a telepath too."

"Oh, yeah, Aunt Zoe told me about him. He has a black wolf, right? My aunt said she's beautiful, and very protective."

My smile faltered. "Uh, he actually pals around with a clumsy grizzly bear these days," I said, forcing a broader smile, and my gaze automatically sought Little Foot, already sniffing around the property.

Annie laughed. "That's so cool. We don't have bears around here, but it still gets pretty crazy sometimes." She glanced toward the horse pasture. "My mom's out with my little sister, Ceara, checking on the baby sheep."

"Oh, yes," Zoe said. The chatter of the group died down. "Dani's going to be so excited to meet you all. She's heard our stories over the years, and now she can finally see your faces."

Though Zoe smiled, glancing between everyone, I noticed the way her attention continued to fall on Hunter. She cleared her throat. "My brother, Jason, and I appreciate you coming all this way. And Harper, the physician," she clarified, looking at Hunter again, "has been talking about this moment all week. They'll be relieved to know you've arrived."

"Let's let them unwind a bit," Jake offered, gesturing toward the house. "You've been driving for days."

"And I have to pee . . . badly," Kat added.

Everyone chuckled like they were used to Kat's unapologetic bluntness.

"Of course." Zoe pointed toward the farmhouse. Kat took off at breakneck speed. "I'll find my own way," she called behind her.

Zoe laughed and rubbed her pregnant belly. She must've been seven or eight months, at least. "We don't host many visitors, you can probably tell. We're all family here and we just help ourselves." She nodded toward the farmhouse again. "How about some iced tea or water—are you hungry?" She glanced between the four of us. Bert was doing his embarrassing lunges, and Alex was chatting with Jake.

My stomach rumbled at the thought of something other than beans, fruit, and jerky. "I could eat—"

"Would you like to go to the clinic now?" Becca asked hoarsely, stepping closer to Hunter. Her tone was warm but her words too formal, much like Jenny's had been. I felt a swell of guilt in my gut as Jenny's crumpled body flashed to mind. *Prophecy,* I reminded myself. Becca saw things the rest of us didn't. I pried my gaze away from Becca to look at Hunter, wondering what she'd seen to make her so thoughtful.

"I would, actually," he said. Hunter seemed tense and hesitant, and my heartbeat skittered as I glanced between them. Of course he'd want to talk to Harper about the vaccine. It was why he'd come all this way to begin with, though Hunter's obvious discomfort made me anxious for him.

Becca nodded like she'd anticipated his answer.

Zoe shook her head. "Yes, of course," she said as if she'd forgotten herself.

"Isn't it kind of late?" I thought out loud.

Hunter looked at me, his expression stone.

"No, it's completely fine," Zoe said, waving my worry away. "I should've thought of that. Of course you'd want to move things along," she told Hunter. I knew Zoe felt guilty for all of this, but I wasn't sure why she seemed frazzled and . . . nervous.

Jake took Zoe's hand in silent reassurance. "Zoe and I will take you into New Bodega," he said. "Jason is there on business, and Harper should still be at the clinic, so he can answer all of your questions."

Zoe glanced among us. "We thought you'd like to stay close together, so we made accommodations for you in town. We can drop off your things at the apartment you'll be staying in on the way."

Alex held up the keys. "I'll drive," he said, and started for the horse trailer. "Bert, help me unhitch this, would you?" Jake stepped in to help.

"I'll stay here with Kat, I guess," I thought aloud.

Hunter eyed me for a moment, and I could tell something was wrong. I was going to ask him why he looked so worried suddenly, when Annie stepped up beside me.

"Is he your boyfriend?" she asked. She and her falcon watched Hunter as he headed toward the truck. Annie was pretty, despite her torn jeans and tomboy appearance, and maybe fifteen, give or take a year.

"Uh, no. That's just—that's Hunter."

"Duh." Annie rolled her eyes, grinning.

"Thank all that is holy," Kat cried, coming out of the house. "I feel *so* much better." She hurried down the steps as Alex started the F-250. "What's going on?"

"They're going to the clinic," I told her, and Kat spun around to Hunter climbing into the truck.

"Oh. Already?" Kat's brow furrowed. "I thought he'd want to rest first."

I lifted my shoulder and shook my head, feeling a little off-kilter in the commotion. "I guess not."

"See you in a bit," Alex called, and Jake and Zoe climbed into the truck with them.

"Good luck!" Kat called, and Hunter nodded from the front seat. His eyes found mine and just as quickly, he looked away.

"Well," Annie chirped. She pointed to the pasture behind her. "We should go find my mom and sister."

"Oh, good," Kat said, and she fell into step behind Annie.

"Come on, Jack!" Annie called over her shoulder. The German shepherd perked up, his tongue hanging from his mouth. But as the dog and I brought up the rear, I turned, watching the truck's taillights disappear down the road and out of sight. Something didn't feel right.

"They're here!" Annie called, and my gaze shot over to the pasture, where a small woman, who I assumed was Dani, came out of the gate. Bays and sorrels and grays loitered around the pasture fence, ears perked up and heads bouncing happily, as if saying goodnight to Dani as she closed them in.

With a final pat on a paint horse's neck, the small woman looked at us, her wild red hair pulled up on top of her head, alive like fire in the dying sunlight. A smile engulfed her face as she registered us. Tilting her head, she pointed at Kat. "Blonde bun and that stride screams no-nonsense," she said. "Which means you must be Kat."

With a chuckle, Kat reached for the woman's hand. "Guilty."

"I'm Dani." Her green eyes shifted to me. "And you must be Thea?"

"Yes," I said, my attention flicking back to the horses. "They're beautiful," I told her, and shoved my hands into my back pockets. There were at least a dozen in the herd, some of them grazing while others, like the paint, watched us curiously.

"Thank you. This old beauty is Wings, she's been with me the longest, since the beginning," Dani explained, and there was a respect and affection in her voice I could relate to. "Annie and I have brought the others up over the years," she continued, squeezing Annie against her. The teen was taller than Dani by a couple of inches, and despite their curly hair, they didn't look much alike. "We try to match them for riders in the community," Dani explained. "And some we just have because, well, horses like to stick together, so why not have an entire herd." She laughed with exasperation. "This place is already a zoo, right?"

Annie shrugged. "Pretty much."

"There's no escaping it with three animal telepaths in the family," Dani explained, and she seemed so happy talking about her Ability, I envied it a little.

"I've always wished my Ability was animal telepathy," I admitted. "It would be helpful *and* awesome."

"You are important, Thea." Becca's voice spooked me from behind. "And exactly as you must be." I glanced back to find her and Bert walking toward us, her violet eyes spearing me. "Never question that," she continued. "Your future will help give rise to a world different than this one."

I felt the weight of her words, even if I didn't quite understand them. "It will?"

Becca stumbled, missing a step, and Bert caught her. "Careful there—"

Becca's gaze shifted to Dani. "I am tired tonight," she told her, her voice a strained whisper. "I will see you tomorrow."

Dani eyed her cautiously. "Annie will walk with you—"

"I will be fine," Becca assured them.

As if knowing her insistence would be futile, Dani didn't argue. "Goodnight then," she said softly.

Annie looked after Becca with concern. "Night, auntie."

Becca flashed the girl a weak smile, then continued down a path that led between the pasture and the garden, toward the settlement beyond the farm. There was a heaviness to Becca's demeanor I hadn't expected. But then, I assumed prophecy would be a heavy burden for anyone to bear.

"I see you've met Jake's sister," Dani whispered, her attention lingering on Becca's retreating form. "She's seen so much over the years . . . I think it's beginning to take its toll." Like Dani suddenly remembered we were standing beside her, she perked up and gestured toward the settlement. "And that's the heart of Hope Valley," she explained. "It's where the Re-gens settled after the rebellion against General Herodson, and they continue to thrive there, thanks to Chris and Carlos, and all the work they've been doing throughout the years to help maintain the Re-gens' Abilities, which is the only way they've survived this long." She turned to us. "You're familiar with the Re-gens—"

"Yes," I said quickly with the flash of a bright, pleading smile. "Elle's sister," I explained. "Jenny." I glanced at Kat, my heart bleeding for her a little as I saw the shadowed memories flash quickly over her features.

Dani nodded as if she understood the topic was a touchy one.

I hadn't realized how many old wounds might open again, coming to this place and seeing all these people that had been connected to us through the years in some way. Becca's prophecies about Nora, and the answers she'd given Kat when she was trying to save Jenny's life, all for naught. Hope Valley was where the General and Dr. Wesley fell during the standoff, and where Zoe and Jason made the serums and vaccines to fix their mother's wrongs. Our lives in Whitehorse were interwoven with this place, and only by being here did I realize how much.

Dani glanced into a copse of eucalyptus trees nestled against the far fence of the pasture. On cue, a little girl with wavy auburn hair popped out with a baby deer. Jack perked up a little when he saw her and trotted along the fence in her direction, like he wanted so much to run and play with her, but his age forced him to the sidelines.

"Time to come in and get cleaned up for dinner!" Dani called, and the little girl frolicked through the pasture toward us, the fawn prancing after her.

"That little munchkin would be my other daughter, Ceara," Dani said. "I'd like to say that crazy child takes after Jason, but between the mane on her head and her fondness for animals, I think it's obvious she's my daughter." Dani chuckled as Ceara galloped closer, chirping and chatting with her fawn friend. The horses looked on, undisturbed.

"Come on, Jumper!" she sang. "It's time for dinner."

"For *human* dinner," Annie told her, much like an exasperated big sister would. I couldn't help but smile as I thought of Beau and me as children. He still looked at me like that sometimes—perturbed and exasperated—but I'd grown to accept it, to count on it, and actually missed it now that he wasn't around as much anymore.

But Ceara didn't seem to care, and with her German shepherd and fawn in tow, we all turned back toward the farm.

"Cute kid," Bert mused. "She's got spunk."

"She's got *plenty* of spunk," Dani muttered. We walked a few steps, taking in the inky evening, and I realized the others sort of just . . . left us.

"I hope you don't mind," Kat started as I wound my arm through hers with an exhausted sigh. I rested my head against her shoulder as she glanced back at Dani. "The others went to the clinic with Hunter, so you're sort of stuck with us for a bit."

I stared at the unhitched trailer beside our truck and wondered how far away New Bodega was and when they'd be back.

"No, we don't mind at all. In fact, I know you've brought some things for us, so we can unload while they're gone, if you'd like? But let's get you something to eat first. You must be exhausted and starving."

As we drew closer to the farmhouse, a guy stepped out of the barn with a lantern in his hand. He looked to be about twenty or so and had grease on his t-shirt and cheek. I noticed his headphones and smiled.

"That's Sam," Annie said. I vaguely recalled someone mentioning once that Zoe and Dani had found Annie and Sam years ago, on the group's journey to New Bodega. Much like Elle had found Beau and me.

His eyes widened as he turned around. "Company," he said, sliding his headphones down around his neck.

"Sam," Dani said, stepping aside as she gestured to us. "This is Thea, Kat, and Bert."

As Sam studied each of us and shook our hands, my gaze lingered on his pale baby blues. "Is that music you were listening to?" I asked. It wasn't very often I met someone with the same proclivities as me.

"Uh, yeah," he said, and glanced down at the contraption attached to his pocket. "It's a Walkman, something old I found a while back. Carlos charges the batteries for me when they get low. It's the only way I can listen to it."

"And who's Carlos again?" I asked, feeling like an ass for not remembering. "His name sounds familiar, but . . ."

Sam chuckled and shook his head. "I doubt you've met him. He's down south with Tom and Peter, Zoe's father and her other brother. Carlos helps at the Re-gen settlement—he's essentially a human battery." His grin widened.

"Oh, wow. Well, that's handy." I gestured to his Walkman. "What were you listening to?"

Sam eyed me carefully. "Garth Brooks." I could tell he didn't think I knew who that was, and he was right. "It's country music," he clarified.

"Oh. I don't have much country on my playlists," I realized.

"Well, you can listen to Garth later," Kat interrupted. "Let's get some grub and unload so that we can skedaddle when the others get back. I'm beat."

24

HUNTER

The night air felt strangely thick as I rode with Alex, Zoe, and Jake to town. It was another thirty minutes to New Bodega but it felt longer, like time was slowing down, prolonging an uncertain fate.

The faint scent of the sea hung on the breeze as it wafted through the open windows, much cooler than it was inland. Like in Whitehorse, a wall stretched around New Bodega, spot lights illuminating the cement and cyclone fencing. Jake waved to the guards from the back seat, and we passed through the gate without having to stop and explain what we were doing there or who we were.

I could see little of the ocean in the darkness, but my mind was too busy to think much more about it. The city itself was lit by lighting that I assumed was solar generated or Ability powered, and the buildings were stacked along the coastal cliffs. Everything was more compact, and with shops and buildings lining both sides of the narrow, winding street, New Bodega felt cramped and suffocating. Or maybe that was my looming future closing in on me.

Alex wound the truck slowly through the unkempt roads, and

what few people were on foot and horseback, moved out of the way, watching us with curiosity.

Glancing back at Zoe from the side mirror, I wondered what her baby would be like, especially since I knew Zoe was an original, or at least, that's what some people in Whitehorse had coined her. She and Jason were ghosts in a way; they were entities that some people questioned really existed or argued whether they were villains in disguise, trying to take over the world, like their mother and the General had tried to do.

Benevolent do-gooders.

Bringers of death.

Propaganda slingers.

I'd heard Zoe and Jason called many things by people who had never met them, and for the first time I questioned whether any of that was true. And if I'd made the wrong decision.

Did it matter? It was a pointless thought because not following through was the biggest risk of all. The end of a people. The inability to procreate. The old would die, the young would too, unless we searched for other Untainteds like us.

As the road straightened and widened, we passed a warehouse and more shops, but it was the unmarked two-story building up on a grassy hill surrounded by cypress trees I stared at. The clinic. I'm not sure what it had been in the world before, but something about its big windows and sterile stone facade gave its importance away. Solar panels lined the roof, and the building itself seemed to radiate with light inside.

We turned up the drive and Alex pulled up next to the only other vehicle parked beside the large sliding doors. Two horses hung their heads low at the hitching post, their manes catching in the breeze, though they seemed indifferent to the brisk evening.

I couldn't explain it, but I could feel Zoe's eyes on the back of my head as the truck's engine switched off.

"I'd tell you not to worry, and that everything is going to be fine," she said as she pushed the back door open. "But I know that's not helpful."

All of us climbed out of the truck, and I reached out to help her the rest of the way. In the darkness, with the light of the clinic casting shadows over her delicate features, her brow lifted with regret.

"No, it wouldn't," I admitted, but I hadn't needed to answer her, she already knew everything I was thinking and feeling. Even if it made me uncomfortable, at least I didn't have to make small talk, prolonging the inevitable.

Zoe splayed her hand on her belly, really looking at me. *Reading me.*

Jake walked around to take her hand, and I got the impression she was more delicate than she was letting on. Fleetingly, I realized she was older than I'd imagined she'd be, and that she was pregnant gave me pause.

"It only took us twelve years," Zoe murmured. She glanced over her shoulder with a wry, waning smile as Jake led her toward the clinic doors, and I felt a strange sadness for her. Had she wanted a child so badly that she'd tried for so long?

I grabbed my backpack from the floorboard and slung it over my shoulder as I headed inside behind them.

"You can change your mind at any time," Zoe reminded me without looking back.

But my decision was made. "I won't change my mind," I told her, no matter the possible outcomes.

Jake peered between us, as did Alex, and we stepped through the automatic doors of the facility.

It was stark inside, with tiled floors and white walls. There was a desk in front, and a gray-haired man with a goatee stood to greet us. "Ah, Zoe," he said with a grin, and he extended his hand to Jake. "Good to see you both."

His eyes met Alex's before they shifted to me. "You must be our special guests this week." He extended his hand to me first, his expression kind and curious. "I'm Chad." I shook his hand with a nod then surveyed the room. There was a walkway that stretched behind the desk, leading to a hallway of doors, and an exposed stairway to the next floor to the right.

"Harper is upstairs in his office with Jason," Chad offered, his eyes meeting Zoe's.

"Thank you," she murmured, and Jake took her hand again, leading us further inside. "I met Harper right after the Virus," Zoe explained as we made our way up the stairs. "He was an Army medic at the time, but has since become one of our resident physicians. He and Gabe, an old friend of Dani's and brilliant geneticist, were able to consult for the initial stages of the vaccine, pointing us in the right direction." Zoe paused as she climbed the final steps. "We also have a few elementals here in New Bodega that have helped us with the more intricate manipulations during the engineering process—specifically with the Ability swiping serum, which was, oh—seven or eight years ago now, I guess. Equipment from before the Ending is hard to find and half the time it doesn't work anymore, so water manipulation has been extremely helpful, as well as telekinesis."

Zoe continued her introduction of the facility as we reached the second floor, but I studied the place that might very well be the last I'd ever step foot in. It wasn't exactly unwelcoming, but it wasn't inviting either.

"Harper?" Zoe called, and she continued toward a partially closed door that opened almost immediately.

A man with an imposing frame and short brown hair stepped out in his street clothes, his eyes similar to Zoe's. When his gaze shifted from her to me, his expression twitched minutely.

"Jason—" Zoe looked back at me. "Hunter, this is my brother."

Jason offered me his hand. He had a firm grip, and I imagined he was every bit as hard and determined as he looked. "Welcome," he said, and glanced at Alex. "Jason Cartwright," he said, introducing himself. "I've heard a lot about your crew." He reached out to shake Alex's hand. "You guys are late."

"Yeah, we had a bridge issue to deal with," Alex told him. "Among other things."

"You're here now," another voice said from inside the office. "That's what matters." A dark-skinned man with buzzed hair and glasses stepped out from behind Jason. "Hey, baby girl," he said with a wide, genuine smile as his green eyes met Zoe's. He leaned forward and kissed her cheek, his white lab coat brushing against her skirt.

His eyes rested on me as he straightened. "I'm Dustin Harper. Welcome to New Bodega."

I stared at him, my mind a flurry of questions and nerves, and the names and faces were blurring together, save for Harper. The doctor. The administrator of my fate.

I shook his hand, peering into his eyes. My mother always said you could see a man's soul in his eyes. She'd known my father was bad news the moment she'd met him, but in her small community growing up, marriages were a lot like they were going to be for me, planned. Strategic. She could see the devil in my father long before he ever put a hand on her.

Harper's eyes were bright with excitement. They were sincere too, and I felt instantly better meeting him. He rested his hands on his hips. "Did you just arrive?"

"An hour ago, maybe?" Zoe said. "The others are back at the farm."

"You didn't take much time to settle in then," Harper mused with a chuckle.

"Becca seemed to think coming over now was a good idea," Jake explained.

Harper's grin widened. "She probably saw Hunter here, running for the hills."

"Or wanted to put him out of his misery," Zoe offered,

glancing at me. I assumed that was exactly why Becca had offered.

Harper's eyebrows rose, and he motioned to a large room next to his office, with a table and chairs around it. "Then have a seat and we'll get started." With a quick, reassuring nod, he headed back to his desk. "I'll grab my things and get you up to speed."

I didn't think my muscles could coil more than they'd been all day, or that my stomach could knot any tighter, but it did as I walked into the large room. At least the windows were wide, making it feel less closed in, and I sat down in one of the seats, trying to ignore the four pairs of eyes on me.

Zoe walked over and opened a window, though I wasn't sure if it was for me or her as I noticed her forehead was glistening as much as mine.

Jason took the seat across from me, a severe expression schooling his features. "Harper gets a little nerdy when he talks about this shit, so if you have questions, ask them."

"Okay—"

"I resent that," Harper quipped as he strode into the room and pulled out a rolling chair between Zoe and Jason. He set a folder on the table, and Alex pulled out a chair beside me and Jake.

"So," Harper started. "The short of it is that we're ready to do this, if you still are," he said, leveling his gaze on me. "After finding out about your community, among others, Zoe was adamant we needed to do everything we could to help make this situation right for all of you who were never infected. Especially with all the knowledge we have about the origins of the Virus and how it works, thanks to our connections over the years."

Harper licked his lips and took a deep breath. "The longer version goes something like this—we've been working on this for over a year, and while I think the vaccine is as close to perfect as it's going to be, we have done no human testing." His focus fixed on me, sincere and kind but also full of warning. "As you can probably imagine, not only are uninfected survivors difficult to find, but ones willing to be tested on are even rarer, and we will *not* force anyone to do this."

Jason leaned forward then, his hands folded on the table. "If you change your mind at any point, you tell us. We won't hold it against you." His eyes flicked to Zoe and she agreed wholeheart-edly. Jason exhaled and leaned back in his chair again. "No matter what the rumors are, we're not like our mother or the General. This is a choice you need to make for you—not anyone else. You get that?"

"I know," I said easily. I didn't feel forced by them, or anyone. Though I did feel obligated. I looked at Zoe. "I won't change my mind," I reiterated, determined; I'd made my deci-sion. "I want to do this as soon as possible." Stewing in my own worry wasn't making anything easier. I needed to get it over with and know my fate.

"All right then." Harper offered me a sketch of molecules and terms I could barely read, let alone understand. "Let me explain what we've done," he said. "I want you to understand the possible side effects this vaccine will have on you before we move forward."

Side effects. I'd seen Wren coughing up blood after Beau infected her. I'd felt her skin on fire. I was very aware of the alternative, if something went wrong.

"The most straightforward explanation of the vaccine is that it's a version of the Virus itself, so you could still have a fever or feel nauseous, achy, and everything that comes with it. That being said, it's a weaker strand, and we've altered it by intro-ducing the devil's club, which attacks the Virus before it gets inside the cells."

Harper took a breath and pointed to the file in his hand. "As I've said, we haven't injected a living person with this vaccine yet, but I wouldn't be offering this as a viable solution if the results we'd found so far weren't promising."

"Or," Zoe started, "had we not had Becca's reassurance that it was ready. She's seen nothing in her visions to raise any alarm, and we rely on that and trust that more than anything. In fact, she's been steadfast in her belief that this next step isn't only plausible, but necessary for your future."

I frowned. I wanted to know her meaning, but another part of me couldn't process that at the moment.

Harper looked at Alex. "With the blood samples we collected from the Ranskins at the last summit—pure, uninfected blood—we've been able to test the vaccine, so it's not as if we're going into this completely blind."

"Don't you need like, a base, or something to build the vaccine off of?" Alex asked. "How did you get the Virus to begin with?"

"The foundation of the vaccine is the Virus in its purest form possible—taken from Jason's blood. Considering their origins, Jason and Zoe have the purest form of the Virus, so it made the most sense, though we haven't taken any from Zoe, uncertain how things might be changing given her unexpected pregnancy." Harper grinned and winked at her, eliciting her smile in return. "That being said," Harper continued, his expression doctorly again, "assuming the devil's club does its job and you come out of this as we expect you to, that's only step one of a two-step process."

"What do you mean?" Alex asked, leaning forward. "What's step two?"

Harper's eyes didn't leave mine. "We won't know if it works until you test it. Meaning, what side effects you have after intercourse—"

"I understand," I said, and moved uncomfortably in my seat. The last thing I wanted to talk about with these people was my sex life or lack of it.

Harper cleared his throat. "But all of that can come later—it's the effects of the vaccine itself we have to start with. We need to make sure it doesn't do more harm than good after administration. We have plenty of devil's club if we need it to counteract the Virus, like what you saw happen firsthand with Wren and Beau. You shouldn't manifest an Ability or change in that way—it's not a true strain of the Virus. But again, we can't know for absolute certain."

"Other than achy joints, what *will* happen?" Alex asked. "You're putting a version of the Virus in him, there has to be some sort of affect." I appreciated Alex's questions. I was too busy absorbing everything to ask any myself.

Harper glanced from Alex to Zoe, then to me. "It's true, there's no way around it. No matter what, whoever takes the vaccine will be genetically different than any of us so far, and as a byproduct, any children will be different as well. What that looks like, I don't know, however, it's something you do need to be aware of going into this. But," he said with a sigh, "in my opinion, it's better than the alternative."

"A celibate, lonely life," Alex muttered, and Jason chuckled under his breath.

I already expected my blood would be different, just as Wren's was. She was a carrier now, and even if she couldn't levitate or speak telepathically, she was different. The blood work Nathan had done on her in Whitehorse proved that much. But considering what affect it could have on my future children was a question mark I hadn't fully considered, and the immensity of what I was doing—the lasting effects of it—settled in anew.

"And if this works," I started, "if I survive this, my brother and mother—my people will be safe? They won't have to think about this or worry about it anymore?" Although I knew Harper couldn't promise that entirely, I needed to see the truth in his eyes that there was hope for my family and my people. I needed to know that *when* I finally convinced my mother that this was the only way forward, my brother, Sutton, and myself wouldn't have to worry about choosing a solitary life or one of potential death.

"If this works," Harper said, leaning forward. "Every uninfected person left in this world should be able to take this vaccine, as long as it's with precaution, ensuring that *all* survivors, regardless of whether they have Abilities, could really, truly comingle, cohabitate, and live without any worry of infection. If we get this right, we can make it available to everyone."

Harper clasped his hands on the surface of the table. "So, if we do this tonight, we wait twenty-four hours for any symptoms to show up. If there's nothing, that's great, but if there is an adverse reaction or negative side effects, we can manage it here, and we'll know what we need to do moving forward." He looked at Alex and Jake. "Having the two of you on hand is an added bonus, since we've seen how your Abilities work together." Jake and Alex exchanged a look of understanding.

"Just to be clear," I said, imagining my mother's tear-filled eyes before I'd left, and the hell she was in now, waiting to know my fate. "If for some unforeseen reason this doesn't work and I survive this, I won't be your pincushion again. I won't do that to my family."

"Understood," Harper said.

I glanced at the radio on a small table in the corner. "Do you have carrier pigeons here?" I joked, straight-faced. "I want my mother to know I'm okay when this is all over."

Harper grinned. "We'll make sure Whitehorse gets word, one way or another."

"Hunter?" I looked at Zoe as she bit the side of her cheek. "I would like to stay with you if that's all right? So that you're not alone."

My chest tightened at the concern in her voice, and for the first time, I realized I did feel alone. I forced myself to swallow and stood. "Okay," I told her, and looked at Harper. "Let's get this over with then."

25

THEA

After sandwiches and iced tea, Dani, Sam, Bert, Kat, and I used the motion sensor lights in the front lot to unload the goods staying at the farm. While some items needed to remain in the trailer for New Bodega, nearly a third of what we'd brought was for Hope Valley. Between the Re-gen settlement and the farm, the community had nearly two hundred people, and was responsible for many of the goods we traded for.

I was listening to the crooning voice of Garth Brooks, singing about friends in low places and beer chasing blues away as I unstacked the jam crates from the trailer, when I felt a nudge against my shoulder and glanced behind me.

Sam was standing there, grinning. I slid his headphones down to hang around my neck.

"Well, what do you think of Garth?" he asked. "And—" he held up his hand, "don't lie because you were humming, which means you can't possibly hate it."

I grinned back at him, uncertain if I should be mortified I was humming, which meant I was close to singing, or if I didn't care one way or the other because he was clearly amused.

"You know," I started, giving a show of uncertainty, "I think I do like him."

Sam's grin widened and he threw his arms up. "Of course you do. Everyone loves Garth Brooks."

My eyebrow lifted of its own accord. "So, you're cocky too, I see." I began unloading the flats of tinctures and powders for them to take next.

"It's not cocky when it's the truth," he said with a wink.

Dani walked up the ramp, her red hair brunette in the shadows. "This rhubarb jam looks *amazing*. We don't have to share this with New Bodega, do we?" she teased, and heaved a crate out of the trailer.

"They have two crates of their own," Kat said, coming up behind her. "And a little extra of everything to sweeten the pot, so I can try Grayson's ale I've been hearing so much about."

"Oh, his ale's good," Sam said with a grin. "You definitely have to try it."

I lugged a flat of Seneca snakeroot and valerian concoctions off the trailer. "Why did we bring so much?"

"The extra dried stuff is for teas and tinctures—for Dani," Kat said. "As a thank you for the extra horse."

"What extra horse?" I set a flat down on the ground outside the trailer and straightened. Even in the cool evening air, I felt the sweat beading on my brow and wiped it away with the back of my hand. Damn, California was warm.

Kat handed Sam a flat of salmon jerky jars, and looking at me, nodded toward the horse pasture. "One of the horses we're bringing back is for Milo."

"Really?" I couldn't help my smile. "He's going to love that!" I lifted my shoulder. "I guess his mother finally came around."

Kat snorted and shooed me out of the trailer so she could close it up again. "I don't think Letty was necessarily on board, but then, Hunter doesn't strike me as someone who asks for permission."

Her words gave me pause.

"What's that look?" Kat said with a wry smile. She brushed her hands off on her pants. "Are you really so surprised Hunter has a heart?"

"No," I said easily, and blew a strand of loose hair from my eyes. "Not exactly." I'd glimpsed a different side of him over the past week. "But I'm a little shocked he felt strongly enough about it that he'd go against his mother's wishes."

Sam reached for the last flat of snakeroot beside me, heaving it against his chest. "Hey, can't you, like, move things with your mind?" he asked.

"Yeah." I stared at him. "Why?"

Sam glanced around as if it was obvious. "Why aren't you using it?"

I peered at the others lugging boxes and crates around. The thought to use my telekinesis never crossed my mind. "Because . . ." I started, but I wasn't sure of the answer anymore. It scared me. Or, at least, it used to. "I don't know," I said instead, and I thought about Hunter.

He'd been encouraging me to use it more the entire trip, insisting it was a strength, not a weakness, and as I thought about the guy with the gun in the woods the other night, I knew Hunter was right. "I should, though, shouldn't I?" I thought aloud.

My gaze fixed behind Sam, on one of the discarded moving blankets in a pile on the side of the trailer, and I tossed it at him with a single thought.

Sam stumbled back, clutching the blanket in his arms, stunned for a second before he smiled, shaking his finger at me.

"Make yourself useful, would you?" I teased.

That earned me another wink from him, and he folded it and dropped it on the gravel drive as the other F-250 rumbled up the road.

"Of course they're back, now that the work is finished," Bert grumbled. I realized my brother was driving, but I didn't recognize the man sitting in the passenger seat, and there was no one in the back.

"Dad's home," Annie said as she and Ceara came out onto the porch.

I glanced at Kat as the truck come to a stop. "Where are the others, at the apartment already?" I asked.

"Probably at the clinic," she said, and the man I assumed was Jason climbed out of the passenger side, his frame and stature that of a well-honed military man.

"Hey, Red." He beamed as Dani sidled up to him. She stood on her tiptoes and gave him a quick kiss.

"I wondered when you were coming home," she said.

"Is everything okay?" Kat asked Alex, and she took a chug from her water bottle.

"So far so good," he said with an exhausted sigh. "And I know where our apartment is, so we can hitch the trailers up and head back."

"What about Jake and Zoe?—And where's Hunter?" I said, scanning the back seat again like they'd miraculously appear.

Alex hitched his thumb over his shoulder. "They're staying at the clinic tonight. I told them I'd check back in after we finished up to make sure everything's okay."

"Wait—at the clinic?" My heart raced as a cold sense of dread washed over me. "Why?" I glanced from Jason, who looked confused, to Alex, who looked curiously at Kat. Then they both stared at me. "Why would Hunter be staying at the clinic?" I asked again, growing more impatient by the second.

"Harper wants to keep him monitored," Jason offered, "and make sure he doesn't have any issues—"

I held up my hand. "Wait a sec—" I couldn't help the angry crease in my brow as I glared at Kat. "Hunter is *taking* the vaccine? What else don't I know?" I bit out.

Alex shrugged, appearing more confused than I felt. "That was the whole point of him coming, Thea."

"No," I said carefully. "I thought it was to learn about it and to take it back—for his *village*."

"He wanted to make sure it was safe before he let the others try it," Jason explained, and I spun around to look at him. "He was pretty adamant about it," he added.

"Why are you so angry, Thea?" Alex whispered, his head tilted slightly.

"I'm not angry," I said far too quickly, surprising myself. I was clearly . . . something. "I'm just . . . shocked. How did I not know this?" While the logical part of my brain told me it made perfect sense to try the vaccine here, supervised, another part of me was worried about him. We all knew how dangerous the Virus was.

Heat unfurled in my chest and up my neck, and I swallowed the lump in my throat before forcing myself to take a deep breath.

Alex stepped closer. "This was always the plan, Thea," he said softly. "It wasn't a rash decision, or something any of us are taking lightly—that's why he's under observation."

"Harper will take good care of him," Dani offered, her voice gentle and reassuring, and while I didn't doubt it, it didn't ease the sudden alarm I felt either.

Feeling all eyes on me, and I forced a weak smile. "Yeah, I'm sure you're right."

With a final look at Kat, I headed toward the truck. "We should go," I called back. "Alex, let's hook up the trailer so we can load up and let everyone get on with the rest of their night." I flashed Dani a grateful smile. "We've bothered them enough for one day."

Alex jumped into the truck and shifted it into reverse. I turned the trailer crank telepathically as I headed over to it without a second thought.

"Thea," Kat said, striding closer. "Harper and Zoe would *never* let him take that vaccine if they thought it was very dangerous. Hunter will be okay. Becca even said—"

"I'm sure he will." I forced a tightlipped smile. Not only had I been clueless, and felt lied to somehow, I was more worried than I was comfortable with. "Make sure the back's locked up, would you?" I asked brusquely.

With a sigh, Kat walked to the trailer gate. I watched the F-250's taillights flash as Alex inched the truck closer, and all I could imagine was Hunter, who'd probably never been to a hospital a day in his life, stuck in a room with strangers, waiting for an uncertain fate.

26

THEA

It was late, and we were all exhausted, but Kat and Alex headed back to the clinic with me, after we dropped off Bert to pass out for the night.

The clinic was a boxy, white building and stood alone on the top of a hill, braced against the wind.

The coastal breeze was frigid, but I ignored it as I walked faster toward the clinic entrance. Only two of the seven windows on the second level were lit up, so I knew where I needed to go.

"Are you still mad?" Kat asked behind me. Our footsteps echoed against the tile floor as we headed through the entry.

I adjusted my backpack against my back. "I'm not mad."

"You're mad," she said with a chuckle. I could feel her and Alex's eyes on me, though Kat said nothing else as we peered around at the empty reception area. With a few chairs along the far wall, it could've been a waiting room too, but there was no one inside.

"Ah." A man of Polynesian descent stepped out of a room on the second floor. "Visitors." He smiled as he hurried down the stairs. He had graying, buzzed hair but no wrinkles to give his age away. "Kat," he said happily, his heavy footsteps resounding in the spacious room. "I thought I sensed trouble."

"Hey, Harper," she replied with a chuckle, and they both leaned in for a hug, like they were old friends.

"And you must be Thea." Harper turned to me. He had an easy, white toothy grin and held out his hand. I noticed a wedding band on his finger and recalled he was married to Chris, one of the Hope Valley gang, though I hadn't met her yet.

Harper acknowledged Alex behind me. "Your brother mentioned you joined the fun this trip. I'm Harper, or H—whatever you want to call me. Just don't call me Dustin, that's reserved for my wife when she's angry with me." His grin widened as he shook my hand.

"Harper it is then," I said, feeling strangely at ease all of a sudden. I liked the open twinkle in his eye.

Harper winked at me as he rested his hands on his hips. "So, I know you didn't come to see me," he jested.

"True." Kat smirked at him. "Is Hunter okay—and awake? We wanted to see how he was doing."

"Of course." Harper gestured toward the stairs. "He's awake and is having symptoms, but I think he's at his worst."

My heart leapt into my throat.

"It came on quickly, as expected, and has leveled off over the past hour. I'll take you to him."

"What does that mean, exactly?" I asked, falling into step behind him and Kat. Alex trailed behind me. "What kind of symptoms is he having?"

"He has a high fever and achy joints so far," Harper explained over his shoulder. "Nothing we need you or Jake for yet, Alex," he clarified. "If at all, since I don't expect it to get much worse than it is."

When we reached the landing, Harper stepped to the side and gestured toward Hunter's room at the end of the hall.

"Zoe's sitting with him now," Harper said. "Maybe with you

here, she'll leave poor Hunter in peace." Though there was humor in his voice, Harper also sounded resolved and sympathetic, which made me curious. "For everyone's sake, though, Jake went to get Zoe and the rest of us some dinner from our friend Biggs down the road."

"And you'll be staying with Hunter all night?" I confirmed, tearing my gaze from the open doorway to Harper.

He winked at me. "I sure am. Don't worry, I'll keep him company and make sure he doesn't get worse. I'm no stranger to long nights here."

While it felt like everyone else looked at me strangely for being so concerned about Hunter, Harper looked at me with a soft, reassuring expression that made my heart swell and the tension in my shoulders ease a bit more.

"Thanks," I whispered, and with a deep breath, I headed down the hall, leaving Harper and Kat to catch up.

When I stepped into the doorway of Hunter's room, my eyes darted directly to him. His head was back, his cheeks flushed, but I couldn't tell if his eyes were closed or if he was asleep.

Quickly, I glanced around the room, surprised how simple and comfortable it was; more homey than I would've expected it to be, not like the hospital in Whitehorse. There was a framed painting of the ocean on the wall, and a potted plant by the window where Zoe stood wrapped in a blanket, gazing out into the darkness. A dresser of sorts and a chair was situated against the wall by Hunter's double bed.

My gaze landed on him again. He looked like he did on most nights, wearing a black t-shirt and pajama pants. He looked unwell, but not like he was dying. I exhaled for what felt like the first time since I'd stepped through the clinic doors.

It was too late to wonder if Hunter even wanted me there, especially since he hadn't mentioned why he'd come on the trip, but I couldn't ignore that he was doing this either, and I stepped inside his room.

"Hey," I said, my voice barely a rasp. Zoe's head whipped around, and Hunter's attention shot to the doorway. His brow furrowed as he sat up, but I tried not to let it bother me.

"Oh, good," Zoe said. She waddled over, one hand clutching the blanket around her shoulders, and the other hand resting on her belly. "A familiar face. I'm sure Hunter's glad for that." She flashed me a smile. I wasn't entirely surprised she was staying with him to make sure he'd be okay, but I could tell she was beyond exhausted. Her bright eyes were dull and heavy.

"I'll leave you to chat." As she reached the doorway, she turned around. "We'll bring you some soup as soon as it gets here." Her gaze met Hunter's, then shifted to me. With another weak smile, she headed out the door, leaving me and Hunter alone.

As I watched Zoe toddle down the hallway and into Harper's office, I realized I hadn't thought this far ahead, and now I was alone with Hunter in his room.

I forced myself to look at him, at his wearied yet surprised expression. Heaving my pack off my back, I stepped closer to his bedside.

"Well, you're alive, I see." He had a flannel sheet covering half of him, but the gray comforter was folded at his feet. "That's good, I guess." I dropped my pack on the end of his bed.

"Yes, I'm alive," Hunter said, his voice hoarse from disuse. "Just tired, but other than that, I'm fine."

I lifted an eyebrow skeptically and crossed my arms over my chest. "Interesting, because Harper said you have a high fever."

Hunter's dark eyes, glistening with sickness, lit even more with amusement. "Careful. It almost sounds like you care."

I reached out and pressed the back of my hand to his forehead. His skin was hot and I could practically feel his exhaustion like it was my own. Remembering the scorching way the Virus burned inside, I could imagine how uncomfortable Hunter was.

"Of course I do," I whispered. That he would think otherwise stung a little.

His brow furrowed deeper, but it wasn't with disapproval or disappointment like usual, more like surprise.

I rolled my eyes. "I'm not heartless," I told him.

Hunter blinked and, slowly, he shook his head. "I know you're not heartless, Thea," he breathed. The longer he looked at me, the more feverish *I* felt.

"Well," I started, glancing around the room again. "Is there anything you need?" I headed toward the water pitcher on the table by the door. "Thirsty?" I didn't wait for him to answer as I poured him some. As the cool water filled the glass, I realized I'd never been in a room alone with him before, definitely not while he was in bed. After telling myself it was perfectly normal to be worried and supportive—that this had nothing to do with anything other than being a decent person—I turned back for his bed.

Hunter wasn't glaring at me so much as he looked perturbed. "What?" I said, handing him the glass. "Why are you scowling this time?"

"You don't have to wait on me. I'm not dying."

I huffed. "Drink the damn water, Hunter."

He eyed me over the brim of the glass as he gulped half of it down, licking his lips when he was finished. "Thank you," he grumbled.

I smiled ruefully, feeling like I'd won that round, at least. "You're welcome."

With a lingering gaze, he set the glass down on the side table. "You're just like Zoe. I keep telling her I don't need anything, but she doesn't listen."

He could say he was fine, and maybe in the grand scheme of things he was, but Hunter was flushed and glassy-eyed. He didn't look himself, and whatever worry I felt, even if it eased a little in seeing he was relatively okay, was still there all the same.

"Well," I sighed, "she's worried about you, as she should be. What you're doing isn't exactly safe." While I hadn't come to lecture him about his decision, I couldn't help the frustration in my voice either.

"I'm fine, as you can see," he said. "And I've already disrupted their night enough, they don't need to fuss over me."

Ignoring his protests, I sat down in the chair beside his bed. "Did you at least bring a book or something to do while you're stuck in here?"

Hunter rested his head back on his pillow. "No, actually. I didn't think about any of that. I've been a bit preoccupied the whole trip."

I could only imagine, and felt guilty for not knowing this had been on his mind, but I forced myself to smile as happy-go-lucky Thea settled into place beside him. "Well, don't worry. I brought you some of my favorite old magazines, and I mean, like early-2000s-old, for you to look at. And a book." I opened my bag and pulled the three magazines I'd brought for the road trip, and set them on the mattress beside Hunter.

"*People* magazine," he read aloud as he picked the first one up. "Who's Jennifer Aniston and Brad Pitt?"

"Some big actors back in the day. I asked Elle about them, I guess they were the 'it' couple for a while. But there's a ton of other people in there too. It's fun to see what funky clothes they wore, what movies and shows were coming out, and what all the drama was about before, well, everything."

Hunter lifted a wry eyebrow, as if it were beneath him to care.

I sighed and waved his disinterest away. "There's a *Nat Geo* about the deforestation of the tropical rainforest in there too." I pulled out the word searches next.

Hunter stared at the stapled pages. "You make your own?"

I snorted. "I don't have much choice. I've pretty much cleaned out Whitehorse. Jackson and Ross get them for me when they go on the occasional scavenging excursion, but mostly I'm left to my own devices."

"But doesn't that defeat the purpose? Don't you already know where all the words are?"

"Not really." I opened to an unsearched page. "I mean, by the time I get the whole notebook filled with letters, I start at the beginning to work my way through them. Beau used to help me sometimes, but, well, he's been busy," I said, feeling the loss more keenly than I expected. "Jackson and Elle used to make them for me when I was little, but as I got older, it seemed silly to ask them since they were so busy all the time."

I met Hunter's gaze. When our eyes held for too long, I forced myself to look away, and I smiled as I pulled out the only book I'd brought with me on the trip. "Also, *Pride and Prejudice*—"

"There's more?" Hunter's brow rose. "How long did Harper say I'd be in here?" he joked.

"He didn't," I said with a chuckle. "But I figured I'd give you some options."

Hunter eyed the sepia cover. "I can't say I've ever wanted to read Jane Austen."

"Well, you might get desperate, you never know." I set the book on top of the magazines and word searches, then looked at him. "You ready for the big one?" I asked.

His eyebrows puckered in question, and I pulled out my iPod. "Boom, baby." I handed it to him. "No one has ever touched this but Jackson, so consider yourself special—oh, you have to plug it into power at all times. It's a relic."

Hunter eyed the iPod in his hand and his expression softened with surprise, tugging at my heartstrings. When he looked at me again, his regard was intent and earnest, and my skin warmed. "Thank you," he said. "You didn't have to do all this."

"I wanted to," I whispered, sitting back down in the chair again. "Though, had I *known* this is what you were coming here for, I could've brought you something more . . . Hunter-ish." I couldn't help the disappointment in my voice, even if I couldn't quite understand it. I fiddled with the backpack's zipper.

"It wasn't exactly a secret, Thea."

My gaze drifted to Hunter's to find his lips pressed into a thin line. "It sort of feels that way," I confessed.

"Why?" The word was more of a breath.

"Because . . . I had no idea," I told him. "In fact, I'm the only one who didn't know."

Hunter's attention shifted to my fingers, playing with the zipper again. "Well, I didn't think it would matter what I was doing," he admitted.

The fact that Hunter, who was stone-faced and reserved all the time, could sound so vulnerable and uncertain made my heart ache for him, and the words fell from my lips instantly. "Well, I guess it does." But before I could overthink that remark or let any awkwardness settle between us—half friends or acquaintances with a truce—I asked, "Why *are* you doing it? A year ago you didn't even want to know us, and now you've put your life in these people's hands—they're strangers to you." It didn't make sense to me, unless he was considering his future, which would make perfect sense, though the thought made my mouth suddenly dry. I swallowed. "Oh," I said dumbly as the realization set in. "There's someone you—"

"It's not about that," Hunter blurted, and his eyes flicked to mine reluctantly. His resolve and severity settled back into place. "I would never let my brother try something like this without knowing the outcome first. Or my mother or anyone else." The words came so assuredly, like it was so obvious, I felt dumb for not realizing it myself.

"Fine," I said, though it was pretty noble and warranted more than a *fine*. "But what if you get sicker than this—what if you wake up tomorrow and your fever is worse, or you don't wake up at all?"

Hunter looked at me as if he was completely unaffected by the possibility. "Isn't that what the devil's club is for?"

I lifted my chin, uncertain how to respond. Yes, it was, but there were no guarantees with the Virus, and just because it worked on Wren, didn't mean it would work on him. But despite my concerns, Hunter seemed unmoved.

"You know," I said, eyeing him skeptically, "you seem pretty confident in all of this."

"Do I?" He huffed a laugh. "I don't feel certain. I haven't for weeks."

"And what about your mother, what did she think about this idea of yours?"

Hunter sighed, as if that was an exhausting topic. "Despite what everyone seems to think, my mother doesn't get a say in this," he said more coolly than I'd expected.

Then it struck me, and I set my backpack on the floor at my feet. "It's why Wren was angry with you," I said, and when I looked at him, he was staring out the window.

"Yes." I recalled the tears in her eyes and the bite in her voice. It wasn't anger, but concern. "That's why I waited to tell her until the end . . . I didn't want her to talk me out of it."

My hands were clammy as I fisted them in my lap. How had I gotten Hunter so wrong? How was it that my mind had gone from disliking him, to distrusting him and always assuming the worst? It was hard to wrap my mind around how differently I felt about him now.

The silence between us stretched too long, and I began to feel uneasy. "So," I breathed, picking at my fingernail. I tried to push the shame I felt in my behavior the past year and a half away. "Now what happens? Will you stay in here for the rest of the trip?"

"Assuming my fever goes away and doesn't get worse, hopefully just a day or two," he said. As always, his gaze was thoughtful and focused, but on me this time.

"Well then," I said, and forced a chipper smile. "What should we do until then?"

He bowed his head. "*We?*"

"I guess not, if you don't want me here," I said as I rose to my feet.

"No—" Hunter reached for my arm, and our eyes met. "That's not what I meant," he insisted. His hand, as warm as if he'd held it up to a fire, fell back onto the bed.

I resisted a smile and sat down again, appreciating how fun it was to tease him—that I felt comfortable teasing him at all.

"Well then," I started again. "How should we pass the time? A word search race?"

He scoffed. "That you would win because you made them?"

I lifted an indifferent shoulder. "I mean, I could give you a head start if you feel you need one."

Hunter's brow rose. "You're competitive too, aren't you? You're practically jumping out of your seat with anticipation."

I batted my eyelashes at him. "I guess you'll have to find out."

27

HUNTER

"*P* lease . . ." *The word was timid and far away.*

Screams and shouting echoed around me, a familiar hell I knew all too well, but this was different. My body was on fire, burning from the inside out.

"Please . . ." I heard her pleading voice again, though it was distant in a vacuous fog.

I'd never felt like this before—torn and confused. Fuzzy.

"Please, Hunter—" She clung to me, and I shook my head, willing myself to focus.

"Please what?" I breathed. Something was wrong with me. I felt like I was burning alive.

Prying my eyes open, I looked down at Thea, scared and shaking.

"Hunter!" Thea shouted, her fingers digging into my biceps. "Wake up!"

M y eyelids shot open, my chest heaving as I peered around the clinic. The room was dark and silent, lit only by a couple of candles on the dresser. My body felt feverish, and my mind was muddled, but I was alive.

A soft moan tickled my ear, and I looked over. Thea was curled up and asleep in the chair beside me. Her pink lips were parted, and her long lashes fluttered while she dreamed. Her hair was loose and mussed, falling over her shoulders, and her chest rose and fell with quiet, little breaths. As if she could feel my gaze, even in sleep, she stirred and pulled the blanket tighter around her.

Again, she was in my dreams and in that house with me. Again, she was in my arms. Her brown eyes flashed to mind, and I swallowed thickly.

I attributed it to getting to know her better and being around her the past week, but deep down I knew it wasn't only that. The curiosity I had about Thea had always existed, and the pull I seemed to have toward her was becoming harder to ignore.

I wasn't sure if Thea had been angry with me for not telling her why I'd come on this trip, or if she'd simply been worried, but she'd definitely been . . . something. That she brought me magazines and games—that she'd visited me—was the most unexpected of all.

Needing to move around and get some air, I peered out the open doorway and saw the light from Harper's office in the hallway. Every part of me ached as I flung the covers back and climbed out of the bed. If felt like I'd been in those train cars that careened into the ravine.

The floor was cool against my bare feet, and I welcomed the chill it sent over my skin as I wandered down the hall. I eyed the door to the room Jake and Zoe slept in as I passed. Whatever part Zoe felt she needed to play in all of this, and whatever drive she had to see this vaccine through, felt akin to why I wanted to take the vaccine to begin with.

I stopped in Harper's office doorway to find him reading a book, his glasses perched on the tip of his nose.

"Hunter," he said, his gaze shooting to me. He set his book down and rose to his feet. "How are you feeling?"

"The same," I rasped. "I think."

Harper walked over, taking my wrist in his hand to check my pulse. "We should probably check you out, just in case," he muttered. "But you're awake, which is far better than the alternative, so I'll take it."

"I had a dream," I said, my head still a little foggy. "More strange than usual."

Harper dropped my arm back at my side and eyed me carefully. "A nightmare?"

"I get them often, but . . ." I glanced toward my room. "This was a little different."

"Well, I can't say that I'm surprised. Most of us had pretty vivid dreams while we were sick too. I should have warned you."

"What did you dream about?" I asked, suddenly curious what Thea's had been too.

"Me? I had dreams about combat—I was a medic, so you can probably imagine the twisted things my mind put me through in those twenty-four hours I was under."

Harper walked back to his desk and poured me a glass of water from the half-empty pitcher beside a framed family photo. "Here," he said, "drink this. I don't want you to get dehydrated." I didn't bother explaining that Thea had already forced me to drink three glasses, but I drank it, and the water felt cool and refreshing against my parched tongue.

When I finished, I handed Harper the empty glass. "Does your family lose you to this place a lot?"

He set the glass on his desk. "Not as often as you'd think. And Chris knows how important this work is—she's actually helped with a couple of projects, and would likely be here now, but she's at the house with our daughter." Harper glanced around his stark office. "This is no place for a five-year-old to grow up."

After a second, he nodded toward my room. "So," he said. "Where's Thea? Still poring over her magazines?"

"Sleeping," I told him. I could still see her curled up in the chair.

Harper chuckled to himself and shook his head. "I haven't seen a magazine in years, let alone thought about the red carpet or the Grammys—I wonder if any celebrities survived and how well they're faring now."

I didn't know much about celebrities, even before everyone got sick. My father hadn't even let me attend school most days, and I'd had to rely on Wren to tell me what was going on in the world and get me my assignments. I used to feel bad for wanting my father to die, and then finally, he did. He'd pissed off the wrong person and, in our lawless community in the middle of nowhere, was beaten to death one night. My mother mourned him, but I hadn't shed a tear.

Hearing footsteps down the hall, Harper and I glanced back at Alex's broad frame and tired eyes coming toward us. "How's it going?" He straightened and gave me a once-over. "You look a little worse for wear, but not like you're dying. That's a good sign."

"I'm okay," I told him.

"The last thing we want," Harper added, "is to think we've got this damn Virus figured out and let our guard down. We might as well check your fever again, make sure it's not getting worse. I'll go grab my thermometer and we can do it in my office, so we don't wake Thea."

Alex's dark eyebrows twitched, and he glanced down the hall. "She fell asleep?"

"About an hour ago," I whispered.

He cocked an eyebrow. "Really? Bert owes me an ale then," Alex said. "I knew she'd pass out. She was extra stubborn today, which means she was *really* exhausted." We headed toward the clinic room. "I didn't want her walking back alone, so I thought I'd come collect her now, so I can get some sleep."

I followed his gaze back to her sleeping form. "I'm surprised she came at all," I thought aloud.

Alex practically snorted. "Don't be." He looked at me skeptically, as if he had a secret. "Whatever's got you two pitted against each other half the time, it isn't enough to change the fact that Thea is the biggest softy—the one you can always count on to worry and make you smile, even if you bring out the fire in her most of us rarely see."

I stared at her, imagining how long and lonely my night would've been without her. "It was nice to have the company." I admired how delicate her features were, and how serene she seemed when her big brown, emotive eyes weren't filled with every feeling that sucked you in, making you want to know what thoughts sparked behind them.

Alex leaned against the doorway, his hands in his pockets as his gaze leveled on me—two pale green orbs that conveyed a mix of things I couldn't quite decipher. I'd heard he was a troubled kid in another life, but now he looked like an observant, concerned older brother, which felt more threatening suddenly. "I'm glad to know you two are getting along these days."

His insinuation was clear, and I shook my head. "We're just trying to be friends," I told him.

"Trying, is that all?"

This time I frowned. "She's with Cal," I reminded him.

Alex shook his head and his brow furrowed, like he was confused. "So she says." He watched Thea sleeping for a moment before he continued. "I don't mind giving the guy a chance after what he did to Kat back in the day, but I still don't understand the connection." A sincere expression of curiosity crumpled his features and he looked at me. "Is it one of those bad boy things?"

"I don't know," I said. "I just know that I don't trust the guy."

"Do you know something I should, or is that a protective, jealous comment?"

Jealous? I shook my head.

Harper came out on stealthy feet with a thermometer and stethoscope. "Come on," he said, heading toward his office.

Alex pushed off the doorframe. "I guess I'll get Sleeping Beauty out of here so you can actually catch some Zs."

I nodded, but hesitated to turn away as I watched Alex wake her. He was right. I wasn't sure when it had happened or how, exactly, but if my dreams were any indication, I was protective of Thea, and though I hated to admit it, a little jealous of Cal too.

28

HUNTER

The morning after my second night in the clinic, after Harper checked my vitals again and made me swear I would take it easy and tell him if I started feeling worse or different in any way, I walked down the hill toward the apartment the others had been staying in. It was a loft on top of a detached garage, beige with white trim and hard to miss on the cliff's edge. The scent of the ocean was indescribable—salty and balmy and unlike anything I'd ever smelled before. The wind was crisp and cold, but felt immensely better than the stuffy clinic. I was still achy, but it was duller than before, more of an annoyance than an ailment, and I was glad to feel more like myself again.

As I drew close enough, I noticed only one of the trucks was in front of the apartment, and I didn't have to wonder who had stayed behind to wait for me. Beyond the truck, Kat stood at a rickety fence, staring down at something. I dropped my backpack on the ground beside the stairs and walked over to her.

My feet scuffed the pavement, and Kat glanced back at me. "Ah, look who survived," she teased. Kat winked at me as she took a sip from the mug in her hand. "Glad you're still sucking air."

I huffed and tried not to laugh as I shoved my hands into my pockets. "Thanks. It's nice to move around." But the longest, most restless two days of my life were forgotten as I noticed the view. The gray-blue ocean stretched into the horizon, as if it was otherworldly and never ended; I could barely pull my attention from it.

"Have you eaten anything today?" Kat asked, eyeing me over the brim of her mug.

I shook my head. "I didn't want to keep Harper any longer than I needed to."

"Good, I'm going to make brunch," she said. "If I can ever get her back up here." Kat lifted her chin toward the water, and I stepped up to the cliff.

Shoeless and with her jeans rolled up to her knees, Thea played with Little Foot on the sandy beach below, the ocean lapping up onto the sand before it ebbed again. She threw a piece of driftwood for him to retrieve and brushed her wind-blown hair out of her face, only for it to whip around again. Thea laughed as she and Little Foot barked and ran from the waves.

"She's mad," Kat mused with disbelief. "Do you know how cold that damn water is, and she's *frolicking* in it." She chuckled to herself. "I forget she's an Alaskan girl, it probably feels like a bath."

With a sigh of amusement, Kat turned back for the apartment, but I couldn't take my eyes off the view below. Little Foot yipped and jumped through the water, running in the waves with Thea like they'd never been more free.

As if she could feel me watching her, Thea looked up, her smile widening as she waved me down to the beach. "Come on!" she shouted. "You wanted to see the ocean, didn't you?" Her voice was nearly lost to the wind, and with a final emphatic wave, she turned back toward Little Foot as he dropped the driftwood at her feet.

What was left of the vaccine's side effects dissolved to nothing, and following a narrow trail in the hillside, I headed down to the water. The scent of salt was thick in the air and I noticed seaweed washed up on the shore. The sand was difficult to walk in, my feet sinking with every step, but I couldn't suppress a smile as I realized I was finally at the ocean, walking on the beach.

"Take your shoes off!" Thea called as she ran over.

I stopped mid-step, staring down at her sand-covered toes.

She rested her hands on her hips. "Do it. You have to, or you aren't *really* experiencing the beach. Besides, it's easier to walk anyway." She seemed very serious about it, so I didn't hesitate.

Leaning against a rock, I unlaced my boots and pulled one shoe off, then my sock, and put my foot in the sand. My smile widened; the dry sand tickled the bottom of my foot.

"Told you," Thea said, her cheeks rosy and her eyes glistening. Her gaze swept over me. "You look better today."

"I *feel* better," I promised, sensing a skeptical lilt in her tone somewhere. I pulled my second boot and sock off, and discarded them beside me as I eyed the sand, scrunching it between my toes.

"Fun, huh?" Thea chirped. Her eyebrows danced, then she glanced at the surf. "Come on, the waves are the best part."

"Thea—"

She lurched forward and grabbed for my hand. "Come on," she said more seriously. "You'll regret it if you don't." Thea knew me well enough to know I didn't want to regret anything else in my life. And when she looked at me like that, I thought I might do anything. "Don't let this be one of your regrets," she said. She squeezed my hand tighter and pulled me toward the waves. "Now, come on!"

We jogged back to Little Foot, loping through the waves.

Even if I should've been taking in the expansive ocean, the gulls cawing overhead, and the waves crashing against the rocky edges of the cliff, it was Thea I couldn't look away from.

I followed her onto the wet sand, appreciating the firmness beneath my bare feet, and watched the way her eyes widened and her laugh turned almost impish with glee as the cold water crashed around our ankles. She tugged on my arm, pulling me deeper into the cresting waves, and as chills ran up my spine, my smile turned into a grin. I'd never felt more content in all my life.

29

THEA

As our week in New Bodega drew to a close, it was time to wrap up what business we still had left. We'd had a group potluck and picnic, which was a nice treat given we'd been so busy most of the trip. And Dani and I had picked out Milo's palomino mare, Sadie. But aside from horses and unloading, touring the settlement, and learning all we could about the vaccine and the Virus, there was still trading to do.

Alex, Kat, Hunter, and I headed into town, Sam joining us to show us the ropes.

I surveyed the cramped city for what might be the last time as we drove through, the wind whipping at my hair and sending goosebumps over my skin. Stacked apartment buildings were cluttered between one bend in the road and the next, and the streets were narrow and winding. Colorful windsocks fluttered in the ocean breeze, and pinwheels glinted from hanging plants on balcony rails. There were people walking on the streets, watching us with interest, and we received a friendly wave here and there.

As we stopped outside the Food Exchange, I noticed the chain-link fence and cement wall continued further down the road, though I only saw a couple of houses. I wasn't sure how far New Bodega continued along the cliffs, but the wall that lined the rolling hills, protecting New Bodega from what lay beyond the mountains, seemed to stretch on forever.

I eyed an outpost at one of the wall joints off in the distance and tried to tally how many people it might take to monitor this place every day. "Do you have someone who can null?" I asked as Sam and I stood up in the truck bed. "I mean, how do you secure such a long wall?"

"You met the lead of all New Bodega security," Sam said, offering me his hand as I jumped out of the back. The asphalt was pitted beneath my boots, like at home. "Jason," Sam explained. "It's why he's here in town so much. Just like you, we have our scavenging and security teams, and Jason runs a tight ship. He's ex-military."

"That explains a lot, actually," I thought aloud.

"Yeah, he's a softy beneath all the gruff, though. Don't tell anyone." With a smirk, Sam leaned closer. "It's Grayson you need to worry about. He runs the warehouse now that he's *retired* from city council." Sam shook his head. "That's what he calls it, anyway."

Hunter, Alex, and Kat opened their doors to climb out of the cab of the truck.

"Anyway," Sam continued. "Grayson's a grumpy old goat these days, but he's like everyone's grandfather. He used to live here before the Ending—he knew Zoe, Jason, and Dani from when they were his students."

"Wow, he's been here a long time," I realized.

Sam rolled his eyes. "Don't get him started. He likes to tell stories. Oh, and don't let his bushy, furrowed eyebrows and grumbles fool you. His bark is worse than his bite."

"So, he's an ornery old coot, huh? We have one of those too," I told him, thinking of Took.

"If things get rocky," Sam joked, "offer him an extra shipment of salmon—he misses the annual Alaskan fishing trips he used to take during summer break." Sam winked at me, as if he'd divulged a trade secret.

"Salmon. Noted." I glanced at Hunter, who was watching us, then at Kat as she slammed the passenger door shut. "Did you hear that, Kat?"

She flashed me a knowing grin. "Sure did." Kat tipped her imaginary hat in Sam's direction. "Thanks for the intel, kid."

"Kat's always haggling," I explained.

Sam grinned. "Oh trust me, I've heard."

Shivering, I followed him up the sidewalk toward the big red doors that led to a warehouse. I couldn't get out of the wind fast enough. Despite the warmer weather inland, the days were overcast, cold, and gusty along the coast. But inside, the warehouse was wind-free and smelled faintly sweet. A potent, herbal tinge was sharp in the air as well, and I noticed assorted bundles of dried basil and thyme hanging from shelves lining the walls as we walked in deeper.

The building was divided into a labyrinth of shelves on one side, and large bins and crates were stacked and spread out on the other; the building clearly housed New Bodega's food stores, and while a couple of townies milled around inside, putting produce and goods into their baskets, my gaze fixed on the bins bursting with colorful fruits and vegetables I'd only ever heard of, but never seen in person.

"Bananas . . . Avocados." I ran my fingers over their foreign skin. *"Pineapple?"* I gasped, eyeing its spiny exterior. I hesitated to touch it.

"If it's sweet stuff you like," Sam said, "you'll love a ripe pineapple."

"You should try the grapefruit, if you haven't had it before either." A girl with golden, waist-length curly hair, and the most beautiful jade-colored eyes I'd ever seen stepped out from one of the aisles. "That would be fun to watch." She wiped her hands off on her apron and smiled at me. "I'm Iris," she said, offering me her hand. Her attention shifted to Sam, then lingered on Hunter.

"Iris," Sam said, "these are our friends from Whitehorse—"

Her eyes widened instantly. "Oh—is Alex here?" She peered behind us as he stepped into view with Kat. "Alex!" Iris called, and hurried over to him. He barely registered her before she wrapped her arms around his neck. "I heard you might come."

Alex chuckled. "It's good to see you," he said.

Iris rubbed his back before stepping away again. "It's been so long. I wasn't sure I'd ever see you again."

"Yeah, well . . ." Alex blew out a breath. "It does feel like a lifetime ago."

Kat leaned closer to me. "I'm going to find Grayson so we can get down to business and back to the farm to start packing." As she disappeared deeper into the warehouse, Iris clapped her hands. Once again, she stole everyone's attention.

"So," she said, "I hear you're married now." She had an alluring confidence, and she was obviously beautiful. "And Alan says you have a baby girl now too." Her eyebrows danced.

"Fi's not so little anymore, but yes, Sophie and I have a daughter." He pulled a family photo from his back pocket. I knew which one it was, from Fiona's birthday last year, and it was faded and paper-thin from being in his pocket all the time. "Lucky for you, Elle is a photographer, so I always have a photo of her," Alex said with a smirk, and Iris fawned over the black-and-white image of his family.

I imagined it was a bittersweet reunion for Alex to see Iris again, not only did she likely remind him of a lifetime ago, before he and Sophie were together, but they hadn't seen each other since Alex, with Jake's regenerative Ability, helped save Iris's father after a massive heart attack.

Alex pointed to me. "Did you meet my sister, Thea?"

"Your sister, oh yes. I didn't realize." Iris gave me a quick wave. "You're the one Woody requests extra honey for at the summits."

"And you're the lavender honey girl that's stolen my heart," I said.

Iris laughed and held up her palm. "Guilty."

"Hunter is a farmer in Whitehorse," Alex continued, and introduced the two of them more formally.

"Hunter," Iris said, and I didn't miss the drawl in her voice, or the way she quickly scanned him up and down, as if she'd never seen anything quite like him before. I supposed he was exotic in a way. I didn't imagine they got many First Nations folks down here. "I've heard about you," she said, and reached out to take his hand.

"Uh-oh," Hunter said offhandedly. "What have you heard?" he asked and smiled—Hunter *smiled*. My chest cinched with annoyance. It had taken me over a year to get even the faintest of smiles from him, and he was flashing her one brighter than the northern lights on the clearest of nights.

"Nothing bad," Iris promised, practically giggling as she batted her eyelashes at him. "You sound kind of mysterious, actually."

I glanced away from them, feeling an unwanted spur of discomfort. "Come on," I told Sam, nudging him toward the back of the store. "Let's find Grayson and Kat so we can get this show on the road."

We walked deeper into the warehouse where there were shelving units stacked ten feet high. Everything had a label and was grouped accordingly. Small, stout jars of preserves were arranged on a row of shelves, while tall jars of dried fruit and grain lined another level.

We had similar food hubs in Whitehorse, but the diversity of what we had paled compared to New Bodega's.

"You have so many different foods," I said with awe. My voice echoed in the warehouse. "Cherries. Rice—"

"We get a lot of goods from a community in Southern California, which is where Tom and Peter are now. In New Bodega, we're known for Iris's honey, Dani's herbal garden, beef, and the Re-gens like to tend to the vineyards—it's constant, hard work and I think they thrive on it. So, they've become our resident winemakers over the years." Sam said it with an unexpected sort of pride. "We trade with SoCal frequently, since they're our closest cohort, especially if you travel by boat, like a lot of us do, up and down the coast."

"Well, maybe you can all come visit us next," I told him.

We heard voices before Kat and Grayson strode around an aisle. "The truck's this way," Kat said.

Grayson looked bristly, just as I'd expected—an old man with long, salt-and-pepper hair and a shaggy beard. I tried to imagine him as a teacher from before, but the mountain man in front of me made it hard to fathom.

"We brought cases of rhubarb jam, cranberry jelly, fifty pounds of moose jerky, and caribou, in exchange for oranges, almonds, and rice. We even brought some potted Seneca snake-root for you to try to grow, so if you're feeling extra generous, you can throw in some ale and"—Kat clapped him on the shoulder—"if you let me take a couple bottles of the wine I saw in the corner over there, I'll send extra smoked salmon home with Jake after this year's summit." Kat waggled her eyebrows, knowing the offer would be too enticing for him to pass up.

"I heard you were a haggler," Grayson said.

Sam chuckled as we followed them back out into the wind to unload the truck.

"It comes naturally, what can I say?" Kat lowered the tailgate. "Elle doesn't know it, but she wants to try that wine." Kat winked at the old man, and he shook his head, all perturbed-like, though I could tell he was happy to oblige her.

"All right," Grayson finally grumbled as they each took a crate of jam out of the back. "Add a pound of the elk jerky in the fall, and you've got yourself a deal. The wine takes time to perfect, you know."

With a self-satisfied smirk, Kat agreed, and she and Grayson lugged the crates into the warehouse. As Sam and I unloaded the rest of the provisions onto the sidewalk, I tried to ignore the trill of Iris's laughter inside.

"Are you okay?" Sam asked, a concerned expression pinching his features.

"Yeah." I straightened and tugged the hem of my shirt down. "Why?"

Sam lowered the crate in his hand and looked at me, confused. "You're scowling."

Scowling? I wasn't scowling. But the way heat flooded through me as Iris's laughter met my ears again, I realized I most definitely was scowling. And I wasn't only annoyed, I was jealous.

I could *not* be jealous. Not about Hunter or anyone else, because I had Cal. There was absolutely no reason for me to have any reaction to Hunter and Iris flirting. Or Hunter and anyone, for that matter.

When I realized Sam was still staring at me, I heaved out a sigh and squatted down to lift a flat of caribou jerky.

"You could use your Ability, you know?" Sam reminded me as usual.

"I like physical labor," I told him, more snippy than I'd meant it to be. I wanted to feel the strain and ache of lifting and moving; it gave me something else to focus on, instead of the looming reality of being confined with Hunter again—along with my startling realization. I needed to get myself in check before we got back on the road, before something even more unwelcome happened.

30

HUNTER

I swept out the last trailer, preparing to load the horses before our weeklong journey back to Whitehorse.

Time had come and gone. The trip had been a surprising one, as chaotic and overwhelming as I'd anticipated, and completely outside my comfort zone, but better than I'd expected too. As much as I liked the idea of a longer trip, I looked forward to getting back on the road even more. My thoughts were generally clear and straightforward, at least they had been before leaving home. Now, my mind was a mess, and I wasn't used to so much distraction.

I watched Thea and Dani as they opened the pasture gate for the horses to walk through, Thea laughing at something Dani had said. That laugh of hers had become a sound I could count on each day—and not just when she was around everyone else, but around me too. And the recent absence of it during our interactions only amplified the fact that something was wrong.

When Thea glanced over to make sure I was ready for the final four, I gave her a thumbs up.

I had no idea why, but she had been avoiding me. I told myself I'd been imagining it, but every time I went one direction she would go the other, and whenever I entered a room, she found a reason to exit. I couldn't ignore it. I didn't want to. So much had changed between us, I didn't like the empty feeling I had when she forced a smile and looked the other way.

"We about ready?" Bert said as he stepped onto the loading ramp. "Alex is refueling the girls' truck."

I wiped the sweat from my brow. "Just about."

"I'll grab Kat then. Knowing this clan, it's going to take us a week to say goodbye," Bert muttered, and he headed toward the farmhouse.

Leaning against the broom, I watched as Dani passed the proverbial torch to Thea, reassuring the horses and introducing them for a final time to their new human, for what would be the foreseeable future.

My chest warmed. As always, Thea smiled and cooed and fawned all over them, a side of her I'd come to rely on to brighten my day. Her love for her family, for her animals—her thrill for life when she let her guard down—was infectious.

My grip tightened around the broomstick. Alex was right. Thea was the most passionate soul I'd ever met, and it kindled the fire in her I experienced at times—her loyalty and her determination. She had a lightness I'd begun to crave, and even if I knew it was dangerous, I couldn't stop thinking about her.

When she laughed with Sam.

When she played with Little Foot.

When she rolled her eyes with grumbled sarcasm.

My affection for her was a terrifying feeling that confused my thoughts and made me anxious. But the more time I spent with her, the more I realized it wasn't going away, and I didn't particularly want it to.

"Penny for your thoughts," Zoe said from the other side of the ramp. Becca stood beside her, both of the women glancing from Thea to me.

"Do you think Dani's teaching Thea how to be a horse whisperer?" I said, my gaze drifting back to the pasture. Thea leaned her forehead against Sadie's, muttering inaudible words with a small smile.

Zoe absently rubbed her hand over her belly as she watched the two of them. "Something like that," she said with whimsical content.

"As I told Thea," Becca said, her raspy voice drawing my attention back to her. Her violet eyes held mine as she continued softly. "You are exactly where you are meant to be. You must embrace the future."

I blinked at her. I thought that's what I'd done by taking the vaccine. But Becca's tone alluded to something more, and as she stared at me, her eyes glazed over, and her thoughts seemed to drift.

"Becca," Zoe whispered, her voice gentle. I heard a hint of concern, or maybe it was practiced patience.

Becca blinked back to the moment. "I apologize," she said, blushing a little. "I find myself lost in my thoughts more and more these days."

"It happens," I told her, wondering what her words meant, or if they were mutterings of a woman whose mind wasn't always her own.

Becca forced a small smile, but there was a distance in her expression I didn't understand. I was about to ask her if she was okay when she started again, "Just something to remember," she said with a nod. "Everyone is important—everyone has a destiny." Her lips curved in the corner as she forced a broader, kinder smile. "Safe travels, Hunter," she said with finality, and glancing at Zoe, Becca turned and headed for the others as they gathered in the gravel drive.

"She doesn't always speak in riddles," Zoe said wryly. "But everything she says is important." Zoe stepped around the ramp. "What you've done here this week has changed everything." She took my hands in hers. "Things will be different now. You'll see."

I stared down at her feminine fingers gripping mine reassuringly, before meeting her jewellike eyes again. "Now you're speaking in riddles too," I told her.

Zoe huffed a laugh. "Saying too much changes things," she admitted. "Besides, it's all part of the fun." She winked, and as her attention held mine, she seemed to focus more intently, her brow furrowing. "It's an endless journey, isn't it, Hunter? I find that as I slay one demon, another one pops up in its place." I wanted to know what she saw in me that had her thoughts drifting so far away, when she shook her head. "Honestly, I'm not sure which is worse, swollen ankles or a deadly virus." She sighed, clearly exhausted, and waved her hand flippantly. "Horrible joke," she muttered, and she took a step back. "I hope your demons are behind you now, though. And that you can focus on what happens next." She glanced at Thea, who was saying goodbye to Sam.

"Me too," I heard myself say.

"And thank you," she added. "I know you came here for your family, but what you did will change everything one day." Her words sobered me, and with a small, knowing smile that sent a chill down my spine, Zoe turned back for the house. "Goodbye, Hunter."

I wanted to ask her what she was talking about, but Zoe's words, whatever they meant, felt as final as Becca's had, and I watched as she made her way over to Dani, Sam, and Thea.

As Thea laughed, wrapping her arms around Sam, I felt my chest ache and my grip on the broom tighten. Whatever the future held was stampeding toward me. That much was certain.

31

THEA

I stood beside the Fraser River with the eight horses as they grazed under a copse of spruce trees. It was late, but the sun was only just setting, and like my equine friends, I was restless after our second day of driving.

Hauling two full trailers meant driving slower, which meant we were making less headway returning to Whitehorse. Still, I enjoyed the company of the horses, feeling a comfort in their presence. Especially now, past the cities, I could allow myself to relax a little.

We'd officially entered evergreen territory again, and with it came the sharp scent of the forest, which reminded me of home. Over the past few days, it had begun to feel too far away. Perhaps I missed my own bed and more than four sets of clothes to choose from. Maybe I missed home because out here, the days were cramped and long, and my thoughts drifted too far away from me. Thoughts about home. Thoughts about Cal and my future. Thoughts about Hunter.

Whatever I'd felt the other day watching him and Iris scared me. I had no reason to be jealous, or any right to be. But I couldn't stop thinking about the hollowness in the pit of my stomach and the ache that nestled there, even if it made no sense. Two weeks ago, Hunter and I weren't even friends, and yet whatever discomfort I'd felt around him before the trip had vanished. He'd become a constant in my every day; a part of all that I did. I knew he preferred mint tea to lemongrass, that he chewed spruce gum when he was restless after too long in the truck, and that he always smelled faintly of basil, especially in the mornings after freshening up.

Sadie clomped lazily up beside me, a blade of wild grass hanging from her lips. "A snack for later, eh?" I chuckled. It was nice the horses knew they were heading to a good home, so we didn't have to worry about locking them up at night; they had no reason to leave, not with enough grass and weeds to munch on until their hearts' content.

Sadie rubbed her cream-colored forehead against my arm with a sigh, her eyes almost crimson in the setting sunlight. "It's not a terrible place to stop for the night, huh?" I said, idly stroking the whiskers under her chin. "Wait until you see what home looks like—"

Sadie's ears perked up and we both peered downriver. Hunter and Little Foot wandered their way up the rocky shoreline, weaving around the trees scattered along the water's edge.

"Way to give us a heart attack," I grumbled, my chest thudding beneath the palm of my hand.

Hunter's attention shifted to me as he walked closer, his hands in his jean pockets and his t-shirt still rumpled from the drive. "Sorry," he said. His voice was quiet as he stared at the herd, a splattering of browns and blacks and grays, as they cloistered around the trees with their heads hung low in sleep.

"Restless?" I asked, though I didn't need an answer. I'd never seen Hunter truly at ease, except for the morning we spent on the beach.

"I guess you could say that," he said, and gazed over my

head at the last rays of the descending sun. He stopped beside me. "Nice view."

I admired the burnt oranges and pinks. "There are definitely worse places we could be." After a moment of companionable, appreciative silence, I looked at him. "Well," I said. "Have you officially met Sadie yet?"

Hunter reached his hand out and rubbed her forelock. "Not officially."

"Hunter, this is Sadie, and apparently she's full of spunk, like Milo. I mentioned he's adventurous, and Dani thought she'd be a great fit. And she's young, so she'll be the perfect companion for him for quite a while, I think."

Hunter ran the crook of his finger gently down her face. "He'll love her," he said with awe. "And thank you for helping with this. Kat mentioned you took over." He smiled ruefully.

I shrugged. "Milo's a good kid. He deserves something of his own. And I'll admit," I said, rolling my eyes, "I might've got a little excited." I combed my fingers through her mane. "I just remember how much happier I was after I got Cinder. She's been with me through a lot. Now, Milo will have a friend like that too."

As dusk set in, a screech owl echoed from the treetops, and Sadie lowered her head and meandered back to the herd. I could feel Hunter's eyes on me, and though I stared at the deepening oranges in the sky, all I could contemplate was what he might be thinking.

"You wouldn't be avoiding me by any chance," he said, propping his foot up as he leaned against the tree behind him. "Would you?"

My eyes shot to his. "Avoiding you?"

His eyebrows rose ever so slightly.

"I'm not *avoiding* you," I started, but I wasn't sure how to finish my statement and looked away.

"It seems like it," he admitted. "And I've been trying to

figure out why, because I feel like I've been on my best behavior."

I couldn't resist a small smile. "You've been fine," I reassured him, sneaking a quick glance at him. "Mostly."

He smirked as he rested his head back against the tree trunk. "Are you glad we're headed home?" Though his question was simple enough, I detected uncertainty in his voice.

"Aren't you?"

Hunter remained quiet for a few heartbeats before his gaze speared me with a gravity I hadn't expected. "Things are different when we're home. They feel more complicated." His jaw twitched. "I wouldn't mind being gone a little while longer."

His brother. His mother. The farm and his village. It was no wonder he needed to escape sometimes. "I always seem to forget how much weight you carry on your shoulders," I admitted. "Being out here where you're free from all of that must be a nice reprieve."

Hunter lifted an indifferent shoulder. "And you—you miss home?"

Tucking a loose hair behind my ear, I tried to pinpoint how I was feeling. "Yes," I said, thinking about Elle and Jackson, and about my bed and a hot shower. "And no." Hunter was right; at home, everything was more complicated. After being around Dani and Jason, Zoe and Jake, and knowing the sort of epic love that Sophie and Alex had, even Kat and Ross, and Elle and Jackson, I didn't know what I wanted anymore. While I was anxious to get back to the familiar, a life I felt more capable of navigating, I longed to stay out here with Hunter too. Somehow, being around him made me feel more content.

"You seem torn," he said as he twisted a twig between his fingers. His dark eyes held mine, sending a warm, fluttering heat through my chest.

"I've—" I licked my lips. "I've been having fun out here on my own adventure," I confessed. "I'm usually the one stuck at home, but it's nice to have stories of my own to share now. Plus," I added, "I've gotten some one-on-one time with Alex, and I always love hanging out with Kat and Bert, so . . . it's been nice."

"And me?" Hunter studied me intently. "My being here hasn't spoiled it for you—"

"No," I breathed. "Nothing like that. I'm glad you came. I don't think we would've ever had a truce if you hadn't, and we'd still hate each other."

Slowly, he pushed himself off the spruce. "I've never hated you, Thea," he said. His voice sounded almost pained, and my pulse quickened.

I swallowed thickly. "Well, that's good."

"I know I can be a dick—"

"We've already talked about this," I told him, feeling a rush of unease as I considered what he might say next. "I'm not an angel, either." I forced a timid smile, my heart a pitter-patter in my throat. "Don't go getting too soft on me now."

But Hunter didn't smile at my teasing, there wasn't even a hint of amusement. Instead, his jaw worked and his gaze hardened.

"Come on," I told him, nodding toward camp. I couldn't stand the charged space between us. "We should probably—"

"I regret how rude I was to you," he said. "In the beginning," he added.

I blinked at him as he took a step closer.

"I regret," he continued, "that I've let you assume things and dislike me because of it. I told myself I didn't care, but the truth is . . . I do care." His words were unsteady, and he licked his lips. "I have for a long time, and I don't want you to have to assume anything with me anymore—I don't want you to draw your own conclusions. I want you to know me—the truth."

Warmth flooded through me. My cheeks flushed, my steadiness wavered, and I had to force myself not to flee under the all-consuming heat in his gaze.

"I'd like to say I haven't been myself around you, but that would be a lie." Hunter's eyes caught the moonlight as he came closer. "Between wounded ego and fear, I was ignorant and blind and—"

"I get it," I whispered. "I have regrets too, but you were just being protective of your people, like I was protective of my brother. So, we were both—"

"Why have you been avoiding me?" he asked again, more urgently this time.

My breath caught in my throat, and my chest heaved as he held my gaze for ransom. I couldn't look away. He was imploring, willing the same honesty he'd given me.

I shoved my hands in my back pockets and shrugged. "Because . . . I saw you talking to that girl and it bothered me."

He frowned. "What girl?"

"Iris," I said, mortification ringing through me as I once again comprehended how utterly stupid I was being.

Hunter's expression faltered, and I held up my hand so he wouldn't interrupt me.

"I have no right to care, and it's totally stupid, I know, I just —I couldn't help it." Exasperated with myself, I threw my hands up and stepped around him. "So, I'm putting some space between—"

"Thea." His voice was a command, forcing me to stop and look at him. "It wasn't like that."

I threw my hands up with a bitter laugh. "That's the thing, Hunter. You don't have to explain. It doesn't matter—it *shouldn't* matter, I just can't help the way—"

In one step—in a single fleeting moment—I felt lightness. A stunned sort of confusion filled me as I realized Hunter's lips were on mine, soft and hot, making my head spin. My eyes closed as my body took over, and I wrapped my arms around his neck, unable to resist kissing him back. I savored the feel of his mouth against mine, and his familiar scent enveloped my senses, warming me from the inside out.

Hunter was kissing me. Frustrating, frowning, angry Hunter. He was earnest and real and virile, and as I felt the brush of his fingers beneath my jaw, I shivered against him. Lifting onto my tiptoes, I kissed him deeper. His fingertips pressed into my back, bringing us closer—his hard chest heaving against mine. The caress of his tongue sent my body trembling. There was never anything so intoxicating. Never a man who tasted so good.

I gasped and pushed Hunter away. "Cal!" I blurted.

Hunter's unfocused gaze floated over me as he tried to catch his breath. "What?"

I raked my fingers through my hair. "I can't kiss you," I bit out, angry with myself. "I'm with Cal." I took a step back. "I'm with *Cal*."

Hunter's brow furrowed. "Cal?"

"Yes, *Cal*," I snapped. "My boyfriend." That I'd forgotten about him made my stomach sour.

Hunter opened his mouth to speak, but thought better of it, and I watched his expression shift from one of shock and confusion, to something more ashamed, as if he had forgotten about Cal too. Hunter composed himself again and took a deep breath. "I shouldn't have done that," he admitted. "I just—I thought you didn't like me talking to Iris?"

"I don't—I mean, no, I didn't, but that doesn't change what I have with Cal."

"Which is what, exactly?" he said sharply. "Why would you settle for someone like him?"

"Settle?"

"Yes, settle." His voice was harsher than I'd heard it in a long time, the old Hunter who made me bristle and see red.

"And what do you know about relationships, Hunter?"

"I know enough—"

"You know *nothing* about Cal. He's a good guy."

"Then why does his attention wander when he's not around you."

I blanched. "What?"

"I've seen him with that girl in town, Thea, multiple times, and he smiles at her more than I've ever seen him smile at you."

My heart stopped, mortification burned through me, and I stared at Hunter, anger and hurt and every emotion in between billowing their way to the surface. "You're being an asshole," I told him, trying to keep the sudden threat of tears at bay. I ignored what might've been a flash of regret on his face and shoved my finger at him. "Two weeks ago, we couldn't even be in the same room together without fighting. Suddenly you care who I'm dating—suddenly you have an *opinion*?"

"Yeah, I do because you were just kissing *me*."

"*You* kissed *me*."

Hunter's lips pursed and his eyes shifted over me. "You kissed me back," he practically growled, and his dependable scowl fell into place. It had been days since I'd seen it and a distant part of me hated that I was the reason it returned.

"Well, I shouldn't have," I told him.

Hunter stiffened, and I took a step back, rubbing my temples. "This wasn't supposed to happen," I murmured.

"Do you love him?"

"What?" I gaped at him. "That's none of your business."

"You just kissed me back, Thea. I think I deserve to know."

My mouth was suddenly dry. The last thing in the world I wanted was to talk to Hunter about my relationship with Cal. "It's complicated—he's one of the best people I know—"

"But do you *love* him?" Hunter asked again, carefully this time.

I loved Cal, but I couldn't bring myself to say it. "If you knew the truth—"

"Then tell me," he said. "What is it about that guy because I don't get it." He opened his arms in welcome. I'd never seen Hunter so angry and calm at the same time, but I didn't know what to say. His eyes scoured every curve and line of my face. "Why are you with him?" he repeated, and his skepticism raked over me like knives against my flesh.

"I told you, that's none of your business," I gritted out, and biting my tongue so I wouldn't cry, I stepped past him and headed toward camp, unable to bear the weight of his gaze—of his words and his mere presence—a moment longer.

32

HUNTER

I stared into the falling darkness as Thea walked away, my heart a sledge hammer against my sternum and my vision still tinged with red. I wasn't sure which stung more, Thea's rejection, or that she wasn't being honest with me, or herself.

Maybe I shouldn't have kissed her, but I couldn't stop myself. Everything about her pulled me closer, making it impossible to get her out of my head. I felt like she might be the only person who really knew how I felt sometimes, who really knew me at all.

Sadie cleared her nostrils, and when I looked at her, she was staring at me. She blinked. I considered for a moment that she might be glaring at me.

What did I just do? Running my hand over my head, I turned toward camp and froze.

Alex was standing at the tree line, his beanie pulled down over his ears, and his hands shoved into his jacket.

Shit.

Eyebrows raised, he stepped around a rock and made his way toward me.

"That seemed . . . intense," he said, and glanced from me to the horses; all but Sadie seemed oblivious to everything that had just happened.

"Sorry about that," I said and heaved a breath.

Alex widened his stance as he stopped beside me. "I can't say I'm all that surprised."

"About what—us arguing?" I shook my head, uncertain there was any coming back from it this time. "I guess I'm not either."

"No," Alex huffed, "that it finally came to this."

His dark features were even darker in the moonlight. "How do you mean?"

"You two have been dancing around whatever is between you since we got on the road, longer, even. It was only a matter of time before you blew the lid off it."

That . . . surprised me. I stared at him, waiting for him to explain.

"Thea's the most non-confrontational person in our family. And yet, aside from Beau, you're the only person I've ever seen her fight with. That's not for nothin'." Alex stared up at the moon. "Do you have any idea how angry she was when she found out what you were doing in New Bodega?"

I shook my head. Thea had seemed concerned and a little snarky that she hadn't known, but angry?

"It was more worry than anger, but still, she was livid."

"What did she say?"

Alex laughed. "She didn't have to say anything. When Thea's pissed, she gets this twitch in her cheek and she forces herself to smile so she doesn't say something she thinks she'll regret. Her nostrils flare too."

I wasn't sure I could feel more horrible for not telling her, until now.

Alex must've seen it in my expression, because he continued. "Like I've said before, Thea worries. Especially about the people she cares about. She worries she'll hurt someone's feelings. She worries she will make waves and rub someone the wrong way;

she worries about her place in the family—I think we all do to some extent. But with Beau—he's her brother, so she's more herself with him, and she has no issue ripping him a new one. And the same seems to go for you."

I didn't know what that meant, but I was stuck on the fact that Alex said Thea worries about the people she cares about. That I was one of them, at least in Alex's eyes, was . . . encouraging.

"I just hope one of these days the two of you will hash it out and get it sorted, because, trust me," Alex said, and he clamped his hand on my shoulder. "It makes things a hell of a lot easier. Now go on. I'm on watch, so get some rest. Tomorrow I'm teaching you how to drive." I scoffed at the idea, and Alex grinned. "Seriously," he said, and he headed back toward camp.

Whatever underlying purpose Alex had for talking to me, he was right about one thing. We needed to lay it all out on the line because our kiss . . . I already craved another one.

I stared toward camp. *No more regrets.* I needed to tell Thea exactly how I felt, because if she was going to push me away, I needed her to reject me properly. It was the only way I'd be able to let it go.

33

THEA

irt and dust kicked up around Kat and me as we loaded the horses into the trailer at dawn. Bert was eager to get on the road so he could sleep in the back, after being up all morning for second watch. I hadn't been on watch, but I hadn't slept much either.

All I could think about was Hunter's kiss. Not how much I should've resented it, because I didn't, though the guilt was gnawing away at me; I promised Cal he had nothing to worry about, and then I kissed Hunter? But what I couldn't stop thinking about most was why—no, *when*? When had Hunter developed those types of feeling for me? I could feel his intensity and the hum that sizzled over my skin when I was near him even now.

Beyond distracted, I slammed the trailer door shut behind Bixby, the chestnut breeding mare we were bringing home with us, and latched it.

"Whoa," Kat said, hand on her hips as she stepped closer. Amusement glimmered in her blue eyes. "I knew you were in a mood this morning, but the way you're manhandling everything, I'd say you're worse off than I thought."

"I'm not in *a mood,*" I told her.

Kat snorted.

"I'm not, I'm just . . . preoccupied."

"I would be too after a blow up like that."

My eyes shot to hers. "You heard?" I sighed, deflating a little, and leaned against the trailer.

"Thea," Kat said, glancing covertly to the guys packing the last of our things. "Everyone within a three-mile radius heard you guys arguing last night." I thought it was a joke, but she looked more concerned than amused.

I brushed the dust off my hands. I already smelled like sweat and horses, and the day had barely started.

Kat's eyes pierced me like a hawk's, watching too close for comfort.

"What?" I quipped, and headed to the other trailer to close the gate.

"Are you going to tell me what's going on?" Kat followed close behind. "Or do I get to guess all of the sordid details and—"

"There's nothing sordid about it," I told her, and swung the left gate of the trailer shut. "Are you going to help me?" I asked, gesturing to the right side. "Or are you just going to pry into my personal life?"

"At the moment, I'm going to wait for you to talk to me, Thea. This isn't like you—what's going on?"

I spun around. "Hunter kissed me, okay? It didn't go well, and now it's really uncomfortable. I'm sure you could've surmised that on your own. But thanks for making me spell it out for you," I deadpanned.

Kat grinned. "You're welcome. Now," she said, her voice softening, "maybe we can figure out what's really bothering you." She latched the right side of the trailer. "Because it can't really be the kiss."

I balked. "Why not?"

Kat rolled her eyes, which should've annoyed me, but I was too muddled to care. "Because Hunter—who shows 'no emotion' and who you *supposedly* hate—kissed you, which means you must've given him the impression you wanted him to. Or, at least that the feelings were mutual. Right? I guess I could have Hunter all wrong . . ."

"No—I mean, yes, maybe I gave him that impression . . ." I stared at her, realizing that's exactly what I'd done when I'd admitted I was jealous of his flirting with Iris.

"So," Kat drawled, "you do, or don't like him?"

Did I like Hunter? The answer seemed obvious that I did, but I knew I shouldn't. And I was scared to think just how much.

"At least blink if you understand the words coming out of my mouth."

I rolled my eyes instead and leaned against the trailer. "Yes."

"Yes, you understand English or . . ."

I would've glared laser beams at her if I could. "Not everything is a joke, you know."

Kat grinned. "But the scowl line on your forehead is gone."

I fought and failed to resist a smile. "I hate you."

With a victorious smirk, Kat winked at me and leaned against the trailer beside me. "You love me."

I leaned my head against her shoulder. "Unfortunately."

She kissed the top of my head. "You realize you should be celebrating this, right?"

"What do you mean?"

"This kiss is what I consider a *finally, hallelujah, thank-the-lord-it-finally-happened* sort of situation."

My head shot up.

"Wait—before you gripe at me, let me explain. Everyone who's been cooped up with you the past two weeks would agree with me. The look on your face when you found out what Hunter was doing at the clinic only solidified it, and the look on *his* face while you were chatting it up with Sam all week was the icing on the cake—" She held up her index finger as I began to protest. "Just because you two are oblivious, doesn't mean the rest of us are."

"But—" I had no words, despite my desperate struggle to find some. "It doesn't make sense."

"And Beau and Wren made sense in the beginning? Like Ross and I made sense?" Kat barked out a laugh. "We hated each other too, remember? I thought he was an unbearable prick. Nothing in this world makes sense, Thea. You should know that by now."

I glanced toward the tents as Hunter and Bert finished putting them away.

"You and Hunter are so much more similar than you think. And whatever you're still holding onto with Cal, for whatever reason, maybe you should let it go."

My eyes shot to hers. "I can't do that."

"Why not? Do you love Cal?"

Why did people keep asking me that? "I might—"

"*Might?*" Kat shook her head. "Then you don't, sweets. It's been over a year. If you don't know by now, then . . ." She reached for my hand. "Look, I know it's tough to hear because you're clinging to him for some reason, but you don't love Cal, and he doesn't love you the way you deserve to be loved back."

"You don't know what you're talking about," I whispered, but I felt defeated, uncertain what I felt or wanted anymore.

"No? Well, Ross and I argue like cats and dogs, and he's the most aggravating man I've ever met in my life, but there's never been a doubt how much we love each other. You can see how Elle and Jackson feel about one another just being in the same room, because it's suffocating," she said with feigned annoyance. "Meanwhile, you and Cal are always off on your own, and none of us really know the two of you together. It's like deep down, you know he's not the one and you're sparing all of us the effort of getting too close or something."

LINDSEY POGUE

"That's—that's not it," I stammered, hesitant under Kat's scrutiny.

"Then tell me." She reached for my hand and squeezed my fingers in hers. "Why are you holding onto Cal so hard?"

My heart was racing in my chest just thinking about that night. Even if the memory felt like it was a lifetime ago, my body hadn't forgotten and my palms began to sweat. But I knew that if I could tell anyone, it was Kat.

Forcing myself to look at her, I felt the tears pricking the backs of my eyes and I pulled my hand away. The emotions were nauseating—the regret mixed with fear, the shame I felt, and the embarrassment.

I glanced at Hunter again, his features hard set and focused as he lugged his bag over his shoulder, completely oblivious to my internal meltdown.

Leaning my head against the trailer again, I stared up at the cloudy morning. "Cal was there for me when I needed him," I admitted. "He's been everything to me since that night with Luna."

"This is about Luna?" Kat asked gently.

"No." I shook my head. "Well, sort of—Beau asked me not to see Donavan after everything that happened, but then Luna died, and Beau left on his trip—" I threw my hands up, uncertain of anything anymore. "I felt alone and I needed to get away from the house—I needed *something*."

"So you kept hanging out with Donavan."

"Yes," I said, "and it was nice to have a distraction, you know? Donavan liked me, at least, he liked me enough that I felt seen. It was stupid and I—"

"Thea," Kat said, more gently than I'd ever heard her before. "Tell me what happened."

My heart pounded in my ears, and my chest tightened. By the time I finally met her gaze, fear and rage simmered in her eyes.

"Not *that*," I told her. "Well, not exactly, anyway."

244

"More details please," she said coolly, her tone on the brink of fury.

"We were together at the old sternwheeler, where everyone meets up, and we were making out, and it was fine at first."

Kat tapped her foot impatiently.

"But things started getting out of control and he wasn't listening to me, and it was all I could do not to hurt him." I felt the tears breach the brim of my lashes. "All I could do was freeze, petrified what would happen if my Ability got out of control—if I thought wrong or made the wrong move." I swallowed the tremble in my voice and cleared my throat. "Cal showed up—we weren't even friends, but he could tell I was uncomfortable, and one thing led to another and he and Donavan got into a fight. Cal broke Donavan's nose. Donavan split Cal's lip—" I shook my head, hating how ridiculously weak I'd been.

I pushed off the trailer and began to pace. "I could've stopped it all from happening," I told her. "It would've been so easy to make Donavan stop, but I couldn't bring myself to use my Ability or my own strength because I was too scared. I didn't want to kill him, so I froze. If Cal hadn't shown up, I don't know what would've happened—I might've snapped and Donavan could be dead—"

"Oh, he'd definitely be dead if he'd taken it any farther," Kat said flatly, then she steadied her breath and her eyes softened. "Thank God for Cal," she whispered, and rested her hand on my shoulder. "Why didn't you tell me this hang-up with your Ability was so bad? I can help you figure out your telekinesis. We've all had to deal with this—I mean, shit, Thea, you don't have to be in this alone, you know?"

"I'm not," I told her, and my heart warmed. "I've had Cal. He helps me a little, when I let him."

Kat dropped her hand back to her side. "So you feel indebted to him now, that's why you're with him?"

"No. Mostly, I was in awe of him. He's a good guy, and he

started hanging around me and making sure I was okay. I sort of clung to him and we've been together since."

"You feel safe with him," she thought aloud.

It took me a moment to decide what it was. "Yes," I admitted, "and he calms me—and he's been by my side through . . ." I glanced at her.

"Is there more?" she asked tentatively.

I studied Kat, wondering if life was always so complicated for nineteen-year-olds. "I've been with Cal," I told her. "I've slept with him."

"That's not much of a shocker. That's why Elle gave you the tincture, so you could be smart—"

"I gave it to Wren," I blurted, squeezing my eyes shut so I couldn't see her disappointment. "When she and Beau got back."

When I peeked at her, Kat's expression was wide and her face was white. With each blink, I saw the pieces falling into place and her attention shifted to my stomach.

"The next time Cal and I were together, or afterward, anyway, I remembered I didn't have the tincture—I'd completely forgotten. I freaked and went to Jade. I told her I'd given mine to Wren and needed more, but Jade didn't have any made."

"Thea, you could've asked Wren—you could've asked *any* of us—"

"And admit to another stupid-ass decision?" I nearly shrieked. "Besides, I told myself it was fine, that it wasn't likely I'd get pregnant the *one* time I didn't use the tincture . . . but then I was late—nothing happened," I rushed to say, though my shame and fear were still palpable. "It was a false alarm, but of course I didn't know that and I nearly lost my mind. Even though Cal was freaking out, he was still Cal, always calm and supportive because he didn't want me to have a nervous breakdown. He told me we'd figure it out—that everything would be fine."

Kat opened her mouth, but before she could say anything, I

said, "Yes, I know, another reckless decision—another dumb move. If I never make another one in all my life, I'd still have plenty to keep me up at night."

"I was going to say," Kat hedged, "that I understand now, why you're with Cal—he's been there for you when no one else has been."

"Right?" I squeaked. "And I made him a promise that nothing would happen with Hunter, and now look." I scrubbed my hands over my face. "Cal's a good guy, and now I've kissed Hunter—I broke my promise to him."

"First of all," Kat said, stepping closer. She braced her hands on my shoulders, and her blackberry lotion filled my nose, comforting me a little. "You're not the first teenage girl to get herself in a situation like that, Thea. You might be the first *super-human* teenage girl to, but reckless, dumb decisions are part of living. It's what you do with those lessons, and remembering that fear and panic, that will keep you from forgetting ever again."

A hysterical huff of laughter bubbled out of my throat. "That's for sure."

Kat smiled. "And second, you don't *only* have Cal, you know? I'm always here."

Yes—sarcastic, tough-love, no-nonsense Kat was always there. She'd always had my back, whether it was to convince Elle and Jackson to get me a horse, or to take me under her wing so I didn't always feel left out. But the walls around her heart were there for a reason. She'd lost so much and I had played a large part in that.

The soft trickle of a tear streaked down my cheek as I peered at her through my lashes. "After Jenny, I didn't want you to—"

"Hey," Kat quipped. She squeezed my shoulders and lifted her chin, her eyes shimmering. "What happened with JJ has nothing to do with you. She made her decision—she wanted to save all of you—her decision wasn't about you or even Nora," she whispered. "All JJ ever wanted was to get back to Elle, and she did. She was happy—she got what she wanted, everything after that was borrowed time." Kat's chin trembled. "Plus, I know better than anyone that when JJ made up her mind, there was no swaying her."

I heaved in a breath, staring into the stormy blue of her eyes.

"You don't get to shoulder any blame for her deciding to do what she did. Her death, her actions—none of that is on you. Okay? Her death is *not* on you, Thea," she repeated.

With a terse nod, I wiped the tear from my cheek.

"And third," Kat said, clearing her throat. She licked her lips and straightened. "Just because Cal's a good guy, doesn't mean you have to be with him."

Her words felt like permission I hadn't realized I'd been waiting for. "And I should be with Hunter?" I shook my head, suddenly exhausted. "He doesn't even know me, not really. If he knew the stupid shit I've done . . ." I forced a laugh. "I'll spare myself that additional humiliation, thank you. His scowls are bad enough now, imagine if he knew the truth."

"What truth?"

Kat and I both startled, and I whirled around as Alex walked up behind me.

"Girl talk," Kat said, and her tone brooked no further questions or arguments.

Alex's palms flew up. "Forget I asked," he said. "Are the horses good to go?"

Kat nodded, and I imagined she was too focused on trying to compose herself to have a smartass remark.

"So are the guys," he said. "And everything's loaded. We should get on the road if we want to make it to the bridge before nightfall."

"Fine, but you get snoring Bert," Kat told him, and nodded for me to climb into the truck with her.

"Don't I always," Alex muttered, and turned and walked away.

Kat's eyes met mine, and her grin faded into a sympathetic smile.

Though I hated to ask, I also wasn't ready to talk to Elle or anyone else about what I'd told her. "Kat, you won't—"

"Wait—if you're about to insinuate or ask if I'm going to tell anyone what you told me, I request that you stop right there so as not to insult me," she said. Then, all teasing aside, Kat wrapped her arms around me. "We all have things we're not proud of, and your past is no one's business, if you don't want it to be. But I *will* keep harassing you about your Ability. I want you to get it under control—I want you to feel safe, and as strong as I know you are."

"I know," I said against her shoulder. "And I sort of do." I thought about us crossing the rail bridge, and what happened in the woods. Then I thought about Hunter.

"Good—but sort of isn't *great*, so we'll revisit this conversation when we get home."

Feeling immense gratitude that nearly brought me to tears again, I nestled closer to her. "Thank you," I whispered, afraid to think of my life without her. "I love you."

"You better," she grumbled. Kat kissed my forehead, and heaving a steadying breath, she turned for the truck. "Oh, and Thea?" She glanced back at me. "Whatever you decide to do about Hunter, I hope you'll still consider talking to Cal. I don't want to see you waste this life with someone you *like*, instead of spending it with someone you could actually love." Her gaze flicked behind me, then she climbed into the driver's seat. "Come on," she called. "We can talk more in the truck. Lord knows we have a long enough drive ahead of us."

I walked toward the front of the truck, feeling as if a heavy cloud had dispersed, and I could feel the full brightness of the sun again.

Opening the passenger door, I glanced back at Hunter. His eyes were on me, his expression thoughtful as always, and filled with concern and uncertainty as he absently stroked Sadie's fore-lock through the trailer window.

Whatever Cal and I were, and whatever feelings I had for Hunter, I knew my decision, despite what it might be, would be life altering and it scared me to death.

"Come on, girl," Kat called. "Time's a-wastin'."

34

THEA

"Can I have some?" Kat said, pointing to my water bottle in the cup holder. "I forgot to fill mine."

"Yeah, sorry about that. That wasn't exactly how I saw the morning starting."

"Don't be sorry, you just have to be my water girl now, is all." She winked at me and I unscrewed the cap. Handing her my water bottle, I let out a restless sigh.

The afternoon sun was high in the sky as we drew closer to the bridge, and I was ready for a bathroom break. Riding on the train rails wasn't helping either; every bump and blunder in the road sent my bladder jostling.

"What the . . ." I breathed, squinting to see in the side mirror. "Is Hunter driving?"

Kat looked in hers to confirm. "Uh—yep."

"Huh," I said, smiling. "I wasn't expecting that."

A sly grin spread over Kat's lips as she handed the bottle back to me. "Is there anything he can't do?" she tittered, batting her eyelashes as she continued around the bend in the rails, toward the bridge.

I rolled my eyes. "Driving is hardly miraculous."

"Isn't it though?" Kat stole a glance at me. "He's lived off the land all his life, hidden away, and he's still so tough and capable." Her eyelashes fluttered dramatically again and she sighed. "He's ventured so far from home, and been experimented on—now, he's learning to drive." I couldn't help but laugh at her jest. "Oh, and have you seen him working on the farm?" Kat began fanning herself. "Yowzers."

"Okay, now you're just being ridiculous."

"I—" Kat pressed suddenly on the brakes, and the truck and trailer lurched to a stop.

I reached out to brace myself on the dashboard.

"What the fuck," Kat breathed, and I vaguely registered the sound of metal and clanking chains as the truck behind us skittered to a stop at the bend in the tracks behind us.

"Geez, Kat," I grunted in confusion, then stared out the windshield, my mouth gaping and my heart hammering against my sternum as disbelief rang in my ears.

"Jesus, ladies," Alex said through the radio. "Who the hell taught you how to drive? Why the hell are we stopped?"

I reached for the handset, my eyes fixed on the road as I clicked it on. "The train cars," I breathed. I had to lick my lips as shock seized me, making me immobile.

Kat's fingers tightened audibly around the steering wheel.

The radio clicked again. "The what?" Alex said hoarsely.

"The train cars are back on the tracks," I told him. "Stay in your truck." I set the handset down and glanced at Kat. "Why are they back on the tracks, Kat? I put them a quarter mile down, at the bottom of the ravine." It wasn't a real question, more of a need to fill the silence as fear gripped hold of me, and I scoured the surrounding cliffs for prying eyes and monsters. The mountainsides were steep and jagged, the scrub oak and evergreens tapering off where the cliff ended and the bridge began.

"The question is," Kat whispered, her hand moving to the pistol strapped to her belt. "Who put them there?"

"It doesn't matter," I whispered. I couldn't take my eyes off the train cars. "We have to turn around."

Kat shook her head. "We can't." Her uneasiness sliced through me. "Not with the trailers in this narrow canyon. We could try to reverse," she thought aloud, staring at the train cars again.

I clicked the radio back on so Alex could hear me. "I'll see if I can move them," I said, and focusing on the steel boxcars, I willed them to move, the mental command almost desperate. But when they didn't budge, I focused harder. I opened my mind and willed them to shift with every fear-fueled fiber in me. My head ached, but finally the train car closest to me shuddered. Barely.

"The vines," Kat said, her voice more of a gasp. "They're covered in vines again—they're holding the train cars down somehow." Kat and I looked at each other, knowing my telekinesis was more powerful than mere vines. Someone was working against me.

I swallowed thickly as dread rolled over my skin, bringing the hairs on my arms and the back of my neck to attention. "Thea —" Alex said through the radio as Kat unbuckled her seatbelt. "We're backing the hell out of here."

"It's too late," Kat said. "Stay here." She checked the magazine of her gun. "Keep Little Foot in the truck. I don't want him getting hurt." His tail thumped loudly against the back seat at the mention of his name, oblivious to the potential danger we were in.

Kat glanced out at the bridge, barely visible with the train cars so close blocking the way. "Whoever they are, they're here, or those vines would've broken like before. I'm going to draw them out. *Don't* get out of the truck."

"No—"

"Listen to me, Thea." Kat's voice was more grave than I'd

ever heard it. "If you need to use that Ability of yours, do it. Do not hesitate, okay?"

"Yeah," I said, nodding automatically. "Okay."

"Keep your eyes open and do whatever your gut tells you to do. And if something happens to me, you get to your brother. You got it?"

My head bobbed again, and I gulped. "But, Kat . . ."

Opening the door, she stepped out of the truck and examined our surroundings. "Tell Alex what's up," she said, but I could hardly breathe, barely focused as panic wrapped around my heart and throat, making it difficult to swallow. She motioned to Alex behind us, to pay attention and stay put, and turning on her heels, Kat peered around, holding her pistol in front of her, posed to pull the trigger as she stepped forward.

It was a distraction, I realized. Whoever was watching might think that was all she had to protect herself. But I could already feel the weather changing, and the charge in the air prickled against my skin. With concentration, she could strike whoever was out there down like the Goddess of Thunder. "We know you're here!" she called. "And this isn't a very hospitable welcome."

I scoured the cliffs as my heart thrummed a mile a minute. I felt eyes on us and knew we were being watched, but I saw no one. More than anything, I needed to get to Alex so he could supercharge me—we could take out whoever was waiting and watching.

Slowly opening my door, careful not to let it creak, I scanned the jagged trees throughout the canyon and the shadows and rocks surrounding us. Grabbing the knife from the cubby in the door, just in case, I climbed out of the truck.

I hadn't gotten two steps to Alex's truck when I heard the hiss of movement and felt the sting of thorns tearing at my skin.

Alex shouted.

The knife flew out of my hand.

Vines wrapped around me from head to toe.

Kat shrieked and cursed, and in a flurry of movement, my shoulder hit the ground, singing in pain. My vision blurred and I made out Kat's faint outline as she hit the ground, wrapped in vines, like me.

35

HUNTER

I ducked as vines shot out, casting flying shadows over the truck and trailer in front of us.

Little Foot's distant snarling and barking barely met my ears, and the horses stirred in the trailer, making the truck quake.

"What the hell—" I called as Alex leapt out of the truck.

"Thea!" he shouted.

Before I could open the door to do the same, vines descended again, seeming to come from all directions, and I covered my head.

Alex's body lifted into the air, the vines curling around him, pinning his arms to his sides as they tugged him out of sight.

"Shit!" I rasped, and pushed at Bert, still snoring in the back seat. "Wake up, old man," I gritted out.

"You—motherfuckers—" Kat's voice was muffled, barely audible over Bert's snoring.

"Bert!" I shouted, my mind spinning with terror and fury as my fist tightened on my Beretta. I had to get out—I had to see what was going on. But all I could think was this could *not* be happening again. No more crazy men. No more Ability-juiced freaks ready to torture and kill us because they could.

As I considered they might be the cult from the river, I reached for the door handle, pausing when I saw movement by the train cars ahead. A guy with a short beard and a dirty baseball cap stepped into view.

"We were hoping you'd come back," he said. Even from far away, I could hear the amusement in his voice. He peered down at the ground, though I couldn't see who he was looking at—Kat, Thea, or Alex. He looked my age, and a little worse for wear with bony shoulders and hollow cheeks. "Which one of you has the telekinesis—which one of you moved my train?"

Bert grumbled from the back as I carefully climbed out of the truck, my heart practically seizing in my throat. "Get with the program," I growled at him. "They need our help."

The cool air did nothing to ease the hot dread beading on my skin as I crouched down to see ahead. Thea and Kat faced my direction, bound in vines on the ground as they struggled to wrench free, the man standing behind them.

Thea was shuddering, like she was trying to move *anything* with her mind—but the vines and whatever Ability was holding them in place, fought against her. *The man.* She couldn't move him if she couldn't see him, I realized.

Red-faced and panicked, she squeezed her eyes shut in concentration. I thought I heard her whimper when she opened them again, and when she registered me crouching by the truck, her eyes widened. She gave nothing away as Kat berated the lunatic nudging her with his foot.

"This is quite the cowardly hello," Kat gritted out, her voice gruff as she struggled.

"Well, it's not often we get visitors, so we're a little rusty. But we *are* sorry we missed you the first time across." He tisked and shook his head. "That wasn't very welcoming of us."

Still crouched and fingers gripping my gun, I aimed, prepared to shoot the bastard through the head, when the hair rose on the back of my neck, and I felt the presence of someone behind me.

I spun around with my gun raised, coming face-to-face with a woman whose hands wrapped around my fingers and the gun with crushing pressure. She squeezed.

I grimaced and shouted, trying to pull away.

The woman's gray eyes smiled at me, more menacing than the rotted-toothed grin that stretched from ear to ear. These weren't the people from the cult. These people were worse.

Tearing the gun from my grasp, the woman flung it, and grabbed hold of my bicep with bruising strength, twisting my arm behind my back as I fell to my knees. "This will be fun," she cackled.

This was it. My fears come to life again.

Bert shouted in the truck, vines wrapping around it, making the vehicle groan and shake.

The horses pawed and kicked from inside the trailer.

Thea and Kat both shouted as blood whirred in my ears.

The woman twisted my arm further as she hoisted me up, a shout bellowing from my chest.

"Hunter!" Thea screamed, followed by a shout of fury. The woman holding me with brute strength flew through the air, nearly taking my arm with her, and my vision flared with white hot pain.

Blinking back to focus, I watched the woman's body slammed against the side of the mountain, then I heard the crack of her skull, and watched the blood drip from stone as she fell to the ground in a heap.

I wasn't even sure my shoulder was still attached as I ducked for cover behind the trailer, biting back the pain.

"My connection's weakening!" A woman's voice called from somewhere by the bridge.

The train cars continued to shift and shutter, and I could hear Thea straining to move them. Brute strength. The vines. I wasn't sure what the man in the ballcap could do, or how many other lunatics there might be, but I knew it was only a matter of time until we learned the answer.

The horses continued to thrash, and a torrent of thoughts tumbled through my mind.

I could let them out as a distraction, or let Little Foot loose, but they'd surely be hurt.

Thea could use the trucks somehow—she could move the trailers—but if she could, she would have.

I considered the woman's brains splattered on the mountain-side as Bert shot through the window of the truck above me, making me cower lower. When the vines he hit exploded, others loosened and trembled.

"I—" There was a strangled grunt in the distance. "I can't—"

"Hold it together, Marta!" Ballcap barked, and while Marta struggled from wherever she was to keep Thea and Kat at bay, I pried and pulled at the vines twisting around the truck with the only arm I could move, the thorns cutting into my hand as I tried to help Bert get out.

"It's you, isn't it?" Ballcap growled. I heard Thea shriek in pain, but I focused on the truck. Gripping the vines tighter. Pulling them harder. They weren't the bramble that grew along the road, but reinforced and surging with energy I could feel vibrating against my skin.

"I've come across a telekinetic before—you can't hurt me because you can't see me," he taunted from behind her.

"I can't—fight her—much longer . . ." Marta struggled to say. "Kill her or—"

"No!" Ballcap shouted, and I glanced over as his head whipped around. Marta stumbled out from behind the rail cars, her dark hair stringy, and her body quaking as blood dripped from her nose. Her fingers were curled inward like claws.

"She's getting tired!" I told Bert as I tore at the vines harder.

LINDSEY POGUE

He shot at another one and tried to kick his way out of the window.

As the vines around the truck continued to loosen, Bert kicked the door open and slid out, heaving a breath. Sweat beaded on his brow and his ears were bleeding.

"Get to Alex," he rasped.

I nodded, but I only had one good arm, and no gun. Bert was our only option. "Distract them," I said, gritting through the pain in my arm and chest.

He motioned to the other side of the truck and handed me the knife sheathed in his boot. "You only have seconds, kid," he said roughly, checking his magazine. "Make 'em count." He winced as he moved, and I could tell he was trying to gain his bearings and stay focused.

"Come on," Ballcap said, heaving Thea to her feet. "You're needed elsewhere." She fought against him, nearly knocking the madman off balance, though he was careful not to let her see him.

Creeping to the other side of the trailer, I glanced around for Alex. He was at the front wheel of the truck, wrapped in bramble, his neck and arms bleeding as the thorns cut into him. But the guy and Marta were too busy worrying about Thea.

One hand. It was all Alex needed to amplify someone. Steadying myself, I waited for Bert's signal, and when he started shouting from the other side of the truck and the first gunshot screeched through the air, I bit back the pain and dashed to Alex, sawing at his binding with a single word. "Kat."

"Oh, you don't like guns?" Bert hollered. "That's too bad." Another gunshot ricocheted through the air.

As the vines loosened around Kat, Alex reached for her, pulling her hand free.

Bang. Another gunshot echoed.

Immediately, the clouds filling the sky turned a roiling black and rumbled. "Die, you piece of *shit!*" Kat screeched, and a

260

crackling, blinding flash lit the sky, the earth beneath me shaking.

The hair on my arms and legs rose, and I cowered in place, waiting for another gunshot or flash of light, but neither came. When I looked up, Alex was gripping Kat's wrist, both of their clothes singed and smoking, their chests heaving. Thea wriggled from her bindings and they fell to the ground.

All of them were bloody, but I barely noticed as I watched Bert stumbling over to the two bodies crumpled under a pine tree at the bridge entrance. One of them heaved, gasping for breath, the other was charred and unmoving.

Pulling myself up to standing, I leaned against the front of the truck and watched as Bert shot the gurgling woman once, then again.

I glanced back at the strong one's remains, ensuring she was still dead from the collision with the mountainside, and Alex helped Thea to her feet. My mind spun as I realized how close we'd come to potential death, and all I could think was, what if there are more?

"You're hurt!" Kat shouted, and hurried over to Bert, clutching onto him as he wobbled, looking for something to lean against. She reached for him, but Bert took a step back. "I won't electrocute you," she huffed, and took his arm, searching his body for wounds.

"I was more worried I'd have a stroke. This is the closest I've been to a half naked woman in years." Bert grimaced as he tried to laugh.

"Even now," Kat said, shaking her head, "you're incorrigible." She continued to scour his body.

"Don't get in a tizzy, woman," Bert grumbled. "I'm just old, probably having a mild heart attack or something." He flinched as Kat smacked his shoulder and helped him back to the truck.

Thea waved Alex's murmuring words away. "I'm fine— I'm . . . fine." As she wiped the blood from her cheek, her attention shot to me. In an instant, she was running over, her eyes wild and panicked. "You're hurt." She covered her mouth, assessing me as I winced, trying to straighten.

I shook my head. "I'm fine—you're the one bleeding—"

"She grabbed you," Thea said, her eyes filling with tears. Her hands hovered over my shoulder. "My Ability wasn't working, but she grabbed you. I didn't mean to—I didn't think—"

"Thea," I said, reaching for her hand with my good arm. "It hurts like hell, but I'm fine. I promise. It's just dislocated."

She kept shaking her head, like she didn't believe me, but this time, there was nothing to regret.

"Hey," I whispered. "Look at me." I held her gaze, imploring her to calm down. "I'm okay. I'm probably still alive because of you. You're the one who's all cut up, and your nose is bleeding." Thea's hand shot up to wipe the blood.

Little Foot hurried over, sniffing and whining as he tried to assess us all, his tail wagging with relief.

Exhaling as my adrenaline finally subsided, I looked at the dead bodies. "What the hell just happened?"

"They set a trap for us and we took the bait," Kat said. "They've been waiting for us to come back."

Alex shook his head. "I can't believe we didn't realize."

"How could we have?" Bert said.

I glanced around, worried more of them would start creeping out of the cliffs. "What are the odds there were only three of them?"

"I don't know," Bert snapped. "But let's not wait around to find out."

"I'll drive," I said, taking in all of their scrapes and bruises.

"Like hell," Thea said. "Your arm—"

"Bert and I will drive," Kat barked, wiping the soot and blood from her cheeks. "Alex, Thea—get the bridge cleared so we can get the fuck out of here. I'll fix Hunter's shoulder." Kat eyed Bert. "Which truck is the big kit in?"

"Ours, if you can wade through the vines." Bert set his semi-automatic on the hood of the truck and rested his elbows on it. "I'm too old for this shit," he muttered.

"So you keep saying," Alex said, clapping him on the shoulder. "Thanks for the distraction, old man."

When I looked at Thea again, she was watching me, her chin trembling and her eyes clouded like the sky above. I could almost see her fears alive inside of her—Luna, her mother, and other shadows I didn't recognize. It was as if they were all she could see.

"I told you, I'm not broken—well, maybe temporarily, but I'll be fine. I promise. I can handle a little pummel." I glanced at the bridge. "Go do your thing."

Alex took Thea's hand. "We should hurry," he said calmly. "Just in case."

With a reluctant nod, Thea turned toward the train.

Unlike the first time we crossed the bridge, Alex and Thea got to work without hesitation. I tried to focus on the vines quaking and tearing around them as each train car began to move, instead of the mind-numbing pain in my near future.

"What do you think they wanted Thea's Ability for?" I asked, glancing at Bert.

"None of that matters now," Kat said, distracted as she lugged a big first aid kit over to us. "The options are limitless when it comes to people like that."

If it hadn't been for the look on Thea's face and the tears in her eyes as she worried about me, I would've lost myself to a whirlwind of unwanted memories and anxieties from over a decade ago. Instead, all I could think about was her. How all this could've ended much differently, and how much I yearned to hold Thea in my arms and feel her heartbeat, suddenly worried I might never get another chance.

"First," Bert said, handing me a bottle of whiskey. "You're

definitely going to want some of this. Take a few swigs, at the very least."

I knew what was coming and took a few long pulls as I held my arm against my chest. My shoulder was a burning, aching mess of pain, but I gritted it down and swallowed another gulp. Getting it back into place would feel far worse, even if it was only for a moment.

"Kat, grab something for him to bite down on," Bert said, more focused and serious than I'd ever seen him. He glanced at me. "I have a sling for you when we're finished, but this is going to hurt like hell."

I took another drink from the bottle, then handed it to Kat.

She handed me Thea's copy of *Pride and Prejudice,* to bite down on in exchange. "We don't have any lidocaine," Kat warned. "So it is what it is."

"I've seen my mom go through this, I know what to expect." I stared at Bert, bracing myself. "Let's get it over with."

36

THEA

M oving the train cars a second time was a blur. And the past couple of hours on the road also felt intangible. All of us were worried, exhausted, and on edge. I thought having the windows down and the wind blowing through my hair as we drove north would help rid me of my nerves, but it didn't. We still had two or three more days on the road, and I hated to think what other *adventures* awaited us.

"Ha." I sniggered to myself and rubbed my fingers over the thorn scratches and what felt like rope burn on my arm. "I've definitely got my own stories to tell now, don't I?"

Kat glanced at me from the driver's seat, her expression drawn with fatigue and smeared with soot, and much like the rest of us, her neck was red with vine marks. "Welcome to the road, Thea. It's nothing if not unpredictable."

I examined Hunter in the back seat, his eyes already on me and glazed over from the booze. "It sure is," I muttered. My heart beat a little faster as his lips curved into a lopsided grin. "How's your shoulder?" I asked, offering him my water bottle.

Hunter took a drink, then handed it back to me. "Better," he said, his grin returning.

I rolled my eyes. "Okay, Mr. McSmiley." I turned to face the front.

"I thought you wanted me to smile more," he said, goading me, and Kat snorted.

"Not because you're semi-drunk and in pain, though," I told him.

Hunter *was* still in pain, I saw it every time he tried to re-situate himself, wincing when he didn't think I was watching.

"They were relatively young," Kat mused. She'd been mostly quiet since we'd gotten back on the road, but the way her thumb tapped on the steering wheel and how fervently she kept checking the side mirror, either ensuring there was no one behind us or that the guys were safe, gave her concern away.

"Yes, they were," I agreed, knowing where her mind was going. "We knew there were still gangs out here." It wasn't a happy thought, but it wasn't surprising either. Not everyone wanted to be good, and Ross couldn't save the entire world, except for maybe our tiny corner of it. "At least we had the element of surprise in our numbers and Abilities," I told her. "They only knew what one of us could do since I'd moved the train. They were cocky, and it bit them in the ass." I shrugged away the magnitude of what we'd just been through, for Kat's sake. And also because I was too exhausted to relive it. "Now they won't hurt anyone ever again."

"They could've done a lot of damage if they'd been more prepared or smarter about it," she said. I knew Kat was going to dwell on it for the rest of the trip, just like I knew what Ross would likely do when he found out what happened to us. They would plan, or at least prep, in case other gangs like them began moving closer to Whitehorse again.

I looked at Kat's profile, knowing she was more shaken up than she was letting on. "What is it?" I asked. It wasn't like her to worry.

Rubbing her temple, she propped her elbow in the window.

"Elle and Jackson would've killed me if something had happened to you," she rasped.

A swell of emotion filled my chest. "Well, I'm fine. And Elle and Jackson wouldn't have killed you—Took maybe would have, because I know that despite how grumpy he is around me, I'm his favorite."

She huffed a laugh and shook her head.

I glanced back at Hunter again. His eyes were closed this time as he rested against the passenger door. Staring at his slinged arm, I felt my own rush of remorse and gratitude. That woman grabbing hold of him was going to tear him to pieces—I'd seen the devilish look on her face and every coiled muscle screamed it. And she almost had. I still wasn't sure how I'd managed it when moving everything else had felt impossible. Yet somehow, I'd done it, and in my haste to pull her away from Hunter, I'd nearly hurt him.

But he's alive. He was still breathing and in one piece, and I tried to let my apprehensions go. "How do you think the guys are holding up in the truck?" I asked, remembering it was shot up and barely functioning. It might not have been running at all if Bert wasn't such a crafty mechanic, and if his Ability melded with Alex's couldn't keep the engine chugging and the truck moving.

"They're still going, which is enough for now," Kat said, sighing with resignation. "But I think it's safe to say Bert is going to tinker all night so we can get back on the road first thing tomorrow."

I nodded absently. "At least we're heading into known territory, and we'll have radio communication soon." More days on the road meant more uncertainty, and suddenly getting home felt more urgent than ever. I glanced at Hunter for the hundredth time. This time his eyes were open and contemplative.

"I'm fine, Thea." His umber irises were glazed over with

drink, but he seemed surprisingly alert. I couldn't shake the daunting *but what-ifs* that kept niggling at me.

The corner of Hunter's mouth quirked up slightly.

"I'm being annoying, aren't I," I said, but it wasn't exactly a question.

Hunter reached toward me with his good arm, barely wincing as he placed his hand on mine. "No," he promised. He squeezed reassuringly and butterflies fluttered through me. I gripped the seat tighter, then relaxed my hand under the warmth of his.

Hunter was fine—we all were—and the horses and Little Foot were safe and settled. This time, I allowed myself a contented sigh and rested my cheek on his hand. I watched the dense woods flash by the window in the dying afternoon as we continued down the highway; the sound of the diesel engine and the squeak of the truck and trailer over bumps in the road had become white noise days ago.

After a few breaths, Hunter pulled his hand from mine. Another wince. Another clench of his jaw. Then he was settled against the door again. "There's nothing like a run-in with a bunch of supercharged crazy people to remind you how useless you are in an Abilities fight," he said humorously.

"I'm not sure if you noticed," I told him, "but we weren't all useful today. If you hadn't cut Alex free, who knows what might've happened." I hadn't realized how true that was until I said it. "Those vines were debilitating . . . I've never seen anything like it."

The three of us seemed to absorb how truly screwed we would've been as we sat in silence.

"You know," I thought aloud, needing to break the tension, "you're handling all of this better than I expected." Despite the whiskey, I knew how horrified Hunter was of people with Abilities—*crazy* ones, at least. It was hard to believe he could seem so calm. "Like, *way* better." I eyed him carefully. "Are you sure you didn't hit your head too?"

Hunter's grin returned. "My head feels a little swirly, but not because I hit it," he admitted. "And I have other things on my mind at the moment." His smile faltered a little, and as always, I wanted to know what he was thinking. I was about to ask when his eyes fluttered shut. Questions. Curiosities. Uncertainties. I could wade through it later. For now, I was content to watch him doze.

———

B y the time we reached the small safe house outside Prince George, full night had set in. Alex and Bert cleared the place, and we made our way inside with our things.

We were all on autopilot, securing the perimeter and unloading what we needed for the night. My body ached as much as I'd expected after wrestling evil vines, and my mind felt heavy. Hunter wasn't exactly sober, but he wasn't drunk anymore.

"I'll let the horses out," Kat said, dropping her and Hunter's packs by the front door. The bandage on her arm was pink with dried blood.

"We should get you cleaned up when you're finished," I told her.

"I wouldn't mind a hot shower, that's for sure," Kat said, wistful. "But that's not happening." She looked me over, appraising my cuts and bruises again, though she looked as bad as I did. Then, she glanced back at Hunter as he slowly made his way toward the house. "Put him in that little room so he can stretch out on the mattress. The last thing we need is Bert smacking his shoulder or something in his sleep tonight. We'll get our scratches and shit cleaned up later."

"Okay," I said as Kat handed me the solar-powered lantern and turned back for the trailer. I met Hunter's gaze. "Tired?"

"Meh," he said, but his heavy eyelids told me otherwise. If

the events of the day didn't wring him out, the copious amounts of booze he'd consumed over the past few hours likely had.

"Yeah, right. You can barely stay awake."

He lifted his good shoulder carefully, as if he was indifferent, and I laughed.

He leaned down for his pack. "Nope!" I said, and slid it out of his reach. "I'll get it." Shoving his sleeping bag under my arm, I lugged his pack up onto my other shoulder and motioned to the little room. "I'm the one with two working arms," I reminded him. "Get moving."

Hunter didn't seem happy that he was being coddled, but I didn't care. "I think I can manage my pillow, at least," he said glumly. Little did he know his annoyance was more endearing than offensive. I conceded, handing his pillow to him, but I didn't budge on the rest.

Lantern shadows flashed across the walls, and the floorboards creaked as we made our way to the single bedroom. The air was stuffy like last time, making me feel a tad claustrophobic.

"I'll open the window," I told him as we stepped through the doorway. I dropped his pack by the foot of the twin bed and opened the drapes. "It's a nice night. There's no sense in wasting it."

The window protested as I pried it open, and when the brisk evening air hit my skin, I pulled it into my lungs, finally allowing myself to exhale a real, calming breath.

Hunter had discarded his sling on the mattress when I turned back to him, and he tried to pull his dirty shirt off with one hand.

"Hold up—" I strode closer. I hated that he was still wincing. "You're really bad at taking it easy, you know that?"

"There are worse things," he muttered.

"Here . . ." I pulled my pocketknife out of my jeans and flicked the blade open.

Hunter stared at it. "I'm not sure what you're going to do with that, but I'm not sure that's a better solution," he said wryly.

"Trust me, it's the easiest, least painful way to get it off." I pulled the hem of his shirt away from his body, prepared to cut it.

"What if I like this shirt?" Hunter's eyebrow arched with amusement.

"It's a black t-shirt," I deadpanned, tearing it up the side anyway. My head was barely higher than his shoulder. "I'll get you another one. Or," I said, carefully cutting his collar so as not to jerk him around. "You can borrow one of mine." I winked at him, earning myself another one of his gorgeous smiles that made me blush. Pleased with my comeback, and the amusement in his eyes, I peeled the t-shirt off him.

I tried not to flinch when I saw the scars on his back, but as always my curiosity was more than I could wrangle, and I found myself staring blatantly at them. "Can I—" I hesitated, not wanting to be rude. "Can I ask what did this?"

Hunter peered at me over his shoulder, his eyes dark and careful. "Glass."

That set my teeth on edge, my stomach turning. "I'm sorry this happened to you," I breathed, imagining what other horrors younger Hunter had been through.

"It's fine," he murmured, his voice quiet.

"No," I said, stepping in front of him. "It's not fine." But whatever conviction I had was lost on my lips as I studied his chest, broad and unmarred, and my gaze trailed down his abdomen. I'd never admired what hard work on the farm could do to the male form, as much as I did whenever I looked at Hunter.

"Thea," he whispered, and my gaze found his again. "It was a long time ago, and there's nothing I can do about it now."

I nodded dumbly and allowed myself to study Hunter's chiseled features—really see him for the first time—without a lens blurred with dislike or confusion. He wasn't as severe as I'd always thought, just serious and honest. His eyes weren't narrowed on me with contempt, but focused and observant. And his voice wasn't rough and deep with judgement, it was careful and thoughtful. Hunter wasn't dark and menacing at all; he was beautiful.

Outside, the horses whinnied and clomped down the ramp to temporary freedom, but I didn't look away from Hunter. I couldn't. There was something pulling me toward him, even before I'd met him. At first it was curiosity, then it was dislike and disdain, and now . . . Now it felt like an enigmatic pull unlike anything I'd ever experienced before, and it was pointless to fight it.

When Hunter's stomach rumbled, however, I peered down at the corded muscle just below the surface of his skin, feeling another flush burn through me, and I stepped past him.

"Finish changing, and I'll bring us a snack." Flashing Hunter a quick smile, I headed out of the room, pulling the door shut behind me so he could have some privacy. Walking back into the living room, I saw my bag by the door and heaved it up onto a wobbly table.

I could hear the others talking outside, so I grabbed my water bottle, unzipped my bag to grab trail mix and what was left of my honeycomb, then headed back toward the room.

I was painfully aware I was treading a fine line that, if crossed, would shift everything into unknown, possibly heart-break territory. But I tried not to question what I was doing because whatever was happening between Hunter and me felt right, even if it scared me.

Pushing my insecurities to the back of my mind as best I could, I knocked on his door.

"Come in," he murmured.

I opened the door to find Hunter in his sweats, but he stared at the clean shirt in his hand before tossing it back into his bag, as if he didn't have the energy to bother with it.

I didn't mind or blame him.

When he glanced over his shoulder at me in the doorway, I

lifted the honeycomb and trail mix. "Snacks," I explained, and walked to the bed. Setting the trail mix, the jar of honey, and my water on the paint-chipped side table, I unrolled his sleeping bag over the mattress and pointed to it. "Go ahead," I told him. "Get comfortable." I handed him his pillow to lean against and preceded to grimace as I watched him ease himself back into the corner. "Maybe you should put the sling back on." The muscles on his good arm flexed as he propped himself up as best as he could.

"Not right now," he muttered, and unlike I would've done with Beau or Alex, I didn't argue with him. "And you should be getting some rest and not fussing over me. You're the one who was manhandled by mutant vines today and moved the train again."

"I *am* tired," I admitted, "but I'll be fine . . . once I eat something," I added, holding up my jar. "This will fix everything."

"You and your honey," Hunter mumbled, and once he was situated, I sat on the edge of his bed and placed the bag of nuts between us.

"Why is it I'm always visiting you in your sickbed?" I teased, thinking of the clinic.

Hunter huffed a laugh. "It's definitely not by choice."

I opened the honey jar and inhaled the scent of it. "Yum," I whispered, thought I was a little sad it was nearly gone.

"You sure you want to share the last of your honey with me?" he asked wryly. "The trip isn't over and—"

"I'm sure," I said, flashing him a smile. "Although, I've never actually seen you eat honey before. Do you even like it?"

"Not as much as you," he joked. "But yes, I do."

Hunter eyed the honey in the jar, his thoughts drifting somewhere else momentarily, then he seemed to remember I was sitting there and looked at me. "Have you ever tried honey with cheese?" he asked.

"*Cheese*? No."

"Goat cheese is best," he said. "Soft cheese."

My mouth watered at the thought. "Cheese and honey? Those are my two favorite things. How did I never think of that before?"

"Add just a drizzle, maybe throw in some fresh lavender—"

I groaned as I imagined it. "Stop, please. You're killing me."

Hunter grinned. "You can get it all at Mr. Murphy's," he said as he tossed back a handful of pine nuts and almonds.

"You surprise me," I said, cracking a smile. "That almost sounds . . . refined."

He chuckled, popping another nut into his mouth. "I wouldn't go that far." Hunter turned an almond over his hand as his thoughts wandered again. Knowing him like I did now made me feel like such an ass for ever thinking I knew anything about him before.

"I'm so dumb sometimes," I thought aloud.

Hunter's brow furrowed with confusion, and I shook my head. "Never mind." I broke off a piece of the honeycomb, loving the feel against my fingertips, and wound a liquid strand of honey around it. "As always," I said, handing the honeycomb to him. "I forgot napkins." And as the honey dripped down my fingers, I panicked. "Open-open-open," I chanted. I leaned closer to prevent it from dripping all over his sleeping bag and chest and practically shrieked as I plopped the honeycomb into his mouth.

His lips closed around my fingers, and a warm thrill trickled down my spine. I pulled my hand away and cleared my throat. "Sorry if I got any on you," I said, breaking another piece off for myself. After plopping it into my mouth, I sucked the honey off my fingers, afraid to look at Hunter in our close, suddenly charged proximity. I tried to smile the effects of it away. "Maybe this wasn't such a good idea. If we didn't already need show-ers . . . now we definitely do." But even those words felt dangerous, and I could feel Hunter watching me, his gaze scalding against the side of my face, and my blood whirred faster.

I broke off another piece of honeycomb, and against my better judgement, I forced my eyes to his. His gaze was burning, and as he slowly chewed the honeycomb, it was all I could do not to stare at his lips; no, it was all I could do not to recall the taste of his kiss. To yearn for another.

I glanced at the door. "I should go and let you get to sleep." I was dangerously close to kissing him, and I wasn't ready for that yet.

"Only if you want to," he said, his voice a low hum.

I blinked at him.

Hunter leaned his head back against the wall, peering down at me through his dark lashes. "I like this," he admitted.

I swallowed thickly. "Like what?"

"This—you smiling at me. Us getting along." Though his voice was quiet with exhaustion, everything we hadn't said sweltered in the air between us—the room was thick and humid with it. Heavy and intoxicating. "It's nice to be on the receiving end of your smiles once in a while."

I didn't know how to respond, so I said nothing. Instead, I watched his eyelids flit shut and his chest rise and fall as his breathing evened out, until finally, he drifted to sleep.

37

HUNTER

As we drove along the Canadian highway, all I could think about was the past two days.

The crazy people at the bridge and the fear in everyone's eyes.

The look of horror on Thea's face when she thought she'd hurt me.

And the past two nights of Thea and I sitting together, talking into the late-night hours about nothing and everything all at once, until we'd finally passed out. I'd never wanted time to stretch longer, and yet the minutes had flown by too quickly.

"Those clouds look like they're about to piss all over us," Bert said, lifting the radio to his mouth and clicking it on. "I need to whiz before the rain starts pouring down," he told the girls. "And we can refuel the trucks while we're at it."

"Ten-four," Thea replied. I could imagine her music blaring as she sang at the top of her lungs perfectly, the window down and blowing through her hair as she drove the truck behind us. I could barely contain my smile.

As we rounded the next bend, Bert slowed the truck and pulled onto the shoulder. The truck's windshield was cracked, the side window was blown out and covered with part of a tarp, and the driver's seat itself was shot to hell, but Bert acted as if it was just another day on the road.

"How does your Ability work?" I asked as the truck shut off.

"Damn if I know," he grumbled. "It scared the shit out of me the first time I saw a spark coming from my fingers, checking a radio a few days after the outbreak. Now, whatever needs a spark or surge of energy to work, does. I don't have to concentrate as hard as Kat and Thea."

"At least it's handy."

Bert took in the vehicle's condition with a sigh. "Yeah, it's definitely saved my ass a time or two. I'm not sure how long it would've taken Ross and I to get to Whitehorse to meet up with Jackson otherwise." He shook his head. "I'm not going to lie," he continued, his voice low with a dark, distant memory. "It took me a while to cope with it though—Ross and I both. I'm an old dog, Hunter. I don't like new tricks." He looked at me, his bushy, gray eyebrows furrowed. "Those were the dark months. I'm glad you've gotten to know who we are now, not who we were back then." I'd heard Ross was a conduit of death, and could only imagine what life must've been like in the beginning, trying to come to terms with so much pain, turmoil, and confusion.

"Well, I'm glad you guys made it to Whitehorse too. It wouldn't be the same without you. And this trip," I said with a smirk, "would've been something else entirely."

Bert chuckled. "I take that as a compliment," he said, and as he nudged Alex awake in the back seat, I shoved the door open. "Wakey-wakey, sunshine," Bert cooed.

Alex smacked Bert's hand away and groaned, and I left the two of them to bicker.

As soon as I climbed out of the truck, my eyes met Thea's as she stood among a colorful line of horse heads sticking out of the trailer. I flashed her a smile, reveling in the way her expression perked up when I did; it was a sight that could never get old.

Thea smiled back, not her open, natural smile, but a reserved, somewhat shy one that made my pulse quicken a little. Deciding it was better to struggle with a bathroom break now rather than to struggle one-handed, wet and miserable in the rain later, I headed into the trees.

Home was only hours away, and I felt a mixture of relief and uneasiness. I missed my mother and brother, and the routines and comfort of home, but I'd thought off and on all day about what would happen between Thea and I once we were back in White-horse. Once Cal was there and we went back to "normal." Would we only see each other in passing? I didn't want that, but it wasn't my choice to make.

Thunder rumbled in the distance, scrambling my thoughts, and my pace quickened to find a tree out of sight. The wind was picking up, and all I could hear were the rustling birch leaves and pine needles around me.

As I dealt with my business, I thought of Thea again—of her and Cal. He was undeserving of Thea, and even if I knew I had no right, I felt a flare of resentment toward her as well. She was drawing me in, deeper and deeper. The draw between us was undeniable, and I knew she felt it too, even if she tried to ignore it.

Stepping out from around my tree, I walked right into her. "Shit—" I hissed as my arm jostled, and Thea stumbled back.

"Crap, Hunter—sorry." She bit her bottom lip, and her amber eyes veered from my shoulder to meet my gaze. "I'm *so* sorry. I was trying to hurry so I could get back and help Kat—"

"It's fine, Thea. I'm really not that breakable," I told her, unable to resist a smile. I had to admit, I liked her fussing over me. It was far better than the alternative.

Ignoring my reassurances, she rose to her tiptoes, assessing my shoulder. With cool fingers and gentle precision, she lifted the collar of my t-shirt and leaned closer. "It looks swollen," she mused, her brow puckering with worry. Thea was so close I could smell the raspberry balm on her lips and feel the soft cotton of her shirt against my hand. "Why do you have to be so tall?" she muttered, but I was too busy staring at her long eyelashes and rosy cheeks to answer.

A gust of wind whipped around us, blowing her hair into her face, and Thea lowered onto her feet. She ran her fingers through her hair and glowered up at the storm clouds. "The *one* day my hair tie snaps," she groused, and when she looked at me again, a stubborn strand lay haphazard on top of her head.

"It's a nice look, but . . ." I reached to smooth it down, feeling the silkiness of her hair against my palm. It didn't matter that my body felt beat to shit, I was practically giddy to be close to Thea. Everything about her lured me in, making the hours we were apart suddenly unbearable. I would dislocate my arm again if it meant that after this trip she'd still fuss over me.

When I realized I was stroking the strand of hair between my fingers, and she was watching me, I lowered my hand. I couldn't look away though. The tip of her nose was pink, her eyes, glistening like honey, were intent on me as she licked her rosy lips.

The wind came up again, whipping around us, but I didn't feel the cold. All I could feel was my heart thudding in my chest and an itch in my fingers to reach out and touch her again.

"Thea," I started, my mind and body pulling me in different directions. She stared at my mouth as I searched for the words. Tension coiled in my groin and shoulders, and my entire body hummed. But as much as I regretted it, I knew we needed to take a step back or I'd kiss her again, and this time, she might hate me for good. "We should—"

"Shh," she breathed, and like the wind itself swept her closer, Thea rose up and pressed her lips to mine, soft and hesitant.

Warmth flooded through me, and in the split second it took for my surprise to wear off, a wave of need stole its place. Leaning down, I wrapped my good arm around her, pulling her closer. I ignored the twinge in my shoulder and the pitter-patter of raindrops on my skin. Her tongue against mine was the soft-est, most arousing sensation I'd ever felt, and whether it was my imagination or not, she tasted like honey.

My arm tightened around her waist as I inhaled her scent, and Thea's fingers curled into my hair, her moan lost in the echo of raindrops on the forest floor.

Slowly and all too soon, she broke away, her eyes shut, her lips lingered only a hairsbreadth from mine. She looked as if she was trying to steady herself before, finally, she opened them.

I could feel it too—my racing heart was soaring, and my body vibrated with an inexplicable feeling; I squeezed a handful of her shirt in my fist and a groan escaped my chest.

Thea looked at me, wildly searching my face, until she took a step back. "I'm sorry," she rasped, brushing an errant hair away.

"Never be sorry for kissing me," I told her, unable to suppress a grin.

"No, I am—I shouldn't have done that." The raindrops dappled her ivory shirt, and she blinked as water trickled down her temple and over her cheek. She shook her head, but her eyes didn't leave mine. "I'm not myself around you," she said, though it sounded more like a realization.

"Maybe you haven't been yourself until now," I countered.

Thea's chest rose and fell as she considered my words, and I tried and failed to ignore the way her breasts heaved in her tank top. Then I noticed the chills covering her arms and shook the lust away.

"You're cold," I told her, glancing toward the truck, which was honking down by the road.

"No," she said with a breathy laugh. "I'm not cold." Another honk pierced the air. "But we should probably get back before someone has a heart attack."

As Thea turned to head back toward the trucks, I allowed myself a slightly victorious grin. Even if she didn't know what she wanted—even if I could tell part of Thea was still torn, thinking about Cal—at least she saw me as a choice, and that gave me hope.

I was about to follow her when the hair on the back of my neck stood on end, and a sickening feeling overcame me.

"Thea—" I rasped, and lurched forward, grabbing her arm. Her wide eyes slashed to me. "Someone's watching us," I whispered. Whether it was my years of tracking and hunting, or a sixth sense, I could feel it. Eyes. Bodies. People.

With a busted up shoulder and my gun in the truck, all I had was my size and grit going for me. I was worthless.

Thea straightened with apprehension, but I saw her resolve too as her hands fisted at her sides and a steely mask of determination settled over her. "We know you're there," she said, stepping past me.

I was about to stop her when I realized seeing the lurkers was our only defense if Thea was going to protect us.

Muscles coiled, I prepared for whatever came next and scanned the dense woods. Had we been followed by one of the gangs? Even this far north, could it be the cult? Boughs blew in the wind and rain fell harder. The forest looked undisturbed around us until I saw movement between the trees, and a man stepped into view.

"Wait, Thea." I clutched her arm. I could feel her tensing and ready to act beside me. "Just . . . wait." My voice was a whisper, and my eyes fixed on the man's skin, the same color as mine. His dark hair was shaggy around his face, and he was older than me, with a scar across his left cheek, and a hard, dispassionate look to him. He had a quiver strapped to his back and his arrow was pointed directly at me.

A woman stepped out next. She was native to the land, too, and her shotgun was aimed at Thea.

"Hunter . . ." Thea leaned into me, questioning my hesitation.

"Who are you?" I asked, torn between fear and disbelief. They were my people. I let go of Thea and took a step closer.

She reached for me, but we both froze as movement deeper in the forest grabbed our attention. I watched a white man, wrapped in furs and wearing worn leather pants, step out of the trees. His beard was peppered with gray, and his eyes were mischievous and familiar.

"What do you want here?" he said hoarsely, and my heart seized in my chest. That voice—I knew that voice.

I stepped closer, vaguely registering Thea's claw-like grip on my arm as the man and woman straightened their stances, prepared for whatever came next. But I shook my head, remembering the lines around the older man's eyes and the bushiness of his mustache and beard.

His gaze narrowed on me, and I smiled. "I know that glare," I said in awe. Shaking my head, I stepped closer, all fear forgotten. "You're alive?"

He studied me a moment before his lips parted in an incredulous gape. "Is that you, boy?" he said, gesturing for the man and woman to lower their weapons.

I stepped forward and wrapped my arm around Sven before I realized what I was doing. "I can't believe you're alive," I breathed, my vision blurred with tears. He was so familiar, so Sven.

Without a word, he pushed me back, inspecting me as if he couldn't believe I was standing there. I shook my head as I imagined the villagers' expressions when they learned about this. "Wren is going to freak," I told him.

Sven's eyes widened to saucers and he took a step back. "Wren—she's alive?" he sputtered, and tears clouded his gaze.

As the past swirled around me and the memories tumbled like boulders, I nodded, reluctant. "She's one of a few," I told him grimly.

Sven's brow crumpled and he pulled me against him. "It's good to see you, son," he choked out. "It's damn good to see you."

38

THEA

With Little Foot at my side, I followed behind Kat, Alex, Bert, and Hunter as we made our way deeper into the woods behind Sven. The rain had turned to mist, coating the woods in a light fog that felt keenly apt. I was anxious around our new acquaintances, but grateful for the movement. My body was vibrating with pent up adrenaline and discomfort after being primed to strike and do *whatever* was needed to protect us in those woods. Instead, I'd stood on the sidelines of a surprise reunion that felt almost too intimate to witness.

Kat continuously glanced back at me as we traipsed through the spruce. She was worried about me, though I wasn't sure why.

The man and woman who had been with Sven led the way, all of us silent, save for Sven and Hunter as they caught up after more than a decade apart.

"I heard you coming a mile away," Sven said, shaking his head. "It's one of those changes that made me think I *had* gone insane in the beginning—hearing things that weren't there, or at least, things that were so far away I shouldn't have been able to. I was convinced I'd lost my damn mind."

Hunter stepped around a pine trunk, careful not to hit his

shoulder against it. "Have you all been sick then?" he asked. I tried to imagine how Hunter felt with so much discovery so suddenly.

"Only a few of us," Sven said from the front of the line. I wasn't surprised some of them were uninfected. I'd wondered as much when first seeing the man and woman in the woods, knowing they might be like Hunter. It was the only reason I'd hesitated to act this time.

"I was trading in Alberta when it happened," he explained. "And a few unwanted run-ins with other survivors later, I got the hell outta there." He shook his head, like the memories were still too close to the surface. "You can't forget things, no matter how much you want to sometimes, you know?" Sven muttered. "Anyway, when I got to Fort Nelson, I met Liam and Elijah, who had been sick too and were hiding in the outskirts of the community. I'd squatted in their house, unknowingly. Together, we figured out what we could do, and we've been traveling ever since, checking different communities for survivors, trying to make sense of things."

We brushed through the low hanging branches of the dense conifers, and I smelled wood smoke before I saw a campfire. Three women were sitting around it, about my age, boiling water and picking stems off berries.

As we stepped into a makeshift camp by a stream, the three women shot to their feet, the berries falling to the ground, and a man rose from his crouched position next to the water's edge, all of them glancing around in panic.

"They're friends," Sven reassured everyone, and he stepped to the side so we could walk into the clearing completely. Little Foot took that as an opportunity to sniff around and explore, and Sven's companions eyed the wolf carefully.

"He's friendly," I told them, noticing a cluster of horses standing lazily in the mist to the left of camp. In everyone's assessing silence, I could hear the plop of waterdrops on the tarp stretched between temporary shelters, covering drying laundry and a deerskin that hung beneath.

"Hunter is a friend of mine from many years ago," Sven explained, and his companions' expressions softened slightly. "They have a settlement north of here, in Whitehorse."

"The boy from the Nahlin region you went looking for?" one of the young women said. She was petite, her dark hair pulled back in a messy French braid.

Sven chuckled. "Yes," he said, "though he's not so little anymore."

The young woman set the pot of boiling water back on the fire grate and stared at Hunter, her gaze lingering on him as if she wasn't sure what to think.

"I went to the old village last summer," Sven explained, glancing at us. His eyes met Hunter's. "I was holding out hope, but you weren't there."

They'd just missed him. Hunter and his people had been there for over a decade, but by the time Sven had finally made it, they were gone. The thought was sad, and I watched the way Hunter studied the new, uncertain faces watching him, the conditions in which they were living, and his old mentor standing there with contentment in his eyes.

This was what Hunter and Wren had been holding out for, finding more people like them. Untainteds. Natives to the land they were living off. Survivors like us in all ways but one—the most significant.

"I'm Avery," the petite woman said, stepping around the fire. She reached out for Hunter's hand. "And this is my sister, Olivia," she said, pointing to a round-faced, skeptical woman who looked a couple of years older. "And that's Anika." She nodded to another curvy young woman with pale eyes.

Anika waved shyly.

"Hello," Hunter said. He sounded reserved and I wondered if he was still in shock.

"You've met Liam already," Sven said, gesturing to the bowman. "And that brutish looking man over there is Elijah." The man from the river walked closer. His jaw was bristled with dark hair, though he couldn't have been more than thirty or so. "And this beautiful creature," he said, pulling the woman with the shotgun closer, "is my partner, Ehwin. Her sense are keen, like mine, and luckily, she never misses what she aims at." Her brow lifted at that, as if in warning. She wasn't pleased to see us, that much was obvious. Or maybe she was only apprehensive, and rightfully so.

"And what about you two?" Kat asked, glancing between Elijah and Liam. "Sven said you've been sick as well. What are your Abilities?"

Liam, the bowman, pulled his quiver over his head and rested it against the trunk of a tree. "I can smell the water," he said with a surprising baritone. "I always know when it's near."

Perfect for survival, but it wouldn't protect them from madmen. I looked at Elijah, who had lighter skin, but the cut of his jaw and his dark features gave his lineage away. He eyed all of us, no doubt wondering if Sven was being careless by inviting us here.

Suddenly, the hair hanging around my shoulders lifted off my shoulders, and floated in the air around me. *Telekinesis.* After a flare of momentary panic, I laughed and met Elijah's gaze. "Me too," I told him. There weren't very many people with telekinesis in Whitehorse, mostly telepathy and sensory abilities, like Sven and Liam and Jackson.

Elijah's eyebrow lifted with amusement, and I thought I might've seen a twitch of his cheek, and fleetingly, I wondered if I was the only one like him he'd met before. "Have you all been sick?" he asked.

Hunter shook his head. "I haven't—no one in my village got it."

Avery's eyes widened. "The three of us haven't been sick

either," she said, gesturing to the women behind her. I wasn't sure if the sudden brightness in her eyes was innocent surprise, or if Avery realized how lucky she was to have found a man like him. "There were more of us," she added, and her brightness dimmed as she shook her head. Whatever the past twelve years had been like for them, I knew it couldn't have been easy, and we could guess the rest.

"Where are you heading?" Alex asked, glancing around their camp. "It doesn't look like you're planning on staying here indefinitely."

"Somewhere south," Sven said. "We move with the seasons, staying away from the roads and towns as much as we can. We head north in the summers because the salmon are easier to find."

"And you can always find water," I said, glancing at Liam.

Hunter looked at me, thoughtful. I knew what he was thinking. In fact, I think we were all thinking it, but Alex said it first.

"You're always in the elements and looking over your shoulders out here." Alex scanned the group of them. "That sounds like a hard life."

Sven glanced between Alex, Hunter, and then at the rest of us. "It's the way it works these days," he said, sounding exasperated by it all.

"You should come to Whitehorse," Alex told them. "It's safe." He pointed to Hunter. "His village is there, and there is plenty of room for you. We have food and electricity."

While Avery's eyes widened, almost hopeful, Elijah and the other girls didn't seem as excited by the idea.

"Of course you should talk about it," Hunter said, and he stepped forward in a way that commanded their attention. "It's not a decision to be taken lightly. I was skeptical in the beginning, but my people have a livelihood now we'd never had living out here." He tilted his head in Kat and Alex's direction. "And there's protection." Finally, Hunter's eyes met Sven's. "And

Wren would hate me if I didn't make you come see her, even if you decide not to stay."

I watched the deep lines and harshness of the years soften as the older man's expression opened and a mixture of relief and excitement settle in its place.

"We have to get back on the road, though," Bert said, more to Hunter than the others. "We have people expecting us back tonight."

Hunter dipped his chin, reluctant.

A sudden wave of dread washed over me. Of course he wasn't ready to leave, he'd only just found Sven again. I'd been shocked and excited for Hunter, but as I studied the women in the camp, then Sven, who was tethered to Hunter's past, it felt like things had drastically shifted and I might be losing him, even if I couldn't explain it. Even if I'd never really had him to begin with.

"You should stay, Hunter," I whispered, and I felt everyone's attention veer to me. Hunter's gaze, however, lingered on Sven a little longer, like he was torn. "You should spend time with them. You can keep one of the horses and ride back when you're ready."

Eventually, Hunter looked at me, his jaw working and his brow furrowing as he considered it.

Glancing back at Avery and the others, I knew it was right, even if it felt wrong. He deserved more time with them, to not feel rushed.

"No." Hunter shook his head. "I need to get home to my mother, she's been worried about me long enough." He surveyed Sven and the others. "But you should consider their offer to go to Whitehorse. I don't think you'll regret it."

"It's about two-days on horseback," Kat said. "Maybe less if you keep a firm pace."

Sven studied Hunter, and I saw the indecision in the older

man's eyes. Maybe not for himself, because it was clear he wanted to see Wren and the others, but for his companions.

"Whatever the group decides," Sven finally said as he walked over to Hunter. "I will join you now, for a little while, at least." He reached out and clasped Hunter's good shoulder gently. "There's a lot to catch up on, and I'd like to see everyone again. Especially little Wren. It's not every day we get second chances like this, not in this life."

Hunter scoffed. "She's not so little anymore either."

The corner of Sven's mouth curved up in a grin. "No, I guess she wouldn't be, would she?"

"I would like to go as well," Avery said, and I couldn't help the warning glare her sister flashed her. The way Avery looked at Hunter made me wonder if it wasn't her curiosity about him that had her stepping forward while the others clearly hesitated.

Hunter stared at Avery. "Of course." Their gazes lingered on one another and I swallowed thickly, uncertain what silent exchange passed between them.

Finally, Avery looked to the others. "You all want to go, you're just scared. But you know deep down we should do this." She was feisty, I would give her that. She and Wren would get along well, and there was an admiration in Hunter's eyes as Avery continued. "Winter will be here before we know it. We need to at least *see* what's in Whitehorse."

Sven winked at her, and Avery peered around at the others. "Well, are you coming with us, or not?"

39

THEA

e passed by the Whitehorse sign, I peered out the rain-streaked window into the side mirror. Bert was driving too far back to see Hunter, Sven, Ehwin, and Avery clearly, but I could imagine all of them chatting about why the truck was patched together, and about Whitehorse and what to expect as we drew closer.

I peeked behind me at Alex, sleeping in the back seat. His neck was kinked to the side with Little Foot taking up so much room beside him, but Alex was too exhausted to care. I smiled when I noticed the worn photo of Sophie and Fiona pinched between his fingers. While Alex was used to these trips, I knew being away from home was hard for him, even if he never complained about it. And until now, I hadn't realized how "on" Alex had been the entire trip, always contemplating next steps and assessing routes for our journey. It was nice to see he could wind down with the promise of home.

My smile faltered a little. Before today, I would've imagined Hunter in the back seat, thoughtful and quiet, processing all that was new and unknown to him. But things were different now. Hunter was taking Sven and his people under his wing—reassuring them and making them feel welcome and safe as they approached a new, scary place. If the others joined us in White-horse, would they look to Hunter as well, as the leader he was always meant to be?

The Hunter I'd seen with Sven and the others today was the Hunter I'd expected to find the day I first met him. It's why I was so heartbroken to find he was someone else entirely. At least, he'd seemed to be. For Sven and Avery, though, he would be the man he always had been. The man I'd come to know and considered my friend. The man I'd kissed in the woods before everything shifted. Things wouldn't be the same after Hunter's discovery today, and the realization made me sad, even if I wanted to be happy for all of them.

I thought of Cal. I had to tell him about the kiss. He was too good to lie to. He deserved more from me—he deserved the truth, whatever came of it.

The windshield wipers squeaked against the window, jarring me momentarily from my impending reality.

"That's the worst sound in the fucking world," Kat groused, and she turned up the Pat Benatar CD she had in the player to drown it out.

Alex startled and grumbled from the back. "We almost there?"

"Yep," Kat said. "Just about."

The power plant came into view first, then the steel walls of the city. We drove past the guarded entrance of Riverdale, and headed toward the prison.

"At least the horses will be excited to finally be home," I thought aloud.

Kat smiled. "Lord knows I am. No offense, but if I had to go one more night with you kicking me in your sleep . . ."

I snorted. "Yeah, sorry about that."

"Something to warn Hunter about," Kat teased, and puckered her lips.

I sobered instantly.

"You didn't seriously think you'd get out of this without a single remark, did you?" she asked, her smile far too smug and satisfied.

"I hoped," I muttered and looked at her askance. Either she'd seen us kiss in the woods or had a sixth sense. "How did you know?"

Alex laughed. "After watching you two the past couple days, you were either making out or fighting, and we didn't hear any arguing."

Flushing with embarrassment, I tried to laugh, but then I realized whatever had happened before Sven and the others was probably the last thing on Hunter's mind now. Maybe indefinitely.

Kat drove through the open gate of the facility. "Finally," she grumbled.

Despite my unease in coming home to the unknown, a swell of relief filled me when I saw both Ross and Jackson's trucks parked beyond the loading dock. Beau's Jeep was parked beside them. Everything was glowing in the dusky, summer light.

"They're all here," I said happily. My family. The familiar. Home.

"We might be late, but at least we made it," Alex said.

Kat pulled the truck up by the horse paddocks and covered arena, and Bert stopped the other F-250 next to it.

The summer rainstorm still pelted down on us as Kat and I climbed out. "Alex, open the arena," she told him. Little Foot fumbled excitedly into the front to jump out of the truck.

Bert, Hunter, Ehwin, Sven, and Avery climbed out of the other truck. My gaze locked with Hunter's until Avery said something to him as she stared at the prison, and Hunter's attention was stolen away.

The floodlights flicked on, and the doors to the prison swung open as our families hurried out. Fiona jumped excitedly beside

Sophie, and Jade and Del waited under the eaves beside the doors, Elle and Jackson coming out behind them. Ross hurried out next, his attention glued on Kat as she ran to him and jumped into his arms, wrapping her legs around his waist as he held her against him.

Beau and Wren were barely out the door when Wren registered Hunter and Sven, and she froze. Even with all the movement around me, the world seemed to slow. The rain darkened Wren's long sleeves as it continued to sprinkle on her.

"Sven?" Wren breathed, her brow furrowed in disbelief.

He took a step closer to her, his eyes shimmering.

Beau stopped mid-step, realizing who the old man was.

"Hey, little birdy," Sven said. It was easy to drown out everyone's confused mutterings as they took in our guests, but I couldn't look away from Wren's expression. Shocked. Confused. It contorted her features as she processed that he was alive and standing in front of her.

In three steps she wrapped her arms around his shoulders, nearly as tall as he was. "I thought you were dead," she said.

"I thought you were long gone too," he admitted, and he squeezed his eyes shut.

Wren's gaze latched on Hunter's behind him. "How did you . . ." She pulled away, Sven still eyeing her with affectionate disbelief. Wren stared at Hunter's slinged arm, and shook her head like she was overwhelmed with questions. "How did you find each other?" she asked them both.

Hunter wrapped his arm around her. "More like he found us," he said, so quietly I almost didn't hear him.

I was too busy taking in everyone's happiness to care that I was getting drenched in the rain, and when my gaze met Elle's glistening green eyes, I hurried over to her.

"You're home," she breathed, and wrapped her arms around me, squealing with glee as she squeezed me tight. "I can't tell you how much I missed you." She held my shoulders and took a step back. "It's been just me and Jackson—that's never happened before, and I barely knew what to do with myself," she teased.

I chuckled softly and wrapped my arm around her again as an unexpected tension in my shoulders eased, and my heart swelled to near bursting. "I missed you too," I told her. There was something so reassuringly warm about Elle, and I suddenly felt the gripping need to divulge all that had happened—the vaccine and how scared I was for Hunter; the lunatics with Abilities at the bridge; Avery and Sven; the people we'd met in Hope Valley . . .

I sniffled and Elle squeezed me tighter. "Oh, sweetie," she said. "I bet you're glad to be home."

I couldn't help my watery smile. "I could definitely use a nice, long hot shower."

Elle laughed, and I felt Jackson behind me before I turned around. He wrapped me in a big papa bear hug that brought more tears to my eyes. "We missed you, squirt." I could hear the strain of emotion in his voice, and I clung to his damp flannel shirt.

"I missed you too. I thought about you every time I listened to the iPod. And every time stinky Little Foot got into the truck, I thought of Elle and how miserable she'd be." Jackson chuckled as I pulled away.

"I definitely haven't missed that," Elle grumbled, and we walked over to the covered arena with the others.

Beau walked over to me, water dripping off his nose, and he smiled, though his expression was less welcoming and more amused than I'd expected.

I frowned. Nothing good ever came from my brother's amusement. "What?" I asked reluctantly.

Beau nodded toward Hunter, whose teary-eyed mother was rushing over to him with Milo in tow. "I take it the trip was . . . interesting?" Beau prodded.

Elle and Jackson glanced between us, and I straightened. "What's that supposed to mean?"

Grinning, Beau pulled me in for a hug. "He's looked over here ten times in the last two minutes," he whispered in my ear, though he was clearly exaggerating.

"Brat," I muttered as I watched Hunter over Beau's shoulder, introducing Avery to his mother. I couldn't help the pang of disappointment as Letty smiled at Avery, knowing Hunter's mother would never smile at me that way.

Beau dropped his arms from around me. "Well, the truck looks like hell, you all look exhausted . . . It seems like you had quite the adventure."

"Hell yeah, she did," Alex said, coming over to give Elle and Jackson a side hug. Fiona held tight to him in his arms.

I was about to tell Beau it wasn't near the adventure he'd gone on, and yet, I didn't think that was quite true. Leaning in, I tapped Fiona's freckled nose with a wink and she beamed at me. "So," I said, admiring all the happy laughter and smiling faces. "This is what it feels like to be on the receiving end of the welcoming committee."

"Yep." Alex grinned. "And no matter how many times you leave and come home, you'll never grow tired of it."

"What," I said, my eyes widening, "like I'm officially part of the team now or something?" I glanced at Elle and Jackson, both of them smiling at me.

"Hopefully," Alex said with a snort. "You're handy to have around, in case you couldn't tell. And this was Bert's last run."

"What?" Mouth gaping, I watched old Bert chatting with Ross and Kat, and I couldn't imagine the trip without him. "That makes me sad."

"It's been a long time coming," Alex reassured me. "But I think the excitement this trip solidified the decision for him."

I couldn't say I blamed Bert. But did I want to do this again? It felt like a huge step, like I wasn't just little Thea anymore, but I was finally part of the bigger picture. And Alex was right, I came in pretty handy sometimes. Even if I'd been terrified at times, I felt a lot stronger for it too.

"Yeah, okay," I said, nodding as I talked myself into it. "I like that idea."

Jackson winked at me, smiling with pride.

"Great. Then welcome to the transport team, Thea." Alex wrapped his free arm around me, Fiona grinning in his other, and he kissed the top of my head. "Kat and I are glad to have you."

Purpose felt good and I beamed, feeling more rooted to Whitehorse, and even to my family.

As everyone continued their hellos, save for old Took who was probably watching the rainfall from his porch at home, a smuggled ale in hand in Jade's absence, I realized Cal was the only other person missing from the welcome committee. And in that moment, I thought I might see what everyone else did when they looked at us.

Why wasn't my boyfriend there to greet me after weeks away, and the bigger question was, why didn't I care?

40

THEA

When we finally got to the lodge, Elle helped me pull my dirty clothes from my pack, a content smile filling her face as she fussed over my being home.

"So tell me, what was the best part of the trip?" she asked, grabbing an empty laundry basket from the hallway.

Kissing Hunter. The thought startled me, and I glanced at her. Oblivious, Elle pulled out my balled up bathing suit from the side pocket. "I liked the beach in New Bodega," I told her. "And Hope Valley. They have a proper farm there, and everyone was really nice. It was cool to see—" Forcing my mouth shut, I looked at Elle again as I pulled out the last of my dirty clothes, forgetting myself.

She looked at me. "To see what?" she prompted, eager and waiting.

"The Re-gen community," I said, turning to her. "They have a huge settlement there."

Understanding shimmered in Elle's eyes, and a small smile tugged at her lips. "I've heard it's wonderful," she continued. "They deserve a second chance, just like the rest of us. I'm glad they have a safe place."

"It's so much more than that," I said. "You would've been awed by it. When you drive past it on the highway, it looks like a village of its own with little cottages." I stacked the few garments that were still clean on my nightstand. "You'd think it was just a normal settlement, and I guess in some ways it is, but their Abilities take farming and production to a whole new level. They're sort of the glue that keeps the whole area running. It's hard to imagine Hope Valley without them."

"I bet." Elle smiled to herself. "What's California like?"

"It's so different from here, you wouldn't believe." I filled Elle in on the mountain peaks that turned to rolling golden hills, the oak trees, and the heat. I told her about the overgrown highways in Washington, and how the coast was just as beautiful in the south as it was in Alaska, only different.

"And about what happened at the bridge," Elle began. "Jackson told me. How are you holding up?"

"Oh, fine. I mean, it was horrifying in the moment, obviously, but . . . that wasn't the worst part. I hurt Hunter."

"His arm?"

I nodded.

"I'm sure Hunter would rather have an injured arm than whatever fate they had in store for him."

Dumbly, I nodded again, but the fear and the unsettling memory of what happened that day felt more like a dull ache than the blaring, ugly one I expected. "I killed her," I said, saying the words out loud for the first time. "I watched her body hit the side of the mountain."

"Thea," Elle said. "This is the world we live in—making quick, sometimes dangerous decisions is what keeps us alive now. Everyone makes their own choices, whether they're of sound mind or not. You have to survive and protect yourself. You can't carry the poor decisions other people make around with you." Elle's gaze simmered with the ferocity I saw in them when she was her most protective. I missed those eyes, and the reassurance only she—a mother—could give.

"I know," I said. And somehow along the trip I'd finally begun to understand that. "I missed you," I told her, and wrapped my arms around Elle's middle for a hug.

"I missed you too," she breathed, and squeezed me against her. We were the same height, and similar in build, but somehow I still managed to nestle against her perfectly.

"So did Cinder," Elle added. "She will be happy to see you. Wren rode her for you while you were gone, but I'm sure it's not the same."

"Of course she did," I mused. Wren was thoughtful like that, though she'd never admit it. And she always needed to keep busy. "I'll have to thank her." I sighed, my attention shifting to the mess on my bed. "I've missed riding Cinder every day. The truck gets so boring."

"And smelly, depending who you're riding with," Elle teased and chuckled softly. "Are these alive?" She pulled my crusted dirty socks out of my bag without flinching.

"There's no telling." I snorted and heaved my smaller backpack up onto my bed and unzipped it.

Elle glanced at me. "How did it go with Hunter?"

My fingers stilled on the zipper. "How do you mean?"

"Well, you've been through a lot together these past few weeks. And you weren't exactly thrilled he would be joining you on the trip when you left."

"Oh, right," I said, and pulled the empty honey jar out of my backpack. "It was fine." *Fine* was a lackluster word for it, but I was too anxious to think about what my situation with Hunter might be now that we were home, let alone process it out loud yet.

Elle snorted to herself and stared at the empty honey jar I turned over in my hand. "That's a new low, Thea, even for you," she teased.

My palm flew up. "Hey, I didn't pack it. It was a gift."

"A gift?"

I nodded. "From Cal."

Elle looked at me. "Well, that was nice of him."

A waning smile parted my lips. "Yeah, it was." And whatever conversation I had next with Cal would be a difficult one. My stomach knotted with guilt as I realized I'd barely thought of him since coming home. And once more, Hunter flashed to mind.

Exhaling what I could of the mess I'd gotten myself into, I tossed my notebook, my iPod, and earbuds onto the bed as Elle flattened out my duffel bag.

"Well, I know you're exhausted, but I hope you're hungry too," she said, unaware of my inner musings. "Jackson was going to make moose steaks, and I made potato salad this morning."

"Seeing how my mouth is officially watering, I'd say it sounds delicious. I could use a break from granola, dried fruit, and jerky for a while."

"But not honey," Elle teased.

"No," I snorted, "definitely not honey."

Heavy footsteps creaked up the stairs, and Jackson appeared in the hallway. His graying beard was longer and less groomed than when I'd left. "What are you two gossiping about up here?"

"Boys," Elle said with a wink. "And steak."

Jackson smiled. "The rain stopped, so I'll get the grill going." He looked at me, almost curious. "You have a visitor," he finally said.

My heart thudded and my hope swelled. "I do?"

Jackson dipped his chin. "Cal's downstairs."

As the excitement drained away, I knew immediately I was a horrible person and I needed to end things with Cal. Tonight. No matter what possible future Hunter and I might have together. No matter what he decided to do now that Avery and the others were a part of his life.

"Go on," Elle urged, motioning toward the door. She handed Jackson the dirty jar of honey. "I'll finish up here."

With a deep breath, I shoved my hands in my back pockets. Jackson moved out of the way, though I could feel his questioning gaze on me as I trudged past him, across the landing, and down the stairs. That Cal had come all this way to welcome me home should've filled me with joy. But it only made telling him what happened with Hunter harder, because the inevitable look on Cal's face absolutely gutted me, and I hadn't even told him yet.

Cal stood on the deck outside, washed in porch lighting, and as I walked across the living room and opened the screen door, he turned around. A smile tugged at his lips, and if I wasn't mistaken, he seemed reticent as he came in for a hug.

"Hey," he whispered. "I missed you." His arms were strong, and his familiarity was as warm and comforting as a winter blanket.

"I missed you too," I said, and even if I didn't get butterflies around Cal, like I did with Hunter, I still meant it. "A lot."

His arms lingered around me before he straightened, and I could feel his sudden distance, like he knew I'd broken my promise. Biting the inside of my cheek, I moved toward the steps. "Shall we go for a walk?"

Cal nodded, but he didn't take my hand in his like he usually did. "I wasn't sure what day you were coming back," he admitted, heading down the stairs ahead of me. "Meghann saw Hunter and his mother go by my house tonight, so I assumed you were home."

"Yeah, just a couple hours ago," I said, falling into step behind him. The stairs creaked and the ground was soggy and wet as I stepped onto it.

Cal glanced at me over his shoulder as I came up beside him. "I had Ross drop me off so I could see you."

"I'm glad you did." We made our way through the property,

toward the river, our footsteps and the sound of the river filling our silence until he spoke.

"So," he started. Our conversation was strange and stilted, or maybe it just seemed that way because of my guilty conscious, but it already felt different between us. "You probably never want to get in a truck again after all of that driving, huh?"

I thought about the company I'd had and shrugged. "It wasn't so bad."

"Really? I thought you would've been glad to get away from Hunter."

I sighed, forcing myself to use this moment to confess. "It's not like that, Cal, not anymore."

My regret was palpable, and Cal stopped as our eyes met. I could see his skepticism in the pale light from the clouded moon, and before he could ask me anything, I remembered the honey. "Thank you for my parting gift, by the way," I told him. "I did my very best to stretch it out during the trip. I barely made it, but somehow I showed unprecedented willpower and—"

"What gift?" he asked.

"The honey," I said, but my gratitude began to waver. "The jar," I added, as if that would alter his confused expression.

Cal shook his head. "I didn't give you any honey, but I wish I'd thought of it." He started walking and I reached for his arm.

"Wait—" Cal turned to me. "You didn't give me the honey? Then who . . ." My mouth gaped. *Hunter?* That made no sense. We weren't friends at the time. Why would he have given me honey, and why hadn't he said anything when I told him I thought it was from Cal?

I blinked dumbly as I considered it, but I really didn't have to; somewhere deep down, I knew it was Hunter. "He'd wanted to thank me," I remembered aloud. But we'd argued and he must've changed his mind. "Kat put it in my bag, but it was from him . . ."

I looked at Cal, his eyebrows lowered in a perturbed expression.

I shook my head. "I'm an idiot," I breathed. Actually, I felt like an asshole, having talked about Cal, and the entire time, Hunter said nothing to me.

Annoyance made my blood simmer. Annoyance and humiliation.

When I realized Cal was staring at me, seeing far too much, my cheeks reddened for a different reason. "Sorry," I told him. "I just—I thought this whole time you had given it to me."

"I'm sorry if I disappointed you," he said, but I couldn't tell if it was regret or bewilderment in his voice.

I waved his apology away. "It was my mistake, I guess." Hunter had been talking to me about honey and cheese and lavender. I shook my head. "Wow," I muttered.

"So, it's been an interesting trip, huh?" Cal prompted, watching me closely.

When I met his gaze again, I knew I had to tell him. "You could say that," I admitted. "A lot has changed."

"Well, since you mentioned it," Cal started. "I wasn't going to say this now, not since you've only just got home, but a lot's changed for me too." His voice was as hesitant as I felt.

My eyes shot to his in a sudden panic. "What do you mean?"

"I know we've been through a lot, and I care about you, Thea, but—"

"You think we should break up," I finished for him. While a huge part of me was relieved, another part of me was strangely saddened. "Why, because of Hunter?"

Cal blinked at me, a few moments hanging between us before he shook his head. "No," he said, looking at me suspiciously. "Wait, you tell me."

I shook my head. "Tell me whatever you were going to say."

Cal ran his hand over his blonde hair and heaved out a sigh, peering around the shadowed property. "I know it's shitty of me, but while you were gone, I spent a lot of time with Marica, and I —I like her." I could feel Cal's unease as he confessed. I felt the knot in my stomach tighten and ease at once. "We haven't done anything or—"

"I kissed Hunter," I blurted. Dread ran like cold water down my back. I swallowed thickly. "So before you feel bad for liking her and *not* doing anything, you should know that I kissed Hunter and I feel like an asshole."

Cal and I stared at each other. "Ouch," he said, his eyes cutting away from me.

I grimaced. "I know. I didn't mean to, it just sort of . . . happened. I can't explain it."

Cal rested his hands on his hips as he stared down at his feet. "I get it—it's unexpected, but . . . I get it," he said, surprising me. "That's how I feel with Marica. I keep finding reasons to stop by the Survival Center to see her, offering to help her with things. I told myself I was bored because you were gone, but then I realized it's just—"

"Different."

He dipped his chin, slow and thoughtful. "Exactly."

Cal and I looked at one another for a minute. He was my best friend, and until this moment, he'd been my boyfriend and the only person I trusted with my heart. "How did things change so quickly?" I said.

Hesitant, Cal shook his head, like he wasn't quite sure. "Maybe they changed a long time ago, we just didn't notice."

"Or," I added with a sudden realization, "they were never what we thought they were."

Cal's eyes held mine as we stood facing each other, letting our new reality sink in. Whatever we'd had together was over, and as sad as a small part of me was, the closing of this chapter in our lives seemed right too.

I heaved a breath, feeling a huge weight lift from my chest. "What a surreal day," I whispered. Cal nodded toward the river and we continued toward it. "I was anxious about telling you, and now that I've told you, I'm anxious about what happens now."

"What do you mean?"

I shoved my hands in my back pockets. "We've brought some people back with us."

"Ah." Cal nodded. "The older guy and the two women—Meghann saw them walking with Hunter's family toward the village."

Sighing, I picked a piece of fireweed with my mind and levitated it to my fingers. "Yeah, and more of them might come."

Cal eyed me a moment, staring between the fireweed blossom and me, then he continued. "You think that changes things—with you two, I mean?"

"Yeah," I breathed. "I think it might." We walked in silence before stopping at the water's edge, a rocky shore I played at as a kid. "It was only a kiss," I told him, though in reality it was two. "But it still feels . . . important, and like I can't ignore it." Discarding my flower, I bent down and grabbed a smooth stone from the bank and skipped it across the water. The moon's reflection rippled and glistened.

Cal bent down and did the same. "You think, what, that Hunter suddenly won't like you anymore or something?"

I shrugged but it felt more earth-shattering than a maybe. "Yeah, I guess."

Cal gave me a sidelong look, like for the first time he didn't know what to think and was trying to figure me out. "It's so weird to think of you two together—you couldn't stand him weeks ago."

"I know. I'm sort of a mess, in case you didn't notice," I said, and a self-deprecating laugh bubbled out of me.

"Sometimes." Cal winked and skipped another stone across the water. "Look, Hunter's been here for over a year, and it seems very coincidental that he chooses now to act like he likes you. There has to be a reason."

My brow furrowed and I glanced from the ripples on the water to Cal. "What do you mean?"

"He just got the vaccine, right?"

"Why?" Cheeks heating, I averted my gaze. "What's that got to do with anything?" Though now that Cal brought it up, Hunter kissing me after going through the procedure did feel a bit more significant.

"The timing is interesting, that's all. Now that you're, you know, an option. Maybe he's liked you longer than you think, but there was nothing he could do about it."

Before I allowed myself to think too much about it, I shook my head. Whatever Hunter's feelings or reasoning might've been when he kissed me was before Avery and the others came into the picture.

Cal shrugged. "It's just an observation."

Forcing myself not to think about that right now, not until I talked to Hunter and figured out where he stood on things, I looked at Cal. "So, what will you do about Marica? I feel like the two of you have always had a connection, one I sort of ruined."

"Nah, you didn't ruin anything, but even if she doesn't like me and has only been flirting, I have to tell her how I feel."

"I get it." And I did. Talking to Hunter was the only thing I could think about. "Why are things always so complicated?" I asked, though it was more rhetorical than anything.

"Because even if we can move things with our minds and look invisible, we are still human," Cal said easily. "If anything, I think it makes us hold on to people harder—any bit of comfort, actually."

It made perfect sense. Cal felt like the best thing I had in the moment I needed him most, which was why I hadn't wanted to let him go. "True. And I know why I've been holding onto you," I realized. "You're my best friend—the only person who knows everything and loves me still." He looked at me, his eyes soft. "But, what about you, Cal?" I worried he had been with me out of pity or fear of hurting me, that I'd been so fragile he'd wasted the last year and a half doing what was right instead of what he really wanted.

Cal stepped closer, his lips pursed and his brow furrowed. "I've never felt like I really belonged here," he admitted. "I've been the bad boy and the poster child, but with you, I just felt like me. I guess I needed you as much as you needed me."

My eyes pricked with tears, happy ones that made me feel as if Cal would always be my friend, no matter what, and I would always be his. I wrapped my arms around his neck. "I do love you, Cal."

"Love you too," he murmured, squeezing his arms around me. We stood there for a few heartbeats, saying a silent sort of goodbye. "Whatever happens," Cal said, "I'll always be here if you need me."

I smiled against his shoulder, feeling like, despite whatever came next, everything would be okay. "Ditto."

41

THEA

The next day, I rode Cinder into town. It was good to get on her again, familiar and comforting in a way I hadn't realized I'd missed over the weeks. But then, she was my traveling companion and had been for years. Every camping and hunting trip, every day on my rides into Whitehorse. So trotting into town should've felt normal, though it felt anything *but* that.

I told myself I was going to check on the horses at the facility to see how they were settling in, and while I *was* planning on it, I steered Cinder toward the village before I could stop myself.

I'd also told myself I was going to take time to think about what might happen between Hunter and me, but I couldn't get him out of my mind after I'd learned about the honey. I kept thinking about our kiss, and about Avery, and how knowing women his own age like him might have changed everything between us.

As Village Row came into view, I noticed the gold-coated, white-maned mare in the pasture with Dancer and smiled. A part of me wished I'd been there to see Milo's surprise when he met Sadie, and also the happiness on Hunter's face in giving his brother such a gift. I could imagine Hunter smiling with genuine contentment.

When I didn't see him in the field, or his mother or brother, I debated whether I should knock on his front door. He was still healing and could be resting. *Or with Sven and Avery.*

Just as I thought better of coming at all, I heard my name in the form of a question.

I glanced at the greenhouse as Hunter stepped out with a basket of herbs clutched in his good hand. I tried to quell the fluttering in my stomach as I took the sight of him in.

He was just as alluring as I'd remembered him, his eyes just as keen and dark, his jaw just as chiseled. He wore his usual black t-shirt, jeans, and boots, though he wasn't sweating or covered in dirt like he often was. It hadn't been twenty-four hours, and I was taking the sight of him in as if it had been days.

Steeling my nerves, I swung my leg over Cinder and dismounted before meeting Hunter's eyes again. His heavy footsteps ceased as he stopped beside me, Cinder sniffing his arm in the sling with curiosity.

"I see Milo got his new horse," I said, tilting my head to Sadie, happily eating from her food pail. "Has he ridden her yet?"

Hunter pried his gaze from me and looked at the mare, shaking his head. "No, I need to show Milo how to saddle her, and—" He lifted his slinged arm a little. "As you can see, I'm still on light duty. I promised my mother I'd wear this today, but it comes off tomorrow," he muttered. "I can't stand it." That he'd worn it even this long was surprising.

"Your mother's right, you're still healing—"

"It's sore, but I'm fine," he said with a huff of exasperation. "And don't worry, I'll still take it easy."

My eyebrow rose skeptically. "You better."

Hunter's eyes shifted over me, so quick I barely registered it, but as a warm tingling shot through me, I thought of the others.

"Where is everyone?" I glanced around. "I don't even see your mom or Milo."

"They're at Otto's with Sven and Avery," he said. "My mother's taken a shine to Avery—"

"Of course she has," I muttered, and Hunter's brow furrowed. A brush of heat licked up the side of my neck and I cleared my throat. "I mean, it makes sense."

Hunter eyed me carefully. "Sven wanted to catch up with everyone," he continued. "And Henni and Wren are there, obviously. They all have questions for one another."

Given the fact Hunter was the head of the community, I couldn't help but ask, "Why aren't you there?"

He glanced at Otto and Henni's house. "I had hours to talk to Sven yesterday," he said, thoughtful. "And they already have a house full, so I figured I'd get some things done out here."

I shoved my hands in my back pockets, wondering if Hunter could feel the unease growing between us, or if it was just me. The way he eyed the house made me curious. "How do you feel about them being here?" I hated to ask, afraid to learn what he was thinking, but Hunter asked me not to assume things about him anymore, so I couldn't stop myself; I had so many stomach-knotting questions.

Hunter's attention shifted back to me, his eyes unfocused. "I'm glad they're here," he said, if a bit distant. "Though it still doesn't feel real—that Sven is actually alive and there are other Untainteds out there."

Ah yes, I was a Tainted. The reference still made me cringe, but I didn't take it personally.

Regret flashed over Hunter's face, "I didn't mean it like that," he said quietly.

"I know." I waved the apology in his voice away. "I totally get it."

Hunter and I stared at one another for a moment, and the

longer I stood there, the more out of place I felt. And the more I questioned whether I should've come.

Finally, Hunter nodded toward the barn. "Come say hi to Sadie."

I smiled as he headed over. "Oh—hold up," I chirped. Hunter stopped as I walked to Cinder's saddlebag and pulled out a clean jar and offered it to him.

"What's this for?" Hunter asked, setting the basket down on the rutted asphalt. He studied the jar as he took it from me.

"It's the honey jar. I figure you owe me a refill for screwing with my head." I told him, lifting my eyebrow wryly.

Understanding dawned on his features, and amusement filled his gaze. "I owe you *more?*" he clarified.

"Yes. And you can give it to me yourself this time—you know, so that there's no further confusion about where it came from."

A slight smile tugged at his lips. "How did you finally figure it out?"

"I thanked Cal, of course. And he was clueless." I shook my head and my hands pinned themselves on my hips. "Why the hell didn't you tell me? Instead, you made me look like an idiot."

"An idiot?"

"Yeah. I'm sitting there acting all happy that Cal got me something, and the entire time it was you. Why didn't you say anything?"

Hunter dropped the jar into the basket of herbs at his feet. "Because," he said, "I thought it would be more awkward. We weren't getting along, and the last thing I wanted to do was argue more. I figured silence was best."

"But then you let me keep thinking it," I told him. "Even after we were, you know, friends." The word felt inadequate and uncomfortable on my tongue.

"Thea, it's just honey. Why is it such a big deal?"

"*Why?*" I repeated. My heart began to race as his question

settled over me. "Because other than my family, no one's ever given me a gift before, and I—I didn't even get to thank you for it. Instead, I looked like an asshole praising Cal for it."

Hunter brushed his hand over his short black hair. "It means that much to you?"

"Yes, it does."

"Then, I'm sorry. I didn't do it out of spite or to make you feel bad."

I eyed him skeptically. "So, you'll get me more then, and give it to me yourself this time?"

He chuckled, making my cheeks warm and my chest flutter with lightness. I loved his laugh—craved it, actually. "Sure. I'll get you more," he said, and snatched his basket up again. "Come on. Say hi to Sadie."

I led Cinder closer to the barn and wrapped her reins around a stall rail.

Sadie's tail flicked as she finished her lunch. "She looks happy here," I said, and walked into the barn behind Hunter.

"Most horses do when their bellies are full."

"True." I smiled and reached through the rail to comb Sadie's forelock with my fingers. "So what else do you need for Milo? A saddle or a halter maybe? We have an extra one of each at the facility we haven't had to use in years. I'm sure Kat would let him have them, or at least borrow them until he gets his own."

Hunter stepped up beside me. "Thanks, but I think we're okay for now."

I nodded and folded my arms over the top rail, watching the way Sadie sniffed around her pail for the last bit of oat dust to lick clean.

Hunter was close, his scent of earth and basil filled my nose, and his gaze was intent, heating the side of my face. When I looked at him, he was staring at me. "What?" I asked softly.

His head tilted ever so slightly. "What did Cal have to say when he found out about the honey?"

"I don't know. Confused, I guess? He didn't have much to say about it," I admitted, and apparently that was the wrong answer because Hunter's eyes darkened.

"Is he even happy you're home?" His voice held a sharpness I hadn't heard in a long time, and it made me bristle.

"Yes," I bit out. "He came to see me last night, right after I arrived. He saw you and knew we were back."

Hunter's scrutinizing stare lingered before he turned and set the basket on an empty table against the tack wall.

"What's wrong? Why are you upset?" I asked.

Hunter shook his head but didn't say anything.

"What?" I repeated.

"I saw him with that girl last night," he gritted out. "So it seems he went to visit you both."

As I realized where Hunter's mind was going, I rested my hand on his arm. "It's fine," I told him.

"No, it's not fine, Thea. You deserve better than this. Cal should care if a guy gives you a gift. And he shouldn't be hanging around other girls—it's like he doesn't care who sees him."

"I'm the one who kissed someone else," I reminded Hunter. "Not Cal."

"That you know of," Hunter muttered.

"He would've told me—"

"Yeah, right."

"*I* told *him.*"

Hunter's gaze shot to me.

"He could've told me then," I reassured him. "And Cal is a better guy than you think, Hunter, so stop assuming the worst."

His eyebrows drew together and he leaned his good arm against the rail. "What did he say when you told him?" he asked, his attention everywhere but my direction.

"We broke up," I said quietly.

Hunter's gaze cut back to me, studying me with a crumpled brow. "Are you okay?" he said more calmly this time.

I was about to shrug because it felt like I should be more upset about it, but I wasn't. Instead, I felt lighter. "It needed to happen," I admitted, and what looked like guilt shadowed the copper flecks in Hunter's eyes.

"It was a mutual decision—Cal wasn't mad." I leaned back against the railing beside Hunter, our arms touching, and exhaled a deep breath. "We've been holding on for a long time, but it's never felt . . . right. When he told me he had feelings for Marica, I was relieved, to be honest. It didn't make me feel like such a jerk for wanting to break up."

Hunter's focus on me was laser-sharp. "Why *did* you break up with him?"

"Because he's not the one," I said simply.

Hunter's jaw clenched, a telltale sign he was battling with himself about something. And in his silence, I continued. "I don't know what happens now, only that breaking up was the right thing to do."

Sadie's tail whipped around as she clomped out into the sunshine, leaving Hunter and I standing in utter quietness. I looked at him sidelong. His eyes were unfocused as his jaw continued to work, clearly lost in whatever mental maelstrom battled inside him.

"Please tell me what you're thinking about," I said. It was a desperate whisper. Some vain and insecure part of me needed him to voice the emotions I hoped played behind those dark eyes of his. The more I realized how badly I wanted to be with Hunter, the more I feared it was too late and he was beginning to question everything.

"I'm just . . . processing," he finally said.

"Processing what?"

His eyes narrowed in consideration. "How new this feeling is."

I blinked at him. "What feeling?" I rasped.

Hunter bit the side of his lip, as if finally coming to a conclusion. "It feels wrong to be glad you're not with Cal anymore, but I've hoped for it for months."

Months? A laugh bubbled out of me. "What do you mean?" But even in my amusement, Hunter's severe expression went unchanged—fixed beyond me, perhaps to a time before or a distant future.

Finally, Hunter stepped closer and my heart crept up into my throat. His chest was inches from mine, his gaze unwavering. "I can't explain it," he said, his voice dark and rich, like the chocolate color of his eyes. "I just know that since the day I met you, I've felt drawn to you, and even if I didn't particularly like you in the beginning, I couldn't stop thinking about you either."

My heart soared hearing such beautifully disconcerting words. Never mind that he didn't like me. The fact that he'd been thinking about me despite himself made me bite back a goonish smile. "Same. But . . ." I swallowed thickly. "What about the others?"

Hunter blinked, his intent focus wavering as he frowned. "What about them?"

"I . . ." My cheeks reddened and I nearly took a step back to escape his scowl already shifting into place. "I wasn't sure if knowing Avery and the others changed things, or—"

"Or what?" he said warily.

"I saw your mother's face when she met Avery, Hunter. I know she would be happier if you wanted to be with—"

"With someone I just met and don't have feelings for?"

Disbelief tinged his words, and I swallowed my embarrassment and unease. "Yeah," I hedged. "I guess."

"My mother doesn't get to decide those things, Thea. You're the one I want, not Avery or her sister—it doesn't work that way, you know." He seemed almost offended by my assumption, but I didn't blame him.

"I know . . . it's just—I feel like so much has changed and I liked how it was on the road. I worry that being home will make things go back to the way they were, especially now that you'll be busy with the others, and I . . ." I shook my head and forced myself to look at him. "I don't want it to."

Hunter's gaze drifted to my lips. I knew that look. I'd come to know it very well in the past weeks. It was desire, dark and dangerous and sending my stomach fluttering.

In a blink. A heartbeat. In the swirl of a second, Hunter's mouth was on mine. Ravenous and urgent. It chased away every insecurity and fear, and every anxious thought clouding my mind since we'd returned vanquished. I could feel his relief and need and hope, as if it was oxygen seeping into me, making me dizzy.

He broke away, his breath hot against my face. "Never doubt how I feel about you, Thea," he rasped against my lips.

I nodded in a frenzy. "Okay," I breathed before my lips were seeking his again. We stumbled back, his solid body pressing mine against the paddock railing. His rough palm was hot against my jaw and cheek, his fingers kneaded in my hair.

My hands roamed down his back, fisting his shirt as I pulled him closer.

"It's Cinder—Mom look!"

Hearing Milo, I pushed Hunter away, my heart hammering and my eyes wide as they met his.

My lips were red; I could feel them, kiss-swollen and pink, and I wiped the back of my arm across my mouth as I spun around, just as Milo ran into the barn.

"Thea's here!" he chirped. "Are you going to teach me to ride?" His face brimmed with eagerness.

I forced a smile and shook my head. "Uh—no, not today," I sputtered. "I wanted to see how you liked your new horse." I glanced at Hunter who was as straight-faced as ever, and for the first time, I envied his collected exterior.

Letty stepped into the doorway behind Milo. Her long black

braid was draped over her shoulder, the crown of her head mussed from wearing her sun hat, and her expression was more severe than Hunter's as she glanced between us. We were definitely busted.

Hunter and his mother stared at one another, something uncomfortable passing between them, and I cleared my throat. "I should go."

Finally, Hunter tore his gaze away from Letty and looked at me. "I'll walk you out."

His mother eyed me without saying a word.

"Goodbye, Milo. We'll go riding soon," I told him.

"Okay!" he said, so excited about his horse he didn't seem to register the suffocating tension in the barn.

"Bye," I said, glancing at Letty as I stepped by her, anxious to be far away from whatever came next.

"Goodbye, Thea," she said, but she didn't look at me. I shuddered as I hurried to Cinder. My name had never felt more condemning as it did passing through that woman's lips.

42

HUNTER

I could feel my mother's glare searing a hole in my back as Thea rode away. My heart was still pounding from the surprise of her news and the touch of her lips against mine again, a moment I'd dared to hope for since our kiss in the woods.

No more Cal. Part of me thought I should've been more remorseful after kissing her that first night, knowing she had a boyfriend. But had I not done it, things would be different. She wouldn't have left with kiss-swollen lips and an impassioned glint in her eyes I already yearned to see again.

When I couldn't postpone my mother's seething any longer, I turned to face her, my eyes barely meeting hers before I strode back into the barn.

"So you leave for a few weeks and come back completely different," she said flatly. Her footsteps sounded as disapproving as her tone.

Milo looked up from grooming Sadie, his gaze flicking apprehensively between my mother and me. I winked at him in reassurance.

"Not completely," I said wryly, and I reached for the herb basket I'd brought from the greenhouse.

"Hunter, this is important," she bit out.

"I can tell," I muttered.

"Look at me," she commanded.

Slowly, I turned around, seeing the hard edges of anger etched on my mother's face, but also the shadows of fear. "You can't be serious, Hunter."

"Serious about what, Mother?" I said flatly.

"About *her.* She can't be your choice."

"Her name is Thea," I reminded her. "And why not her? Because I promise you, no matter who I chose to be with, you'd feel the same way. In fact, I thought you'd be happy because you didn't much care for Wren either."

"I like Wren just fine," she said, taken aback. "She's a hard worker."

"So is Thea."

"Wren is smart, I know her family, and she's—"

"One of us," I finished for her. "That's what this is about."

My mother swallowed and shook her head, but she wouldn't look at me. "I just thought that, now that there are others, now that we know—"

"Know what?" I gritted out, resenting how easily she thought she could plan my life in whatever way suited her. "Because there are more people like us, I'm supposed to just pick one and pop out some kids?"

Her eyes widened and flicked to Milo. "Watch your tone," she warned me. "And no, this has nothing to do with that."

"Yes, it does. I had to be with Wren because she was the only option, and now that I want to be with Thea, who I actually have feelings for, suddenly you think Wren was a better option because you dislike the idea of Thea even more."

"And now that you've taken that dangerous vaccine, you would be so reckless as to risk your life for a pretty girl you're infatuated with? You've barely spoken to her. You can't have *real* feelings for her—"

"Don't tell me how I feel," I bit out. "How would you even know?" My eyes narrowed on her. "You've never once asked me what I want, Mother. You've never let me decide anything for myself. You mistake my wanting to help my people all of these years with a control you don't have over me. And you definitely don't get to decide my future. I'm old enough to make my own decisions, I have been since I was a boy. You have no say in what makes me happy. Not when you've never cared before— not when you don't even know what happiness is."

My mother's eyes rounded, and she gaped at me. "But our people—"

"Which I've only *ever* worried about," I reminded her. "Until now."

I stepped closer and lowered my voice. "You're intelligent, Mother. You know as well as I do that things are different now. We don't live in a bubble anymore. Wren is with Beau. Wren and I never felt about each other what I feel for Thea, and *that's* what's real. I pick what and who makes me happy. Not you." I forced myself to take a deep breath, a desperate feeling clawing at me as I realized my mother might ruin this for me. I took a much-needed step back. "I would've thought my happiness counted for something," I said, unable to keep the hurt from my voice. I glanced at my brother, staring between us, and exhaling my frustration, I shook my head. "I care about Thea, Mother. You can either accept it or not, but she's the one I want, if she'll have me."

My mother blinked at me, ire lighting her eyes and her jaw working. She had too much control to look hurt by my words, but I saw the sheen of it clearly.

"If you love me," I said more calmly. "Don't get in my way."

43

THEA

C inder clomped down the street toward the grocer's. All night I'd only been able to think about Hunter, feeling giddy and restless at the same time, and torn between confusion and glee. I didn't know what would happen next, but I was excited to find out. Not even Letty's glower yesterday could dampen my mood.

I brought Cinder to a stop outside Mr. Murphy's. "I'll be back," I said, patting her neck. "Maybe he'll throw in an apple for you while we're here." Cinder's dark ears perked up, and I headed into the shop.

"Ah, Thea," he said, handing Meghann a basket of potatoes. "You're here for some sugar for Elle's raspberry jam, right?"

I nodded as Meghann spun around. "Thea," she said in surprise.

After he finished up with his customer, Mr. Murphy disappeared into the back.

Meghann's expression was downcast as she appraised me. "How are you holding up? Are you all right? Cal mentioned what happened between you two the other night."

"I'm fine," I told her, glad there wasn't anyone else in the shop to listen in. "It was a mutual decision. We're still friends."

Meghann nodded, but she still looked sad. "Oh, all right, if you both say so. I hope you won't stop coming around every so often. With Cal always with Ross, it's nice to have some company every now and again."

I smiled, if a little weak. "Of course I'll stop by," I told her, wishing Hunter's mom had even an ounce of affection for me the way Meghann always had.

"Okay, well, I'll leave you to your errands." Meghann lifted her basket. "I'm making potato salad for the scouts' campout tomorrow. If you see Beau, will you tell him for me?"

"Of course I will," I said, happy to have a reason to stop by Village Row to see Hunter on my way home.

As I stepped up to the counter to await Mr. Murphy, Meghann stopped short behind me. "Oh, Letty, I didn't see you."

A wave of nausea churned inside me.

"Meghann," Letty said tightly in greeting. It was unnerving how naturally her voice conjured so much anxiety.

"And you must be one of our newest guests—Avery, is it?" I didn't have the nerve to look back at the exchange and meet Letty's gaze, not after what she'd walked into yesterday.

Meghann and Avery had a brief exchange before Letty said, "Have a good day," and I heard Meghann's retreating footsteps. Then it was just them and me, and I could feel Letty's dagger-like attention spearing me from behind. I couldn't ignore her though, not forever, and I had to try to make peace with her for Hunter.

Slowly, I turned around. Letty didn't look angry, per se, but she didn't look pleased to have crossed paths either. Avery, on the other hand, smiled, if a little awkwardly, and waved.

"Here you are," Mr. Murphy said as he brought a sack of sugar over for me. "You—" His words fell short when he saw

Letty, and he cleared his throat. "Oh, good afternoon, Letty. I didn't expect to see you today."

She blinked, and her attention on me wavered as she looked at him and dipped her chin with a twitch of a smile. "Gus," she said.

Gus? No one called Mr. Murphy by his first name, and if I wasn't mistaken, Letty averted her gaze a little too quickly, as if she felt uncomfortable under the weight of his stare. I glanced curiously between them.

"I've run out of willow bark," she explained, taking a step closer to the counter.

"Yes, of course. I have some in the back. Let me go grab some for you. I still owe you for the extra carrots last week, so the willow bark's on the house."

"Thank you, Gus," she said, and lucky for me, Letty began her survey of the store.

"Oh, and Mr. Murphy?" I called back to him, remembering a last minute item. "Can I get some popcorn kernels for Jackson—whatever will fit in a jar?"

As he came from the back with Letty's willow bark, he winked at me, his cheeks rounding with a smile. "You got it, Thea." The storekeeper opened the sack behind him and poured four scoops of corn kernels into a mason jar. It was from Hunter's fields, I realized.

"So," I said, aware that Avery was still standing in the center of the small store as Letty shopped; she didn't seem to know what to do with herself. "Have you heard from the others, Avery? Will you all be staying?"

Avery sighed and shook her head. "I am, but I don't know about the rest of them. My sister may come, but she's stubborn. And I think she likes Liam, so if he doesn't, it's going to take some persuading."

"Oh." I thought about Liam and Elijah. Both had been infected. "Did Hunter tell you about the vaccine we brought back?" I asked quietly. It would be the only way they could be together.

Avery leaned closer, glancing at Letty who, as far as I could tell, was oblivious to our conversation. "Wren did. Apparently Hunter felt it would be weird coming from him, which I actually appreciated. He's the last person I'd feel comfortable talking to me about sex," she said with a snort. "He's very . . . intimidating. It would've been really awkward."

I tried not to laugh. "I used to think so too," I admitted. "I'm glad Wren talked to you about it."

"Here you are, Thea," Mr. Murphy said, placing my items down.

"And can I steal an apple for Cinder?"

He winked at me again. "You know where they are."

"Thank you!" I chirped, sliding my sugar bag off the counter and snatching the corn kernels with the other hand. I turned back to say goodbye to Avery. "I know you don't know me very well, but if you have any questions, or if you need anything, just let me know."

"Thanks, Thea." Avery looked a bit relieved, and I waved a little goodbye as I skedaddled out of the shop.

But it wasn't fast enough. I was putting the corn kernels in my saddlebag when I felt a presence behind me, and I knew instinctively who it was. With a deep inhale, I turned around.

Letty was standing a few feet back, her ashen eyes assessing me as her grip tightened around the basket in her hand.

I braced myself, knowing that whatever future I might have with Hunter was worth fighting for, whatever might come next.

Letty's eyes held mine a moment. "You care for my son?" she finally asked, her voice low, but not quite a whisper.

"Yes," I admitted. "I do."

"And you want to be with him," she clarified.

"Yes." I forced the memory of his lips against mine from my thoughts.

"And you would risk his life to be together?"

This time, the answer fumbled on my tongue. "I—what?" I frowned. "No, I wouldn't risk his life—"

"Isn't that what the two of you risk being together?" Her eyes narrowed minutely.

"I . . ." *Risk Hunter's life?* An overwhelming sense of dread washed over me. She was talking about sex. The vaccine. The fever. I shook my head, hating myself for forgetting about the possible outcomes. I'd been so focused on Cal and Avery, I hadn't thought about what being with Hunter in that way would risk. He'd taken the vaccine, but that was only part of it. We didn't know what would happen next—not even Harper did. What if Hunter hadn't had severe side effects from the vaccine because it hadn't worked completely, and the Virus could still be deadly to him?

As Letty stared at me, watching the reality of a relationship with Hunter settle in, I knew she was right. "No," I said again, my voice breaking a little. "I would never risk that." The words felt like they'd been yanked from me, even if I knew it was true. I would not risk Hunter's life. I would *never* be able to live with myself if something happened to him.

"He accuses me of being heartless, but it is his life I worry about. Nothing more. And seeing you here . . . I knew I must say something. You did not see Wren that day, Thea. You may care for Hunter, but you don't know what the possible outcome looks like." Despite Letty's straight face, I heard the emotion in her voice, rattling ever so slightly like she was trying to remain in control. "You and Hunter are young and you are ruled by feelings, but the reality of whatever future you see together is a dangerous one. I simply wanted to remind you of that."

Letty turned on her boot heels, heading briskly back into the store.

A reminder. As much as I resented it, I'd needed one.

I felt numb as I climbed up into the saddle. Suddenly, the

past twelve years came flooding back, along with the death I always seemed connected to in some way. The suffocation and heaviness of it. I couldn't possibly risk bringing that on Hunter, and I hated myself for forgetting the gravity of our situation.

I led Cinder out of town at a trotting pace, needing space and air, needing to think as the tears welled in my eyes. What had been such a light, hopeful day now felt consumed by an invisible torrent that filled my heart to aching. It wasn't the end of the world, but it felt like I was falling as my future with Hunter seemed more precarious than ever. And the longer I thought about it, the more my fear doused what little optimism I had left, and it felt like Hunter was already slipping away from me.

His intent, obsidian-like gaze flashed to mind, as did the memory of his small smiles that were so few and far between, they felt like a gift, just for me. The man who never opened up or gave himself to anyone was giving part of his heart to me, and a cry caught in my throat as I realized I wasn't sure I could accept it.

I could hurt him. Considering all he'd been through already, I refused to risk it.

The moment the road opened up and the town fanned out behind me, I let Cinder take the lead and we ran, like she could feel the frantic energy coursing through me. My pulse was pounding, my heart breaking, and before I knew it, the wind was pulling at my hair, and Cinder's hooves fell heavy against the earth. Shutting my eyes, I let my mind soar along with it.

44

HUNTER

For two days I stewed, wondering what to do about Thea. It didn't help that, despite my shoulder, only tender as it finished healing, I felt listless, making her far too big a distraction.

"Are you going to see Thea ever again?" Milo said from the greenhouse doorway.

I looked over my shoulder at him, my hands covered in dirt from potting tomato seedlings. Milo's dark hair hung in his eyes, and freckles dotted his cheeks from so much sun.

"Why do you ask?"

Milo shrugged, but like me, he hadn't been quite the same after the argument I'd had with my mother. She and I hadn't talked much, save for pleasantries. She was no doubt angry at me for being foolish and reckless and selfish. And I was tired of her trying to control everything.

I turned to him fully. "A shrug? That's not good. You don't want me to see Thea either?"

Milo frowned. "No, I do. But . . . I don't want you and Mom to argue anymore." Anger toward my mother bloomed hotter again. She had made my life and future more about her than about me, and now Milo was internalizing it, and all it did was make me want to go claim Thea, as if I had the right to, just to spite her.

"Mother will come around," I told him. She had to because I would not tailor my life to her whims anymore. Not when I felt what a semblance of happiness was like. Not when I yearned for it now more than anything else.

Milo leaned against the doorframe, picking at a sliver of wood.

"Don't worry about me and Mother," I told him as reassuringly as I could. I grabbed a rag off the potting table and brushed off my hands. "Milo," I started again, and waited for him to look at me. "Sometimes our elders don't always know what's best. Mother is scared, but we came here so we didn't *have* to be afraid anymore. We get to be happy and have a full life with friends and protection"—I nudged his shoulder—"and a horse." I smiled, earning a small one in return. "There's so much here— it's why we came, and a happy life is what I want for both of us. And for Mother. I'm just waiting for her to see what I see." I lowered my head, looking him in the eyes. "Mother *will* come around eventually, Milo. It won't be like this between us forever."

He studied the splintered wood again, picking at it before he finally conceded. "Okay."

"Good." I tossed the dirty rag back onto the table. "Now, speaking of your horse, let's go for a ride."

Milo's downcast expression faded. "Yeah?"

"Yeah, before Avery and Sven get back with the others, and we'll have to get them settled in. I glanced at the bucket beside the door. "Help me water these and we'll go see Thea. I need to take her something."

"Okay!" Milo grabbed the bucket and disappeared around the side of the building to fetch water. Mother might not be happy, but I would see to it that Milo and I would be.

W e rode the horses up the gravel road to Thea's. It felt presumptuous to show up uninvited, but I didn't want another day to go by without seeing her, and for our routines, families, and ways of life out here to interrupt what was evolving between us. Even if Thea and the unknown was making me a restless ball of nerves.

Milo was oblivious to any of that, and seemed just as intrigued by the property as Sadie and Dancer, all three of them glancing around at the thick woods cast in fading sunlight.

I'd only been to the lodge once, but Wren had mentioned Thea spent the evenings tending to the animals. I just hoped Thea would still be outside so that Milo and I didn't interrupt the family.

"Look!" Milo pointed to the top of an old telephone pole. "There's an eagle's nest!"

"That's pretty big," I said, gaping up at it.

"Yeah, and Krissy told me there are sixty different kinds of eagles."

"Oh yeah?" I lifted an eyebrow. "Who's Krissy?"

"A girl Jasper teaches sometimes. She's really shy and doesn't like the big classrooms."

"But Krissy isn't shy around you?"

"I wish." Milo's features twisted with exasperation. "She talks to me *a lot*. It's kind of annoying. I think she likes me."

I grinned. "What's not to like?"

He huffed and rolled his eyes. Even if Milo wasn't old enough to realize it, he didn't have to worry about bloodlines and the Virus anymore, which made my trepidation in New Bodega worth it. Now the vaccine was tucked away in Nathan's hospital, ready to administer when Milo was old enough to make his choice. He wouldn't have to worry about whether he was *allowed* to like Krissy back, or any other person, because it wouldn't matter; there was no more risk.

Lie. I'd been ignoring the sex part of the equation. There was still the question of what might happen if I slept with Thea, which I desperately wanted to do. Even if it made my palms sweat thinking about it. Thea wasn't sheltered like I'd always been. I wasn't dumb enough to assume she'd be as inexperienced as me. It wasn't enough to drive the hopeful idea from my mind though.

"What's wrong with your face?" Milo asked.

My eyes shot to him, and I chuffed a laugh. "I don't know," I said. "You tell me."

He frowned. "You look . . . weird."

"*You* look weird."

"Do not." Milo's eyes narrowed on me. "You're not freaking out because Krissy likes me, are you?"

"No," I said with another laugh. Krissy definitely wasn't the girl I had on my mind. "Why, should I be freaking out?" I watched him carefully. "You're not thinking about proposing or anything, are you?"

His face crumpled. "Gross. No."

I couldn't help my grin. "Why is that gross?"

He shrugged again. "I dunno. It just is." Milo played with the fringe of Sadie's mane as we crested the hill.

"Okay, well that's probably a good thing for now. Let's make sure you can take care of Sadie before you start thinking about a wife." His lip curled at the thought of a wife, and I shook my head. *Oh, how your tune will soon change, Milo.*

Finally, the front of the lodge came into view through the trees.

"This place is really hidden," Milo mused.

"I'm sure that's a reason they chose it," I told him. "Thea's family were the first ones here, so they didn't have walls to keep them safe, like we have now. They didn't have a town of people with super Abilities either—it was just them and Woody, I think."

Little Foot trotted out to the road as we approached, his white and gray tail wagging as his ears perked up, curious. And just as quickly, he turned back for the lodge, and Milo and I urged our horses to follow.

As we rounded the side of the house, Jackson's truck was parked in a circular gravel patch, which we guided the horses around. Chickens clucked in the distance, and a few small cabins and a greenhouse came into view. The two-story barn was tall, sticking out beyond the trees down the hill, and livestock paddocks surrounded it. Goats lounged in their pens in the dying afternoon, and Cinder and a small red pony stood at the trough, eating their evening meal.

The lodge was a little village of its own, with outbuildings and animals scattered around. The trees were thicker here than in town, and I could imagine living in a place like it one day—I could imagine a family and a farm . . . and Thea. That I could even hope any of that was possible made my chest swell with something indescribable.

"There she is!" Milo pointed to Thea down the hill. We pulled our horses to a halt beside the greenhouse, but I watched her for a moment before dismounting.

Her long hair was up high in her ponytail, swaying as she bent down to brush something off her leg, and mouthing inaudible words, probably to one of her songs. Her purple tank top and jeans hugged every one of her curves, making my body stiffen.

She chatted with one of the chickens, mouthing what looked like a "pardon me" as she eased the gate open with her mind, making me smile. That she had grown more comfortable with her Ability made me glad for her. The chickens fluttered out of the way as one by one the eggs floated out of their nest and into her basket.

I couldn't explain my draw to her, only that when I saw Thea, I wanted her and no one else. I wanted to be playful with her, to see the world the way she did and make her smile. I wanted to sit with her all night when the world was quiet and talk about her favorite songs and drawings and her love of honey. I wanted to hear all her little sighs, and watch the way her face crinkled with every barely-there expression she couldn't hide. I wanted her to fuss over me when she was worried. And I wanted those impassioned, brown eyes of hers to look into my soul the way it felt like she did sometimes, and know how much I cared for her. She was the most aggravatingly beautiful person I knew, and my heartbeat quickened and my palms began to sweat as I realized she was the one. She'd always been, I felt it in my gut. Fate had sent us down two incredibly different paths, and yet, I felt like I was exactly where I was supposed to be.

"So," Milo drawled. "Are we going to talk to Thea or just stare at her?"

I glowered at him. "You're hilarious."

Milo chuckled to himself, far too pleased, and we dismounted our horses, my boots hitting the ground with a thud. Dancer and Sadie peered around excitedly, and Cinder's head popped up in the pasture below as she realized there were visitors.

Thea closed the chicken coop door behind her, counting the eggs in her basket when Milo called her name.

She glanced toward the house, and something flashed across her open expression when she registered us. Something didn't feel right. Thea wasn't smiling, and my insides twisted. I hadn't seen that look of discomfort around me in so long, I'd forgotten how instantly it affected me.

We walked our horses down the hill, between the greenhouse and the cabins, toward the center of the property.

Basket in hand, Thea met us halfway. Her eyes were locked

on mine, but her expression was one I'd never seen before, and I couldn't tell what she was thinking.

"Hey," she said, and offered me and Milo a small wave. "This is a surprise."

"A bad one?" I asked, holding my breath.

Her brow furrowed slightly and she shook her head. "No. Not at all, I was just finishing up my chores." But even if Thea was being pleasant, she didn't exactly look happy to see us either.

Clenching my jaw, I turned toward my saddlebag and pulled out the jar I'd brought with me.

"Honey," she said with a small smile. Her eyes brightened a little.

"You said I owed you some," I reminded her, though I handed it to her hesitantly. "And Milo needed to get some riding in."

Thea's smile widened as she glanced from my brother to Sadie. "And, how do you like her? You look pretty handsome sitting up there, like she was made for you." Thea tucked the jar of honey under her arm and reached out to pet Sadie's head.

"I love her," Milo said with pride. "She gets along with Dancer too, and she's not as big as Dancer so she's easier to ride."

Thea's smile widened. "Good. She's perfect for you then."

Little Foot trotted over, his tail still wagging as he sniffed and licked at my hand for attention. I scrubbed the top of his head, not taking my eyes off Thea as I tried to work out where this sudden awkwardness was coming from.

"Visitors?" I heard a male voice and turned around.

Jackson closed the door to what looked like a smoke shed and latched it as he looked at us. Seeing him in his home felt strange, like he was suddenly more formidable. Or maybe it was because I'd come to see his daughter.

"Hunter," he said as he approached.

"Hi, Jackson." I glanced from Thea to him. "I hope you don't mind us visiting."

"Not at all," he said with a grin, his eyes twinkling in the sunlight as he stopped beside the palomino. He looked at my brother and his smile broadened. "I heard you got a new mare, Milo."

"Yeah, her name's Sadie."

"That's a good name. Come on." Jackson nodded behind him and patted Sadie's neck. "Let's get these beauties some water." He reached for Dancer's reins, which I handed him gratefully, and motioned for Milo to follow him.

With flicking tails, the horses headed toward the water trough, leaving Thea and me alone in thick silence.

"You don't seem happy to see me," I said.

Thea's expression softened a little, and a sympathetic gleam filled her eyes. I didn't like that look. Nothing good ever came from a regretful look like that.

"Is it about Cal?" I asked, wondering if they might've gotten back together. My chest tightened at the thought.

"No," she whispered, and she turned the honey jar over and over in her hand. That Thea wouldn't meet my gaze was a bad sign, and the dread I'd been feeling dropped like a lead balloon in my stomach.

"Then what's wrong?" I tried to keep the edge from my voice as I took a step closer. "Two days ago we were smiling and kissing, and now you won't even look at me."

Her cheeks flushed, she licked her lips and peered up at me through her lashes. "I'm sorry, it's just—I've been thinking," she started, and a chill ran through me. "Maybe we should slow down and really think about what we're doing."

"Why? I want to be with you. If you want to be with me, I'm not sure what there is to think about." She turned the jar over in her hand once more, watching the way the honey dripped from the sides. "Thea," I said, stepping closer until there were only inches between us. "What changed—did my mother speak to you?" It was the only thing I could think of.

Finally, she met my gaze, and my impending heartache solidified into anger.

"Unbelievable," I grumbled, and ran my hand through my hair. "Don't give weight to what she says, Thea. She's meddling and she—"

"She's concerned about you, and I don't blame her," Thea explained.

"Concerned?" I found that hard to believe. "Why?"

"Because the two of us together is dangerous, and not something we should take lightly."

I shook my head, my jaw aching as the pieces fell into place. "I thought we were on the same page. Suddenly you're what, scared to be with me?"

"No—I mean, yes, but it's more about what I might do to you."

"You're talking about infecting me?"

"Yes," she said, as if she was exasperated with me.

"I know there's risk, Thea, but I'm not going to never have sex or be afraid of it. I knew what I was doing when I took the vaccine, and there's only one way to figure out if it works. It was half the reason I did it—so that we could be together." Her mouth parted and I realized what I'd just admitted. "It crossed my mind at one point," I amended.

"You thought about this when you took the vaccine?" I could tell she was cataloging the past few weeks, the past few months. The past year and a half. "But we weren't really even friends—"

"There was a fleeting moment when Harper was talking to me about it that I considered the possibility that one day it might become an option," I said, feeling my cheeks turn crimson. The words felt uncomfortable on my tongue. "Look, I can't explain it, Thea," I rasped, taking her hands in mine. How did you articulate something that had no words, only feelings? "I get that the vaccine is a scary unknown, okay? It's my life—trust me, I know what I'm risking. But I also know that whatever happens is worth it to me because I want you—I want whatever comes next in my life to happen with you."

I glanced behind her to make sure Milo and Jackson were still out of earshot. "Do you have any idea what it feels like to be tethered to someone you're supposed to spend the rest of your life with, but feel nothing other than brotherly affection for? It feels hollow and miserable, and like there was something wrong with me. Wren was miserable too—look what she did to herself because of it." I ran my hand through my hair, willing Thea to feel what I did, and know that it was worth any risk. "It's different with you. I felt guilty when I *wanted* Wren and Beau to be together. But this—you pushing me away—feels ass-backward."

"I know," she said in a rush. "And I'm sorry. It's not that I won't be with you or that I don't want to, but I just—it's different for me, Hunter. I need time."

The torrent of uncertainty in her eyes felt like a blade to the chest, and I squeezed her hand. "Time for what?" I asked more gently.

"To think." She rubbed her temple. "If something happened to you—it would break me, Hunter." Thea's voice strained as her eyelashes flitted shut. "I would never forgive myself and I just . . . I have to be sure I'm ready to do something like this."

"I'm not rushing you," I promised. "And I don't expect anything from you, not if you're not ready, but I don't want you to push me away out of fear. Please." I swallowed the thickness in my throat as I thought about her fleeing in the other direction. "Thea," I whispered, gently taking her face in my hands. Her nostrils flared and her watery gaze met mine. "Becca told me to let go of the past and embrace the future, and that's what I want to do. And I know you're supposed to be in my future, I can feel it with every heartbeat. Even if something does happen to me, it would be worth it."

Her eyes searched mine wildly. "I want you too." She licked her lips. "But you know about my past, and . . . I don't want to hurt you. I *can't* hurt you."

I leaned in and pressed my lips to hers. "Then we'll figure it out when you're ready." It didn't feel right to imagine whatever came next without Thea in it. "And please," I breathed, resting my forehead against hers. "Come to me before you start talking yourself out of *us* again, okay?"

With a hint of a smile that made my unease fade away enough that I could breathe, Thea tilted her head with steely resolve. "Promise."

45

THEA

Hunter. Us. The future. His *life*. It felt like there was a little devil on one shoulder, telling me that everything would be fine. *It's worth the risk, Thea.* But the little angel on the other shoulder was uncertain and kept my feet moving as I approached the marked graves in our little cemetery.

I plucked a few fuchsia wisps of fireweed from the leafy earth with my mind, not thinking much about it as my thoughts drifted.

Since telling Hunter this was my special place, I'd been asking myself why. The cemetery called to me when I felt off-kilter; it had always been that way, almost like these beings tied to my past were a comfort for me.

Luna's headstone came into view first, then I saw Jenny's and Rocky's, and guilt niggled its way closer to the surface. *No.* Not a comfort, I realized. A sort of penance.

I sat beside Jenny's grave, remembering her gray, shimmering eyes. *"You will take care of Elle for me,"* she'd rasped, trying to smile. *"Won't you?"* A giant lump formed in my throat. I could still hear Elle's sobs as Jenny said her goodbyes.

No, I didn't come here to feel better; I came here to grieve—

it was self-punishment. It was like I was forcing myself to remember them. Though, it wasn't as if I could ever forget.

I placed the fireweed bouquet on Jenny's grave. She'd been on my mind a lot during the trip south. Seeing the Re-gen camp in Hope Valley. Traveling the same path she and Kat had used to get to Whitehorse years ago to find Elle. And struggling against those vines, feeling my Ability waning, I thought I might've glimpsed an ounce of what Jenny felt as her powers drained the life from her that day with Nora.

"I wonder if you'd still be alive if it wasn't for her," I thought aloud, but Kat's words tugged at my memory. *"All JJ ever wanted was to get back to Elle, and she did. She was happy—she got what she wanted, everything after that was borrowed time."* The reminder that Jenny's health was deteriorating long before she came to us was a necessary one, something my little girl mind had forgotten in what befell us after. Sadness. Emptiness. Regret.

"You don't get to shoulder any blame for her deciding to do what she did . . . Her death is not *on you."*

I glanced at Luna's hand-carved gravestone, wondering if she still looked in on Beau sometimes, and my eyes blurred. Luna had been Jenny all over again, only worse. I wasn't some little girl who'd been tricked and gotten herself into trouble. I was a young woman, choosing to make dumb decisions, to act without thinking, and I'd torn out a piece of my brother's soul in the process.

"Even if I know I have to forgive myself, I can still be sorry about it," I told them. With a watery laugh, I blinked the tears away. "It feels like I'm saying goodbye, but you've all been gone for what feels like a lifetime."

I stared at Jenny's moss-covered headstone, remembering what Becca had said to Hunter, about embracing the future and forgetting the past. That he was important. And then I thought about what Becca had said to me.

"I know this is who I'm supposed to be, and that seemed important to Becca, which means all of it—the heartache and guilt—must all have been for something." I picked at the lichen growing on the stones covering her grave. "And I can make better decisions in the future, starting with Hunter."

Minutes. An hour. I'm not sure how long I sat there, but all I could think about was Hunter coming to see me—the panic in his voice, and his earnest expression as he thought he had to convince me we should be together. There was never any question that I wanted to, only my fears of what would happen if we were.

My mind fogged with exhaustion and I realized how tired I truly was. The past month had been a long, confusing one, and as my eyes became heavy, I laid my cheek on the warm stones that covered Jenny's grave and watched the sun descend behind the trees.

It dawned on me that in the end, despite the hurdles and danger, Luna and Jenny both had gotten what they'd wanted— endless sleep. As a result, Kat had found Ross, and no one could argue they weren't made for each other. And Beau had finally connected with Bear, his brother and friend in a way that Luna never had been.

Telepathically, I picked another wisp of fireweed from the forest floor, too exhausted to move, and laid it on Luna's grave. Then, I picked another for Rocky and lost myself in a swirl of possible futures, all of which I saw Hunter beside me. He was always there, no matter what.

Eventually, I noticed a fireweed bouquet lying on each of the graves, and I smiled, realizing my mind had done more than wander. *See, you're not so broken.* I heard Hunter's reserved yet self-satisfied snark in my mind, and my smile widened. "No," I thought aloud. "I'm not so broken." A few weeks ago, the inclination to use my Ability at all never would've crossed my mind, and now it felt almost natural, like it did when I was little.

I sat up. So many things in my life had been out of my control over the years, but my relationship with Hunter wasn't one of them. In fact, he made me feel stronger.

I looked toward the house, remembering him by the chicken coop. He was right; we knew what we were getting into—Hunter knew the risks and he still wanted to be with me. And despite how scared I was to hurt him, being together made us *both* stronger. More than that, being with Hunter felt destined. It was the first thing in my life that ever felt right.

Unlike all the times before, I wasn't helpless or being rash. And with an unexpected surge of resolve, my heart felt a little lighter, the dread unfurling to something a lot more like anticipation, and I knew instantly what I needed to do.

46

THEA

The spinster sisters waved from their basket weaving on the porch as I rode through Village Row, and Otto bowed his head in greeting from his wheelchair, no more judgement in his eyes, like he'd had months before. As Elijah and Liam moved what possessions they had into one of the empty houses that now belonged to them, I realized how much had changed in the past year. Hunter and I being the most unexpected.

As I approached Hunter's farm, I peered past the barn and toward the fields, noticing Hunter and Milo at the cornstalks. Milo waved excitedly when he saw me, and I waved cheerfully back. And when Hunter's gaze met mine, I couldn't help the fluttering in my chest. His steely exterior was so misleading, and as his lips spread into a smile, my chest warmed, and my own smile grew into a giddy as hell grin.

I nodded down the road, waving a quick goodbye, and Cinder and I headed to the greenhouse, hoping to find Henni. She wasn't only Wren's grandmother, but the village's healer and matriarch. Like Hunter, Henni was everything to their people, and what I was about to do felt epic; the conflicted part of me needed her approval and to know that however Letty felt about

Hunter and me, Henni, at least, was on our side. She'd been on Wren and Beau's side from the beginning, wanting the village to relocate to Whitehorse, so I thought just maybe she'd be on my side in this too.

Bracing myself for whatever might happen next, I glanced at the greenhouse. The door was open, and one of Henni's crates sat on the step, only partially full of tincture bottles, and I hoped I'd find her working inside.

I eased Cinder to a stop and dismounted, giving myself a quick internal pep talk. Henni was like Jade in so many ways, but she was built of tougher stuff and had lived a life that had hardened her around the edges. She was reserved on her best days, and could slash you with a single look on the bad ones. But I needed to talk to her because I needed her help.

Leaving Cinder to wait patiently for my return, I tugged the hem of my shirt down and, combing the wayward strands of hair back with my fingers, I walked to the greenhouse.

Laughter emanated from inside, and I stopped just before the doorway.

"—admit it," Bert said, his rough voice all too familiar. "You missed me." My eyes widened, and I leaned closer to listen.

"I wouldn't go that far," Henni countered, but not as stern as usual; in fact, there was an amusement to her voice I'd never heard before. It sounded as if she was trying not to laugh. *Henni laughing?* I couldn't really imagine it.

The floorboards creaked. "No?" Bert murmured. They creaked again. "Not even a little bit? I almost died, you know."

Henni practically snorted. "I couldn't get rid of you if I tried," she teased, and Bert chuckled softly.

"No, probably not." His voice was a playful whisper.

Hand splayed over my mouth in shock, I took a step back. They were flirting.

"Hey, Thea!" Milo jogged up behind me and Cinder, a carrot in his hand.

I cringed inwardly and heard Bert clear his throat. "Hey, Milo," I said, forcing a defeated smile. I was totally busted. "Will you look after her a moment?" I handed him Cinder's reins.

"Sure!"

As I stepped into the greenhouse doorway, Bert lifted a vial, nodding to Henni. "Thanks for the tincture. My sciatica appreciates it." He looked at me next. "Hey kiddo," Bert said in greeting, and with a wink, he stepped past me, the scent of chamomile wafting off him.

Henni, on the other hand, stared at me, shrewd and straight-faced. "Thea," she said, brushing her hands off on her apron as she took a slight step forward.

I wasn't sure how Henni really felt about me, but even if she was brusque and harsh sometimes, she had a worldly understanding, and if anyone was going to give me the brutal truth or put my mind at ease, I knew it would be her.

I could practically see her mind trying to explain the reason for my visit, and I considered, briefly, that she might already know. "I was wondering if I could talk to you . . ." I hedged.

Her expression gave nothing away as she pointed toward the sidewalk. "I should stretch my legs a bit anyway."

I stepped away from the door to wait for her, reveling in the breeze against my clammy skin.

As Henni came out of the greenhouse, she glanced at Milo and Cinder retreating to the barn, as if she were trying to determine if Hunter was a part of my unexpected visit. Then, she began walking the opposite way down the sidewalk, motioning me to follow. "What's this about, Thea?" she said, her voice curious but guarded.

I bit the inside of my cheek. "It's about me and Hunter," I confessed, though I'm sure it was no real surprise.

Her gaze drifted to me, her arms clasped in front of her as

she took unhurried, easy steps that matched mine. "I'm surprised you've come to me then."

"Once you know why I've come, you won't be."

"Well then, girl, spit it out." She stopped and turned to me. "What's this about?" she repeated.

I glanced down at Hunter's house, remembering his mother's disapproval, and braced myself for a tongue lashing. "You know what Hunter did in New Bodega," I said.

She dipped her chin in answer.

"You know why?"

"I can imagine a few reasons," Henni answered, and continued walking. "Hunter is very protective and very decisive. And despite how much it scares Letty sometimes, he's a leader. I couldn't imagine him doing any different, especially when it comes to his brother's future."

"I know, and now that he's taken the vaccine," I continued, inhaling a steadying breath, "we want to be together."

Her head whipped to me, and her thin gray eyebrow lifted.

"I know it's dangerous, and while he's giving me time to get used to the idea, I want to be prepared. Obviously, I don't want to hurt him, so I need your help."

"And he knows you've come to me?"

"Well, no," I admitted, shaking my head. "I'm more worried about it than he is, so that's why I'm here. You saw what it did to Wren. It probably won't be like that since he got the vaccine, but I still want to be prepared, just in case."

The old woman was thoughtful and said nothing as we walked for a few more heartbeats.

"Why not ask Jade to help you?" she asked, her eyes fixed on the end of the road. "Why come to me?"

"I don't know," I told her.

"Yes, you do." This time, Henni looked at me, expectant. "Why did you come to ask me for help when your own grandmother could've helped you—when your mother could have?"

345

I licked my lips, feeling the weight of her stare keenly. "Because I know how much you care for Hunter. I know you would do everything you could to help me, especially since you've seen what could happen."

"And," she said, as if there was more. I was about to tell her that was all, but it wasn't.

"And, I can't go to his mother and talk to her for obvious reasons, but it feels like someone should know how I'm feeling about this." I shoved my hands in my back pockets. "I want to think of every possible outcome—I want to do the right thing. I don't want anything to happen to him."

"Of course you don't want to hurt him, child." The certainty and appreciation in Henni's voice was a relief I hadn't expected to feel. She continued walking.

"I just . . . I need help. Please."

After a thoughtful moment, Henni nodded, the wrinkles around her eyes softening. "I will help you, Thea, but you must do something for me in return."

47

THEA

Lying on a pallet of blankets I'd made, my sketchbook in front of me, I peered around the master bedroom of the abandoned house Hunter squatted in when he needed time alone. The ceiling was water-spotted, and there were cobwebs in the corners, but I'd seen far worse in the other homes left to ruin.

When I heard the crunch of heavy footsteps in the backyard, I closed my sketchbook with my mind, setting it on the floor beside me.

Hunter walked by the window, and in three steps, he filled the crooked doorway. "I got your note—" The words died on his lips as he took in the candles lit throughout the room. The entire space was glowing. "Wow," he said, peering around as he stepped inside. A small smile tugged at his lips. "What's all this for?" He was still wearing his dirty, gray t-shirt and work pants, as if he'd come straight from the field.

I climbed off the pallet. The freshly swept wood floor was cool against my bare feet. As nervous as I was at how silly this might've seemed to Hunter, I wanted everything to be perfect. Our first time together. *His* first time.

"It's for us," I said, drawing closer. My eyes locked on his, my heart pounding in my chest as I waited for him to understand.

Realization flashed across his feature, and he looked from the bed of blankets to me again. His brow furrowed.

"I know that my planning this is probably strange to you," I blurted, squeezing my eyes shut. Even if I knew how Hunter felt about me, this wasn't exactly what he'd asked for. I took a deep breath. "I just . . . If we're going to do this, we have to do it the right way—*I* have to do this the right way, for my sanity's sake." When I opened my eyes to find his questioning gaze locked on me, I rushed to continue. "We don't have to do it now, if you don't want—I don't want it to be weird, but I do want to be prepared, in case this goes terribly wrong." I blew out another breath. "I *have* to be prepared." The words were more of a desperate plea for him to understand.

Hunter's features softened and he shook his head. "Thea, it's you I'm worried about. Not me. This is—" He glanced around the room again and a slight smile curved his lips. "This is really nice—it's perfect, actually—but there's no pressure. I don't want this to be another regret for you. I can't live with that."

"I know, but . . ." How did I explain that he'd chosen *me* to be *the one* and that felt so special and momentous, I could refuse him either, nor did I want to. "If it wasn't for the Virus inside me, I wouldn't even think twice about it," I confessed. "But . . ." I took his hand in mine.

He stared down at our fingers laced together.

"Something Becca told me while we were in Hope Valley has been playing over and over in my head, and after you told me how you feel, like we're meant to be, I'm starting to think you might be right. That this"—I waved around the room—"might be right."

"What did Becca say?" he asked, his voice quiet but curious.

"That I shouldn't be afraid of what I am because I'm important. And I think she might've meant that I was important for *you.*" Somehow the fear had faded after talking to Henni, like if she didn't freak out, then I shouldn't either. And all I could think about all day was that if we were meant to be, then this couldn't be wrong.

Hunter searched my face, trying to gauge if I was wavering.

"I've already taken something for myself," I told him, refusing to have a pregnancy scare my first time with him. "And Henni gave me a tincture," I explained. "It's devil's club, cayenne, and white willow, for you to take after, just in case."

His eyes widened infinitesimally. "Henni knows about this?"

I glossed over his question, knowing it wasn't ideal, but I had little choice in the matter. "And I have a tea you can drink if you have symptoms, and a cream too, for the fever. Just in case," I reiterated, but I wasn't sure if I was reassuring Hunter or myself.

His lips twitched like he were resisting a smile. "You've thought of everything," he said with quiet awe.

I took a ragged, tired, desperate breath. "I tried." There was no point hiding my fear; Hunter already knew how scared I was, and yet somehow, his smile crept wider and wider. "You think I'm hilarious," I groaned.

"No," he whispered as he peered around the room again, like he was seeing it through a fresh lens—the pallet, the candles, the snacks and water, and the slew of vials on the crate I'd upturned as a table. "I can't believe you did all of this . . . for me." The amazement in his voice made my heart soar, and I wondered how there had ever been a time I couldn't stand him.

I inched my shoulder up, as if it was nothing. "Of course I did. You make me feel special, and I want you to feel special too."

Eyes gleaming in the candlelight, Hunter leaned in and kissed me, more gently than he ever had before. It felt like a thank you that started with the brush of our lips before he pulled me into his arms. That scent of his—the basil, earth, sweat, and everything a virile, hardworking man should smell like—made my insides quiver.

Hunter lifted his head, his gaze scouring me for a hint of apprehension as his fingertips trailed over my jaw. "We're really doing this?" he breathed.

My hands moved down to the button of my jeans, and Hunter's jaw slackened as I shimmied the denim over my hips. He drew in a sharp breath and licked his lips, making me feel more powerful than I ever had in my t-shirt and underwear. I stepped out of my pants, slid them out of the way with my mind, then moved closer until my chest pressed against his. "Yes, we're really doing this," I told him, and kissed his lips again, growing less anxious and more starved for him as his body relaxed against mine.

He brushed his nose against my cheek, and a thrill twirled inside me, an unrestrained hope and anticipation. "Come on," I whispered, and tugged him toward the pallet. Bedrolls, blankets, and old cushions weren't ideal, but they would have to do.

Hunter didn't move as I crawled onto the bed. In fact, he didn't budge for what felt like the longest time, as he stared at me. The claw-like fingers of insecurity began to rake over me, until finally, Hunter lifted his arms and pulled his t-shirt over his head. His shoulders, his chest—the way he stood before me, like an offering I didn't feel I deserved—sent butterflies flitting around inside me again, and I nearly lost my breath.

What I had with Cal wasn't like this. It just . . . *was*. It happened, and it was fun, but this was more. This was Hunter and me. This made my stomach knot in a tangled web of terror and unbridled need.

Slowly, Hunter lowered to his knees, his gaze shifting down the column of my neck and over my chest, heaving in the expectant, charged silence hanging between us. He swallowed thickly and his Adam's apple moved like a lazy drip of honey down his throat. I licked my lips.

"I'm nervous," he admitted, and if I hadn't grown to know him better in the past weeks, I would've called him a liar. His expression gave nothing away, but his jaw clenched and that was his tell.

I rose to my knees, our heights matching for once. His eyes shifted frantically over me as I lifted my hand and traced my index finger lightly over his lips. I watched the invisible line my finger drew down his chin and throat, following the curve of his collarbone. The muscles of his shoulder tensed and his bicep flexed as I traced further down his arm before running my fingertips over his and taking his hand in mine.

My heart beat recklessly in my chest and my blood was whirring in my veins to the point of distraction as I placed his palm against my heart. "You're not the only one who's nervous," I whispered, and flattened my palm over his. "I'm terrified."

A twitch of a smile pulled at Hunter's mouth, and his reticence was chased away by something more primal and determined. His focus sharpened and his fingertips pressed into my chest as if they were staking their claim. The warmth and heaviness of his palm over my heart sent a delectable wave of chills running through me.

Leaning forward, he brushed his lips against mine, his eyes open and watching me, and with a steadying breath, they finally closed and he claimed a kiss. More covetous than before. And as he explored my mouth with his, my thoughts swirled to nothing.

Hunter laid me back against the pillows and lowered himself down beside me. His thigh pressed between mine, the pressure igniting a spark through me. He kissed my lips and my jaw and lingered by my ear. "I want you," he rasped, each word a rushed whispered.

I arched against him. "Then take me."

As I reached for the button of Hunter's pants, his hesitation vanished. I could feel the moment he lost himself to the pull between us, and without faltering, he pulled the hem of my t-shirt up over my head.

Our panting breaths were all that filled the silence as his firelit gaze raked over my body—over my bra and panties. His mouth parted and he licked his lips. "I can't believe I ever thought I didn't like you," he groaned, and I giggled as he ran his finger beneath the strap of my bra, down to my breast.

"And I can't believe I used to curse your existence," I countered.

And as a wry smile pulled at Hunter's lips, and a ravenous hunger burned wild in his eyes, I knew I was done for.

48

HUNTER

I woke to a featherlight touch on my back. As my eyes opened and the flickering glow of a single candle illuminated the room, I smiled to myself. *Thea.* Her legs were warm, tangled with mine, and she traced the scars on my back with her fingertip.

"Have you slept at all?" I asked, my voice hoarse from sleep.

She sat up on her elbow and peered down at me, her long hair tickling my shoulder and chest as it slid over me. "You're awake," she quietly chirped. She kissed my shoulder, the blanket she held against her grazed my back.

I craned my neck to look at her. "And so are you, apparently."

Her shoulder bobbed with a slight shrug. "I wanted to make sure you were okay." Candle shadows danced in her eyes, warm with affection.

I was more than okay. I was perfect. I never wanted to leave this dirty old house and the lumpy pallet bed. Ever.

Turning onto my back, I peered up at her bow mouth and into her wide, beautiful eyes that shone every emotion so bright, I could feel it inside my soul. She *was* worried. And adorable. "I'm okay." I lifted my hand, brushing my thumb over her lips—I could still feel them against my skin, and the undeniable ache in my groin returned.

"Are you sure you're all right?" she asked, skeptical as she studied my face.

Easing her down to my side, I pulled her against me, sighing with satisfaction as her body wrapped around mine and her head nestled perfectly against my chest. "Don't I feel like I'm all right?" I ran my finger down the length of her arm and drew little circles on the back of her palm.

"You're warm," she said.

"So are you," I countered, knowing the heat I felt had nothing to do with the fever. At least, not the kind she was thinking of.

Her finger swirled the sprinkle of hair around my belly button, making my stomach tighten, and I pressed a kiss to her forehead. "I'm okay, I promise. My heart's been beating erratically, and my muscles are tight from using them in ways I never have before," I teased. "But I'm not sick. In fact," I said, suddenly aware I hadn't had a single dream, "I actually slept."

"Good," she said, but Thea sounded distracted.

Squeezing her tighter against me, I tilted her chin up to look at me. "What's wrong?"

She bit her bottom lip, and I couldn't help my body's response. Her brown eyes scoured mine. "What happens when your mom finds out we're together and—"

"Let me worry about my mother," I told her, hating that even in her absence, my mother could possibly ruin this moment for me. "But—where exactly does your family think *you* are right now?" I asked, suddenly afraid they might be worried.

"Elle knows I'm here. I'm not sure what she told Jackson." A flush of unease came and went, knowing Henni and Elle were aware of where we were and what we were doing. But that Thea was able to be so open with her family left a sense of longing in the pit of my stomach.

"Are you worried about my family?" she asked in my silence. "I mean, you don't have to be, but I know they can be intimidating, especially Beau when he gets prickly."

"Thea," I said with a chuckle. "You're far more intimidating to me than your brother is," I teased, but it was also true.

She rolled her eyes. "No, I'm not—"

"Yes," I promised. "You are."

Her brow furrowed and she pouted her lip a little. "How do you mean?"

"Well," I started. "First of all, you make me feel things that scare me."

She licked her lips, her gaze shifting to my mouth and back. "I do?"

I tried to think of a way to explain how my entire life had been a woven tether of people and experiences I'd known and conformed to. "Until you, I had perfectly constructed armor that I thought would protect me from everything. I thought it made me stronger for my family and my people." I savored the contours of her face, the column of her neck, and the fullness of her lips before meeting her gaze again. "But you . . ." I swallowed thickly. Suddenly all the wasted months around Thea felt gut-wrenching.

I tucked a strand of her hair behind her ear, and sat up on my elbow, peering down at her. "I'm sorry I treated you the way I did." I thought about every cross word exchanged between us the past year and a half, and how even then, something unexpected and frightening churned inside me. I could still see her freckled, pink nose perfectly in my mind, and the way her hair danced in the breeze around her beanie on that cool winter afternoon on my front porch. "The first time I saw you, I'd never wanted to kiss and curse someone at the same time so bad in my life."

Slowly, a smile part her lips. "Me too."

My eyebrow arched of its own accord. "Really? I didn't get that impression."

She giggled and rolled her eyes again, a nervous habit I relished. "Well, let's just say I can't believe I wasted countless hours of my life detesting you."

"I feel so honored," I said with a grin, and I pressed a kiss to her lips.

Thea rested the back of her hand against my forehead. "Are you sure you're okay?" The flirtiness was gone from her voice. "You do feel a little warm, but I can't tell if it's a fever or the blankets." Her sincerity and unease made my chest tighten.

All I could do was nod. Thea thought I made her feel seen and special, but the reality was that she made me feel like someone else entirely. Someone with hope and an unexpected need for life outside of everything I'd ever known—a life with her. A lover. A friend. A soulmate.

"No one's ever worried about me like you do," I whispered. And as she studied me, searching for a shred of hesitation, I couldn't help the flood of heat that washed through me, and the sudden need I felt to have her again. Every part of her. To show her in some small way what this feeling was inside of me.

Leaning in, I brushed my nose over the smooth round of her cheek, sending a tendril of toe-curling need through my body. "Thea," I breathed and pressed a kiss beneath her chin and then the nape of her neck, eliciting a soft mewing moan from her throat.

"Hunter," she rasped.

I wrapped my leg around her, pulling her closer, and smiled against her ear. A low growl rumbled from my chest as my lips kissed a trail toward her breast.

Her head fell back, her fingers gripped my shoulder with bruising pressure, and she arched her body against me. "You . . . definitely don't . . . seem sick . . ."

I grinned against the supple skin of her breast and took it into my mouth. As she squirmed beneath the weight of me, I knew sleep was a distant memory. Gripping her hips, I rolled her on top of me. "We better find a way to stay awake, though, just in case."

49

HUNTER

When the sun finally rose, and Thea and Cinder rode back to the lodge, I forced myself to head the opposite direction, back to the village. It wasn't more than a fifteen-minute walk from the abandoned house, and the minutes passed quickly as I thought about tonight, when I would go to Thea's place for dinner.

Mother wouldn't be happy, but that was of her own making and I tried not to let that ruin my morning high.

The village was shrouded in mist as it came into view. I walked up the street toward the house, passing the horses in the barn. When I reached the front porch, I opened the front door quietly so that I didn't wake anyone. I was unsurprised to find my mother sitting at the kitchen table, already dressed with a tea mug gripped in her hands.

I glanced at her, taking in her perfectly braided hair, her work pants, and her scowl. Though, it wasn't as severe as I would've expected.

"Good morning," she said, her voice flat but quiet.

I headed for the faucet and the fruit basket. "Good morning,

Mother." I grabbed a peach and took a glass out of the cupboard to fill with water.

"Dare I ask where you've been all night?"

"You could ask," I told her, "but you won't like the answer."

She said nothing as I filled my glass, downed it in a few gulps, then took a bite of my breakfast.

"So, you've made your decision then," she whispered.

"Decision? I've made many in the past few months, you'll have to be more specific."

Finally, she looked at me.

I leaned against the counter, my arms crossed over my chest as I took another bite of my peach. It was crisp and barely ripe, exactly the way I liked them. "Your decision to be with Thea," she clarified.

"Yes," I told her. "But you already knew that."

I waited for her to look away in disgust, but she didn't. Instead, she rose to her feet and walked over to me, her steps unhurried and her lips pursed.

"I already know how you feel about it," I told her. "There's no need to remind me."

My mother leaned against the edge of the island across from me. "The vaccine works, then," she mused. She didn't need my response, nor did she wish it, so I held her gaze instead. "What do Jackson and Elle think about all of this—you and their daughter?"

I glanced away, feeling a flush of uncertainty. "I don't know," I admitted. I didn't know what the proper thing to do was in a situation like this. Thea was the one in control, and if Elle knew where she was . . . "They're okay with it, I guess."

"And you don't care what they think, just as you don't care what I think," she said.

I took a final bite of my peach and opened the lid to the compost bin, tossing it in. "I care what they think," I told her, realizing how callous my words must sound to her. "And I care what you think," I added. "But unlike you, they aren't trying to stand in the way of us being together. We're not children, Mother. It's not some passing infatuation. I love Thea."

My mother's lips parted in surprise, and her eyes widened. "Love?" She swallowed, quickly collecting herself, and her surprise faded. "That's a powerful word, Hunter."

"Yes it is, and you know me well enough to believe me when I say it. I know it's difficult for you to contemplate life beyond me and Milo, but we can't live like that anymore. We deserve a life. Just like you do. And Thea makes me feel like I'm not alone anymore." When I registered the wounded pride shining in my mother's eyes, I shook my head. "I want more than a mother and brother who love me. I want a partner and a friend."

It took her a moment to soak in my words, but I saw them playing through her mind as her nostrils flared, and disbelief, hurt, and an unexpected flash of regret shone in her eyes. "I've never wanted you to be unhappy, Hunter," she whispered. "I've only ever wanted the best for you—both of you—I just—" She peered down at her dirt-stained fingernails. With her hands, she'd taught me how to till and work the earth, the same hands that, since my father's death, had always worked as hard as my own to keep food on the table and the village fed.

"I know," I told her, guilt washing over me as my mother's hands, so capable and worn, began to tremble. "But I need space to be a man and not just your son. Milo is going to need that one day too. You have to accept it—"

"I know," she said, a tear striking down her cheek. Unable to stand the distance that had been growing between us for months, I stepped closer and wrapped my arms around her.

"I just," she started with a sniffle, and her hands clenched my t-shirt. "I just don't want to lose you—you and Milo, you're everything, and I need you."

"You won't lose me, Mother," I promised, kissing the top of her head. "I will be here, always. I'm not leaving. I'm just trying to find my own path too. And Thea doesn't want to take me from you."

"I know," she rasped, nodding against me. She cleared her throat again. "And I'm sorry."

I stiffened. My mother never uttered those words, and I knew what they must've cost her, just like I knew how hard it was for her to let go after spending a lifetime afraid we would be taken from her, many times coming far too close.

"I'm just happy you're all right. If I lost you to this Virus after everything else—" She sobbed into my shirt, her arms tightening around me.

"I know," I whispered. "I'm okay though. Thea and Henni made sure of it."

My mother pulled away and wiped her cheeks and chin with the back of her hand, looking both curious and confused.

"Thea came prepared with tinctures and creams and teas," I explained, refraining from a smile. "She was just as worried as you."

I wasn't sure what emotion flashed across my mother's face, though I thought it might've been a mixture of surprise and gratitude.

"You would like Thea. I wish you'd give her a chance," I said, handing her a folded towel from the counter to dry her eyes.

"She has a temper to rival yours, I'll give her that," my mother conceded, dabbing the moisture from her cheeks.

"It's true," I agreed, and gave her a moment to collect herself. I wanted this to be a turning point in our relationship. For my sake and for Milo's. My relationship with my mother was the only thing left that felt skewed. "I'm going to her house tonight for dinner," I told her. "Would it be too much to hope that you and Milo might come with me?"

My mother froze from folding the towel, her expression unreadable.

"Never mind." I tried to bite back my disappointment. "You don't have to," I told her, pushing off the counter.

She reached for my arm. "Do you want me to?"

"Of course I do. But if it's too much, too soon, I understand."

As my mother studied me, I could tell she was reticent, but she battled against it, knowing I needed her to make an effort for me. After a contemplative moment, she lifted her chin, as if she was decided. "Of course I will," she said.

My eyes narrowed on her. "Really?"

She rested her hand on my arm. "I don't want to be the one who makes you unhappy, Hunter. And if Thea and her family are willing to take such good care of you . . . I can't ask for more than that."

My throat tightened, and the weight of the world seemed to ease from my chest and shoulders. I cleared my throat. "Can I ask you one more favor?" My tone was cautious.

My mother tilted her head, a reluctant, fearful gleam in her eyes.

"Will you make some of your honey-glazed fruit salad to bring? It's Thea's favorite."

She sighed and chuckled with what looked like relief. "I can manage that, I think." Her voice was soft, exhausted even, and she shook her head. "Let me guess, extra honey?" she said wryly.

Smiling, I kissed her cheek. "Thank you, Mother."

Her gaze held mine, full of fatigue and fear, but I saw relief in there too. She bowed her head. "You're welcome."

I glanced toward the hallway. "I'm going to change for work. It's going to be hot today."

My mother nodded, and as I turned to leave, I heard her sigh.

I paused, glancing over my shoulder to find her gripping the countertop as if her life depended on it. "Mother?"

She looked up at me.

"I love you, you know?"

She smiled tightly. "I know. I love you too. And I'm very proud of you."

50

THEA

lle and I made our way toward Village Row, our special friend in tow as the crisp breeze grazed my skin. It was a relief after the fifth day of working long hours with Kat, our riders, and the new horses. Despite the hour, though, the sun was still high in the sky and the clouds churned in golden hues.

All Took had wanted for his eighty-seventh birthday was to grumble alone and hide away at home, whittling wood and stealing a few sips of Huck's ale when he thought Jade wasn't looking. But that's not what Took got.

With his birthday falling on the summer solstice, the brightest day of endless sunlight, Henni insisted a true celebration was in order. And as always, no one would argue with her. But while Beau and Wren embraced her sudden hospitality and desire for a friendly gathering, I knew she had ulterior motives as well.

I looked sidelong at Elle, her cheeks rosy from the walk. A bit of mischief glinted in her green eyes, and I couldn't blame her.

She glanced behind us. "How are you doing back there, Mr. Murphy?"

He met her gaze with a polite smile. "Oh, it's Gus—please, Elle," he said as he strolled along. His footsteps were unhurried, and his expression was a mask of calm indifference, but I could practically feel his nerves as if they were my own. "I'm just taking in the view. It's nice to get away from the storefront once in a while. You know," he added, pushing his glasses up the bridge of his nose. His face was freshly shaven and he was dressed in trousers and a leather vest that looked like one of the spinster sister's handiwork. "You really didn't need to go out of your way to invite me. I don't want to intrude—"

"Oh, don't be silly." Elle stopped and turned to him.

"Yeah, Mr. Murphy, don't be silly," I echoed. "We have an IOU list with you nearly a page long," I reminded him. "Thanks to Jackson's popcorn addiction."

"The least we can do is invite you for dinner on a beautiful evening like this," Elle added. "Besides, it's a gathering for friends and family. You are our friend, so you aren't intruding."

"If you say so," he drawled, and continued to stroll behind us. If Mr. Murphy wasn't the most talkative, amiable shopkeeper in town, at least when Bear wasn't devouring his produce, I would've thought he really was taking in the view, but his thoughtful silence gave him away.

We turned the corner and Village Row came into view. I smiled instantly. There were so many people moving around, and chatter filled the air, I could barely contain my excitement.

"Look!" I chirped. "Everyone's already here." A moment like this, with all of us together, was what Beau and Wren had always pictured, and finally, Henni was making it happen.

Woody, dressed in his best, and Stanley, in his trousers and bow tie as always, helped Beau and Hunter move the last of the picnic tables into the row down the center of the street. Aria, Milo, and Fiona set lanterns on the tables, and the spinster sisters decorated the tabletops in evergreen garlands and fireweed bouquets behind them. Aria and I exchanged a quick glance, she smiled, then went back to situating the lanterns.

Jackson, Ross, and Del stood at the roasting pit, created for the night's festivities, dressing meats at the prep table beside it. Wren, Susan, and Avery readied the food tables with bowls, trays, and platters, and Anika, Ehwin, and Olivia followed with pitchers of drinks.

Jade fussed over Took, already sitting under the shade of a spruce at the sidewalk, in what appeared to be the camping chair of honor, complete with a mug of ale. Otto sat in his wheelchair beside him, watching everyone with a sharp eye.

"The horses are fed," Elijah said as he and Liam made their way from the barn. "We'll grab the adult beverages from the house." Elijah winked at Took, as if they had a prearranged agreement, and I smiled to myself.

Alex, Kat, Bert, and Sven strung the last zigzag of the bare bulb lighting from one side of the street to the other, and at the helm of it all, was Henni, straight-faced in her apron and linen skirt, and her long, silver hair hanging loosely around her shoulders. I didn't miss the way her eyes met Bert's.

"She took your advice, Elle," I said, pointing to the string lights. They might not have been a necessity on the brightest night of the year, but they were beautiful and perfect.

Elle winked at me knowingly. "I still remember a thing or two from working on the cruise ships. It's *all* about the ambiance."

I glanced at Mr. Murphy, who was oblivious to Henni's intentions for tonight, and slowed to wait for him. "Care to escort a young lady to the party, Mr. Murphy?" I asked playfully.

He grinned. "As long as that man of yours doesn't get any ideas about us," he said with a wink.

I gaped at him. "Are you flirting with me, Mr. Murphy?"

He chuckled and offered me his arm. "I'm too old for flirting," he said, and I thought he might've believed it.

"You can never be too old to flirt," Elle told him. "Just ask Took." The three of us chuckled, and Mr. Murphy offered Elle his other elbow as we walked toward the party. But as I peered around, I didn't see the person I was looking for.

At first, I thought it was a horrible idea, exposing Mr. Murphy to Letty's cold shoulders and curt comments, but the more I was around her, the more I saw the softer side she hid so painfully well, and I decided Mr. Murphy and his obliging gentleness might be exactly what Letty needed. Like Henni, I began to hope a little nudge was all it might take for her to find some happiness.

Hunter met my gaze as we reached the festivities, his eyebrow rising with curiosity as he registered Mr. Murphy.

"Thea, you're here," Henni said when she noticed us. The corner of her mouth twitched. Smoothing down her apron, she made her way over.

"Henni!" Letty called, bumping the screen door to her house open with her shoulder as she stepped out with a pot in her hands. She froze on the porch as she noticed Mr. Murphy standing with us. Her expression twisted, confused at first, then turned to something more panicked before it sharpened again. There was no denying where Hunter got his seriousness.

"Over here, Letty," Henni said, waving her over.

Hunter popped up to take the pot from his mother, and when Letty's hands were free, she made her way over, reluctant.

"We brought a friend to dinner," I told her as she walked closer.

"I see that," Letty muttered. Her eyes weren't narrowed on me so much as concerned.

"Good evening, Letty," Mr. Murphy said, bowing his head politely.

"Hello, Gus." Her eyes cut to Henni, who ignored Letty's accusing stare completely.

"I hope you brought your appetite, Mr. Murphy," Henni said. "There's plenty of food."

He nodded, but his gaze fixed on Letty. "I brought you a little something," he told her. I held my breath as he pulled a folded envelope out of his back pocket.

"What for?" Letty asked, a bit breathy as he handed the creased envelope to her. She looked utterly bewildered and almost fearful, and my heart broke a little for her.

"I've heard you say you always wanted some, and I thought, well," he shrugged, glancing to the envelope. "I thought you might like them."

Letty's brow furrowed. "That's completely unnecessary," she told him.

I cleared my throat and eyed her with silent reproach.

"Um—but," she said, her voice wobbly as she tried to collect herself, then flashed Mr. Murphy a tentative smile. "It's very thoughtful." She stared at the envelope as her smile faltered. "What is it?"

"Maybe you should open it and see," Elle gently prompted her with a reassuring smile. I wasn't sure which was harder to watch, Mr. Murphy's obvious affections, or Letty's awkwardness. When was the last time someone—a man or friend—had given her something, expecting nothing in return? Not a barter or a trade, but a gift.

The moment she opened the envelope, the uncertainty etched in her features softened with surprise and her eyes rounded. She looked at him. "Cherry seeds?" she asked, dumping a few into her palm.

"I came across them a while back, and I've been holding onto them. I'm not sure why, but I remembered you telling Hunter it's the one thing you always wanted to plant but never did. I thought since you're putting down roots here, you might try." Their eyes met again, and my heart leapt with adoration for him.

Elle and I looked at one another, realizing we had overstayed our welcome, and as if Henni realized the same thing, she looked at me. "Well, get over there and see Hunter, Thea," she commanded with a sly wink. "He's been eyeing the road for you all afternoon. Elle—" Henni pointed over her shoulder. "I'm sure Jackson needs you for something."

Elle and I stood at attention, and like the good little helpers we were, we left Mr. Murphy and Letty to their stilted, but engrossing conversation.

"Letty, don't just stand there," I heard Henni say. "Thank the man and get him a refreshment—Mr. Murphy, make yourself at home. If you're left wanting anything tonight, it's your own fault."

"Yes, Ma'am," he said. "Thank you."

I nearly burst into laughter as Elle and I glanced at each other one last time, beyond amused. We gave each other a high-five, then went our separate ways.

Hunter straightened from stacking wood beside the barbecue pit when he saw me coming, his eyes latched on his mother a moment. "Is it just me, or does she look . . . panicky?"

I watched as she led Mr. Murphy to the refreshment table. "Panicky is a word for it, but let's hope that by the end of tonight, they finally have a conversation that doesn't revolve solely around produce."

Hunter chuckled and shook his head. "I *knew* you and Henni were up to something. She never leaves the village if she can help it, and suddenly she wanted to go with me to 'see the horses' at the facility." He shook his head again. "You two have been scheming." The corner of his mouth lifted as he glanced at his mother again, and I thought I saw more than amusement on in his eyes, but a shimmer of hope too.

"Everyone deserves a little bit of happiness," I told him, admiring the way his gaze softened as he looked at me. "Even your mother."

"Especially my mother," he said quietly and kissed my forehead. I knew Letty had been through a lot, even before what happened to their village all those years ago. Hunter chuffed a laugh. "Who better for her to be with than the grocer, who is as obsessed with citrus as she is?"

"I know," I said with a snicker. "If they get married, we can send them to New Bodega for their honeymoon. Imagine how much fun they'd have in Grayson's food warehouse." My eyebrows danced impishly and Hunter laughed, a deep, genuine sound that sent my heart into a tizzy.

"Now you're just getting crazy," he said.

I rose on my tiptoes for a kiss. "But a cute kind of crazy," I murmured.

Hunter shrugged playfully and snaked his arms around me. We stood contentedly by the fire pit, watching everyone else who was oblivious to my perfect moment.

Bert nudged Henni with a wry smile and inaudible whispers that made her eyes widen and her cheeks flush as they collected the empty decorating baskets on the sidewalk. Alex played tickle monster with Fiona as she finished laying napkins on the table, and Sophie tried not to laugh at his ridiculousness.

Elle and Jackson smiled as they whispered together in their own secret moment by the barbecue. Woody, hair as crazy as ever, stood with Stanley, Letty, and Mr. Murphy, likely discussing Stanley's ability to grow the most beautiful green beans in Whitehorse, and how Woody had given up trying years ago.

Aria and Milo came out of Henni's house with Little Foot yipping at their heels, and my brother and Wren laughed with Took and Otto, the old men's grumbles carrying on the breeze. I wasn't sure I'd ever seen Otto smile, and the fact that he was made the moment all the more perfect.

No matter what the last twelve years had brought, now, my

family was happy and together, I had Hunter, and I wondered if life could possibly be any better.

"And what about you," Hunter said, his arms squeezing around me.

I peered up at him. "What about me?"

"What would your ideal honeymoon be?" He brushed a loose strand of hair from my face, and his grin widened. "Let me guess, running in a field of horses, toward a wagon full of honey?"

I barked a laugh. "Pretty much. But that wouldn't be very fun for you."

His eyebrows lowered. "It could be," he said more suggestively. "There are lots of things you can do in a field . . . with honey."

Blushing, I tried to bite back my smile. "True," I whispered. I expected Hunter to smile or lean in for another kiss, but he studied me intently instead, his jaw working as it always did when he was contemplating something.

"What is it?" I asked, squeezing his hand. It was rough and warm, and I still wasn't completely used to the reality that I could touch him whenever I wanted. That I could talk to him and it felt completely natural.

"What *do* you want, Thea?" he asked, his serious, velvety tone drowning out the chatter around us.

"Is that a trick question?"

His lips curved into a small smile. "No, but I do think about what happens next."

I lifted my shoulder. "You're going to marry me, of course," I told him. "And we're going to see what happens after that." Having kids was still a scary topic. The biggest unknown that remained between us—Untainted and Tainted bloodlines commingling.

Hunter's smile stretched into a grin that lit his face, and he leaned in for a kiss. "Good. Just making sure," he whispered, and as I kissed him back more eagerly, my name boomed over the crowd.

"Thea!" Took hollered. "It's not his birthday, it's mine. And you haven't even said hello yet," he grumbled.

Biting back a laugh, I looked at Hunter. "Sorry, but I better go say hi to Mr. Grump before I never hear the end of it."

Hunter lifted his chin. "All right, but only because I'm afraid of him."

With a laugh, I kissed his lips once more, feeling like the luckiest girl in the world that I got to spend every day for the rest of my life with Hunter. "I love you." The words fell from my lips in an effortless whisper, and Hunter's expression softened.

He beamed at me. We'd thought the words and danced around them, so there was no reason not to say them. "I love you too," he said in earnest. After another lingering moment and final kiss, I hurried over to Took. It was in that moment I realized I'd never felt so full in my life, and for the first time, I was excited about the future.

EPILOGUE
THEA

One Year Later

Staring at my reflection in the cabin mirror, I wondered who the woman was staring back at me. Her hair was French-braided and crowned with blossoms. Her cheeks were rosy, her eyes were glistening, and on the outside, she looked like a bride ready to start the first day of the rest of her life.

Inside, I was a ball of nerves and trepidation. My stomach lurched, and my hand moved to it automatically as I glanced furtively around the cabin. Elle and Sophie were getting ready in the cramped bathroom, and Jade braided Fiona's hair on the bed.

"I want it to be just like you did Auntie Thea's," Fiona reminded her for the seventh time.

"How about I make it even better?" Jade said, our gazes meeting in the mirror. She winked at me.

"With more flowers?" Fiona chirped as she handed Jade another fireweed blossom.

"Of course with more flowers." Jade smiled, patient as always, and she tucked the wisp into Fiona's crown.

Sophie peeked her head out of the bathroom, her strawberry blonde hair knotted prettily atop her head. "You're not being too demanding of Grandma, are you, Fi?"

"Nope," Fiona promised.

Sophie looked at me, then back into the bathroom at Elle, who was pinching her cheeks for a little added color. "She's going through a bossy phase," Sophie muttered.

"Ha! Jackson says I'm still in that phase," Elle said with a laugh.

I chuckled to myself and watched as Fiona drew shapes with her fingertips on Jade's ivory linen skirt, all of us nearly ready for the ceremony. *My wedding.* But the longer I watched Fiona, the more uneasy I felt.

Needing air, I rose to my feet, my bare feet pattering across the floor toward the door. "I just want to sneak a peek," I whispered, flashing Jade and Fiona a quick smile.

Everyone I knew was at the lodge. Mr. Murphy, Letty and Milo, Sven and the rest of the villagers—even Cal and Marica had come to celebrate Hunter's and my big day.

Vehicles and horses filled the gravel drive, and laughter and congenial voices echoed from down by the reception area, meeting my ears.

Walking to the edge of the porch, I glanced toward the lodge, where I could hear Took grumbling from the deck, to the lanterns hanging from golden-leaved birch and evergreens in the clearing by the river.

Wren, Stanley, and Beau hustled around the tables, ensuring they were set. The mason jar centerpieces practically sparkled in the waning afternoon, and the fuchsia bouquets inside of them trembled in the slight breeze. Everything was beautiful, everything was perfect—exactly as I'd imagined it—except for this.

Squeezing my hands into fists, I forced myself to ignore the feeling I had in the pit of my stomach, and took a deep breath.

Everything is fine.

I exhaled.

So what if children between Tainteds and Untainteds was uncharted territory. And that Wren and Beau hadn't even had their first child yet. So what if I'd been responsible—that I'd done *all the things* and somehow, here I was, pregnant on my wedding day.

"Everything will be fine," I whispered.

I glanced toward the gravel drive, wishing Kat were back. The summit was taking longer than usual this year, and I was a panicked ball of nerves. I didn't have to take a test; with each passing day, I felt more and more certain, like my blood rushed with an extra whir and my skin tingled at the slightest sensations. I'd been brushing it off as butterflies for one of the biggest days of my life, but it wasn't working anymore. I couldn't deny it now that my wedding day was here, and I didn't have any nerves or apprehension or second thoughts about marrying Hunter.

I was pregnant; I knew the truth with every fiber in me, and I was scared to death.

Jackson headed up the hill toward the cabins, donned in a fresh, forest green button-up shirt and slacks. It was a visage of him I'd never seen, and it brought a smile to my face.

What I thought might be a mixture of awe and pride filled his hazel eyes as he took in the sight of me. "You look beautiful," Jackson said, stopping in front of me.

"Thank you." But my dress was forgotten as my mouth started moving again before I could stop it. "Do you have—any —you know, weird feelings, by any chance?"

Jackson's brow crinkled slightly. "Bad feelings—about your wedding?"

I shook my head. "About anything at all?"

As if Jackson thought he understood, his lips parted in a heartening smile and he leaned in and kissed my forehead.

"There doesn't always have to be something wrong, Thea." As he pulled away, I met his gaze, which was so certain and reassuring, even if he didn't have the faintest idea of what I was talking about. Somehow, I thought he might actually be right.

I wrapped my arms around him, needing the steadfast energy he always exuded. When I was seven, Jackson had been a stranger, and now he was the best father I could've hoped for in this life.

With a sharp inhale, he hugged me back, squeezing his arms around me. "I love you, squirt," he said hoarsely, emotion thickening his throat. "I'm so proud of you."

"I love you too." My vision blurred with unshed tears. "No crying before the wedding!" I chirped, reminding myself. "The last thing I need is a red, puffy face." I blinked and blotted away my tears with the back of my hand.

Jackson chuckled. "You look perfect." He sighed and glanced past me. "Is Elle still in there?"

I nodded into the cabin. "She's finishing getting ready."

"I better hurry her up. I think she's more nervous than you." He winked and stepped past me, nearly knocking into Fiona as she ran out.

"Auntie Thea!" she chirped, and swirled in her eyelet dress and fuzzy sweater. "Look at my hair—it's got flowers in it like yours, but way more."

"It's beautiful," I told her, crouching down to kiss her cheek. I stared into Fiona's crystal blue eyes and tucked a strand of her umber hair behind her little ear. I lost myself in the slight slope of her cute little nose and the roundness of her cheeks.

"Fiona!" Sophie called. "Come put your shoes on, please."

Fiona scuttled back into the room, and fireweed petals floated to the ground in her wake. I stroked one between my fingers.

What would our baby be like? Would it be perfect like

Fiona? And would it have Abilities like me, or none like Hunter? Or something in between, something different? Something . . . dangerous?

"Thea?"

Hearing Hunter's voice behind me, I turned around. "You're not supposed to see—" But the words died on my lips as I took in his stunned expression.

"Beautiful," he breathed, his gaze raking over me as he took a step closer.

"Thank you," I said, a bit sheepish. "Your mother and the spinster sisters did a wonderful job, didn't they?" I felt like a princess.

Hunter nodded dumbly. "I was looking for Jackson, but I'm happy to find you instead."

Grinning from ear to ear, I leaned in and kissed his lips. "That's reassuring," I whispered against his lips, and took a step away, running my hands over my dress.

"What are you doing outside of the cabin, anyway? You're not thinking about running, are you?"

"No," I said with a nervous laugh. I couldn't help how unsteady I felt.

"Hey," Hunter said, taking my hand. As always, his eyes saw too much. "What's wrong?"

Forcing another smile, I glanced toward the commotion down by the river. "I just wanted to see how it all looked."

But Hunter's expression was unchanged, and running his hand down the back of my arm he took my hand in his. "Serious-ly," he said, brushing his thumb over my cheek. His eyes were alive with sudden worry. "You look pale . . . or sad."

Licking my lips, I shook my head. "I'm fine, I'm just—" I searched for the words. "I was just thinking, is all."

He turned his head slightly, as if he feared my next words. "About what?"

"About our children," I admitted reluctantly.

"You mean," Hunter started with an amused smile, "the one's we don't even have yet are already stressing you out?" He tried to joke, but as I told myself now didn't feel like the right time to tell him, I knew I had to or he'd know I wasn't telling him the full truth.

"Not about our future children," I said quietly. "But about this one." I rested my hand on the lace of my dress. As I spoke the words aloud for the first time, tears formed in the backs of my eyes. "And I'm scared," I admitted.

Hunter swallowed, his shock evident, until he seemed to understand my concern and leaned in to wrap his arms around me. "It'll be okay, Thea," he whispered.

"I'm sure it will," I said because I *wanted* to believe him, but not because I did. The Virus changed everything, making the world and the people still living in it unpredictable. Lunatics, Regens, evil power-wielders, people like us . . . people like Hunter. And then there was whatever was in between. There was no telling what our child would be like—there was no one like us, not that we knew of anyway. There was no guarantee that everything would turn out okay.

"And you're certain?" Hunter whispered.

I met his gaze. "I can feel it."

The sound of a diesel engine rumbled up the drive. Wiping the tears from my cheeks, I registered Kat, Woody, and Ross climbing out of the truck.

"We're not too late, are we?" Kat shouted when she saw me, and practically loped toward the cabin. She was wearing her cargo pants and long sleeves, her hair pulled back in a blonde bun on top of her head. "Thea—"

"No," I said with a relieved smile. "You're not too late. I was just finishing getting ready."

"Thank God. I told Ross I would never let him live it down if he didn't get me here in time." Kat's brow furrowed as she glanced between me and Hunter. Then Kat glared at him. "What the hell did you do already?" she chided.

I snorted. "He didn't do anything, Kat. I'm just—" I looked at Elle and Jackson coming out of the cabin with Sophie and Jade, ready for the ceremony. They looked at Hunter and me, confused.

"What is it?" Elle asked softly. Everyone glanced around at one another. "What's wrong?"

Meeting Hunter's reassuring gaze, I swallowed and braced myself to say the words for them all to hear, and with a sudden laugh of a sob, I said, "I think I'm just hormonal."

It took a moment for my meaning to sink in before there was a collective gasp.

"Wait—what?" Kat said, as if she needed me to clarify. But Elle took my hand, rubbing my arm in tentative excitement. She understood my reservations, we'd discussed it before, but there was supposed to be more time to get it figured out. Hunter and I hadn't been planning for kids so soon, though we hoped one day they would be in our future.

"You're pregnant?" Kat reiterated.

"Yes," I told everyone. I blinked the tears away. "It's so dumb. I know I shouldn't be worried. I'm sure everything will be fine, I just—what if it's not?" I met Jackson's gaze again, hoping this time he'd give me *something* to put my mind at ease.

"No bad feelings, squirt," he said, trying to sound hopeful, but he couldn't hide his own uncertainty of where this was going to lead, and there were months ahead in which anything could happen.

"Oh, sweetie—" Elle pulled me into her. "You're going to be fine. There's still plenty of time to figure things out."

I nodded, hoping she was right, even if I couldn't seem to stop the tears from dripping down my cheeks.

"Babe!" Ross said, trudging down the hill with an exhausted *I-just-rode-twelve-hours-with-Kat-barking-in-my-ear* expression.

"Don't forget to give Thea Becca's present. She seemed adamant —" When he looked at me, he froze and his face crumpled with confusion.

"I'm fine," I told him. "Everything is fine." I straightened and flashed Hunter, who looked worried sick about me, as reassuring a smile as I could muster. "Seriously. It's totally hormones." I cleared my throat and dried my cheeks.

"What's wrong with Auntie Thea, Mommy?" Fiona asked sadly. "I thought she was supposed to be happy—"

"She is, love bug. Come on, let's go tell everyone Auntie Thea's almost ready, okay?" Sophie met my eyes with a soft smile. "Love you," she mouthed before they padded off.

"Fi's right. This is our special day," I said aloud. I didn't have to dwell on things out of my control, today of all days. "I have eight more months to figure out what happens next. I won't worry about it anymore today."

Hunter gently stroked my back, as if he didn't believe me.

"Well," Kat said as she shoved the gift at me. "Ross is right, Becca was adamant we give this to you as soon as we got here this morning, but we're clearly late, so—here . . ."

I glanced between Kat and Ross, then down at Woody as he met the others down by the river. I was glad no one else seemed to notice the blubbering bride.

I looked at Hunter. "It's a gift, so it can't be that bad," he said, both of us equally confused and afraid. Nothing was ever straightforward with Becca, and I wondered if there was another one of her riddles inside.

Untying the twine bow, I pulled the top off of the box and lifted the note resting on the tissue paper. Unfolding it, I handed it to Hunter.

His eyes scanned over it first. "It says, never forget, and congratulations." He looked from the note to me, and I pulled back a piece of white cloth. A knitted, heather green garment was folded inside. I held it up. "A baby sweater," I breathed.

Hunter read the note again. "Never forget, and congratulations."

Becca's words from last year echoed in my ears. *Never forget. You are important and exactly as you must be.*

"Everyone has a destiny," Hunter said, his voice distant. I watched him as my own memories began to fall into place, and he took the sweater in his hand. "Zoe told me the vaccine was necessary for my future. I thought she'd been talking about Milo, but Becca said something that stuck with me on the last day we were in Hope Valley."

"What did she say?" I asked, the words barely a breath.

"She said that everyone has a—"

"Destiny," I finished for him. "Becca told me that too."

Your future will help give rise to a world different than this one. I stared down at my stomach, my thoughts reeling before a bubble of laughter escaped my throat. "She knew. She'd seen it all already." I still didn't know what sort of child was growing inside me, but that Becca had knitted a sweater was as good a sign as I needed. I met Hunter's watery gaze. "The baby," I started. "Whatever happens next . . . It's going to be okay." I said it with far more certainty this time.

Hunter's chest rose and fell, and relief seemed to wash over him as he exhaled a ragged breath.

"She wanted you to know," Elle realized. "She wanted you to have peace of mind."

The fear seeped from me as I thought about Becca's words over and over. Her certainty rang true, and I sniveled an excited laugh.

Awestruck by Becca's words, Hunter and I stared at one another. Her prophecy was heavy, but not a burden, and the more that settled in, the more I allowed myself to be happy. "A baby," I mouthed to him, as if I couldn't believe it.

"Congratulations," Ross said, clapping Hunter's shoulder. Hunter grinned as the others exclaimed and applauded the news, and after a whir of well wishes, everyone was gone, leaving Hunter and I standing there, silent as we gazed into each other's eyes.

"A moment ago, I thought our children might be something —wrong," I admitted. "But now . . ."

He tugged me against him, holding me as we absorbed each other's relief. "I've thought about this for so long," he said, his voice almost inaudible at my ear. "My future has changed more times than I can count, and yet this—all of this feels perfectly right."

With a happy sob, I blubbered into his shoulder. "We're really doing this."

"We're really doing this," he echoed. When he pulled away, I admired the unbridled excitement in his eyes, an indescribable happiness that made it impossible to imagine a darker future. "We'll make it work, whatever happens," he promised.

"I know." Squeezing the little green sweater against my chest, Hunter and I turned toward our family and friends gathering below. We had all the help we'd ever need.

Sighing, I rested my head against Hunter's shoulder. "And to think," I said, "you didn't want to come to Whitehorse." I peered up at him through my lashes.

Hunter shook his head with a knowing smirk. "You're never going to let me live that down, are you?"

"No, probably not."

"Wait—" He stiffened. "Is Fiona already digging into your honey cakes—"

"What?" My gaze raked over the crowd. When I saw her riding on Alex's back around the dinner tables, I glowered at Hunter. "That was low, Hunter, even for you," I told him.

With a chuckle, he whisked me up, and I shrieked as he cradled me in his arms. "I guess you'll have to punish me later."

I wrapped my arms around his neck. "Looking forward to it," I whispered against his mouth.

Hunter brushed a featherlight, lingering kiss against my mouth. "Come on, beautiful. Let's get the party started. We have a lot to be grateful for and celebrate tonight."

THE END

Keep reading for a bonus scene with the Hope Valley crew.

BONUS SCENE
THEA

Hope Valley

We spent our fourth afternoon in New Bodega at the Hope Valley farm. All of Hunter's symptoms from the vaccine had finally fizzled to nothing, I'd gotten a sunburn from the deceptively overcast skies while exploring the beach with him and Little Foot, and it was time to get back to work.

I stood at the pasture with Dani to officially meet all eight of the horses we'd be taking back with us—one horse in particular.

"This is Sadie," Dani said as the palomino mare came trotting up to the fence. It was natural to assume Dani had beckoned her with her mind. Sadie whinnied and nudged her, requesting a quick pat.

"She's beautiful," I said. Sadie's coat was the color of Hunter's wheat field in the afternoon sunlight, her mane a blonde tangle that hung around her eyes.

"She loves the kids too—I think she relates to them more than us old farts." Like Sadie knew exactly what Dani was saying, she meandered back out to the pasture to join the other horses with a bit more spunk in her step.

The warm breath of a black gelding fanned across my arm as he inched closer, his ears perked toward us in curiosity. "And who is this beauty?" I asked as he scented my skin, no doubt smelling a mixture of sweat and herbs and summertime goodness from a day of my helping in the fields.

"That's Peanut," Dani explained. "Ceara named him."

I grinned. "Well you're a tall, handsome boy—aren't you, Peanut?" There was movement by the barn and I noticed Hunter walking toward us.

"Oh, geez," Dani groused. She glanced at Ceara, splashing with Jack at a small frog pond between the apple orchard and the farmhouse. "Of course the munchkin's soaked right before the picnic." She flashed me a regretful grin. "I better get her inside and cleaned up before we eat. Zoe's been extra sensitive to smells lately." Dani mimicked a big belly and grimaced. "I don't want to be responsible for Zoe's gag reflex when she gets a whiff of Ceara at the picnic table."

I laughed as Dani jogged toward the pond, Ceara completely oblivious as she giggled and splashed through the mud with Jack. I recalled the warm days of summer when Little Foot and I would play in the Yukon River.

"I remember those days," I said wistfully, my chin jutting toward the pond as Hunter walked up to me.

He followed my gaze.

"Warm summer sunshine. The boggy scent of the water in the shallows, and wet dog, which I knew I'd get an eye-scolding for later." With an exaggerated sigh, I smiled. "Those were the days."

"You had a happy childhood then," Hunter seemed to think the thought out loud, and his slightly pinched features told me he was surprised.

"Yes, I did." I tilted my head, waiting for him to say whatever thoughts perplexed him.

"It's just . . . It's good to know that. After what happened with your mom and—" My brow crumpled, and Hunter shook his head. His cheeks flushed slightly as he glanced away. "I don't know why I brought that up. That was insensitive." He reached through the fence and stroked Peanut's mane absently.

The fact that Hunter cared much about my past at all was worth more than any discomfort in him bringing it up. "It's fine," I said. The wood poked into my back as I leaned against the pasture fence, but I barely noticed. I'd been thinking about what Becca had told me, about how I was exactly who I needed to be, and I realized that, regardless of my future, I knew she was right, even if I struggled to forget the past sometimes. "We both have things we don't want to remember, but sometimes we don't get the choice," I said.

Hunter's head angled slightly, as if he was surprised by my sudden optimism.

"It's part of who we are, right? The good and the bad parts."

He practically snorted and draped his arms over the fence. "I don't think you have any bad parts, Thea."

"Ha! Oh, I do, trust me. In fact, I think you're one of the only people who's seen some of the worst in me, and not always for good reason."

"Maybe, but you've never said anything to me I didn't deserve at the time."

"That's not true," I admitted, staring into his eyes. They shined like liquid amber in the afternoon, yet were clouded like wood smoke too, housing so much pain and longing and strength, all at the same time . . . I couldn't have forced myself to look away if I'd tried.

"Well, your intentions have always been good, at least," he said, and he was the one who looked away, breaking the spell.

"Oh, and yours haven't?"

Hunter glanced at me, his chiseled jaw slightly dusted with scruff. He paused from petting Peanut's nose and dropped his hand.

"Uh-oh, I've said something wrong," I muttered, only half joking. "And we were doing so well."

His gaze swept the pasture and he shook his head. "No, nothing wrong. But you do make me question a lot of things," he mused. I had to bite my tongue from asking more questions. As much as I wanted to know everything there was to know about the mysterious Hunter, it didn't feel right to ask either, and the tension was already thickening between us again.

"Come and get it, guys!" Kat called to us from the picnic tables they'd moved out onto the lawn. Bert was spreading out blankets, and Jake and Jason carried racks of meat out to the buffet. Becca, Annie, and Alex followed behind them with other dishes, setting food along the line of picnic tables so the fourteen of us could eat together.

Hunter and I said goodbye to Peanut and made our way around the pasture.

"They wouldn't even let me help move tables," Hunter grumbled, glancing at the cluster of people hustling around, getting dinner set up. "I'm not sure if they think I'm contagious, or if they think I might break."

I nudged his shoulder, trying not to laugh. "Hey, just accept it. You're taken care of here, instead of taking care of someone else. This is what it feels like." I inhaled a deep breath and exhaled. "Relish it."

Hunter looked at me, unmoved, and was about to say something snide when we heard a familiar chuckle behind us.

Glancing back, we found Harper swinging his daughter, Zayleigh, up onto his shoulders. She giggled. Her tawny hair was in pigtails with wisps that fluttered in the breeze, and her eyes were bright green, like her father's.

"She's adorable, isn't she?" I asked, my attention shifting to Hunter.

He watched the little girl and nodded, and I saw a spark of

amusement in his eyes. "As if you've ever found a kid you didn't think was adorable."

"Ha! That's a fair assessment," I conceded.

A small smile tugged at Hunter's mouth.

"She looks just like you, Harper," I said as he and Zayleigh drew closer.

Harper's grin widened as he eyed the both of us up and down. "Wow, it's amazing what a little sleep can do," he joked. "You both look reborn."

"It's not the sleep," I told him as he fell into step beside us. "It's the ocean." I looked at Hunter. "Don't you think? It's rejuvenating."

Hunter smirked, an expression I found myself craving. "Sleep helps a little, though."

With a chuckle, Harper shook his head. "I wouldn't know anything about it." He glanced up at Zayleigh as she pulled at his hands.

"Hurry, Daddy."

"Dustin . . ." The three of us paused.

"Uh-oh, Daddy's in trouble," Harper muttered. I knew immediately it had to be Chris, because, according to him, she was the only one who called him by his first name.

She walked toward us, distracted as she pilfered through the bag slung over her shoulder. She wore cargo pants, a tank top, and her hair was up in a blonde bun, just like Kat's always was. "Where's Zay's drops? Did you bring them?"

His expression fell. "Shit."

"Daddy!" Zayleigh giggled and leaned forward to look at Harper, her hair flopping in front of him and hanging in his face.

"I mean, poop," he corrected himself. He moved Zayleigh's curtain of hair to the side. "We used the last of them the other day—I forgot to get another with everything going on."

"What's the tincture for?" Hunter asked. "If you don't mind my asking."

"Headaches," Chris groaned. She sighed, as if she'd given up looking for a hidden or forgotten vial tucked away somewhere. "She has Harper's *gift*, and sometimes it's too much for her."

Fleetingly, I thought of Fiona's Ability, which resembled both Alex and Sophie's. Being a conduit for amplified feelings and emotions wasn't exactly easy for a five-year-old either. Suddenly, growing up with my Ability didn't seem all that bad.

"I brought a flat of salves and tinctures from Henni," Hunter said. "I know there's some of her iris-cayenne remedy in there. It helps with headaches. I'll go grab you one."

Chris's blue eyes lit up. "Oh, would you? Thank you. It would make me feel better."

"It's the least I can do," Hunter told her. "Especially since I was the distraction."

"Hey," I said, grabbing onto his bicep as he turned away. Hunter stilled, his eyes shifting from my fingers to me. I dropped my hand and cleared my throat. "The stuff from the village is inside the barn." I shrugged. "A person could get lost in there, if you don't know where to look." I figured Hunter could use the warning, since he hadn't been around when we'd unloaded them. "The flat of tinctures is on the ground, next to the jams."

Hunter's lips pursed. "Thanks." With a dip of his chin, he headed in that direction.

"Come on, Zay," Harper said, spinning around. "We'll go help him so you can see the kitties while we're at it."

"Okay!" she squeaked, and they walked back toward the barn.

Chris looked at me with an exhausted sigh and shook her head. "Sorry, I'm Chris," she said, extending her hand.

"Thea." I grinned. "You have a wonderful husband," I told her. "And a beautiful little girl. She has your freckles. I *love* freckles."

Chris laughed. "Thank you to both, and yes, she does have my freckles. And my temper."

We started toward the picnic again; the group was already serving themselves food. "She has a prophecy Ability then, like Becca and Harper?"

"Yes," Chris said. "Of course it keeps getting stronger. Zay gets headaches sometimes when she has visions. And when I'm around, they aren't so bad, because I can generally help soothe her a bit with my cerebral fingers, but—" Chris shook her head. "I'm not always around."

"I never thought about having to worry about something like that," I realized.

Chris laughed. "Me either. It's definitely different, worrying about these sorts of things now. With my boys—" She paused, as if she hadn't meant to broach the past. "Well, you didn't used to have to worry about developing Abilities and remedies." She flashed me a weak smile.

"True, but at least you have Harper around. He'll come up with some magical elixir for her one of these days."

Sam and Ceara scuttled past us with pitchers of ice tea. "Sorry, sorry!" he said, and they set them on the tables. Ceara's hair was in a damp braid after getting cleaned up, but I noticed she already had a wet stain on her shirt. "We had a bit of a setback, but it's all fixed now," Sam explained. "Drinks are ready." He winked at Ceara, as if they had a secret, and she looked sheepishly at her father as he walked up.

"Trouble again, you little rascal?" Jason said, and he leaned down to kiss the top of Ceara's head. "I'd have it no other way."

"Yep—come on, Jack!" she called, and she ran off again.

"Don't worry, I'll get your plate ready," Jason muttered, and he glanced at me with a smile. "Grab some grub, Thea. There's short ribs over there, and a birdy told us you love honey. Zoe made her famous honey butter corn on the cob over there. It's about the only thing she can make, but—"

Zoe stopped beside him and punched his shoulder.

He glared at her. "Where the hell did you come from?"

"Pregnancy gives you supersonic hearing, Jason. Didn't you know?" With a smirk, she poured herself a cup of lemonade.

He looked at me, shaking his head. "I don't know how she does that."

"I'll never tell," Zoe said, and surveyed the food on the tables. "But I *am* ravenous." She rubbed her belly and licked her lips, as if her mouth was suddenly watering.

With a chuckle, I got into line behind them. "I'm definitely going to have some corn. And the ribs—I can't remember the last time I had beef anything."

"I'll tell you what," Jason said, plopping a blackberry from the fruit salad into his mouth. "You eat all the beef you want, and I'll eat your portion of those moose meatballs you made."

I laughed. "You've got yourself a deal. Those are one of Jackson's signature dinners."

When I finished heaping food onto my plate, Zoe and I sat at one of the picnic tables out of the way.

"Don't mind me," she said as she squatted down on the bench across from me. "I'm just going to pig out now."

Sam was already sitting beside her. "Thanks for the warning," he muttered, and scooped a spoonful of potato salad into his mouth. With his baseball cap on backward, his blue eyes gleamed in the sunlight.

I hadn't had more than a few bites when Hunter plopped down on the bench beside me, he and Sam glancing at one another before we all fell into companionable silence. I eyed a strawberry from the fruit salad on my fork, imagining how much sweeter it would taste with a bit of honey.

As if he were in my thoughts, Hunter slid an open jar of it toward me with a barely-there smile.

My breath stilled.

"I snagged the jar from the other table," he said.

"You—are awesome. Thank you."

"You're welcome." Hunter's cheek rounded with a grin, and my heart melted, just a little.

———

I hope you enjoyed the final installment of the Savage North Chronicles. It's been a wild, fun, and heart-wrenching ride, and I loved every minute of it. I hope you did too. Please consider leaving a review of the book and/or series.

The post-apocalyptic and dystopian adventures continue in my Victorian weather-ravaged world, Forgotten Lands.

ALSO BY LINDSEY POGUE

WWW.LINDSEYPOGUE.COM

Survival/Post-Apoc Adventure:

SAVAGE NORTH CHRONICLES

The Darkest Winter

The Longest Night

Midnight Sun

Fading Shadows

Untamed

Unbroken

Day Zero: Savage North Beginnings

THE ENDING SERIES

After The Ending

Into The Fire

Out Of The Ashes

Before The Dawn

Beginnings: Ending Series Origin Stories

The Ending Series: World Before

YA Dystopian:

THE ENDING LEGACIES

World After

Victorian Post-Apoc Adventure:

FORGOTTEN LANDS

Borne of Sand and Scorn - Prequel Novella

Dust and Shadow

Earth and Ember

Tide and Tempest

New Adult Love Stories

SARATOGA FALLS LOVE STORIES

Whatever It Takes

Nothing But Trouble

Told You So

Science Fiction (Charity Anthology)

Beyond The Galaxy - At Dawn

For more information visit: www.lindseypogue.com

ABOUT LINDSEY

WWW.LINDSEYPOGUE.COM

Lindsey Pogue has always been a sucker for a good love story. She completed her first new adult manuscript in high school and has been writing tales of love and friendship, history and adventure ever since. When she's not chatting with readers, plotting her next storyline, or dreaming up new, brooding characters, Lindsey's generally wrapped in blankets watching her favorite action flicks with her own leading man. They live in Northern California with their rescue cat, Beast. You can follow Lindsey's shenanigans and writing adventures just about everywhere.

Free stories & a monthly email:
https://www.lindseypogue.com/newsletter

You can find "Author Lindsey Pogue" here: